Wicked Words
An erotic short story collection

Look out for the other **nine** volumes in the
Wicked Words series

Wicked Words

An erotic short story collection

Edited by Kerri Sharp

BLACK LACE

Black Lace books contain sexual fantasies.
In real life, always practise safe sex.

This edition published in 2004 by
Black Lace
Thames Wharf Studios
Rainville Road
London W6 9HA

First published in 1999

Typeset by SetSystems Limited, Saffron Walden, Essex
Printed and bound by Mackays of Chatham PLC

ISBN 0 352 33363 4

Contents

Introduction　vii

Exit Stage Left Felicity Salten　1

Shoot Anya Ross　19

Frozen Violets Leona Rhys　33

Shadowlight Kitty Fisher　48

Secret Kitty Fisher　68

Lepidoptera Helena Ravenscroft　84

The Chrome Man Maria Lloyd　97

Pussy Willow Liza Dallimore　112

Loaded Miranda Stephens　124

The Bargain Kathryn Anne Dubois　131

Primal Scream Sophia Mortensen　146

Office Politics Tina Harden　159

Bloody Grunge Love Airyn Darling　169

The Western Whore Kristina Lloyd　189

The Best of Hands Portia Da Costa　207

Sweet Revenge Wendy Harris　217

Private Dancer Magdalena Salt　228

The Red Petticoat Rhiannon Taliesin　245

Mindless Raptures Larissa McKenzie　258

Mistress Sheila Kate Dominic　273

Introduction

I am delighted that these wonderful Black Lace erotic short story collections are getting a new lease of life, and in such fabulous eye-catching new pop-art covers, too! The series has been hugely successful, and sales of *Wicked Words* anthologies have proven how popular the short story format is in this genre.

This was the first book in the series, and was launched as something of an experiment – so the stories in this collection are a fascinatingly diverse mix of imagination and thematics. It has been great fun compiling these collections, particularly when serendipity played a part and one could see a coincidence of themes emerging. Curiously, there are three nature-based stories in this book: *Primal Scream*, *Frozen Violets* and *Lepidoptera*, and one can see elements of Angela Carter and A. S. Byatt creeping in. Part post-modern fantasy, part ethnic folk tale, they lend a mystery to the flavour of the book and provide a counterbalance to the more down-to-earth explicitness of stories like *Exit Stage Left* and *Office Politics*, while *Loaded* is guaranteed to shock, mixing uniform fetishism with a hardcore element of danger. Well, you can't go wrong with a female highway patrol cop . . .

As from February 2005, we will be publishing themed collections – which will be a fun way of diversifying the list. The first books will be *Sex in the Office* (Feb) and *Sex on Holiday* (May), and after we will be publishing *Sex at the Sportsclub* and *Sex in Uniform*. But in the meantime, *More Wicked Words* is also published as of this month – July 2004 – to be followed by *Wicked Words 3–8* through

August to November. If you never got the chance to buy all the books when they were first published, you can now complete your collection and be the envy of your friends! Look out for the colourful covers – guaranteed to stand out from everything else on the erotica shelves in bookshops.

Do you want to submit a short story to Wicked Words?

By the time these reprints hit the shelves, it will be too late to contribute stories to the first two themed collections, but the guidelines for future anthologies will be available on our website at www.blacklace-books.co.uk. Keep checking the news. Please note we can only accept stories that are of publishable standard in terms of grammar, punctuation, narrative structure and presentation. We do not want to receive stories that are about 'some people having sex' and little else. The buzzwords are surprises, great characterisation and an awareness of the erotic literary canon. We cannot reply to all short story submissions as we receive too many to make this possible. Competition-style rules apply: you will hear back from us only if your story has been successful. And please remember to read the guidelines. If you cannot find them online, send a large SAE to:

Black Lace Guidelines
Virgin Books
Thames Wharf Studios
Rainville Road
London W6 9HA

One first-class stamp is sufficient. If you are sending a request from the US, please note that only UK postage stamps 'work' when mailing from the UK.

Exit Stage Left

Felicity Salten

'Now, please only attempt this if you feel sure you can get to the top. It is a long way up, and there's no stopping halfway once we get everyone moving.'

A silence had fallen over the group as we looked up into the dark shadows where the rungs disappeared into blackness. Dave, the head of department, continued to speak.

'I'm going up first. If you think you might be a bit slow, please wait till last.' With that, he took an agile swing at the third rung of the ladder and hauled himself easily up the clanking bars two at a time. He was quickly followed by a steady stream of students, all eager to see the stage from the bird's nest.

I felt the sweat already clamming up my palms as I strained to see the steel riggings swinging high above my head.

'You coming up?' asked Paul.

He was flirting. That golden skin and the late summer tan specially nurtured to catch all the girls off guard at the beginning of the autumn term – well, it wouldn't wash with me.

'I'm keeping my feet firmly on the ground,' I sneered. 'And anyway, I've seen it.' Lie.

'Chicken shit,' he crowed, and disappeared with a speedy silence. I looked around me. I was left with the spotty girl and the dweeb. Not cool, but I knew I'd fall if I got on that ladder. Voices faded into distant chat as they paraded above us. I saw Paul's blond head leaning dangerously over the railing, seventy feet above us.

'Come on up, Nat!' he shouted. I heard the faint high pitch of Dave's angry voice, giving him a bollocking for messing about.

What a twat that guy was. I'll show him, I thought. I took a step towards the ladder. My palms were dripping hot. I held on to the cold rung at eye level, and tried to get my leg to bend at the knee. My foot hit the bottom bar with a clang which I heard but couldn't feel. My feet were like rubber stumps on resisting blocks. Somewhere behind me the spotty girl was speaking.

I hauled myself up with my arms and clung on, looking straight at the brick wall behind the ladder. Someone had carved their name in the unimaginative 'I woz ere' pen. I wished I wasn't, and swung up another rung. Three up! I looked down. I was about three feet off the ground. Four, five, six, seven. I peered up into the black, and my head reeled. I gripped my hands together through a rung and froze, my breathing quickened and the sweat prickling out in beads across my forehead. I was too heavy to lift myself any further, and my arms were weakening with the effort of holding on. I froze.

Minutes seemed to drag by, and all I could hear was the breath pumping out of me, and then softer rhythmic soles echoing through the grid from somewhere below. A hand gently took my ankle.

'I'm going to put your right foot on the next rung down,' said a calm voice while a hand gripped firmly.

'Do you trust me?' it asked.

'Yes,' I heard in my head. My leg was pulled downwards.

'Talk to me. What's your name?' he asked.

The spotty girl butted in. I heard some commotion high above. 'Is she all right, Dan?'

'She's doing fine!' the voice behind me called back, as though I were some great ship sailing out of dock. I was aware of my position, my bum looming down towards him, this stranger with the softly spoken authority, getting an eyeful of my greatest assets. They didn't call me lard arse for nothing! I had to get out of there. I tried to rush the next couple of steps, but the rubber stumps that were my feet hadn't regained feeling, and my boot heel skidded over the rounded bar. I fell.

It was really all too embarassing. The last thing I remembered was seeing Paul's face, high in the darkness like a comical moon, struck dumb as he saw me falling. Then I was fighting for breath, winded and bruised with a throbbing in my backside and the sensation that the back of my head was being pushed through my eyeballs. The spotty girl was hysterical. I passed out.

I remember the ice, so cold it numbed the pain, and a finger carefully wiping a trickle of ice water from my cheek. 'We'd better get her to the nurse,' he said, and I felt his hands supporting the weight of my head as I was covered with a blanket. Hands I could trust. Fingers that had touched me.

I was OK. A few days in bed and it was back to college, ready for the onslaught of jokes about me pulling any stunt for some attention. Well, we were on a drama course. Luckily I had suffered no side effects, although I had a strange sensation the next time I went into the theatre. There was a rehearsal onstage, and the lighting was undergoing last minute technical detail.

I began to feel the same urgency in my breathing as

the moment before I crashed to the floor. I felt sexually alive and excited in a way I had never experienced, and I sensed I might find the release my body needed.

I smuggled myself into a dark seat in the furthest corner, threw my coat over myself and settled down to watch. The actors were badly under-rehearsed, even if they were only first years, and I couldn't help laughing. Gradually, though, I became bored with the scene before me. I looked around at the empty seats sloping down the auditorium and, checking there was no one else about, I unbuttoned my jeans and slid my hand into the warmth of my knickers.

I smiled at the idea of being a dirty old woman on the back seat of the theatre, rummaging under my huge overcoat for some urgent relief, and this image was reinforced when I drew out my hand and smelt my spicy juices on the tips of my fingers.

I tasted the salt.

I felt a little more daring, and swung my boots up on to the seat in front, catching the heels on the back of the chair so that it pulled at my ankles and arched my feet within the leather. My jeans were loose now, and I pushed my hips forward to ease them over my bum, pushing my fingers into hot folds of cunt.

I didn't know why I was feeling so horny, but a recent conversation with close friends had led me to divulge that I'd never experienced an orgasm, and this confession was met with disbelief. I was eager to dispel it, and keen to prove to myself that I was neither frigid nor prudish. I twisted my pubes round my fingers, pulling them upwards so my slit became an elongated gash, and stroked the edges where hair met silky wetness, probing deeper.

Pushing my cunt lips apart, and stretching my labia, I teased the delicate surface with my nails, running them up to my clit and pressing it in small circles until I had built up a steady rhythm.

My clit was responding, and I circled harder, waiting for the inner, deeper sensations that friends had told me about. I couldn't feel it. In my frustration, I plunged two fingers into my cunt, and pushed them up high to try to find my G-spot, while keeping two fingers rolling on my clit. I had pushed myself further off the seat to do this, and was unaware of the motion my heels were causing to the chairs in front. The whole of row B was rocking. A head stuck out from behind a seat four chairs down.

It was a face I liked, and one I hadn't seen before, framed with ruffled black hair. The dark eyes stared at me from the gloom, and he smiled at me in recognition.

'How are you?' came the calm, strong voice.

I felt a stirring of excitement inside me, and a significant tremor of pleasure. It was my rescuer. We hadn't formally met, but I knew that voice, and now I found myself staring back hard to see that face. He was suddenly on his feet and climbing over the back of the seats towards me. I shifted uneasily under my coat, quickly crossed my legs and folded my hands piously on my thighs, but I couldn't hide the steaming smell of my pussy as it drifted from my fingers.

He fell into the seat beside me and swung his legs so they dangled over row B. I was subtly hemmed in. I smiled. I kind of like to feel trapped.

'How's your climbing technique these days?' he asked, raising an eyebrow. I noticed the light crinkling around his eyes as his expression changed. He was easily 35.

'Which year are you in?' he asked.

As we exchanged chit chat, I was aware of the ripening perfume on my fingers. If I could smell it, he surely must be able to, and I searched his face for any signs that he might. I told him I was in my final year, and had opted for the technical theatre module with performance and set design.

'I'll be seeing a lot more of you then,' he said. 'I'm the new technician. Good with lights ... wiring ... plugging.' His lips parted slightly, and I saw the flicker of his tongue as it ran slowly over the inside of his lip. He stared hard at me.

I felt my pulse quicken and, as if instinctively wishing to reassure me, he placed a hand on my arm and gently tightened his grip. The same strong grip which had guided my numb, leather-clad ankles down the ladder rungs. For a second I remembered the image of my big, rounded arse in tight jeans above his head, moving slowly down the narrow iron rungs. This time I held on to that thought. Maybe he had enjoyed it.

The lights went up. 'Dan, we need a blue gel on number twenty two and a redhead on five!' someone shouted from the lighting box.

'I've got a redhead here,' he murmured, 'and she's a bit of a handful. I hope.' He jumped out of the seat, over the orange sea of chairs, and was enveloped by the swish of the brown velvet curtains – exit stage left.

I buttoned up my jeans and slipped into my coat, leaving the theatre with the satisfaction of an actress who has just had a fulfilling rehearsal, and the tingling anticipation that I might get to do an encore.

I wanted to learn every aspect of theatre life, and now I had a secret reason to loiter after hours on the bare stage. Paul was still pursuing me, getting intense about a love role we were rehearsing for his final piece. I had already agreed to be in it, and our names had been entered on the examination register, so I was obliged to endure his wet, sucking mouth which clung to mine for longer with each rehearsal, until I was forced to push him away. For me it was acting, but with each refusal he came back with greater persistence, turning a simple kissing scene into a full-on grope of my breasts.

One evening I'd had enough, and pushed him off so hard he staggered backwards and fell awkwardly on to his wrist. Dan happened to come into the auditorium for a sound check as Paul hit the deck with a strangled cry.

'Cunning stunt!' he shouted from the back row of the stalls. Paul was not amused.

'That was not a stunt. She's a bloody headcase!' he spat, and stormed out through the fire doors, swinging them with a bang and setting off the alarm.

'Shit!' Dan hissed, and bounded down the aisle. The orchestra pit was open, a gaping five-foot hole falling twenty feet under the stage, and he leapt it without hesitation. I was impressed.

He clambered over some canvas backdrops and flats, caught the handle of the fire alarm and silenced it. He unlocked the lighting desk and flipped the house lights down, plunging the stage into darkness, but leaving me in my own personal suffused pool of light.

I stood watching as he climbed back down, watching his older but fit body, clad simply in jeans and a black T-shirt, unaware that I was absent-mindedly rubbing my tender breasts which had just been roughly grabbed during the love scene. Paul's words, panted as he had roughly pulled at my nipples, echoed with the shriek of bells round my head: 'Why do you wear those tight shirts for rehearsals, then? Come on, let me see your tits, Natasha. Come on, hold my cock.'

Dan was walking towards me. 'You OK? There's always trouble when you're around!' he said with a smile. 'You love it, don't you?' He had dimples when he grinned. I noticed his eyes straying down to my hardened nipples which were now pushing hard at the crêpe-like fabric of my fitted shirt. He was trying hard to look me in the face, and failing miserably. His gaze fell on my nipples again.

'What was all that about, then? Is he your boyfriend?'

'No! He thinks he is. He also thinks that just because I agreed to rehearse after hours I'm begging for it!' I snapped, suddenly finding an outlet for my anger.

He took a step closer. 'And are you?'

He reached out a tentative hand and traced the outline of my breasts with one finger. I noticed it was long and lean like the rest of him. He circled my stiffening buds, shifting his attention alternately between my face and his finger, paying careful attention to what he was doing.

'You like twiddling knobs?' I smirked.

'Yeah', he replied without laughing. 'Do you?' I fell right into my own joke there, and inwardly cursed my childish stupidity.

The main door into the theatre swung open, and I could just make out the dimly lit features of Dave, the head of department. He stood at the top of the stairs, squinting down at the two of us in the spot of soft yellow light, Dan's outstretched hand on the full curve of my breast.

'Why did the fire alarm go off?' he shouted. 'Dan, what are you doing down there? Have you taken up acting now?'

'Just reading me through my lines,' I called back, before he had a chance to reply.

'So who started the fire, Natasha?' Dave quipped, obviously aware of what was really going on.

'Fire safety officer,' Dan shouted into the darkness without taking his eyes from my tits.

'Don't get your fingers burnt.' Dave's voice faded out. We heard the muffled slam of the swing door and the safety bar rattled shut.

I turned my attention back to Dan's fingers, which were now running lightly up my cleavage and on to my neck. He smoothed the hair away from my face, every brush of his flesh against mine running through me like a red heat. And then his mouth was fixed on mine, his teeth biting at my eager lips. I wanted to explore his mouth, curl my tongue around his, and suck the lust from his lips. I was turned on.

I made the second move and eased our frantic bodies

towards the floor. I fell to my knees and began to unzip his well-worn jeans. He was naked underneath. A dark pattern of hair ran up the smoothness of his abdomen to his navel, and I reached down to touch, pulling his jeans over his hips with my other hand. I could feel the hardened mound in the crotch of denim, and I pressed it rhymically in with the palm of my hand to make it as hard as I could before freeing his cock.

Dan had unbuttoned my shirt, and I cursed the fact that I was wearing a rather shabby old bra beneath it. But he was in biting heaven, and sucking furiously at the silky flesh above my breasts. I tried to remember if I had put on clean knickers; to my initial shame, I realised I had not.

One glance down at his bulging erection, still pushing at the palm of my hand, told me that, clean knickers or not, he wanted me more than all of my old boyfriends put together. I laughed.

'What's making you smile?' he asked, tearing his mouth away from the lovebite that was forming in a purple-red bruise.

'I've got yesterday's knickers on!' I whispered like a naughty tart. I'd never experimented with talking dirty, and I was unprepared for the reaction it would cause. He pushed me back on the floor and began to pull roughly at my jeans. I was aware of space beside my head, and I realised how close we had moved to the open well of the orchestra pit, but something excited me about the risk of plunging over the edge. A button had got stuck and he was tugging furiously at the denim, making the curve of my creamy belly jiggle in response.

He made a low moaning sound and turned his attentions to the gentle ripple of flesh which lolled over the top of my waistband, kissing and caressing my rounded hips while I released the stuck button. I lifted my bum and pulled my jeans down, revealing my grubby white knickers, which were also torn slightly at the narrow lace band. His hand slid under the tight elastic and touched my cunt lips for the first time. His fingers moved quickly over my wet pussy, stroking and probing at the hot, soaking folds of my centre, and he pushed them into me as I lay my head back on the floor and opened my legs.

I stretched my hands above my head and touched a cold metal object. My distracted fingers toyed with with it, and I sensed a circle, a ring in the floor to pull up sections of the stage. I slipped two fingers throught the ring and used it to push myself deeper on to Dan's fingers, which were now sliding in and out of my dripping minge. He caught sight of my little invention, and with most of one hand still inside me, began to tear my knickers off with the other.

He shifted his weight forward to pin me down with his body, and I ground my pussy deeper on to his hand, trying to reach the solid bump in his jeans with which I wanted to make contact. I couldn't reach his groin, but the pleasure his fingers were causing inside as I writhed wildly in my efforts made the attempt worthwhile. I concentrated on trying to push harder and felt a wave of intense pleasure, the beginnings of my first orgasm.

He was fumbling around over my head, and I felt something pull at my wrists. He had tied my hands to the ring with my knickers, and now as he rolled on top me, he thrust himself upward and pressed his face into the still-warm gusset. He sniffed them hard, thrusting his fingers deeper inside me the deeper he breathed in my scent.

He stopped suddenly and sat back on his heels, and I thought for a moment of the sight we must have been making on the stage. There was I, flushed with sensual urgency, hair tangled and tied to the floor by my knickers with my shirt thrown open, legs askew, and Dan, pausing now, with his fly undone and his T-shirt pulled up at the back.

He had a strange expression on his face.

'Is anything wrong?' I asked, catching my breath.

'Wrong? God, no! I thought I was going to come, and I don't want to yet.' He winced slightly, and the dimpled grin flashed for a second. 'You're too much! You and those dirty knickers. I can smell you. The same smell as that day when I came and sat next to you at the back of the theatre. The same smell I caught a hint of when I was behind you on the ladder.'

'What! You could smell me then?' I blushed for the first time since I was a kid.

'Aw, you've gone all pink! Come here.'

He slipped an arm round me and lowered himself on to me, kissing me intensely. We remained locked in each other's mouths for several long, beautiful moments. Christ, I'll be falling in love in a minute, I thought. But what I craved was his body on top of mine, right there, right then.

'Take your jeans off, Dan,' I pleaded. 'I want to see you.' He slid them off. I hooked my ankles together behind his back and pulled him down on top of me, feeling the solidity of his cock against my cunt, and the tickling of hair, unfamiliar and new and exciting.

I freed one hand. Turning my head so I could see his cock, I slipped my hand down to feel all of it before it went inside me. I closed my fingers around the shaft and gently moved my wrist to and fro so I could wank him to bursting point. Not too much too soon. I wanted him in me before he came.

I cupped his balls in my hand and then slid upwards with long, deliberate strokes, watching the tightening skin of his hard dick. He shuddered slightly as I increased my speed, my hand slapping on the top of my thigh on the downward strokes. Then I eased myself into position so he could push himself into my pussy. I spat on my hand and lubricated his cock, and grabbed a

11

bum cheek, urging him in. Then I tugged at the dirty knickers round my wrist, wanting to be tied up again.

'Tie me up and fuck me!' I whispered.

'I will,' he gasped. 'But what will you do for me?'

'Huh?'

'If I do that, will you do something for me?'

Oh, here we go, I thought! Time to really open myself up to some degrading perversion or act of utter depravity. The thought occupied my head for less than a second. I wanted him too much.

'Anything! I'll do anything!' I uttered, beyond my sense of decorum now anyway. He spread my legs and entered me. It was the best fuck I'd ever had, but although I came close, I didn't come. He did. Twice.

The autumn term was almost at an end, and since that evening in the auditorium, I'd only managed to flirt with Dan during tech lessons when the other students were present. The most contact we had was when he squeezed my arse in the lighting box after I'd made sure I was the last one out.

Then, after the Christmas show, when everyone had gone to the pub in a noisy crowd, I slipped backstage and found the big old brush used for sweeping the stage, which was a thing I loved to do.

'Do us a little dance, then!' a shout came from high above me. I swung round and threw my head back to look straight into the dazzling lights.

'Dan! I can't see you!'

'I can see you! Wait there, I'm coming down.'

The purple blind spots were just clearing when his arms were round me.

'I've been watching you.' He flashed his dark eyes wolfishly. 'I've had you in mind for something . . . and you did promise,' he said, taking me by the arm and leading me over to a dark recess of the wings.

'I hadn't forgotten.' I turned and caught him by his

slender waist, slipping my hands under his white T-shirt and pulling him to me. I lifted his top to his shoulders, and bent forward to kiss his naked chest. He smelt of fresh sweat and the musky linger of old aftershave. I teasingly bit at his dark-haired nipples, flicking my tongue over them as I ran my nails down his back. I licked a trail down the centre of his body and began to unzip his jeans. He gripped my shoulders.

'That's not what I want,' he sighed. 'Come over here.' I followed him to the back wall of the theatre, and found myself once more at the foot of the narrow ladder.

'Up you go.' he spoke closely into my ear, and pressed his erection firmly into the crack of my arse. 'I'll be right behind you.' He patted my bottom.

'You have to be kidding!' I stammered, half turning to see that it wasn't a joke.

He pressed into me, squashing my soft body between his eagerness and the cold iron grid which dug into my back. I felt myself weakening under the wonderful pressure of his body, and he persuasively rubbed his bulging crotch against me – his hardened and demanding, mine already melting.

'I can't!'

'You said you'd do anything I asked,' he said firmly, taking my face in his hands and forcing me to look into his eyes. 'You trust me?'

'Yes', I muttered feebly, drawn in by his steady gaze.

'And anyway,' he said, 'I want you to help me fix a light up there. You really ought to be able to do that as part of your course, so just look at it like that. Think of this as a perk of the job!'

I turned and looked high into the blackness, just making out the platform grids which criss-crossed over our heads. A queasy sensation wobbled my knees, and churned in my stomach.

'I'm sorry, I – I just can't! I'll fall. I'm not strong enough to pull myself up.' I heard myself whine. I hated

13

being the whingeing female, but heights just did that to me. At the same time, I knew I should really try to conquer that bloody ladder, and my self-resolution was telling me not to be such a spineless coward.

'But I'll try.' My words conveyed the fears of one who is resigned to their fate, and I turned and faced the iron rungs before me. Adrenalin flooded my veins, and I began to climb.

Tentatively I placed one foot higher than the other, watching only my white-knuckled hands as they gripped the wrought-iron rungs. Up, and up, a hand, a foot.

'Keep looking straight ahead,' Dan encouraged me.

'The brickwork doesn't make an inspiring view.' I tried to laugh, but couldn't hide the tremble in my voice.

'You should see what I can see!' He smacked his lips.

'Thanks!' I liked the compliment, even if it was an inopportune moment. 'Oh, God, my arms and wrists are aching. Are we halfway yet?'

'Not even close. Let your legs push you up, don't rely on your arms. Anyway, I like the way it makes your arse swing.'

'You're a cheeky bugger,' I laughed with a sudden confidence, and I turned to look at him.

The floor spun at least 25 feet below, and I shuddered, grabbing the ladder close and hugging it to me. I froze.

'I want to go down!' I breathed, not daring to move my body an inch.

Dan pulled himself up so his lips were close to my neck, and the feel of his breath, combined with my utter terror of letting go, made me shudder with a deeply sexual tremor which stirred my blood and throbbed through my cunt. I was breathing hard.

'Come on,' he whispered. 'We've been here before. I'll guide you.' Taking each hand in turn, he began to inch us slowly upwards again, but keeping me distracted from the fear by whispering filthy nothings in my ear. And they were filthy – so filthy my pussy was throbbing more and more with the succulence of being so turned on. I'd almost forgotten that we were 70 feet in the air. I suddenly found myself at eye level with the meshed platform which made a gangway to the lights.

'Ha! I did it!' I laughed, exhilarated. 'Are we going to shag in the bird's nest? How do I get on to the platform?'

'Just hold on a second, you sweet little fuck! Stay right where you are.'

He disappeared from my shoulder, and I felt his presence moving down a few rungs, but still pressed closely to my body. I was drifting in mid-air without him behind me, and I could feel myself swaying off the ladder.

'Dan? Where are you? Come back!' My fear turned into a sickening excitement which shook every nerve-ending in my body. It was a breathtaking scariness which froze my limbs, but made my cunt ache with the thrill. I felt his hands unbuttoning my jeans.

'Not here!' I half-shrieked, but he wasn't listening, and he knew I was too scared to even try to move off on my own. A rough tug and they were mid-thigh, then my knickers followed, exposing my great, curvaceous mound of bum.

'You're mad!'

'Hold on tight,' he replied, ignoring me, 'I'm going to move your feet. Bend your knees and put your weight on your right leg.'

It took me a couple of seconds to co-ordinate this move as I clung on, and every inch I moved felt like much further. He took a firm hold of my left ankle, and, bending my knee, hooked my foot around the bar on a higher rung.

'Transfer your weight to the left,' he said, and I did, slowly, until my body had shifted position. Then he took my right ankle and anchored that foot round the opposite bar on the same rung, so I felt like I was frozen

15

in a plié, and semi-squatting with my boots firmly locked around the ladder.

My naked arse was now hanging out for all the gods to see, but the feeling of such exposure set my pussy throbbing again, and knowing that there was nothing beneath me made it almost unbearably, dangerously sexy. So unbearable, I began to tremble with the need to feel a tongue or a finger on my cunt. Instinctively, as if in reply to my thoughts, I felt Dan's face pressed against my buttocks.

I had a little more leverage because of my position, so I was able to push against the sliding of his tongue as he moved it along the length of my arse crack. I could hear him breathing harder as he buried his face in my wet cunt, lapping at my juicy hole. I pressed down harder, and his tongue wiggled inside me.

'You taste fantastic,' he moaned and, taking one hand from the ladder, he parted my bum cheeks to get closer in. The smell of my cunt and warm arse drifted up to me.

'Suck harder,' I gasped, feeling the waves of pleasure turning inside me.

He slipped his hand under me and began to lubricate the whole of my pussy with my stickiness, rubbing his fingers slowly over my clit. I let my knees bend furthur so my body was sagging over his face. While his fingers worked on my cunt, his tongue found my arsehole, and he ran it in small circles over the ring of my anus. This was a new one for me, and my virgin arse ring responded with a tightening ecstasy. He pushed more spit in with his tongue, going in deeper until his face was pressing hard up my bum, and then I could feeling him sucking his own saliva back out, swallowing hard and tasting my arse.

I was helpless within my metal bonds, free to move, and yet tied by the drop which fell away beneath me. My arms were numbing, and the ladder was biting hard into parts of my bared thighs, but I wanted him to go on.

'Dan, make me come!' I wailed in a voice I hardly recognised as my own.

He lapped harder at my tight little bumhole, making it sensitive and ready for more contact. He gave it a final sloppy lick to make sure it was properly lubed, and then he pushed his middle finger right up inside me. My body jerked involuntarily and, as my head fell back, I saw space all around. It increased my sensations, and I began to rock harder on his finger.

He thrust in and out of me, pressing on the outside of my pink hole just before the finger slid in to heighten sensitivity. He stopped for a second, re-lubricated my arse with his tongue, and then I felt more fingers being inserted. A second of pain mixed with a throb of an orgasm made me cry out, and he thrust into me with increased speed.

'Put all your fingers in,' I called back to him. 'Make it hurt!'

I heard him spit.

My thighs tensed as I felt his hand forced inside me, and it literally brought tears to my eyes. I could feel a spasm building up inside me, and I let my body drop the final few inches so I was resting fully on the ladder. Now, as Dan quickened his pace, the force of his rhythm had begun to shake the iron frame.

'Oh, God!' I cried, half in fear of the ladder coming away from the wall and half in ecstasy as I felt a deep tightening in my cunt. The ladder shook violently, rattling the bolts against the brickwork where a small amount of powdered brick was crumbling.

I gripped the ladder, and stretched my arms, locking them at the elbow, so I resembled Boudicca riding her chariot, my head flung back and leaning into fresh air. I tensed my thigh muscles as the tingling inside pulled me closer to my climax, and Dan's fingers moved faster, filling the whole of my arse with his hand. I was going to come. The feeling that he was right up inside my body overwhelmed me. I was suddenly sucked in by the clenching of my vaginal muscles, and then released on a pulsating, rapturous arc.

I flopped against a rung, breath coming from deeper than my lungs as I sagged, spent and motionless. I couldn't moved even if I had wanted to. Dan climbed up beside me and kissed my cheek, wiping away a trickle of sweat with a finger which smelt of me.

'Did you enjoy that?' he asked.

I tried to nod, and a tiny sigh escaped from my lips.

'Don't worry,' he grunted, heaving himself over my inert body and clambering on to the platform, 'We can go down in the hydraulic lift.'

It took a second to click. I stared at him.

'You mean there's a lift?'

His dimples were showing like an actor after giving a great performance. At that moment I began planning an exquisite revenge at Dan's expense – but one I knew we would both enjoy.

As it turned out, the view from the top of the bird's nest was worth the climb. I fixed the bulb on a 2k, mended a barn door, re-wired a junction box and passed my course. And, strangely, heights weren't a problem after that.

Shoot

Anya Ross

A cameraman with pretensions to write, and a writer with intentions of photographing him naked. It should have worked out beautifully, but I realised too late that he wanted a girlfriend without the sexual complications, while I just wanted his body, and some of his mind. The alarm bells were switched off for two months when they should have been screaming in my ears from the start.

Flashback, a Friday night: I left a message on his mobile, unknowingly saying the key words, 'Let's go out to play.' He called back and got straight to the point: 'Get in a cab and meet me at the Metro Cinema on Rupert Street.' His forcefulness immediately turned me on. The film started at nine. I leapt into the bath, washed my hair, shaved my legs, dressed, called a cab and got to the cinema by 9.15. So we missed the beginning of the film, which, like seafood, was to become a habit, one of those little intimacies that seem so relevant at the time.

Kissed is not a film most people would choose for a first date, since it's about a beautiful young woman who works in a mortuary and has sex with dead men. It was surprisingly erotic. Joe said that if his screenplay had a genre, *Kissed* would be part of it. What he didn't say was that his story was deeply twisted.

Several times during the film I laid my head back, closed my eyes and smiled: I was utterly content, if slightly giddy, sitting in the dark next to a gorgeous man, watching a strangely sensual film. I was picturing him naked, of course, but even fully clothed he emanated sex. Tall and thin, he was not conventionally handsome despite his near-perfect features; it was the combination of short greying hair, the bluest eyes, an almost feminine nose, dagger cheekbones and the kind of mouth you want to thrust on to your left nipple right now.

As we left the Metro and stepped into the Soho mêlée, he took my hand, placed my arm in his and said with a worldly smile, 'This is much more civilised.' I managed to smile graciously but my thoughts were far from gracious; they were in the gutter. The Joe I thought I knew was adorable, funny, overly animated and, at 41, very boyish. The man holding my arm was sophistication in a pair of Levi's: charming, urbane and outrageously sexy. The sexiness had always been there, but was masked by his childlike enthusiasm. There was nothing at all childlike about him as we strolled through Chinatown and the theatre district.

So we had dinner at Café Fish, a prime date restaurant with low lighting, myriad water images on the walls, intimately small tables and unobtrusive but efficient staff. How perfect; I'll never go there again. We pulled the film to pieces, me from the writing side and Joe from the technical. I learnt more about tracking shots, POVs and reverse angles than I actually needed to know. My curiosity waned after a while, but I didn't show it. At least he had the good grace to ask about writing techniques. I realised later that it was entirely motivated by self-interest; it wasn't *my* writing he was interested in, it was what I could teach him. He brought out my daring side, so I made an analogy with sex: 'Basically, good writing should be concise, clean and as close to brevity as you can get. So, it's the exact opposite of good sex.' His eyes widened and he laughed.

'You're very direct.'

'That's where the line between writing and sex becomes blurred.' I felt I was about to go too far, so I explained that Journalism-One gem, 'Eating your darlings', which, surprisingly, has nothing to do with sex. He found the term highly amusing and, on that note, paid the bill.

As we strolled arm in arm along Piccadilly to Green Park to catch the last tube home, I thought, Who is this man? I should never have asked. That first evening and for the next two months I thought he was a gentleman, smoothly insisting on paying for everything (I won only once), taking off his scarf and putting it round my neck because I was cold, always calling when he said he would. He was even solicitous with doors. But it was all on the surface; beneath that shiny veneer he was a seething mass of damage and poison. I hadn't realised there was such a fine line between chivalry and misogyny.

Back at my flat we talked about past loves. I was the optimist to his defeatist. I should have listened and looked harder. With misplaced compassion, I felt sympathy instead of suspicion; what I took for real pain in those pale blue eyes was actually hatred and venom.

We were both amazed when 5 a.m. rolled around; we weren't ready to stop talking. I called a cab, then we held each other close and kissed briefly on the lips. It was a tender and slightly awkward moment; had we shifted from acquaintances to potential lovers?

I went to bed, stunned and outrageously turned on. I woke up three hours later with the searing desire to make love very slowly; fucking was at that point out of the question. Out of nowhere I recalled a line of nonsense poetry: 'Oh, how you made me come, when you told me you were forty-one.'

He was there with me the whole way. My hands were his as he stroked my neck. My nipples were already hard when his hands reached them. I heard him whisper, 'If you want me to hurt you just tell me.' Where the hell did that come from? It wasn't part of my usual fantasies. I rephrased it: 'Just tell me you want to make love until you can't take any more.' I had the feeling he would be a talker. His dialogue was border-line dirty; so was mine. That beautiful mouth travelled down my body slowly, kissing and licking me all the way to my hips. When I wanted him to bite me he did, but gently, just enough to tell me he knew I wanted to go close to the edge.

He pushed my legs apart and said, 'Look at me.' I gazed down at him as his fingers teased me. 'Don't close your eyes, I want to see how it feels.' We spoke silently as he slowly slid two fingers inside me. His smile said, 'I can feel how turned on you are.' I don't think I had ever been that wet.

His face disappeared between my legs. I gasped as he licked me and his fingers pushed deeper. My hips moved with him as he sucked me hard. I knew he wasn't going to let me hold back: he wanted me to come right then, in his mouth. So I let go and went with him. My back arched as he forced my legs even further apart. His mouth was so hard on me it should have hurt. I felt the rush rise through me so fast I lost control and let it all go into his mouth. I was shaking and shivering as I came down. The intensity brought me to tears. He smiled at me and said, 'You taste like honey.' He licked the tears away and kissed me softly. 'Salty tears on your face, honey between your legs.'

* * *

I decided not to call, no matter how long it took. He gave in first, two weeks later. By the second date he had progressed from arm in arm to hand in hand. The flirting was subtle on my part, and progressively explicit on his. It took me a while to figure out what it was about him that was so seductive: it was the way I felt when his eyes were on me. At times I could barely hear what he was saying – I just wanted that mouth on me. Yet by the fourth date he still hadn't given me a real kiss and my patience was running out. I rationalised: 'He's shy, he's intimidated, he's old-fashioned, he's gay, he's a secret misogynist and is getting a twisted thrill from winding me up.' Of all those, 'shy' was the one I fell for. I was wrong. It was the final option that almost brought this story to an end.

On the sixth date, when I couldn't bear for a moment longer the ache throughout my body as he kissed me on the mouth and went home in the early hours of the morning, I said, 'Joe, I am utterly bemused by you.'

He smiled, knowing exactly what I meant, and said, 'Collect your thoughts and we'll talk next Saturday.' His assumption that we would spend almost every Saturday evening together was implicit.

He knew precisely what was coming later in our conversation. We were sitting in a restaurant with hard wooden benches. He noticed my discomfort and, touchingly considerate, folded his jacket and said, 'Here, sit on this.' Then he laughed wickedly, 'Mmm, I'll enjoy putting that on later.' In the car on the way home, as a prelude to another subject, he said, 'This is foreplay.'

The message seemed unambiguous. I was totally confident that within half an hour we would be in bed, or on the floor, having outrageous sex. There was not a flicker of doubt in my mind as I said, 'So, shall I get to the point?'

'Shoot,' he said, smiling.

I took a deep breath and said, 'I don't want to give too much away, but I can't be just friends with you, it would be physically impossible.'

He folded his arms and, without changing his expression, said, 'Well, we can have closure on that right now.' His body language told me, in a word, 'No'.

I was too stunned to respond when he said, 'I thought about it the first few times we went out, but I realised we weren't going to be a long-term item.' He shrugged his shoulders. 'It was just instinct.'

'So what were you doing holding hands with me and flirting?'

He laughed and said, 'That was 2.5 on the flirting scale. Anyway, holding hands doesn't mean anything.'

The conversation continued along these lines for another hour. I was so shocked, humiliated and wounded that I couldn't respond, let alone defend myself. My mind was blank and I became inarticulate as his words hit me like fists. He twisted the knife deeper with every sentence: 'You don't talk enough'; 'The spark just isn't there'; 'I'm looking for someone different, just different to you'; 'You're just not . . .' 'Not good enough' was what he meant. 'I don't do short-term relationships any more. Three years ago I would have steamed in there with you and six months down the road it would have ended, it would have been angst-ridden and messy. So I just don't do it.'

'At all?'

'Well,' he said and grinned as if he had a secret to tell. 'There's this woman. I go to her house, we do the business and I go home. No complications. But it's kind of sordid.'

'Then why do you do it?'

'Because it's sex and it's uncomplicated, and it doesn't cost me anything, financially or emotionally.' So it wasn't even fucking; it was just coming. Outwardly he had the perfect set-up: clinical sex with his 'receptacle' and toying with me, an alluring woman, all dressed up for him on Saturday evenings – hand-holding and affection, yet no emotional expenditure, no physical exchange: basically a date without the effort.

'You should thank me, I'm saving you from all that angst.' I didn't feel at all grateful, I felt sick. 'Read my screenplay. I *am* a bit of a misogynist,' he said, and laughed as if it were funny. He couldn't hide the smug smile on his face as he landed several more verbal punches, from which I couldn't defend myself.

I finally said, 'Well, there's nothing left to say.'

He got up and said breezily, 'I'll hit the road then,' as if we were acquaintances who had just had tea. I walked him to the door. We had a replay of our first goodnight kiss; it was a surprisingly tender moment. Until he made sure that I would read his screenplay.

So, he had turned out to be all fantasy and no trousers. Anger hit me the following morning and he was so lucky not to be in the same room with me. His rejection was brutal; there was no sensitivity or thought for my feelings. I needed to vent my anger, so I sat at the computer, the one place where I am never inarticulate, and wrote him a letter. I was as nasty and brutally honest as he had been, but far more eloquent. Then I read his screenplay straight through, taking notes all the way.

It had some moments, but it was an amateur and sloppy attempt, self-indulgent and autobiographical to the point of laughter; one of the main characters was a boyishly handsome cameraman. The women were sluts and the men losers, and the sex scenes were predictably nasty. One of the stereotyped female characters actually said my line: 'Let's go out to play.' There was no depth, there was barely even a surface. His lack of personal life had killed his perception. I could have been kinder in my criticism but I felt he deserved an honest opinion, and that's all he deserved. I ended the letter with a veiled challenge. I had the feeling he would fall for it.

As disgusted as I was at myself for allowing him to affect me so deeply, I was even more disgusted that I still wanted him; we had unfinished business. I relegated him to the role of Fantasy Man, exploiting all those base things I could never do for real, hearing the words that ignited me when I was with someone who wasn't turning me on. The dialogue in his screenplay echoed in my head; I had temporarily sunk to his sexual level.

Over the next two weeks he left three messages on my answerphone in response to my letter; I'd been at home to hear two of them. I stopped screening my calls when I finally couldn't bear the anticipation a moment longer. He called at about 11 p.m. 'Did you get my messages?'

'I've been busy.'

'So, what are you doing right now?'

I cut the retribution and said, 'Joe, get over here right now and fuck me slow and hard.' He paused, then hung up. Either I would be alone in twenty minutes, or not. I leapt into the bath and dressed like a slut. This was about to be my revenge-fuck.

The door bell rang. My nerves had disappeared the second he'd hung up; I was in the fantasy. I opened the door and we stared at each other with hatred and lust. I grabbed his leather jacket in my fists and pulled him inside. Up close to his mouth I whispered, 'I hate you so much.'

He looked at me as though he wanted to hurt me and said, 'I hate you too.'

'Perfect,' I said. Then his mouth, that mouth, was on mine, soft and gentle, just as I had imagined the first real kiss. His hands were tangled in my hair as he pushed me against the wall and the kiss was suddenly not at all gentle. His long, lean body crushed into me and his mouth and mine were fighting. I scraped my nails along his neck and his shoulders shot back. I pushed his jacket to the floor and tore his shirt open, buttons flying.

'Rules,' I said. 'This is *my* fantasy. So, I get to come first, you go slow and you talk dirty.'

'Done.' And he lifted me until my legs were around his waist and carried me into my bedroom. He lowered me to the floor, undid the zip of my dress and let it fall. He stepped back to take in my body and the black underwear. 'Beautiful bitch,' he hissed. His words shot through me like hot ice. It suddenly struck me that he might lose control; I'd virtually given him permission. It was exquisitely frightening.

He kicked off his shoes and, like the gentleman he wasn't, bent down to take off his socks. I undid his belt and the buttons on his Levi's, pushing his jeans slowly down his long legs. He wasn't wearing any underwear. I closed my eyes in anticipation as I went down on my knees: I still had no idea whether he was a throbbing hunk of masculinity or hung like an adolescent.

'Do it,' he said and pushed my mouth on to him. Slowly I took him in and I knew – rock hard but well below average. Somehow I wasn't surprised. I'd think about it later. Right now I was in the fantasy: I could pretend he was huge.

Since I wasn't in a generous mood I stopped after less than a minute. I could feel his size precisely and it might have swayed me out of the pretence. I stood up and kissed him hard for a moment then pulled him on top of me on to the bed. He played with my bra straps as his mouth teased around my nipples. I was breathing hard as he got closer. Another second and I would explode. I reached around and undid my bra and, after two months of knowing how it would feel, I thrust that beautiful mouth on to my left nipple. My breath left me as he sucked hard, his hands on my back forcing me into his mouth. He bit me just enough to feel good. I held his face and pulled him back.

'Say those things you wrote in the script. Say them to me. Fuck me like the bitch you think I am.' Our eyes locked and he started to say them silently.

'Out loud. I want to hear you.'

He took my hands and forced them above my head, then held my face in one hand and said, 'Do you really want to hear me?'

I nodded slowly.

'Do you think I do this all the time?' he said. I nodded again.

'You're wrong.'

'So do it now. If you're bastard enough to write those words –'

'Oh, I am,' he said with a bastard smile. 'You *are* a bitch. I thought you weren't. You seem so . . . ladylike.'

I scraped my nails down his cheek and said, 'Shut up and start talking.'

It crossed my mind that he was verbally impotent but he put his mouth to my ear and whispered, 'If you want me to hurt you, just tell me.' Déjà-vu.

'You've already hurt me, so just fuck me.'

'Hard and slow?'

'Oh, yes.'

He ran his hands down my torso and traced the contours of my hips. I watched him smile as he studied my body and I nearly faltered; this was too much like making love. He kissed my stomach and licked my navel, which is not a big turn-on for me. Time for an order. 'Turn me over and kiss my back.'

Slowly he kissed the full length of my spine and up again. As he reached my shoulder blades my back arched and my head shot back. 'Bite me,' I said. And he did, but not for long. I could only take so much; my spine is my most sensitive erogenous zone. I've been known to come full throttle by a propitiously placed mouth. As he bit me between my shoulder blades, I held back and shouted, 'Stop!'

'I want to fuck you from behind.'

'No way. I don't trust you.'

'I know you want to come like that.'

'So fuck me like that from the front. I want to see your face when you do it.'

'I want your pussy first.' He spread my legs open and I gasped as two fingers slid deep inside me; had I ever been this wet? He took my right hand and pressed it between my legs, then pushed my wet fingers into his mouth and sucked, my second favourite thing; how did he know that? 'Mmm, sweet,' he said as I lay there moaning and gasping for breath as he forced his fingers deeper inside me. I could have come at any moment, but I held back.

'I want your cock inside me now, you bastard.'

In one thrust he drove his cock into me; another couple of inches and I would have screamed. He ground himself into me hard, then pulled out and pushed a finger into my mouth. 'Make it wet, it won't hurt so much,' he whispered. I was so turned on, I wanted to get to the main event as much as he did. Slowly he slid his wet finger between my buttocks, into that forbidden place.

I gasped and whispered, 'Don't hurt me.'

'Sshh, I have to hurt you a little, but it'll be so good.' He played gently with me then pushed his finger deep inside me. 'No backing out now. I'll force you if I have to, and then I'll really hurt you.'

I had the feeling he wanted me to say, 'Make me.' So I did.

He held my hands above my head with one hand and pushed my legs further apart with his knee. 'Give it to me, make it easier on yourself.' As I lifted myself towards him, breathing hard and scared, he eased his cock towards me with his hand. 'Real slow now, take it real slow.' I held my breath and tried not to tense. When he entered me I dug my nails into his shoulders and gasped.

He pulled out and said, 'Look at me.' I opened my eyes and looked into his. I saw fear, mine and his. Fear that he would lose control and that I couldn't stop him. I also saw tenderness, as if he was asking me if I really wanted this.

'Yes,' I whispered. The tenderness left his eyes: I saw only blue ice and felt it shiver down my spine.

'All the way now, take it all the way.' Slow and hard he forced his cock inside me, all the way. I gasped for breath and moaned so loud he put his hand over my mouth. I had never been this turned on with anyone. I could have come in a heartbeat. I was his: totally vulnerable and in his control.

Slowly he pulled out again and pushed my legs further apart. My back arched as he thrust into me again. Not yet, hold back. I wasn't ready to come, I wanted more of him before I gave in.

I held his face in my hands and looked into his eyes. 'Do it now,' I said. 'Say all those things you wrote in your script. Say them to me while you're fucking me. Say them.'

'You want to come like that?'

'Oh yes.'

He closed his eyes and his expression said, 'Don't make me do this.'

I stroked his face and said, 'Do it.'

He took a deep breath and put his mouth to my ear. 'You asked for it, you bitch. Come on, take it like a whore. I want to hear you come so loud. I'm gonna fuck you so hard it'll make you cry, you dirty little slut.'

The force of his words left me breathless. I murmured, 'Fuck me . . . Fuck me harder.'

'Fucking bitch. I'll give it to you harder. Tell me what it feels like . . . Tell me . . . Tell me.'

'It feels so bad, you bastard.'

'Good. I want to feel it hurt you.' If he'd been any bigger I would have been in real pain but it felt so dirty talking like that I didn't have to fake any of it.

I was close now. 'Stay right there, right there.' I arched my back and opened my legs as far as I could and ground myself hard against him.

'Fuck me . . . Fuck me,' I said over and over. I could feel it close now. I lost his voice as I felt the deep thrill well up. I cried out his name as it all came rushing through me. I came like I never had before. It seemed to go on and on as he had total control over me. Eventually I came down and I held on to him tight.

'I need a minute,' I said. He stayed inside me and held my face in his hands as I caught my breath.

I kissed him softly and moved my hips under him as he said, 'Say it again. Say "fuck me".' I shook my head. I'd got what I wanted and couldn't be bothered to talk dirty again. It didn't take long. When he came I could barely feel him inside me. As his breathing slowed, I stroked his face, looked into his eyes and said softly, smiling sweetly like a lover, 'I hate you with all my heart.'

His face crumpled and the breath caught in his throat. He buried his face against my shoulder and cried. I held him tight and stroked his hair, 'It's OK, I know, I know. Go on, cry your eyes out, let it all go.' And he did.

Eventually the sobbing stopped and I reached to get him a tissue. He blew his nose and wiped his eyes. 'I'm sorry, not for crying, but for everything. I'm just fucked up, I'm a mess. I'm so sorry.' I knew he wanted me to hold him and comfort him as he told me everything, every sad, sorry moment that had made him like this. But I'd heard all I needed to hear. I'd got the fantasy and the apology. With Joe I'd been as low as I ever wanted to be; only once. I slipped from under him, turned the light on full and said, 'Get dressed and get out.'

Frozen Violets

Leona Rhys

*I*n Northern lands there has always been a tale whispered, one in which a brother and a sister leave their cruel family and follow a trail deep, deep into the woods. There, it is said, they find a fantastic house, and in it a witch. This story is older than it seems, for in the eleventh century in the cold Viking mountains the tale was already being told. The siblings were already present in this early rendering of the legend, as was the strange house in the woods. There was an evil stepparent; a trail that the siblings followed through the forest. But the story then was not how people whisper it now, made careful and safe in the retelling. The old story was more curious, the story of how Oshu and Ola once met Skathi, the Norse goddess who lived alone in the hills to track and hunt.

It was the story of how a brother and sister left a warm house to escape a cruel father, and then were alone in the bleak landscape of the Scandinavian mountains, two figures moving between the blue shadows cast by the trees on the cream-white snow. The sister had huge black eyes that were serious and thoughtful; full, lush lips and ebony skin so dark it shone nearly purple in the starlight. Her tight-curled hair was woven into an inky rope of braid, intertwined with threads of silver and gold. She had once been a rich man's daughter, and beneath the rough foreign furs and cloths she wore a small amethyst tucked into her navel. She thought of it as a secret; a reminder of the life she had before she came to this cold land. She was the older of the two, proud and confident and brave.

Her brother was fairer in skin but just as beautiful. His eyes were green; his hair loose curls that skimmed his neck. He was seventeen. In this barren country, people counted time by cycles of seasons rather than by shifting alternations of rain and drought and it seemed a crude process to her. She did not like it.

They had a mother in common.

At first, they moved quickly, but when they realised that they were not being followed they stopped to catch their breath. It was then that the brother noticed the trail. They stood nearly immobile, their leather-bound feet just breaking through the first crisp layer of snow. Over them the heavens trembled out patterns of weird colours. It looked to the girl as if the whole sky were transforming to an ocean: surely the wavering blues and greens in the heavens were found by rights within the slippery panorama of the sea. The sister lowered her eyes from the sight. It was not the first thing that she had found disturbing in this land to which their mother had brought them; not the first sight that had disconcerted her.

She turned to her brother and said, 'Let us follow this trail; see where it goes.'

'Yes.' The brother looked out over the mounds of snow behind them, in front of them and to both sides of them.

She wondered whether his back still stung from his father's beating of the day before, and wondered if he knew that it had been worse for her. Still, here was the trail strung out before them, an escape of sorts. Yes, it was he who had first picked up one of the objects that had made up the trail and shown it to his sister. It was a frozen petal of a flower she had not yet seen in this country, but she had recognised it immediately as the petal of a violet.

He had laid the purple chip in her hand, its colour in stark contrast to her light palm. She had raised her hand and licked at its flat glassy surface, feeling its fragile structure crumble at the warmth from her tongue. For just a moment then, she had felt that her brother was watching her intently, strangely. But that was before the two of them had noticed a whole line of frozen violet petals dotted through the snow, leading into the curve of the white forest. Evidence, it seemed, that someone else was near. Perhaps someone that could help them.

They followed the trail of frozen violets, which looked like a line of bruises on the snow. The girl thought of the bruises on her brother's arms, and she winced. It had been her idea to leave; had been she who had gathered food and clothes and woken him while her mother and stepfather lay sleeping. The whole time they had crept out she had been afraid of the assault that would follow if her brother's father woke, but she had whispered a prayer and they had left him sleeping in the house.

The moon and stars made things look eerie in the blue woods; the shadows were more violent and sharp-edged against the white snow. And her brother's face was even more haunting: delicate, beautiful, wistful; lashes juxtaposed like black feathers against his heavy lids as his eyes moved to survey the dark forest. She cleared her throat, reached for her brother's covered hand and they passed by trees piled with blankets of sparkling, dustlike snow.

She was bitter. She had been betrayed by only one parent, but he had been betrayed by both. She had been right to suggest that they leave. No more beatings, no more excuses mouthed by their ashamed and weak mother, so hopelessly in love with her husband that she ignored her own children.

'The trail continues here,' the girl told her brother, showing him how the petals led between the overladen branches of pine, through the papery frozen skins of the cold birch trees.

The girl was turning cold now; it felt as if her skin was freezing painfully from the inside. Her cheeks were no longer cold – just numb skin over the chilled blood beneath. Even the amethyst was growing cold, a frigid pit caught deep in the indentation in her abdomen. She did not wish to alarm her brother, but she feared that they would have to return if they did not soon find the source of this trail. It had to be a human and not an animal; to leave a trail of frozen petals seemed a peculiarly human thing to do. She shivered, remembering how her stepfather had told them tales of the angry Northern gods even before he had taken them north by treks and sea. It was then that they saw the house.

They stopped in shock, their feet sinking into the snow. At the same time as she felt relief, the girl's heart sank. For here was warmth and shelter, but here was also what was obviously the abode of one of the Northern gods of whom her stepfather had spoken.

The house was between two arcing pines and the trail stopped right at its door. She had not yet seen such a wondrous sight in this cold, ugly land and, thirsty for beauty, despite herself her eyes were drawn to its details. When she could not explain the coloured ice, her mind made up explanations for her: in place were blocks of frozen crimson wine, crystallised rivers of green-gold honey and purple blueberry juice suspended in the frozen house. She whispered this explanation to her brother, and for him it was enough that his sister offered a reason for the colours; he did not question further until he pointed to the fruits embedded in the ice, dotted along the length of the house. The girl was not sure of their proper names.

'What are these?'

The girl scoured her imagination for answers. 'Sweet-meats of raspberries,' she told him, 'strawberries, orange *hjortron* berries placed at the ends of the eaves.'

'Why does the house shine so?'

'It is the thousand candles from within the house that make it glow with colour and light.' It could be the truth, she told herself. She looked long at the ice house, and held her brother's hand tightly. Her mind kept on explaining silently: the house was yellow where pine pitch had been swirled into the ice; glowing sun-coloured spirals decorated with small flowers: blue forget-me-nots, little buds of roses just kissed with scarlet, the separated petals of dandelions. It was as if a summer garden had been caught, preserved within the house itself. When she had arrived in summer, she had thought the Norse flowers small and inadequate, but that was before winter had come and there were none at all.

'What is it?' said her brother.

The girl knew very well that it was one of the houses of the Northern gods, but she was reluctant to let her brother know that – he would be able to tell that she was frightened.

'I'm not sure,' she said.

'Can I go touch it?'

She watched silently as her brother began to circle the house of light, running his hands against its melting sides, licking at the honey-coloured walls, his hands flat against the structure. The girl watched him do this; she could almost feel the wetness on her own palms. They could not return now; they would freeze to death, and so she must gather courage and knock on the door of the angry Northern god. She wondered if the god would be as terrible as the people of the country had been, whether he would laugh and scorn her beautiful dark skin. She would spit at him and leave, she decided, if that happened. Even if it meant her death in the snow. She was too tired of the cold country and its cruel people.

She pushed open the door, and saw with relief that there was no angry male god within but rather a woman who sat at a hearth whose fire burned and licked and curled red flame, lighting the house inside as well as outside.

'There are no thousand candles,' her brother whispered behind her, but she ignored him.

The pale woman stood up. She had short hair, and she was nearly as tall as a man. She had a strange necklace round her throat of small twigs that were fused together in the shapes that these Northern people called runes, and the woman fingered them slowly as she spoke. 'Where have you come from?'

'From far away,' the boy answered. His sister would have gestured for him not to speak, but he seemed enthralled by the woman. The girl knew, however, that it was dangerous to speak to strangers. She waited for the inevitable questions as to their origin and the questions as to the colour of their skin. She didn't want to tell the same story all over again, of how her Nigerian mother had met her Viking stepfather in the distant trading lands to the south and then borne a son to the Northern stranger. The girl felt angry when she thought of how her stepfather had forced her mother north, and only grudgingly permitted his new wife to take her children: a daughter from a previous marriage and a half-Viking son. Relating the familiar information made the girl tired; it would be the same questions, the same clucking disapproval.

But the short-haired woman was quiet for a moment, touching her twig necklace, and merely looked sad. 'I, too, come from far away,' she said, and then fell silent.

'From where?' the boy prompted. His sister wanted to shake him for being so forward; it had earnt him many a beating in the past. Who knew what this strange Northern woman was capable of?

'The land of the frost giants,' said the woman, and the girl felt a chill run up her spine as she recalled again her stepfather's stories. 'But that was long ago,' the woman added. 'Long ago and far away.' She looked piercingly at the siblings, each in turn.

The girl felt herself go hot despite the snow piled in layers on her clothing. She knew who the woman was, and she and her brother should leave right now if they were to be saved from her clutches. She knew the story from her stepfather; this woman was the solitary goddess in a house of ice and the girl cursed herself for having ignored the clues to the woman's identity. The woman was still looking at her, straight in her eyes. They had to go now. Now. She turned to her brother, but he was smiling at the woman, and the girl felt her heart sink. They were lost. She would never be able to convince her brother to leave to a sure death in the snow.

'You're wet and cold,' the ice woman observed. 'Take off your clothes and draw close to the fire.'

The girl hung back, watching as her brother did as the Northern woman asked, as if he were hypnotised by her voice. She watched him take off the soaked bright woollen shirt to reveal his taut stomach; and the youthful, wiry muscles of his arms, and she also watched the woman's pale blue eyes grow bright. The ice woman saw what she herself did: that her brother was a beautiful man. The girl closed her eyes and swallowed.

'You, too.' The woman's voice was low and persuasive.

The girl kept her eyes closed, hearing the crackle of the fire and the breath of both her brother and the woman. Finally she sighed, reasoning that if they were doomed it was better to be dry and warm. She stripped, revealing her high breasts and hips, still as slim as a youth's. She thought she saw the woman's eyes shining as they had before. The girl joined her half-brother before the fire, crouching low and feeling the heat on her chest and throat. Her brother laid a hand on her neck and stroked her there, as if in reassurance. Perhaps he was right. Perhaps she had no cause yet to be suspicious.

The ice woman's voice broke in. She was standing some distance behind them, evidently still observing them. 'My name is Skathi.' It was a statement; it did not seem that she was asking for a similar revelation from them.

A moment passed, and the girl felt her toes grow warm again as they began to unthaw. Her brother removed his hand from his sister's neck, and the girl sensed that he was hurt; that he did not understand her rudeness to the woman. It's not rudeness, she thought, just caution. But nothing yet had happened in the house of ice, nothing like what her stepfather had warned her about. Her stepfather had said that Skathi cracked the bones of children with her teeth and drank the blood of men. Skathi had come from the land of the giants; had married one of the Northern gods and then left him behind, in order to live alone in the mountains where she hunted and skied on skis formed from long antlers and ate disobedient children – and even disobedient young women, her stepfather had added. Skathi lived in a house of ice and could never go home. She was banished from the gods, and banished from her own people, the giants, as well.

The girl heard her brother sigh beside her; she knew that he would not speak again until she herself had said it was all right. The amethyst in her navel began to grow warm again.

'Oshu and Ola,' she finally said, pointing to herself

and her half-brother in turn. She gave the Norse approximations. She didn't tell the stranger their real names; it was not a gift she would willingly bestow upon a stranger. She stretched her fingers out before the fire and did not look behind her. Already she regretted speaking.

'Oshu,' the woman said, and the girl heard her approach from behind. The woman put her hand on her bare shoulder, and the girl shut her eyes for the death blow that was coming – but it did not happen. Skathi's hand felt soft and safe, as her brother's hand had felt. 'Oshu,' the ice woman said again, 'what brings you here? Why is there such pain in you?'

The girl turned around to face the woman, goddess or not. Her own eyes were filled to the brim with tears, and she could only imagine what her brother was thinking. He had never seen her cry. 'I never wanted to be here.' She stared at the pale woman, as if daring her to deny it.

'Nor did I,' the goddess – if that was what she was – said softly. She stepped closer, and the girl saw that her eyes were kind. For a moment she wanted only to succumb; she was tired of holding in all the exhausting pain, tired of being the strong one for both her brother and herself. Out of the corner of her eye she saw her brother watching silently, saw his skin shining in the light from the fire. Then she exhaled, her eyes closed. A single tear ran down her cheek. Then she leant forward, nearly falling into the woman's pale arms.

The Northern woman ran her hand down her braid, and for a moment the girl shuddered, remembering how her Viking stepfather used to yank at it. She was away from that now, she told herself. Skathi put her lips to the dark girl's throat, cool skin against cool skin, and licked a warm trail down to the sculptural frame of the girl's shoulderblades and collarbone. The girl was briefly and desperately reminded of the trail they had followed, and wondered if they would ever claw their way out

41

again. But heat was surging through her, heat that she hadn't felt since the day her mother had forced them on their journey north. She was reminded of home: the rich scent of vividly coloured flowers, of bright laughter and brilliant sun.

'You remember your home,' the woman whispered in her ear, and the girl knew then that she was indeed a goddess, or at the very least a priestess, able to see what was in a person's heart.

Yes, she thought, I remember. But Skathi drew away, and left the girl standing on the fur-covered earth floor of the ice house, pondering how her memory of home had suddenly flared back now, after so many months in this cold, ugly land.

Her mouth was dry, and she was aware that there was a wetness between her legs. And now this strange woman was doing the same to her brother, kissing a gentle track down his skin; and the girl watched how her brother shut his eyes, clenching his hands into fists at his side; watched how the swelling at his groin grew beneath the alien clothes that they both hated.

'Ola,' Skathi said, and whispered something in his ear. He licked his lips, and his sister trembled with emotion. Her brother was beautiful. She felt a light sweat beading on her body, and irrationally wondered whether the tall cold woman would notice. She watched as the woman ran her hands over the displaced cloth below her brother's waist, stroking and caressing at the hardness that the girl knew was there. This seemed safe and right and the icy room was bright and hot. She thought that she could smell the sweet, heavy fragrance of living violets, all the way from home.

Her breath was coming quicker now as she watched the woman, naked except for the necklace of twigs, leaning over her brother, now also naked. The girl pressed a hand against her crotch and a sweet sensation began to stir there, so she rubbed her fingers roughly up between her legs. She kept her eyes on her brother and the strange white woman. She couldn't help her jealousy: what if the woman were to touch her like her brother was being touched, to stroke her softly between her legs? Would she like it, or would she feel frightened?

The fire crackled higher. There was a scent of musk in the air, and the girl slipped her hand to the curls of her own sex-hair. She pushed a finger down into the stickiness there, the sticky warmth she had felt gathering ever since the woman had licked at the flesh of her throat. She pressed down on her little bud and moaned; when she opened her eyes seconds later, her finger still on the bud of her sex, both the woman and her brother were staring at her. To her surprise she felt no shame whatsoever, and held their gazes while she continued to move her finger, slipping it over the hard little centre of her sex. All around her was the heady fragrance of violets.

'Come,' said the woman called Skathi, and she motioned them down to rug of fur spread out over the whole of the ice-house floor. The woman laid herself down on the rug, stomach against the dark pelt.

Both siblings stared at her, and then at each other. The girl's pulse was racing wildly in her breast, and she saw her brother's excitement from his hard cock, thick and ready, jutting from his young body. If I were a man too, she thought, I would look like that. Ready. I feel ripe, ripe as violets in bloom. She ran her hands up over her stiff nipples. She felt tight all over, as if her skin was too small for her body. Her brother was still looking at her, but neither moved, as if they were afraid to move either closer down to the woman on the rug, or closer to each other. Then all at once her brother reached for her, and she felt his breath before his wet, slow kiss, and she felt desire rising up through her as he held her, his arms tight around her. There was the scent of violets in his curls, she noticed, and for a moment they both forgot about the woman Skathi as they lost themselves in the kiss.

But she broke the kiss eventually, breathless, and stared down at the short-haired woman, who was watching them intently but still, it seemed, patiently. When the ice woman saw that they were both staring at her, she moaned gently, and just the sound of it sent a thrill through the girl. She felt just like the Northern woman, as if she were lazy and creamily wet, so ready and ripe. She was not surprised when her brother stepped forward to the Northern woman; indeed, if he had not, she would have done so herself.

The fire, she noticed, was making the walls of the ice house run, but nothing about either heat nor cold could scare her now, as she watched her brother slowly kissing the white woman's haunches, the curve of her arse, and rubbing his fingers in the valley between her legs. He raised his hand, and his sister could see it shimmering with wetness, then he licked at it and sucked at the moisture, and this time both women moaned at the same time.

The girl found herself walking closer, around to the front of the woman, and she crouched before the Northerner, her thighs on either side of the woman's head. The woman's face was flushed, and she moaned again. The girl saw that her brother had entered the woman from behind, his cock forging deep into her, and the girl heard the wet sounds as it entered the woman: sloppy, lusty sounds. She thought of her brother's beauty, and she felt her face grow hot again.

'Oshu.' The woman murmured her name, and ran her hands along the younger woman's thighs. 'Come closer, Oshu.'

The girl shut her eyes; the overpowering scent of ripe violets stinging through her head, and moved her wet crotch closer to the stranger, then slowly opened her legs to her. The woman began to lap at her, at first gently, and then the ice woman was lustily drinking from her, as the girl's brother pumped into the woman from behind. The girl was at first nervous, but then pleasure began to pound through her from the woman's mouth, and eventually she fell back, the woman continuing to lap, and her brother continued to fuck the woman, his hands on the woman's limber athletic legs, and the girl smelled violets everywhere, violets and her own ripe arousal, the scents swirling together in a musk of perfume. She was blind to them, though, as the pleasure tightened and then exploded though her, as she shoved her sex down against the woman's mouth, the woman's face glistening with juices. The woman was also bucking, her hand down on her own sex as the girl's brother lunged and then finally withdrew, his pearly come spraying over the woman's buttocks and thighs. The woman continued to move her hand against her sex and lick deep inside the girl, and she groaned deeply as she reached her climax.

They lay there together, panting for a long while, the girl listening to the walls of the ice house drip from the heat of the fire. Then Skathi moved, got up and quickly dressed herself. 'Come,' she said, and helped them to dress. The house was melting quickly.

'I don't want to return to my mother and my stepfather,' the girl said, knowing that she must assert herself quickly, as it looked as if the woman was getting ready to lead them away.

'Nor I,' her brother quickly added, his face still glowing with excitement. He said it in the tone of one who felt it necessary to break at last from a beloved sibling and find his own voice, the girl noted with a touch of sadness.

'No,' said Skathi, ushering them quickly out before the house began to crash in on itself. She stretched out a hand to each and led them to a sled, which was fastened by sinew to a great elk. The snow was beginning to fall softly and the girl looked behind to the melting spectacle of the ice house, now crumpled into a mass of coloured ice blocks and frozen flowers, covered by the gentle flakes of snow spinning slowly from the grey sky.

For once her brother moved without his sister's approval, climbing up into the sled, which was piled high with furs. He pulled his sister up into the curving sled, and they nestled in amongst the furs, warm and safe. Snow melted on the girl's long lashes. The liquid blurred her vision for a moment, but then she saw Skathi throw herself up on the huge horned beast and give out a piercing whistle. The sled began to grate against the rocks beneath the snow before it hit its glide on the cool white drifts.

She held her brother's hand tightly as the elk began to race. The sled went faster and faster down the hill, pulled by the beast, until even the blue, drift-covered trees became a haze before the girl's dark eyes. The speed was so tremendous that she and her brother shut their lids against the slash of the cold wind but, just as they had done so, the sled abruptly stopped.

The sister and brother opened their eyes. In the air was a searing, beautiful, sexual scent of wild violets, and she still held her brother's hand tightly. It was clear morning, a beautiful winter day. They sat within the heaps of furs lining the sled, but both Skathi and the great elk had melted away; the sled's sinew leads dangled limply in the snow, unattached.

Up ahead there was a village and the girl knew that they would be able to get board there and eat before continuing their long voyage home. For a moment she tried to remember home, her true home: bright sun and palm trees. But behind her she could still sense the presence of the lonely goddess, perhaps watching from the woods.

'Look,' the girl's brother said to his sister before he climbed down from the bowl of the sled, 'she's left us food as well.' He had been looking through the furs; had emerged with his hands cupped full of the same summer fruits that had decorated the house of ice: the same fresh berries and edible flowers. For the first time in a long while, the girl saw hope upon her brother's face.

The girl thought for a moment before she climbed down and began the trek to the village, trying to understand the witchery that had brought them both safely here. She tried to remember the burning hearth, the woman's thin, slightly bitter but kind smile, her short hair. She tried to visualise the house they had escaped from, but it already seemed to be solely a bad dream. The only image she could summon was the trail of violet petals, but in her vision they were no longer frozen chips but soft and tender; bruised, but still alive.

This is the older story, and it is the truer one, as well.

Shadowlight

Kitty Fisher

*P*aul Fenton slumped back on to his sofa with a weary sigh. The last week had been one of nail-biting tension, too little sleep and a constant anxiety that had been resolved only that morning; a morning that was eight long hours of debriefing ago. Wrung dry of the last dregs of his energy by the intense interrogation that had followed his successful mission, Fenton had returned home on autopilot, changed out of clothes he never wanted to see again and collapsed in an enervated heap.

He should have felt happy, or at least content, at the victory. Yet the high cost in terms of lives lost, hardware irreplaceably damaged and morale lowered meant that it was almost as hard to bear as a defeat. Still, at least the enemy had eventually backed off, a fact that couldn't be guaranteed these days. Winning was becoming progressively more difficult as the aliens' skill and ingenuity increased, their knowledge of Earth and humans growing with each encounter, with each mind overtaken.

Even though he'd gone far too long without sleep, adrenalin still sped around his system. Living with fear, danger and the half-acknowledged dread of being absorbed by the freakish skills and intelligence of the intruders left him drained but incapable of relaxation. Thoughts and ideas milled about his mind, denying the lithe sprawl his limbs had fallen into of their own accord; the metronomic tap of his finger on the arm of the sofa was the only outward sign of tension. He knew he should take one of the small blue pills prescribed by the doctor for such occasions, but he wanted to wind down without the artificial benefit of drugs. Especially as tomorrow was an officially sanctioned rest day.

A whole day off. It was becoming a luxury.

Closing his eyes, a frown creasing between his brows, Paul wondered if the commander would be taking a day off too. If he was exhausted, then the same and more must be true of Anders; the commander liked to pretend he was made of steel, but there had been dark shadows biting into the pale skin under his eyes that morning. Not that anyone could tell him to rest.

With a sigh Paul stretched, trying to work tension out of his muscles. With no luck. Subsiding he stared blankly at the tier of ambient lighting, willing himself to get up and do something useful, even something as banal as some housework – anything that took him away from work and its problems.

He didn't succeed. Half an hour later he was jerked out of a precarious half-sleep peopled with the shadows of horrific dreams by the insistent beep of the telephone. Scrambling to reach the receiver he answered, 'Hello?'

'Paul?'

'Commander.' Fenton found he was breathing shallowly, expectancy banishing sleep and exhaustion from his thoughts.

'I wondered if you fancied having dinner tonight?'

Fenton swallowed excitement and smiled at the soft drawl. 'Yes, I'd love to.'

'Great! I'll pick you up in about ten minutes.'

'Fine . . .' Paul went to answer but his words were lost in the dial tone.

Ten minutes. He looked down at the casual clothes he'd changed into. They wouldn't do; not for tonight. He suppressed a grin and headed for the bedroom, already stripping off his tunic, his thoughts skittering past the tricky problem of which suit to wear, and onward to the possibilities of what the night might bring. Perhaps Anders would be in the mood for simple, unadulterated sex tonight. Then again, and Paul shivered at the thought, maybe not.

The restaurant was one of the most expensive in the city. Each table had a pool of privacy around it; discreetly arranged screens meant that conversation was kept totally private. Softly lit black wood, ivory linen and chrome created an exquisite atmosphere. The waiters were summoned by the press of a hidden button. No interruptions were allowed to disturb the illusion of intimacy granted to the diners.

Swallowing the last mouthful of a very light meal, Paul Fenton sat back with a creak of leather as the chair moved with his weight. He stared through his lashes at his companion, trying to absorb every detail of the man seated before him. It was always startling to see Ed Anders dressed entirely in black. He usually sported the lighter colours that fashion and his complex cover role demanded, and a dark, midnight blue was as close to the richness of this sable that he allowed himself.

Fenton thought that the commander looked good in whatever he wore. But not as perfect as this.

In the muted light, Anders was a slim, darkly mysterious figure. The tight-fitting, high-collared cashmere jacket moulded his fine musculature to perfection, the narrow trousers taut over his long legs. Yet there was little difference here to the commander's usual style of dress. Certainly not enough to warrant the difficulty Paul Fenton seemed to be experiencing in breathing.

That was entirely due to the colour.

The light-absorbing black enhanced everything about Anders, from the strange silver hair that seemed almost luminescent, to the pale smooth skin and lithe sensual body. The only feature untouched was the cold eyes; their blue was as remote, as difficult to read as ever. But then Fenton was quite aware that the only place they really changed was in the privacy of the bedroom; the commander had himself under too harsh a discipline to allow anything else.

He smiled to himself, starting slightly when Anders asked, 'What are you thinking about?'

Fenton shrugged. 'You.'

'I'm duly flattered.' Anders sat back, drawling his words, a smile flickering around his mouth, visibly easing some of the tension that the last week had caused. He waited for the waiter to clear their plates, then leant forward. 'But what exactly?'

Fenton hesitated, then quirked his lips wryly: 'I was thinking that I like it when you wear black.'

Anders rested his hand on the tablecloth and spread his fingers, inspecting their long, elegant lines. 'I know. But you know why I only wear it sometimes. And I've always given you the choice.'

'It was never a choice, you know that; you knew long before I did what I wanted. Even how natural –' Paul slowly shook his head, searching for the necessary word '– how right it would be.'

'It's certainly not that.'

Paul started, 'What? Not right? Don't say that. If it isn't right, then how come I enjoy it so much?'

'Because you're like me, because it gives you a chance to let go, to forget. Besides, you shouldn't confuse something you like doing with something society would find acceptable. They're often very far apart.'

'But I still say that doesn't make what we do wrong.'

'I don't think so either. I'm merely reminding you that not everyone thinks the same way.'

'You mean at work.' Paul considered, then looked up through his lashes, suddenly unsure. 'Is this a warning?'

Anders shook his head. 'No, not about work. I wouldn't be madly keen for what we do to become public knowledge, but it isn't against the law.'

'Then what are you saying?'

'I'm saying that despite the liberality of this society, despite the fact that sex between consenting adults in all its forms is supposed to be acceptable, that prejudices die hard. That discretion is the better part of valour.'

'I've no intention of broadcasting what we do to anyone. It's private.'

'Good. You might find a few of your friends reacting differently if they did find out. Not everyone can see that what we do is only a variation of sexuality, a different expression of love.'

'More fool them.' Paul grinned. 'I think everyone should try it.'

Anders took a sip of iced water then shook his head. 'No, I don't think I'd want everyone to be the same. Meeting someone who feels the same way I do is such a rarity that it lends an added excitement to the occasion. If I could find a perfect partner in just anybody –' his eyes narrowed in amusement '– I don't think it would be quite the same.'

Fenton bent forward, the movement taking the muted brown of his hair and touching it with bronze where it caught the restaurant's shadowy light. 'You know why? Because you're a hunter. It's as simple as that. The day you show signs of being anything else I'll probably faint.'

'I think it would take a bit more than that to make

you pass out.' Anders leant forward and smiled. 'In fact I know so . . .'

The direct stare sent a spike of lust down into Fenton's groin. He shifted slightly, swallowing as saliva filled his mouth. Suddenly the nearness of other people was too much. He shivered and said thickly, 'Let's go home.'

'In a while.' Complacent, his eyes smiling wickedly, Anders lounged back, sliding something shiny out of his pocket. 'Go and put this on.'

Fenton stared at the circle of silver that sat so benignly in the elegant palm. After a moment, he reached forward and took it into his own fingers, feeling its weight, feeling that the inside rim was ridged. The circle of metal was smoothly hinged for quick release. 'Now?' It was all he could say, his mind and tongue tied by the intensity of his arousal.

'Yes.' Anders was watching intently, his attention focused hard on the expressive face before him. When Fenton stood up, his hand closed tight on the ring, he relaxed.

'Here?'

'In the men's room: I don't want to scandalise the natives.' He almost smiled.

Fenton was back within four minutes, his long jacket firmly fastened from top to bottom. Anders was still seated as before, though he'd lit a cigar and his expression was clean of any emotion. Paul cautiously sat down and waited, his thoughts spinning around Anders, the centre of his universe. Their intimate life was so clear – demarcated in black and white. It was perfectly suited to each of their temperaments. Fenton may not have known before Anders that he needed to be mastered, but he was sure now. Sure enough to trust Anders with his life, with his sanity, even with his love.

'Tonight, I want you. All of you. Understand?'

Fenton nodded jerkily at Anders' words, the constriction at his groin painful.

There was a silence. Anders watched intently the passage of sensation and emotion over Paul's expressive face. After a moment he asked, with something like a frown in his voice, 'What does it feel like?' Fenton closed his eyes, letting his senses feast on the sensation. A slight prickle of sweat dotted his upper lip. When he spoke it was very quietly. 'It feels tight. It must be smaller than the last one; I can feel the ridges. It feels as if you're touching me.' He shivered in anticipation of the reality to come. 'When I move it gets tighter.'

'What you mean is, as you get aroused it gets tighter.'

Fenton sighed. 'Yes.'

'Do you like it?'

'It is ... delicious.' Fenton opened his eyes and tried to lean forward, thinking better of it as the metal bit down. 'Please, I'd like to go home.' Expensive as the restaurant was, there were still other tables, other diners beyond the screens. What he wanted was to be naked, to free his arousal, to be on his knees. Here he couldn't even talk loudly.

'And I'd like a coffee.' Anders signalled for a waiter, ordering a cafetière before muttering for Fenton's ears only: 'I'm sure the exercise in patience will be good for you.'

Fenton knew there was no point in arguing – unless the point was to push Anders into doing something like this. He was quite aware that on occasion Anders' subconscious moved in mysterious ways. And most of those occasions seemed to be when he was wearing unrelieved black. The coffee was curling its steam into the air and they were alone again.

Fenton had his body under slightly better control, though the tension in his blood was just as fiery. The simple knowledge of what Anders had planned for later had kept his cock part-aroused all evening. Locking himself in the men's room he'd had to fight for control in order to obey instructions, taking deep breaths until it was possible to slide the cock-ring on. He knew quite well that giving the presence of a hard-on as an excuse for failure would have got him nowhere with Anders. And despite appearances he didn't court pain. Not all the time, anyway.

As a signal of Anders' intentions, the black clothing was such a simple yet effective idea. Most of the time they met and indulged in pleasant, delicious sex. This abberation from their normal routine had only been introduced by Anders after about six months. Quite why he hadn't seen it coming, Fenton wasn't sure, for there was a deep need in Anders to be in control – even in bed. Perhaps especially in bed.

The pale eyes were staring again. Paul deliberately moved until he was sitting very straight, broad shoulders pulled back, gaze lowered, both hands folded neatly into his lap. He didn't need to say a word. Anders laughed, and ignoring the plea, poured a cup of the strong coffee, diluting it with a hefty dose of cream. 'Drink that.' Fenton obeyed, wiping his mouth afterwards on a linen napkin. Then he returned to the posture of waiting.

'When you went to the bathroom did you relieve yourself?'

Fenton was momentarily startled by the question, but he shook his head in denial; he'd been too involved in other things to consider the state of his bladder.

'Good. Have another cup.'

Wicked, very wicked. Fenton smiled in acknowledgement at the mercurial glint in his lover's eyes and took the proffered coffee, drinking it all. Already the pressure of liquid inside his body was causing discomfort. Wine and coffee. His cock was hard and the constriction of the tight silver ring distracting. So much for Anders wanting simple sex tonight. Except that for Anders this was simple. Sex and Fenton's pain. A simple combination.

Fenton sighed, quite happy.

Anders crushed the butt of his cigar into a glass ashtray and signalled for the bill.

Paul Fenton's mouth had been the first thing that attracted Anders' sexual interest. It had been just after Paul had fallen prey to the aliens and tried to kill Anders. They'd come into such close proximity then, learning far more about each other then most men learn of their friends in a lifetime, that maybe for the first time they looked at each other as well.

Once he'd noticed Paul's mouth, in its bruised and bloodied promise of unbounded sensuality, it had been his undoing. It had taken all the willpower at his disposal to continue that particular conversation. Anders had lost track of what they were discussing and he was sure that Fenton had been momentarily unnerved by his lack of concentration. It had taken three weeks and remarkably little effort to persuade the colonel into his bed, and from the first there had been no doubts as to their compatibility.

Now, a year later, he knew that sensuality intimately. More intimately than he had ever known anyone's – even his wife's – because Fenton had given himself totally to his lover. At work Fenton was professional, adept, strong-principled, arrogant. Here in privacy it was different: there was nothing that Anders could do that would incite rebellion or even a question. This was Anders' domain; one he ruled with all the passion that he poured into everything he did.

For Anders, it was almost as if for the first time in his life, the sex was real, the games not really games but soul-deep truth. Even when the sex they indulged in was vanilla it was better than anything he'd previously experienced. And he'd thought himself adept before.

He strolled into the dimly lit bedroom, stripping off his jacket as he walked. Dressed in his skin-tight body-suit he stood in the centre of the room and slowly turned, seeing the wide bed with its satin sheets; the discreet restraints; the water ready by the bed. No lubricant. Perfect. He caught a flash of white against the shadows as the bathroom door opened and closed.

Standing there, quite still, was Fenton. Apart from the cock-ring he was naked.

Anders took a deep breath and nodded to himself. 'Come here.'

Serene, aware with every cell in his body of the ritual of this moment, Fenton paced slowly across the floor, his feet silent on the deep carpet. At his commander's side he stopped and cautiously raised his eyes, though he didn't look any higher than the smooth curve of Anders' shoulder.

With one hand Anders felt the velvet-sheathed heat of Paul's erect cock. It was smooth, sensual to the touch, dry except for a drop of liquid nestling in the slit. Anders smiled and pressed his palm to the flatness of his dark belly. Fenton breathed in sharply as the need in his bladder became insistent.

Anders smiled, a silver-haired hunter, sloe-eyed with lust.

'Kneel down.'

With a whispering sigh of willing submission, Paul knelt.

Anders stepped back and took in the whole of the kneeling body. Paul was so beautiful: the clean, strong lines of his body; the honey-tinted skin that reacted so easily to the slightest touch; his face. Praxiteles would have fought to sculpt him; Ganymede would have torn his eyes out. Anders paced around, watching as the inspection increased Fenton's arousal, the already hard cock pulsing, lengthening, a pearl of arousal glistening enticingly at the tip.

'What do you want, Paul?'

'To please you, sir.'

'Then put these on.' He held out his hand, dangling shimmering metal from his fingers.

Paul shuddered, for a moment fighting his own unwilling flesh, then nodded. 'Yes, sir.' He sounded breathless, though not from running. Anders could have set the clamps to any tension he felt like: from a light clasp to a pressure so tight as to be almost unbearable, anything was possible.

Unknowing, Paul took them, his stomach tight, half wanting, half fearful of their touch. They were warm; Anders must have held them in his hand for a while. The thought made Fenton sigh. The devices were linked by a length of fine, supple chain that slipped through his fingers with a metallic whisper. He hesitated, fingers hovering over his breast.

'What do you want, Paul? Do you want me to fasten them for you?'

Fenton held his breath, fighting between wanting desperately to be touched, yet knowing how wicked those hands could be – what destruction they could wreak on his self-control. In the end he waited too long and the decision was made for him.

'Stand up.'

They were almost of a height, though Paul's naked feet took away some of his advantage. Anders licked forefinger and thumb, caught a nipple tight between them and pulled it hard away from the still body. When it was taut, he paused, then clamped the metal down just under the rock hard bud.

Paul gasped, the shock of contact – of pain – flooding through his nerves.

'Too tight?'

'No, sir.' There was intense strain in his voice. Paul licked his lips and finally took a breath as the first wave of pain died away. Just as he relaxed, the process was repeated on his other nipple. The pain rose through him and peaked, swiftly translating into sweet pleasure as his cock pulsed with sensation at every beat of his heart. He closed both eyes, giddy, transported. Sweat was already sheening the lightly tanned skin of his broad chest and when Anders pulled hard on the linking chain, Paul moaned – the fine line between hurt and arousal blurred, indistinct, lost in a vast, shadowy cavern of need.

'Paul, you're just so damn sexy,' Anders growled, pulling the parted slightly lips to his own. He kissed deeply, hungrily, pressing himself to the solid length of his lover's body, wanting its strength, needing its need. Digging his hands through the soft brown hair, he forced his tongue deep into the eager mouth, sighing as Paul opened his jaw wide, offering all of himself.

When Anders pulled back, his arousal was quite clear through the tight fabric of his clothes.

He stripped efficiently, then came back to stand close to the other man. Very gently he touched the tip of one nipple where it extruded from the clamp. Paul flinched, biting his lip, expecting more.

'What do you want, Paul?'

'To please you, sir.' The words came out as a whisper that was echoed by the shiver of metal as the long chain was brushed against his chest.

'No games tonight.'

'No, sir,' Paul hissed as the hand skimmed down – still linked to the length of chain – barely touching skin as it went.

Anders curled his body around the shivering man, resting his left hand on a curve of arse. With his right he pulled hard on the tight curls of dark pubic hair. Both of them were totally involved, this strange sensuality running wild through both their blood; this knife-edge of desire as familiar as breathing.

When Anders finally touched him, Paul's knees went weak and if it hadn't been for the nearness of the other body he would have fallen.

The commander smiled, looking down at the spear of over-heated skin, loving its length, its beauty. The silver ring was constricting, digging viciously into the soft flesh of shaft and balls, engorging it all with blood, making the testicles high and hard within their tight-drawn skin.

It was time. His own erection was almost as painful as Paul's looked. Quickly, he snapped open the cock-ring and let it fall to the floor.

Paul moaned again as the pulse of fresh blood into his cock made him shiver, the room darkening around him. The release reminded him his bladder was full, and the completeness of the sensation sent him teetering to the edge of orgasm. Knowingly, a thumb dug hard into his glans and orgasm receded, leaving sweat glistening wetly on his skin.

'Go and lie on the bed.'

In a trance of desire Paul obeyed, settling himself in the way he knew was preferred. He spread his limbs wide, face pushed into the silk cover, wincing as the scrape of fabric tore at unbearably sensitised nipples. The burning need to piss throbbed through his erection. When the bonds were fastened around his wrists and ankles he sighed in relief; when the cool weight of his lover settled against him, he moaned in need, in an agony of desperation, every cell of his body craving the fullness of cock inside his arse.

But it wasn't to be yet. Anders reached underneath the bound man and pulled at his cock until it lay flat to the bed, then he knelt back. The strength of the muscles bound firmly for his use set his heart beating fast. The beautiful body caught in perfect tension, skin damp, craving possession, never failed to stagger him with its erotic power. Perfect.

Paul swallowed as Anders' weight left the bed. He wanted to plead that he was too near the edge, that tonight was just right as it was, that all he wanted was to be taken and fucked until he screamed. But the shifting of the bed as the other man resettled himself told him how vain such an attempt would be. Anders was kneeling by his side.

'Look at me.'

Paul stared up at him wide-eyed, sweat trickling down the hollow of his cheek.

'I love you.'

Fenton shivered, his body bowstring taut, his eyes flickering to the length of black leather held so carelessly in Anders's hands. He licked at dry lips and whispered in return, 'I love you, sir.'

'What do you want?'

'To please you, sir.'

'What do you want?' The voice was more insistent.

'For you to beat me.' There, it had been said. Fenton closed his eyes and knotted his hands into fists around their chains.

'Look at me, Paul.'

His eyes opened and widened as Anders bent to gently kiss his lips, tonguing them with a restrained intimacy that reassured and aroused. Anders smiled. 'I'll fuck you when I've finished.'

Fenton barely had time to nod before the first blow landed. Anders worked the crop with easy skill, marking the pale skin with a crisscross pattern of fire that had Fenton writhing, crying out with each successive blow, pressing his nipples still bound by the clamps into the bed, the pain shocking, enlightening.

After a while, his own breath fast and erratic, Anders stopped and rested the sweating palm of his right hand on the curve of arse where he had landed the crop. The underlying muscles trembled at his touch and Paul moaned as the fingers traced each welt across his skin. Anders could see that Paul's cock was still erect, pressed wetly to the sheets. The pain had only enhanced the arousal and it was dark red, swollen. When he ran a nail across the fiery pattern, the shaft pulsed and, impossibly, seemed to lengthen.

Anders almost growled, lust spearing his own cock into the air. Throwing the whip to the floor he slid himself between Fenton's outstretched legs, pushing the thighs further apart with his knees.

Paul cried out as Anders sheathed himself in one hard movement. Even though his arse was prepared, the possession was still almost too much to bear – Anders' cock was long and thick, seemingly too big for the lightness of his frame. Paul lay still, his bound hands clutching at the sheets, tension knotting his shoulders, pain from his abused skin riding through the arousal.

Then Anders slipped his hands under them both and removed the clamps.

Fenton bucked wildly beneath him and called out, the fire of pain ripping through him like a meteor. Flicking hard with his thumb Anders moved again, sliding his cock out slowly, feeling the shudders of Fenton's body as if the pain were his own.

For a long heartbeat Anders waited. He could feel the urgency in the erratic breaths, in the sweat that slicked both their skins and in the heat that tantalised him. He pressed his hands to the raw nipples, to the curving swell of buttock, pressing until a moan of desire and pain was muffled by the sheets. Then, eyes half closed, he let himself slide back inside, savouring the tightness, the heat, pressing deep into responsive flesh.

Fenton felt his own need consumed by this spear of need that split him in two, fragmenting then remaking him with each stroke. He wanted more than anything to feel the man above him lose control, to sob out loud as he came, to become as abandoned as he was himself. The size of the cock inside him no longer mattered, nor the pain, nor the urgent requirements of his bladder. With a ripple of muscle he pushed back, drawing a gasp of hunger from Anders.

It was all Paul needed. Without any thought for himself he fought for Anders' orgasm, using all his strength to coax the man above him into desperation, until Anders let loose, pumping hard into the willing flesh.

But each stroke battered against tissue made unbearably sensitive, pounding against his bladder until he was shaking, every muscle gripping down hard to stop himself from giving in to the unbearable compulsion. He bit down on the cover, tears escaping through tight-closed lids as Anders ravaged his body. The sensation was beyond pleasure, sending him into a realm that was ruled by darkness and pain.

Finally, with a shuddering cry the commander lost control, the extreme tightness of bunched muscle around his cock too much. Biting into the softness of skin, Anders came hard, the pulsing sending him deeper into the tight second skin of his lover's body.

When he opened his eyes, he found himself still plastered down the length of well-muscled back. There was an agonised moan and Anders knew what had brought him round. He slid the softening length of his cock from Fenton's arse and moved to release the bonds at his wrists and ankles.

'Turn over.'

Slowly and carefully Fenton obeyed. He was wide-eyed with desperation, his cock soft against the skin of his thigh.

'What do you want?'

The answer came out as an uneven croak: 'To please you, sir.'

'You do that, most certainly you do that.' Anders leant forward and kissed the parted lips very gently until Paul moaned in despair and the kiss was returned. Pulling back, his eyes hooded with the return of desire, Anders nodded. 'Stand up and walk to the bathroom.' Fenton obeyed, lightheaded with need, unsteady on his feet. At the toilet he stopped and waited, he could hear Anders following.

'Go on, you can have ten seconds.'

Ten seconds. It sounded an age. Fenton held himself and tried to relax his muscles but they had been tightened for too long, and only a trickle of liquid emerged. He groaned aloud in frustration. Anders was counting off the time.

'Nine, ten. Not long enough, or has the urge gone?'

'No! No, sir. I just can't . . .' He was almost sobbing.

'Yes you can. I'll help.' And two fingers slid their way into the semen-soaked tightness of Paul's arse. 'Perhaps this will encourage you; when you've pissed, then you can come. Better?'

Paul nodded, not knowing if it was or not but incapable of disagreeing, feeling the return of arousal despite the agony in his gut. He concentrated very hard, knowing that if he got a hard-on it would be even more difficult. He tried to ignore the skilful fingers as they played so gently inside him, to ignore the tantalising scent of Anders's skin, the animal musk of semen, the pain, to ignore everything but the most basic of needs.

'Go on, I won't tease anymore, you can have as long as you like.'

A second hand rested on the flat plane of his belly and pushed. It was too much and with a gasp his body relaxed, liquid streaming into the waiting bowl.

Afterwards, he stood, head down, breathing heavily as a hand reached and pulled his head around. The intensity of the look took his breath away and he fell at his master's feet, mouth searching blindly for the comfort of skin against his mouth. But strong hands forced him on to his feet, pushing him hard against the wall.

'Didn't I tell you it was your turn to come?' Anders waited for a bemused answering nod, then with a wicked laugh fell elegantly to his knees to take Paul's cock into his mouth. Instantly fully erect, the long arousal combined with the sight of the blond head bent to service him were too much, and with a cry Paul shuddered into release. His hands held tight to Anders as he forced himself deep into the accommodating throat, screaming silently as he came.

Slumped against the wall, he blinked sweat out of his eyes and jerkily relaxed his grip on the kneeling man. Almost in wonder he stroked the sweat-damp hair.

Letting the softening cock slide from his lips, Anders rested his cheek against the damp prickle of darkly curling hair at Fenton's groin. He sighed, quite happy.

'Why?' Paul let the silky, ice-white hair slide through his fingers, the feel sensuous, hypnotic, fascinating.

'Because I love you.'

'But . . .'

'But what? It's not as if I've never done that before.'

'No, but not when we're in the middle of a scene, not when you're . . .'

'Topping you? No, I suppose I haven't.' Anders sighed and closed his eyes, breathing in the strong scent of masculinity.

'Then why?'

'You're so damned persistent. OK, I felt like swapping roles with you, I wanted to feel what you feel for once.'

Paul swallowed and tried to think about this in a coherent way. In the end he could only croak, 'For once?'

Anders opened his eyes and pushed away from the support of Paul's legs. He knelt very still, acknowledging the importance of the moment, then shook his head. 'No, not just the once, but I don't know how often. Don't even know if I'll like it.'

'Yet you want to try.'

'Yeah, why not?' Anders smiled and stood up. 'Turn around.'

'Sometimes, having a conversation with you is like talking to the mist.' Paul sighed but obeyed.

Anders examined the welted skin. 'I'll put some cream on these after you've showered.'

Paul nodded. His skin burned and he knew that it

would need something on it before he could sleep, but as an issue it was far less important than their other topic of conversation. He turned around.

'And on these.' Anders lightly touched the sore-looking nipples. He tutted at Paul's sigh of frustration. 'I feel like trying out something a bit different.'

'Very different?'

'No, not as different as you think. But I don't think it's going to be today.' He kissed Paul lightly on the lips and walked into the bedroom, oblivious to the consternation left in his wake. 'Come to bed for a bit before you shower.'

Paul obeyed, despite the fact that he'd have been glad of the interruption. He was unsure of his reaction to Anders' words. Unsure if he'd be up to whatever Anders might need of him. Unsure if he approved of the searing arousal that had burned him on realisation of what Anders planned.

Silver hair bright against the dark pillows, Anders was a relaxed sprawl under the sheets. Fenton slipped in beside him, taking the lighter body into his arms, wrapping them together in the way that was right.

Anders curled against him, arm heavy across Fenton's chest, fingers contentedly stroking him. He shifted his head on the heavy muscle of Paul's shoulder and peered at the sensual face, seeing the eyes already half-closed, sleepy. Anders yawned and asked, 'Are you all right? Not too sore?'

'No, I'm fine.' And he was, the aches and pains were nothing to the overwhelming sense of peace that weighted his limbs. Even Anders' statement was pushed to the back of his mind, not important enough to disturb his serenity. It was always the same. Here in this bed, with his lover wrapped so trustingly in his arms, Paul Fenton had found the essential peace that had eluded him all his life. Nothing else mattered, not here. And if what was needed to keep this was a reversal of their roles, then so be it – after all, he'd had a good teacher.

'I love you, Commander Anders.'

'I know.' The words were muffled, their speaker almost asleep.

Fenton smiled gently into the air and spoke the voice command that turned off the lights. In darkness he waited, the edge of pain dulled by his love, the discomfort of cold semen seeping from his body ignored. Anders liked to be held after they'd made love. So held he was. It was the least Fenton could do.

Secret

Kitty Fisher

*H*e listened to the sound of a door opening and closing, and groaned silently. Not again. Surely not this soon. It was too much. He found that breathing was difficult. Fear, icy as a winter's night, drowned what little warmth there was in his veins.

'Hello again.'

Even blindfolded he could see the grin that went with the mocking voice. Anger flared through the fear, lifting his head off the bed to swear blindly, 'Go fuck yourself, Curran!'

'Jack, don't be like that.'

'Why not?'

'Because you're all tied up and, quite frankly, as I can do whatever I want to you, I'd be a good boy and keep that smart mouth shut.'

'I thought you'd already done what you wanted.' Silence. Though to Morrow it was as if he could hear Curran laughing. 'Didn't you, you bastard?'

'You mean I fucked you?'

Morrow heard soft footsteps as his captor came closer. He tugged uselessly at his arms, biting the metal cuffs that cut deep into his wrists and held him flat on his back. Panic. This was close to panic; his heart fluttering painfully in his chest. 'Yes.'

'Or would you prefer to call it rape? More emotive, perhaps even more accurate, but just as much fun. Rape or sex – or what about making love?' Curran's voice softened slyly on the words. 'The trouble is, as someone once said, once just isn't enough.'

'Alex . . .'

'Oh, Alex is it?'

'Curran.'

'Be quiet! I like to fuck, Morrow; I especially like to fuck men like you: so smart, so condescending, so god-damned horny. I wanted to get at you from the day they showed me your photo, and you know something? Having you was even better than I imagined it would be.'

'Why? Can you only get it up when your partner's unwilling? Christ, you're a sick bastard.'

'Yes.' The voice smiled again. 'I guess I am.' A hand touched Morrow's chest, making him tense, then it pinched his nipple, hard. 'Though it takes one to know one.'

Morrow fought as panic rushed adrenalin into his blood. No. There was no way Curran could know. He hadn't come before. Hadn't let himself . . . A mouth encompassed his nipple, shockingly warm, caring, gentle, before the teeth bit down and he arched in a wasted effort to escape the pain, a low sound crawling from his tightly closed lips.

'You know something, Morrow?'

He knew lots of things, none of which were much help here. A shiver ran through his limbs, making the cuffs rattle loudly against the barred headboard. Flat on his back and helpless. Shit. The bastard could answer himself.

Not that Curran wanted a reply. 'You look good naked. Your body is better than I expected. Always knew you had a great ass, but here –' a hand touched Morrow's belly '– and here.' It dipped down to his cock. 'Great. You know, I wish I could keep you here, as a plaything, but they won't let me do that. Shame really, especially as once they get you you'd probably rather be here as well.'

'Don't bet on it!'

'Why? Do you look forward to being interrogated?'

Sickeningly, there was serious interest in the voice. 'No!'

'Shame, because that's exactly what's going to happen. After I've finished with you.'

'Who are they?'

'Don't ask questions you know I can't answer.'

'You could if you wanted.'

'But I don't. Now be quiet.' An almost gentle slap enforced the command.

'What are you going to do?'

The laugh was soft, and oh so amused. 'Whatever I want . . . whatever I want.'

There was the sibilant rustle of clothing being un-peeled then falling to the floor. Tied, hands cuffed above his head, feet chained loosely apart, Morrow could only curse loudly.

'Don't!' A hand tight around his balls held the string of obscenity in check. 'You like to talk dirty? OK, but not yet.'

'Not yet?' Incredulous, Morrow almost laughed.

'Not until I want you to.'

'Fuck it . . .' Morrow stopped speaking abruptly as the hand pulled hard.

'Ever worn a ball-stretcher? It would look good; pull these beauties down, give just enough pain to keep you keen.'

'I don't . . . like . . . pain.' Morrow hissed the words, gasping as the hand twisted.

'No?'

'No.' He managed to sound firm, convinced. Then, just as the pain shot through him, heat encased his cock. Curran's mouth; that sulky, little boy's mouth, that told such lies, sucking him in, shockingly erotic. Breath fled from Morrow's lungs, he threshed wildly; panic there again, as the pain and pleasure shot into his brain. A keening sound threaded its way into his hearing, and he knew it for himself, for his own voice. It shocked him into cold sanity, and he knew where he was, remembered who was manipulating him, and what had been heat and desire turned arctic.

After a moment the mouth slid away. 'I had you then,' Curran tutted, though he loosened his hold, stroking the abused skin reflectively. 'Almost.'

Morrow was somewhere else; somewhere very cold. He spoke very slowly, very softly. 'I don't want you to touch me.'

'I don't suppose you do.'

'Leave me alone. I won't respond to you. I won't play your games. Let your friends at me.'

'In a while.'

Morrow swallowed dryly, and tried not to think of what his body wanted. He felt shaken, frightened by a monster he didn't dare name. He started violently when a hand touched his face, making him jerk away, tension snapping at every nerve in his body.

'Shush. I could hurt you so badly, Jack. I could kill you . . .'

'Then do it!' It even sounded like a sane alternative to this captivity.

'No, not yet. Not yet.'

The kiss was so swift that Morrow had no time to react, no time to show his revulsion; only time to flinch.

'I'd kiss you properly, but I know you'd bite my tongue off.'

'And anything else!'

'I know that.'

The laughter was back. Morrow wanted to scream.

Curran was moving about, doing something. Morrow didn't know what. It would be better to be deaf as well as blind. He knew his pulse was speeding, sweat slickening on his skin, pricking under his arms, itching his scalp. Then fingers were touching his ankles and he knew that Curran was going to do the same as he had earlier. Frustration, knowing what was going to happen, but not being able to do a single thing to stop it, made him squirm on the bed, the mattress rough against his skin.

The chains were lengthened. Morrow tried to curl up, but Curran was there, effortlessly holding him flat, his weight warm against chill skin, fingers bruising where they held, a knee threatening, stilling any threat of fight.

'There.'

'Curran . . .' Morrow gnawed at the fullness of his bottom lip, though it was already worn raw.

'Will you beg?' Curran was shifting the long legs, making room for himself.

Morrow answered, 'No.'

'Will you tell me what they want to hear?' A hand stroked through his hair, gentle, kind.

'No.' Despair, threaded into the single word.

'Oh well . . .'

Morrow arched as his body was penetrated, hating every moment of the cock sliding slowly into his body, every soft sound of pleasure that escaped from his tormentor's lips. It all took longer than it had the first time. He lay still under the assault and let the pain wash around him while he fought the need to feel pleasure. Treachery was there in his own body, sliding around the shame and the bitterness, finding a path that led straight to his cock.

At the first stirring he tried to back away. But there was nowhere to go – the mattress hard against his back, the cuffs solidly tethering his limbs.

'That's it, Jack. Let yourself.'

'No!' Morrow twisted, howling denial, careless that blood dampened his wrists as he fought, not feeling the warmth trickle between the straining tendons of his forearms.

'I can make you come, I know I can!' Triumph was there in Curran's lust-tight voice.

And it was true. Morrow was hard, close to the edge, so fast – faster than he had ever been. When his knees were hoisted higher and the coupling became savage he was screaming again, and this time he was convulsing too, his body racked as he came, semen splashing on his curled belly as Curran cursed and cursed again, the obscenities a fitting soundtrack to his loss.

A long time later, or so it seemed, he still lay where he was, semen drying cold and tight on his skin, the other's seeping like disease from his body. Despair cocooned his every thought, buffered him, though his face was wet, and he had no memory at all of tears.

Curran was dressing. Going away. Morrow wished himself free of the chains, for all he wanted to do was to curl tight on himself.

'The others will be here soon.'

Morrow flinched at the abrupt sound of speech.

'Tell them what they want. Do what they want. It will be easier.'

If anything there was some sort of pleading there, in that soft command. Morrow shivered, very cold, hating the sympathy, wanting the hatred more. It was hard to find words at all, but he was strong enough – though that fact surprised him. 'Go away.'

'I'm going. Just thought . . .'

'Don't!'

'No.' Curran walked to the door, his shoes softly squeaking with each step. He seemed to pause. 'You know, I could make any man come, not just you. Physiology . . .' He left the word hanging as if that explained it all; made it all right.

'Go to Hell!'

'Maybe, probably.' The sound of footsteps, quite fast, brought him back to the bed, and his breath was warm, sweet as almonds against Morrow's face.

'I understand your secret, Morrow, but even if I didn't, I could still have done the same.'

Hands held his face, thumbs wiping away the wet from his cheeks. The kiss was light, scarcely a touch of skin against skin. 'I won't let them kill you.' Breath, warm; the feel of close lips moving. 'And I'll be back, when they aren't watching.'

And he was gone, leaving Morrow cold, waiting in darkness.

He shifted slightly, the darkness behind the blindfold finally beginning to settle. They hadn't been so concerned with the cuffs this time, merely binding wrist to wrist and then by a chain to the bed. His legs were free. Though even at his most optimistic, Morrow would have agreed that he was hardly a threat. Not today. Against this, maybe never.

At the sound of the door, his skin shivered. It was too soon. Footsteps came close.

'Did you tell them the truth, Morrow?'

Curran. It was such a relief that he could have wept.

Somehow Morrow held on to an unconcerned drawl, fighting desire. 'What is truth, Alex?'

'Ah, Pilate's answer. He was a devious bastard; I'm glad to see they haven't broken you yet.'

'Go to Hell.' Morrow gave up, his head falling wearily back on to the mattress.

'Really?' A hand touched Morrow's shoulder; it was very warm, making him realise quite how cold he was. 'I could be good for you . . .'

'Go fuck yourself.'

'I would if I could. Sounds great to me. I could fuck you instead though; that sounds even better.' He gave a small laugh. 'Or I could just hold you.'

'No!'

'Scared, Jack?'

Morrow fought a wave of fear as Curran climbed on the bed and curled against him. He was fully dressed, in what felt like a lightweight suit. His shoes were hard against the soles of Morrow's feet. Arms enclosed him, and Curran leant his head into the curve of Morrow's neck. 'There.' He stroked a hand gently against skin.

For Morrow it was, appallingly, the most comforting thing anyone had ever done for him. And the most frightening. He fought to stop shivering, and failed. 'Why are you doing this?' He spoke between gritted teeth, trying not to let himself ease into the embrace, to not show how unsettling kindness was after everything else.

'You always have to have reasons for everything, don't you?'

The hand was still stroking, warm as velvet against his skin. 'Me?' Morrow laughed shakily, without humour. 'That's rich coming from you! Why are you here? What can you want?'

'Sarcasm.' Curran tutted. 'Trust me, Morrow. Have I asked any questions?'

'Then why are you here?' Morrow was having trouble keeping the shiver out of his voice.

'Why not?' Curran shifted, drawing his body even closer. He was hard, though he did nothing but tuck his hips neatly into the curve of Morrow's ass.

'Because you –'

'Shush! I'm not here to argue with you. Just be quiet for a while, will you?'

'Just leave me alone, Curran. I haven't the energy to play your mind games.'

'Leave you alone?' The hand stilled, though it lay, warm against skin.

'Yes!' There, that was better; firm and in control.

'Oh, Morrow . . .'

The loss of the warm body was shocking. Miserably, Morrow understood his own sense of loss far too well. It was good Curran was leaving now. For the best.

'I'll come back another time.'

'Don't bother.'

'I want you, Jack Morrow.' The bed creaked as Curran leant over it, his breath warm against Morrow's cheek. Then he spoke again, louder, no longer in the soft whisper that made Morrow want to cry. 'I want to fuck you again; I'll be back for that.'

'I'll count the hours.'

Curran laughed, and the sound of the door opening and closing brought silence to the room.

Time lost its coherence. Morrow counted hours, then lost them. Food came, then again, long before he was expecting it. Either that, or it didn't come at all. There were trips away from the room, and he knew from the sounds that he was in an old house, somewhere suburban, almost rural.

They still asked the same questions; wanted the same things. Yet, despite himself, unless he lied, he could never give them an answer.

He thought of Curran more than should have been possible. The minutes they had lain together became a mnemonic for remembering there were ways he could be touched that didn't inflict just pain. Even the times before that, when he had been fucked. At least it had been Curran – whom he hated and thought about more than anything. Unless it was to wonder if anyone knew he was missing.

He knew he shouldn't have taken that vacation.

It had been a long time since Curran had been in the

room. A long time, though he would never be sure of
the exact measurement of hours and days. When they
touched him now, he tried to think only of a warm arm
encircling his body, of fine wool cloth scratchy against
his skin. Comfort, in a world of unease.

'Morrow . . .' The whisper, and the touch of a hand,
startled him from a light, dream-scattered sleep. 'Don't
say anything!'

'Curran?'

'Who else. How are you tied?'

Hands felt his wrists, tied together above his head,
then his ankles, somehow cuffed together. Then he was
shifted on to his side, and a soft, bitten-off moan of
protest was stifled as a naked body curled wonderfully
into him.

'There.'

An arm was around his waist, an anchor. Curran.
There were worse things in Heaven and Hell. Morrow
blinked behind the thick blindfold. His voice was raw
when he spoke. 'Why are you here?'

Curran giggled softly. There was some sort of alcohol
on his breath, and something else – honey, as if he'd
been eating Greek pastries. 'They're all asleep. I just got
back, and I don't want to disturb them. They've left one
guard and he knows me well enough to let me in here. I
told him to go and get some supper, so he won't be
watching. I wanted you all to myself.' He wriggled
closer. 'Fuck, it's cold in here. No wonder you're
shivering.'

It wasn't the cold. He was used to that. No, it was the
heat at his back, the soft voice, the hands that touched
so easily. 'You've been away.'

'Mmm, so you noticed.'

Morrow nodded. 'Yes, I noticed.'

'And you're still alive. Shit, sorry, was that a bruise?'

Morrow let out the trapped breath. 'Guess so.'

'You're a stubborn bastard, I'll give you that.' The grin was there again. 'Is your secret still safe?'

'I don't have a secret.'

'You'd be one in a million. Well, I won't argue. But do you want me?'

The sudden question was shocking. Spinning Morrow off track. 'What?' He tried to twist from the encompassing arms, but was held easily in place. 'Why should I want you?'

'Because.'

Curran's mouth was so close to Morrow's ear that he could feel the lips moving as Curran spoke. 'Because nothing! I don't want you.'

'But you do. Don't lie to me.' Curran's head moved, the mouth nibbling, finding where his arms were twisted above his head. He was laughing again. 'You smell like sex.'

'Don't!'

'Then be good. Now, just lie a bit more on your side and curl your legs up ... that's right.' Curran wriggled, positioning himself. 'I brought some stuff with me; you'll be fine.'

Morrow wasn't worrying about lubrication. 'Curran, please, don't!' He was close to panic, breath coming hard around small sounds of distress, but something wet and cold was pushed into him by probing fingers.

'I'm not doing anything you don't want. Admit it.'

'Jesus,' Morrow gasped as the head of Curran's penis pushed blindly at the curve of his ass, sliding between his legs.

'Be quiet. I'm not going to hurt you. I only want this to please us both.'

The whispers were the devil in Morrow's head, but he denied it all. 'Please us both? What are you, insane?'

With a soft grunt, Curran forced his cock in the first couple of inches, his hand covering Morrow's mouth before he could cry out. 'No, not mad. Just wait, Morrow, relax a bit.' He shifted and wriggled until he was as far in as the position would allow. 'And straighten your legs, not too much.' To his surprise, Morrow obeyed. 'There.' He slid almost all the way out, then pushed back in one long even thrust.

'Curran . . .'

'Yeah, told you it'd be good.'

There was no fight in him anymore, and Morrow surrendered to his body. There was little difference between the pleasure of being held and this. Curran was still there, warm and alive, close. Comforting. That he was being fucked as well . . . that was pleasure, too, in its own way. He didn't get hard, but after a while he moved slightly to accommodate Curran; did slight things with his hips that seemed to be good. When Curran came, Morrow was crying, his own body shuddering with release.

Curran held still for a long time after he'd come, his cock slowly softening until it slipped of its own accord from Morrow's body. There was the sound of a rubber being stripped off, a soft kiss brushed against his shoulder, then Curran was gone.

Morrow cursed into the darkness. Despair tasted of bitterness, and was scented with honey.

Seemingly, they lost interest in him. Whatever it was they wanted him to be, he had failed. Or succeeded. Maybe they'd just found a different source. Still bound to the bed he wondered if his failure meant his death, for he was very alone.

Darkness cocooned him. The lack of hands to hurt was a blessing. But he yearned for Curran. And that secret burned.

They had let him go, taking him to his apartment without a word. He had healed, as he always did, but work was still a week away. He lay on the sofa and watched TV instead. Sometimes he slept. Though all he would dream of, relentlessly, was Curran wrapped around his body, holding him; comfort from a comfortless place.

One day he drove himself back to the house: a near-derelict Victorian place in one of the city's outer suburbs. He sat for a long time in the car, engine running. It had got colder, and he shivered, even with his overcoat on, when he finally stepped outside.

A small flight of steps led up to an acid-etched glass door. He took the stairs slowly, letting himself into the house with a key. More stairs went upwards; he trod them lightly, as if afraid to disturb ghosts. They led him to the room.

The door eased back on oiled hinges, the sound of the handle enough to curl the hairs on the back of his neck. The bed was still there, his blood dark, ugly. The cuffs were gone.

He touched the metal frame, running a finger along the shiny newness. They must have bought this just for him. He wondered if it had been worth it.

Hands deep in his coat pockets, he sat down. He blinked slowly at the room, miserably aware of nothing in the world but loss.

Then a sound cracked softly through the silence. Morrow was on his feet as the door swung slowly open. Curran looked the same, though he wore all black, the darkness taking in the light, making his face seem very pale. He seemed to hesitate, then nodded. 'I wondered when you'd come back.'

'How did you know I would?'

'I know you, Morrow.'

'Do you?'

'Yes.' He seemed to consider the fact. 'Or I did, once. Before this, this . . .' He sighed. 'Was it worth it?'

Morrow shook his head. This, what had happened here, had been what he wanted – thought he wanted.

Yet the reality had been so different from his dreams. He shook his head, the winter light slanting into the room blurring his sight.

'Morrow, what do you want now?'

He couldn't say; didn't know. He swallowed hard and looked away, silent with need. When the other man spoke he started.

'If you still want me, you can have me.'

Morrow would have been laughing if it wasn't all so sad. 'Curran . . .' He broke off, shaking his head in denial.

Curran stepped into the room, his leather jacket creaking softly as he pushed the door to and closed the distance between them. 'I mean it.' Without waiting he took hold of Morrow's face between his hands and kissed him.

Morrow moaned and opened his mouth. He knew this was sick, but if this was disease then he never wanted the cure. He kissed back, opening his mouth and taking possession of something he had never been offered before. The mouth tasted of honey; honey and cloves. Morrow licked into the warmth and moaned as his tongue was met, flicked against, dominated. He would have gone to his knees there and then, knelt like a whore, but he was not allowed to. Instead, Curran held him still and, rather than demanding obedience, slipped to the floor himself.

Dazed, Morrow looked down at the tousled hair, and as if the hand reaching out was not his own, touched it. Soft and clean, it ran like water between his fingers. He concentrated on it, aware vaguely that his flies had parted and his pants and boxers were pooled around his ankles.

The heat of Curran's mouth was shocking.

'Alex . . .'

The secret was here. Morrow shuddered as his cock hit the back of a long throat and was held there, muscles

81

contracting around it. Fire streamed into his blood, and forced his fingers to dig hard into hair and bone. Curran moaned and Morrow knew it wasn't from pain. He understood everything; his fingers reaching into Curran's skull linked them need to need. There was madness too. But he didn't care. Nothing mattered but the mouth. And the throat. He shuddered violently as Curran's fingers dug into the skin of his thighs and, beyond hope, he spilled seed into Curran's voracious heat, feeling him swallow it down with a cry that shivered in the air, unrecognisable as his own.

Unsteady, he stood unmoving while Curran dressed him.

'Come on.'

Morrow blinked at the command, unsure of what was required of him. 'What do you want?'

'You. Us. Come back to me?' Curran came close, and rubbed the back of his fingers against Morrow's stubbled cheek. 'Whatever you sought here, you didn't find it. Did you?'

Morrow saw the flicker of doubt and shook his head. 'No. I'm not what they wanted. This wasn't what I wanted. It was nothing like –'

'Pleasure?'

'No.' He hesitated. 'You were that.'

'I wondered. Hoped.' Curran seemed to gather himself. 'I want you so badly . . . but not here.'

'Where?' Not that it mattered. There was no doubt he would have gone anywhere.

'Away. I came back because of the secret, Morrow. It is mine too.'

'I thought I'd hidden it so well.' Amusement was there, and something of the old Morrow.

'Not from me, sweetheart.'

'No.' Morrow sighed and took the hand in his own, bringing it up to kiss the knuckles. 'I hated you for so long.'

'Maybe.'

'I still do.'

'Hate is like love; close as brothers.'

'Or as lovers.'

Curran smiled. 'Come with me. I want to fuck you so hard.'

'Alex . . .' Morrow shivered; a ghost walking over his grave.

Curran went to the door, hardly looking at the room around him. He reached his hand out and waited. Until Morrow came to him.

Lepidoptera

Helena Ravenscroft

*T*he wall beneath her hands was smooth. She slid her fingers across the surface seeking imperfections, but there were none. A plain wall. Simple, smooth and as cold as ice.

The whole room seemed cold. She knew she was naked, although she couldn't see for her eyes had been bound with a wide satin ribbon that made her world eternally dark. Her arms were stretched wide and fastened to the wall with immovable leather straps, her legs spread and manacled. The only movement permitted by the bindings were the tip and tilt of her head and the slide of her fingers on the wall.

'How beautiful you are.' His voice was low and dark, a caramel-soft caress. She could feel the warmth of his breath on her shoulder as he stepped forward to tighten the leather circlets at her wrists. His fragrance washed over her and she flared her nostrils, desperate to catch more of him, to suck in the scent. Rosemary and berries, brandy and tobacco, a hint of lime and the merest touch of something darker and more sensual. It had been this perfume, this part of his own sexual signature, that she

84

had found more alluring than his face or physique when they had first met so very long ago.

'Do you trust me?' he breathed. She stayed still, waiting. He moved closer and she felt the brush of his hand on her waist. Her skin prickled at his touch, a shiver of anticipation and longing that shimmered through the bare skin where his fingers had made the briefest contact. 'Do you trust me, Illona, my beautiful captive? Do you trust me this time?'

She sighed, and it was the softest sound. She ached for his touch, longed for his hand to be firmer on her skin, wanted him to lay the length of his body against hers; but she knew that he wouldn't be hurried.

'I trust you.' Her own voice sounded strange to her, foreign, tinged with desire and hunger but tremulous with the cold and the waiting. She had hung there for a long time, growing chilled as the minutes became quarter hours and the quarter hours ticked by in steady quartets until she had lost count of time. It was always thus. He caught her. He pinned her. He left her to grow hungry and cold.

He gave her chips of ice to moisten her lips, occasionally pressing the larger pieces to her nipples until she gasped and strained her breasts towards his hands. Once he'd fed her a peach, biting and chewing the fragrant flesh and kissing it between her lips. Twice he'd dripped warm honey on to her tongue, following this with his own burning, crushing mouth.

'This time we will go further than we have ever gone before, Illona. You're so beautiful, so proud. You will be the perfect specimen.' His hands smoothed down the curves of her body as he spoke. 'Come. Are you prepared to begin?'

She nodded, her whole body tense and expectant. She stayed very still, listening to him, hearing his voice move away and the whisper of silk over flesh as he removed his shirt. She didn't hear his near silent approach and was surprised by a sudden piercing sting. It was sharp and fine and it pressed against the tender flesh of her earlobe but did not break the skin or wound her. He held it just close enough for there to be pain, but not so forcefully that pleasure eluded her.

She sighed and shifted a little, feeling the warmth of his skin very close, soothing the length of one side of her body.

'Do you feel that? Is it enough?' he asked. She nodded.

'No more than that. Please,' she whispered.

'You must feel some pain.' His face was close to hers now, his lips almost brushing her cheek and she could feel the beat of his heart in the close air between them. 'It will purify the experience. Like the dizziness of hunger that you feel – it will intensify every sensation. Open your mind and feel with your soul.'

His hand swept down her neck to her breast. His palm was roughened and when he brushed her nipple her body shivered with arousal. She sucked in her breath and pushed her ribs upward and outward, fitting her breast to his hand so that he was forced to cup it and she could feel his thumb rubbing over her nipple. As he bent his head the warmth of his hair fell on to her skin, then her mind clouded with a sensuous heat as his lips closed around her nipple.

He sucked the taut bud, teasing it with his teeth. It was as if a satin glove had been folded around her breast; the power of his tongue and lips drawing her inside him. She gave a low moan, her body arching against the coolness of the wall behind her so that her breasts were pushed up to his face. When he withdrew she sighed and called his name.

'No. Please don't stop. Oh, please. More,' she said.

This time the thin sting, the pressure of the needle, was lower, just to the left of her throat. Again, not enough to pierce the skin – but only just. He held it there then removed it and she waited until she felt it again, trying to anticipate where he would choose, to discern a rhythm to his prickling stings. It was briefly on her fingertip, then quickly on the fleshy pad of her thumb, piercing her skin this time, she was sure, for he followed it with the pressure of his mouth and she heard the low sharp intake of breath as he tasted her blood. His tongue traced back over her hand, snaked over the leather cuff and trailed in a warm wash up her arm. He buried his mouth in the hollow of her armpit, breathing and licking. Then he was gone again.

The needle was next at her breast, scratching a complete circle around her areola where the pale flesh became dark, and her nipple sprang to prominence. The muscular nub strained and swelled as he darted faint pricks around it, then she gasped and arched her neck as she felt him apply the sharp point of the needle to the tiny ducts at the end. He stung them and pricked them until her nipple was like fire, then he enveloped her breast with both hands. He pulled and squeezed so that she made herself swell towards him, then his hot mouth covered hers, his tongue probing her throat. She almost gagged with the sudden deep penetration of his tongue, but recovered enough to kiss him back; a gush of creamy arousal slicking her already damp thighs as she felt his hands slide from her breast to her hips.

'Your responses improve every time.' His voice was so low that she had to strain to hear him. His fingers played lightly over the satin skin of her lower belly, then descended to the velvet hair that darkened the flesh between her thighs. The manacles at her ankles held her feet wide and her knees were spread so that she couldn't evade his hand, even if she wanted to. She tilted her pelvis towards him, suddenly desperate for the hard thrust of his fingers inside her, or the brush of his thumb over her clitoris. But there was nothing. Just cool air fanning her suddenly abandoned body.

'Where are you?' she cried.

'Ask no questions, or I will have you gagged.' His voice was suddenly hard and unfamiliar, the caramel caress replaced by granite tones that echoed against the cold walls. Illona shuddered, a prickle of unease running up her spine. She heard him approach, his feet soft on the wooden floor, and her skin tingled with a mixture of excitement and fear. His fingers were firm on her breasts as he pinched her subsiding nipples to cork-like hardness, then she felt the cool kiss of metal as he squeezed silver nipple grips on to them.

Before she had time to protest his hand burrowed into her pubic curls and she felt his hot breath on the front of her thighs as he squatted before her. His thumb brushed her clit, pressing the fleshy hood back, and she let a welcome flood of milky juice wet his hand. His hands were firm and cool as he gripped her labia and spread them wide, using tiny jewelled clips to pin them like butterfly wings so that she was exposed and vulnerable. His tongue was searing as he lapped her; she could feel her juices flowing on to his nose and mouth, and she gasped and shuddered, her heart racing feverishly and her mind spinning. He exhaled his hot breath on to her open sex, then came the needle, silvery and piercing, as he pricked repeatedly and quickly all over the inner surface of her tenderest parts.

'You hurt me like that,' she protested. There was no reply. If anything the pricking was firmer and she feared that the needle would pierce her flesh soon.

'Please, Lotharian, you hurt me.' It was barely more than a hoarse whisper and she didn't know herself whether she was pleading for him to desist, or continue. She hung in her bonds, her head drooping slightly so that the silkiness of her long hair cloaked her full breasts. Her sex was fire and ice, and she could feel herself swelling towards the source of the sharpness as he stabbed and pricked the juicy, fleshy, petal-soft creases.

His hands withdrew and were suddenly smooth on

her thighs, stroking and coaxing, his thumbs circling and moving to her knees and then back up. In the split second before she felt him test her inner creaminess, she remembered that his fingers were impossibly long and slender. He slid a forefinger deep within her sex. She felt her whole body tighten, her muscles clenching at his hand in an attempt to retain the single probe. He pushed into her until the knuckles of his other fingers pressed against the soft contours of her buttocks, then he pulled out and was gone.

'More,' she cried, her body tense, her hips thrust wantonly forward, her breasts and sex swollen and blushed. She heard him move in the room and a door snap closed, the sound brittle in the cold air. There was a movement at her side and she felt soft lips suckle on to her breast while gentle hands placed something smooth and slender between her legs.

The dildo. She had seen it once, long and silver and gleaming with the rime of her own juices. He did not use it every time for he was capricious in his desires and liked to change his instruments regularly. She felt its rounded nose press against the pout of her sex; then it was thrust quickly into her, twisting and plunging until she could hear the slick of her cream on the smooth surface. Hot desire and a trembling, shuddering pleasure washed over her and she felt the sucking mouth increase the suction on her silver-starred nipple. It was a glorious sensation, pure and sweet, and she moaned as the dildo began to move rhythmically in and out of her warm, grasping flesh.

His fingers crushed against her clitoris with an abruptness that made her gasp, then she felt the tips of his nails lightly score her skin as he worked his hand under her, around the plunging dildo, to her bottom. He gave the tiniest pressure with a single, moistened finger and she felt herself flare and open to him, used to his tutelage of her most secret place. He eased in, past her tight little sphincter, and she felt him crook his finger forward slightly and rub her inside, increasing the pressure until he almost met the smooth surface of the dildo through the thin membrane that separated her front and back.

His hands moved first together, then alternately. Slow, slow, then fast, fast, fast until she heard a harsh cry that sounded like pain – but she knew that it was her own shout of rapture. She would come; she would come soon, she knew. His mouth on her breast sucked harder and seemed to dart from one nipple to the other – so quickly that it felt as though he had two mouths that sucked and licked.

She felt her body stiffen and a jolt of sheer ecstasy thrust upwards from her belly. But before she could drown into the beginnings of her climax, his hand was rough at the back of her head and the satin ribbon was suddenly torn from her eyes. She blinked in the candle-light and saw that Lotharian was standing before her, his dark features sober and intense and his arms spread wide like a pagan priest.

The sucking of her nipples and the plunging of the dildo and finger remained, however. Confused and aroused, she looked down and saw the twin heads of his sisters, one dark, one fair. Their slim hands were buried between her thighs and their tongues and lips worked in unison upon her breasts. Illona stared up again into his eyes and felt herself drown into the blackness of orgasm. Shuddering, sinking, dissolving. She sobbed and gasped, her hips thrust forward and her knees splayed outward to absorb every nuance of their touch.

He observed her intently, his eyes hooded and watchful, his chin sunk almost to his chest. Slowly he lowered his outspread arms until his long fingers brushed the leather-clad sides of his muscular thighs. She saw that he wore the amulet around his neck, the leather thong twisted and black as it snaked between his coppery nipples, the amber crystal pendant making a fiery shadow against his skin. As he moved closer, she could just make out the butterfly captured within, preserved forever – beautiful for all time. Its wings were a delicate apricot and its slender body a sliver of dusty charcoal that matched his dark eyes.

'Perfect,' he said softly. 'Stop now. You will have her again in time.'

The girls dropped back on their heels, leaving the dildo buried deep inside her swollen sex. Their faces were flushed, their lips soft and pouting. She could hear them breathing, soft little sighing sounds that made the downy hairs on her arms lift and prickle. She had never been this close to them before and she gazed down at them both, studying them intently.

Amaryllis was pale, her cloud of white-blonde hair like moonshine around her face, and her mouth was petal pink, the lower lip full like a swollen rosebud. Her body, folded in an attitude similar to prayer, was tiny and lithe with gleaming limbs that shone with oil and little breasts that fluttered under her rapid panting. Illona could see that she had shaved every inch of herself, even her rounded pubis and her eyebrows; the curiously denuded skin had the translucency of a frozen pool.

Hellebore was dark, her skin golden and sun-kissed, her hair straight and captured by twists of ivy into raven plaits that curved over the undulation of her breasts. Her nipples, red and puffy like exotic fruit, had been pierced by black bars that looked like two thorns in her flesh; and, glistening in the barely visible pout of her sex, there was a black iron ring that pulled at her clitoris and made it constantly engorged and huge, like a miniature penis peeping from her black pubic hair.

Lotharian stood between his sisters and she thought how beautiful they looked as the candlelight flickered on their skin and hair. They were like fallen angels. Ravishing. Lascivious. Decadent and debauched.

His hands rested lightly on their heads and he spoke softly.

'My beautiful butterfly is hungry. She must feed on the flowers. She must seek their nectar and it will make her more lovely, more powerful, more perfect. The Amaryllis has a beautiful scent; she exists only to perfume the world. The Hellebore was once believed to cure madness; she exists solely to cure mine. Observe, butterfly.'

The girls moved slowly, their limbs intertwining and smoothing as they lay on the wide crimson cloak that he spread on the floor. She watched their hands touching and stroking, lightly fingering puckered flesh, and she sensed a quicksilver pull at her own sex, a shimmer of desire that pinched at her and swelled in her belly like hot treacle. She sighed and shifted against the wall, feeling the perspiration that beaded behind her knees and in the cubit of her elbows. Her sex was thick and heavy between her spread thighs and she imagined how open and juicy she looked, how inviting and welcoming. Her eyes sought his and he paused for a moment, one hand resting on Hellebore's rounded shoulder.

'Wait,' he said, simply. Then he bent to devour his sister's mouth with his own, his hands crushing and kneading the softness of her breasts, his knee jerking between hers and forcing her legs apart. Hellebore sank on to the cloak, her plaits entwining her neck like two dark serpents that seemed to writhe and tighten. Amaryllis cradled her sister's head in her lap, her shaven sex nudging close; her small white hands slipping and stroking over the golden skin until her fingers found the black piercing in the swollen nipples. She pinched and pulled until Hellebore cried out with pain.

This seemed to inflame Lotharian, for he grasped Amaryllis by the hair and forced her face up to his, biting and tearing at her lips with his teeth until she too cried out. His fingers seemed everywhere: holding Hellebore's tiny waist, plunging into her juicy sex, pulling at the buttons of his own leathers. He gasped as he released his cock and gripped it in his fist, his fingers sliding around to pump and massage his tight balls. He was so close that Illona could smell his animal odour. The male fragrance of his sex mingling with his fresh sweat made her head swim; desire and frustration pulsed through her veins until she thought she would faint.

She twisted her hands but the bindings were firm and she could do nothing but watch as he twisted Hellebore over and anointed her bottom with his spit and generous fingerfuls of Amaryllis's slick juice. He parted the rounded curves of her buttocks and paused for a moment, as if admiring the tightly puckered bud of her anus. Then he placed the head of his cock on her, the glans shiny and polished. She seemed to open for him, as if he had tutored her in the same way he had Illona. The captive felt a surge of jealousy thrust up through her chest, so strong it almost choked her. Her eyes seemed to smart and burn and she felt her breath come quick and fast as she watched.

Unhesitating and smooth, he slid his length into Hellebore, broaching her gently at first but then – as she flared around the granite hardness of his straining cock – he plunged deep and quick and Illona heard them both groan. Her own arousal was so pervasive now that she heard herself panting in time with their bucking, almost as if she was the recipient of his rigid thrusting. She remembered the dildo still embedded deep in her sex and she squeezed on it, rhythmically pulsing on the hard silver rod.

She could see Amaryllis sitting lotus fashion, her depilated sex gleaming and open just beneath Hellebore's nose. Her petal-fresh perfume obviously pleased her sister, for the dark head leant forward and Helle-bore's tongue smoothed and licked until Amaryllis trembled and sighed, her eyelashes dropping to cast dark shadows over her pale cheeks.

Realising that she was near to climax, Lotharian reached out and grasped one of her breasts in his hand, his fingers crushing the translucent skin until a violet bruise spread from under his gouging thumb. Then he pushed Hellebore away and jerked Amaryllis towards him, his hands tight on her waist. Without pause, he thrust her legs up so that her thighs were almost resting on her shoulders, and then plunged into her, his face contorted and flushed.

He fucked her hard and fast until she screamed her orgasm into his shoulder, then he withdrew and pumped his fist along the length of his cock until he came. His hips shuddered and jerked with the intensity of his climax, sweat beading his smooth chest and his biceps corded and twisted. Beneath him, Amaryllis and Hellebore crawled and twisted, mewing like cats as they caught the hot spray of his come and licked it from each other's lips and cheeks.

Illona shuddered and writhed in her bindings, desperate for release. She begged him with her eyes, gazing at him with mute appeal as he stood and gestured to his sisters.

'Unbuckle her arms and lower her forward.'

They did as he bade them, their fingers soft and caressing, secretly stroking the tender insides of her wrists where he couldn't see. They lowered her slowly, keeping her body straight and leaving her ankles fastened to the wall. When her chin was in line with their hips, they stopped and held her there. She raised her head and saw that he had become hard again, his cock dark and shadowed as it rose from the tangle of night-black hair at his loins. The amulet glowed and swung against his chest as he advanced and he gripped it between thumb and forefinger, studying it for a moment before lifting it to his lips and kissing the cold amber jewel.

'You're thirsty,' he said. 'Drink. Quench your thirst with the nectar of my flowers. Lick my sisters from my cock, beautiful Illona, my papillon.'

He moved until he was level with her nose and she could smell the dark, secret scent of sex mingled with a light lily perfume and sweet rose fragrance. The heat of his body curled up to her face and she could feel her cheeks grow warm and flushed at his proximity. He smelled divine. Delicious. And a thirst that demanded to be assuaged settled around her dry mouth.

'Suck me,' he breathed. She could do nothing, just obey. Desire and love throbbed through her as she opened her lips to welcome him. He tasted better than he ever had before; her tongue tingled and all the tiny nerves in her palate gushed with fresh saliva as she drew him in deep. His hands cradled her head and his fingers moved softly over her hair, cupping her ears, stroking her jaw, smoothing her brows. Beneath her, Amaryllis and Hellebore trembled like flowers in the breeze, their arms taut as they supported her weight and held her arms wide, spread like the wings of a butterfly.

The last thing she heard before the white-hot spurt of his come seared her throat was their tender whispers and sighs as they gently tongued the rounded under-curve of her breasts.

'Open your mouth. Drink this.'

The taste of warm wine and honey was sweet on her lips and she swallowed, feeling the liquor spread its welcome heat in her throat and down inside her chest. He kissed her tenderly, his eyes open and fixed on hers so that she could see his pupils – they were so dilated that they almost obscured the darkness of his irises. His breath was warm and syrupy as it washed across her face and she felt her belly contract with love for him.

He released her and closed the glass door across her face, carefully fastening the little brass latch. She could feel that her arms and legs were pinned wide to the velvet bed, her sex open and creamy, her breasts still aching from the needle-pricks and the silver grips.

When he moved back she saw him throw his arms wide in an exaggerated gesture of blessing and the two sisters came to kneel at his feet, each entwining like ivy around his muscular legs. As the candles flared and the shadows receded, she could see – to the left and to the right – a collection of varnished wooden cases, glass-fronted and carefully hung, each with a beautiful specimen pinned to a velveteen board. Preserved. Forever beautiful.

His butterflies.

The Chrome Man

Maria Lloyd

Miranda pulled into the quiet cul-de-sac by Regents Park and finished the letter she'd been composing while crawling along in the Euston Road rush hour. She placed the Dictaphone in the glove compartment, climbed out of the car into the city heat and clicked the Saab's remote locking and alarm into action before pocketing her keys in her thin linen jacket. She crossed the road and her high heels struck against the pavement purposefully, her dress swaying against her slender body. Then she slowed, turning into the alley that led to the gallery and its grounds.

It was a discreet building overlooked by tourists and locals, who often assumed it was part of London University. A mock cottage, miniature against the Georgian townhouses, with the ground floor sheathed in reflective plate glass as an attractive yet alien feature. The lawns and the shrubbery were neat and well kept. Rustling chestnut trees and a high brick wall protected this haven from the outside world. She had gained access at the wrought-iron gates by a credit card swipe and a smile at the surveillance camera. She sighed, feeling the tension of the drive dissolve from her shoulders as she strolled up the winding pathway to the gallery's entrance.

The gallery was obscure. Very few knew of its existence. She had only gained an admission card after she had been a member of a certain ladies' club for two years. Now she found herself drawn here more and more frequently – whenever she needed some quiet time en route to sales meetings or between appointments with clients. She found the cool, restrained atmosphere of the place hypnotic. The minimalist rooms, smooth parquet floors and large canvasses on pale walls reminded her of a temple. In the current exhibition each canvas displayed was an interpretation by a different woman artist of one of the positions depicted in the *Kama Sutra*. Some were practically abstract, some pornographically exact. She enjoyed focusing on each one in turn, as a kind of meditation.

Max, the gallery attendant, looked out from his small office near the entrance as she passed through the lobby.

'Good day, Ms Percy.'

'Hello, Max. And how are your studies going?'

'Very well, thank you. May I recommend the sculpture room today? There is a new installation.'

'Thank you, I'll take a look.'

She smiled at the blond young man, a German student studying philosophy, who worked here weekends and during vacations. He often waylaid her for short innocuous chats when she dropped by. 'I want to practise my colloquial English,' he had once explained, but it was also clear that he desired her. There was a time when such attentions would have embarrassed Miranda, but now she welcomed the attraction, and would have liked to have tested it to its limit. Perhaps Max was one major reason she had visited the gallery so often lately.

Max gave an uncertain smile. He paused in the doorway to his office for a few moments. He seemed about to ask her something but he simply returned to his post behind a bank of surveillance cameras showing each area of the gallery. Miranda noticed a folded-back copy of *Justine* by the Marquis de Sade on his desk, and wondered if it was required reading for his course or just a matter of taste.

She strolled along the parquet floor, glancing at each canvas flanking the gallery as she passed, until she reached the sculpture room at the end of the corridor. Full-length windows on three sides allowed for a light and airy atmosphere in which to exhibit sculpture.

There was only one piece on exhibit in the centre of the room: a life-size chrome male nude, with full erection. He was seated on a plain, high-backed chair of polished wood. Opposite the sculpture was a chaise longue for viewers to sit if they so wished.

Miranda approached the statue. The sculpture's face was blank and smooth, and the highly polished chrome reflected back her own features. She liked the look of curiosity and faint arousal which spread over her elfin face, her cupid-bow lips. Her long lashes and chestnut fringe shielded the newly kindled lust in her grey eyes as she reached out to stroke the smooth muscled contours of the chrome abdomen, the pectorals, the lavish erect prick. The prick was slightly jointed at its base so it could swivel when touched.

The air conditioning in this room was switched off, and the afternoon sun slanted in, giving a hothouse atmosphere which made the smooth coolness of the sculpture refreshing, inviting. With all the greenery and high blue sky on three sides of the room, it seemed as though Miranda were in the garden itself. But here there were no annoying insects, no worry about lack of privacy.

The ideal setting.

Miranda knew the surveillance camera, set high in the corner of the room, was working, and Max could see everything that went on. She quickly glanced up at it and shrugged. It had never stopped her before.

She unbuttoned her linen jacket and red polka-dot dress. Cotton folds pooled around her ankles before she stepped out of them. She let her hands smooth across the raw-silk brassière that cupped her full breasts, before her fingers sought out her clitoris through the silk of her panties, and fondled its swollen base into sweet hot stiff expectation. She was wet just thinking about how young Max would be watching her, too shy to intervene. He would ensure no other visitor to the gallery disturbed her.

She had to do it. Stroking the large chrome prick tenderly, she was reminded of the phallic appendages on mediaeval armour. She had always had a fantasy of being screwed by a crusader. Quickly she wriggled free from her bra and panties. Her well-toned body glistened with a fine moisture, and her nipples protruded like fresh berries, rose coloured against her honeyed skin. She could watch herself as she manoeuvred herself into the statue's lap, admire her nakedness in the contours of his mirrored chest.

Slowly, gently, she eased herself on to the cold, hard phallus. It felt so smooth and slick against her, cooling her insides, making her vaginal walls twitch at the strange sensation of welcoming a metallic prick, which swivelled and butted but did not yield like flesh. As she became used to its generous size she felt her excitement growing. She gently rocked against the prick, circling its smoothness, testing how securely the sculpture was fixed to the chair.

Very securely, by the feel of it. And the feel of it was heavenly. Soon she rocked and bucked against her still and silent lover, holding on to his smooth shoulders and caressing his chest with her breasts, stroking her nipples into harder arousal on the glossy chrome. She watched her eyes dilate, and her lips become smudged while kissing the metallic sheen of the blank face. Then she closed her eyes and thought of Max, watching a few metres away on his surveillance screen, wondering if he would be aroused beyond self-control and finally come on to her. But she was too turned on to wait much longer and find out. She let out a fierce cry of satisfaction as she came, then nestled against her chrome lover to recover.

Eventually she disentangled herself from the sculpture and dressed. The chrome sculpture was smeared with her saliva, her lipstick, her sweat, her come juices.

She walked back along the gallery. Max popped his head out of his office. He looked slightly flushed, and his piercing blue eyes held a glitter she had never seen in them before. She thought he would say something now, but at the last moment he seemed to change his mind and merely smiled.

'Goodnight, Ms Percy.'

'Goodnight, Max.'

Bastard, she thought. She had treated him to a floor show and he had not even asked her out for a drink, let alone offered to screw her senseless. 'I think you may need to clean the sculpture installation before anyone else sees it, Max,' she added coolly. 'I would hate for you to lose your job on my account.'

'Quite so, Ms Percy,' Max murmured as the door swung closed behind her.

Max wanted Miranda too much, that was the trouble. She made him feel unequal to her challenge.

He burned for her. Whenever she visited he used his own special video tapes to record the footage, then took them home and watched and re-watched as she made love to herself, screwed the chrome nude.

Max was so jealous of that sculpture. Miranda felt more lust for that inanimate figure than she could ever feel for him. The chrome man became his obsession. Polishing it for her, cleaning it after her visits, cursing it.

There was a girl on his course at college, Carol, who had been after him for weeks. She was a thin sporty type, with fair curly hair and prominent front teeth. Not his usual sort, but his friends Colin and Nick had both been out with her and reported she gave good head. They thought he should snap out of his mooning over Miranda, and go to it with a girl of his own age. So he invited Carol to visit him at the gallery one Friday evening, fifteen minutes before his shift ended. They could go out for a drink, take in a film afterwards maybe.

Carol turned up shortly after Miranda had gone through to the sculpture room. Carol wore a tight black T-shirt that exposed her midriff, and shorts and trainers. Her long brown limbs folded around him eagerly in greeting.

'I thought we could take a quick stroll in the grounds? There's no one here to mind,' he said, before she could notice the surveillance screen for the sculpture room.

'OK.' Carol bobbed down the hall ahead of him. He had to hurry to catch her up. He put his arm around her waist.

'This way.'

They took the path around to the back – to the secluded lawn and shrubbery that surrounded the mirrored glass of the sculpture room. White butterflies danced between the blooms. The roses gave out a languorous perfume. Easily, Max paused, and began to hug and kiss Carol, who responded hungrily. He moulded Carol's pert breasts under his palms, and rolled the bullet nipples between his fingers until she moaned softly with pleasure.

'Look, it's like making love in front of a mirror,' he murmured into her ear as he turned her towards the reflective window, pulled off her T-shirt and sucked and nipped at her bare breasts. He had paused in the exact spot on the lawn where he had calculated Miranda would get the best view. He wondered what she was doing now in the sculpture room. Whether the sight of him caressing Carol had made Miranda pause as she rode her chrome Romeo.

'Cool,' Carol crooned, and sank to her knees in the clipped grass.

'I've always wanted a man in uniform,' she laughed, unbuttoning the flies to his dark trousers. She helped him take off the crisp white shirt and dark silk tie and smoothed an appreciative palm over his hard brown flesh. Then she released his straining prick from the folds of his boxer shorts and began to fondle it, taking it into her mouth, letting her tongue tease its tip. Max moaned, gently entwining her blonde curls between his fingers as her pace quickened. Then he looked into the reflective glass again, willing an invitation to the invisible Miranda.

Soon he halted Carol's attentions, and she quickly stripped. He watched as Carol went down on all fours, waggling her smooth little arse to him in invitation.

'I'm hot, baby,' she said. 'Take me now; don't make me wait any longer.'

He knelt and gradually eased his prick into her, doggy fashion. He paused as she gripped him eagerly, rotating the tip of his dick inside her to make her want more. Then he quickly entered her fully, and they both gasped in satisfaction as he fell into a slow and steady rhythm.

He looked up at the clear blue sky, listened to the sirens in the distance, wondered how many other people in London were fucking at exactly this moment. He tried to slow his crescendo. It had been a long time since he had made love and it took all his self-control to delay coming long enough to make Carol orgasm too.

He hoped that Carol – and Miranda – appreciated his expertise. Then he groaned. He stared at the point he felt Miranda would be, thinking of her full firm breasts, her long legs, that honey skin. The very image of Miranda, naked, on the other side of the reflective glass, made him come.

Afterwards, Max and Carol lay on the grass for a few moments looking up at the swaying treetops and summer sky. Then they dressed and Max returned to the gallery to lock up while Carol waited for him at the entrance.

Miranda had already left. Max touched the phallus of the chrome sculpture. Still warm and moist. She had orgasmed here just moments ago, watching Max and Carol fucking in the garden. He could still smell Miranda's Clinique perfume. He glared at the blank sculpture, an obscene techno-Pan, his rival. Then he bent and sucked its metal phallus swiftly and noisily.

He had to. It tasted of her.

Miranda did not visit the gallery for a fortnight. She had been away in the States at a conference, she explained, when she finally dropped in on a Friday evening. The weather was still hot and sultry and she wore a scoop-necked silk shift dress and high-heeled strappy sandals. Her chestnut hair was pinned high in a top knot. Max admired the nape of her neck, her fine-boned sloping shoulders. A gold crucifix nestled against the naked upper portion of her breasts, in the scoop of her dress. Her nipples were contoured against the thin ivory fabric. Her tanned legs were long and slender under the short flared skirt. Max felt a physical pain in his chest just looking at her, chatting to her, wanting her.

'Is the sculpture still here, Max?' Miranda asked casually after their exchange of pleasantries.

'Yes, along with a few other items the artist has put on display.' Max grinned, his blue eyes clouded a little. 'The artist requested that I explained to people what they were, but I think they are all fairly self-explanatory.'

'Still, I would like to see the exhibit as the artist intended. So please, Max, accompany me.' She asked this in her huskiest plummy voice, and was gratified when he coloured slightly.

'Very well.'

He followed a little way behind her and she jutted out her bottom, swinging her hips so he could appreciate her curves. Then he moved ahead to introduce her to the new-look room.

The chrome male nude was seated as before, his permanent hard-on taunting the rose bushes and trailing wisteria blooms in the garden beyond. Around the edge of the room, however, were a series of pedestals. On each was an erotic implement. A PVC blindfold-mask with bridle and bit. A pair of nipple clamps, held together by a thick chain. A short leather cat-o'-nine-tails. A saddle. A riding crop. On the final pedestal was a bottle of twelve-year-old Islay whisky and a tube of KY jelly.

Miranda wandered from one pedestal to another, fingering the articles displayed on them.

'And the explanation?' she asked.

'Simply that it's a riddle which shows the best way to appreciate the sculpture.'

Max swallowed hard, watching Miranda's svelte body in silhouette against the windows. She looked even better than all the fantasies he had entertained while she was away. He had watched the latest video tape of her fucking the chrome man. Watched as she had paused, playing with her breasts, undulating against the chrome phallus, to gaze at the couple on the lawn making love. Then she had ground her fanny against the chrome man harder and faster than ever before. The very thought of it made his cock stir. He had wanked to the replay every night for two weeks. He had already told Carol he could not see her again. Miranda consumed him too much.

'I see.' Miranda broke in on his thoughts, considering

this explanation a moment. She stole a sideways glance at him. 'I think I can solve that riddle, but I would need a willing and amenable partner. Would you help me, Max?'

'Yes,' Max replied faintly as the truth dawned.

'Say "please", Max.'

'Yes, please.'

'Then strip,' she ordered bluntly.

Miranda picked up the mask, bridle and bit as Max took off his clothes and placed his uniform in a neat pile on the chaise longue. Then she strolled over to him and circled him deliberately. She was admiring his body in the same way he had watched her admire the sculpture. Appraising him. He could feel himself breaking into a light sweat with the excitement, his prick growing hard under her gaze.

Miranda liked the look of his body. So taut, so effortlessly healthy and powerful. She reached out hands with long red fingernails to scratch gently at the surface of his tanned skin. She clawed across his nipples, the ribbed muscles of his abdomen, his firm buttocks. She liked the tender expression in his piercing blue eyes as she fixed the mask over his face, then placed the bridle bit in his mouth.

'Now kneel.'

He obeyed, swaying slightly as his knees pressed into the hard parquet. She continued to circle and fondle him, pleased that he was blinded to the bright day and would not know which part of his body she would choose to caress next. His prick had leapt into full erection as she gently stroked its tip and he took a sharp breath with the unexpected pleasure.

'You have been a naughty gallery attendant, Max. First you spy on me, and then you engineer that sex session in the garden to distract me. Don't you realise that visitors should be allowed their privacy? Don't you realise bringing that girl here was a breach of security? You could lose your job for less.' Miranda fetched the nipple clamps and carefully attached them to him as she talked. Then she gave the reins a small sharp tug, pulling Max on to all fours.

'I'm sorry,' Max replied in muffled tones that betrayed his rising excitement.

Miranda rested the Cuban heel of her sandals on his right shoulder.

'Say "I am very sorry, mistress".'

He repeated her words. Miranda stroked Max's neck with her sandalled foot.

'That's all right, Max, because now I'm going to teach you how to behave. You are going to enjoy it so much you'll just want to be naughty all over again. So I can teach you all over again.'

Miranda pressed her thonged foot against his lips. 'You can start by licking the tip of each toe. Carefully.'

Max put out an experimental tongue, gently lapped and suckled each dusty toe in turn. Miranda closed her eyes to fully enjoy the sensation, swaying slightly. She wondered if the contrast between her skin and the cold metal bit inside his mouth felt pleasing to him.

'That's enough,' she said. 'I'm now going to saddle you up and ride you. You had better be a good stallion between my legs, or you shall be punished. Do you hear me?'

'Yes, mistress.'

Miranda took the saddle and slung it across Max's broad back. She lay on the floor beneath his crouched body to buckle the saddle tightly against his abdomen. She let her breasts brush against his erect prick and hard balls as she did so, rolling his penis against her hardened nipples. She loved the sensation. It made her throb between the legs. Her abdomen hardened as her loins stirred and her labia swelled in expectation of pleasure.

It almost made her impatient to fuck him now, but she had to play this out to the end.

So she straightened up and sat astride the saddle, striking Max's right buttock with the riding crop, tugging on the reins.

'Gee up.' She jabbed his flanks with her heels and he crawled about the room, turning in obedience to her orders and tugs on the rein and use of the riding crop, until they had made a full circuit of the gallery and returned to the chrome man.

The undulating movement of his body made the smooth leather saddle rub lasciviously against her clitoris and labia, and stroke the insides of her naked thighs provocatively. The sensation was exquisite.

'Good, but not good enough,' she said as she removed the saddle, bridle-mask and bit. 'Go fetch the cat-o'-nine-tails so I can punish you.'

Max obeyed, moving a little stiffly after his equestrian experience. Miranda took the whip from him, letting the leather thongs trail across her silk-clad breasts.

'Now, bend over, and rest on the sculpture's knees for support. In fact, why don't you suck on the chrome man's dick? It will act as your gag while I punish you. And don't try to tell me you haven't done it before.'

Miranda could almost hear Max's heart thud with excitement as he obeyed. Miranda walked around the homoerotic tableau she had created. Very Greek. The sight of Max's lips stretched around the chrome phallus, his own cock proud and aroused, his buttocks quivering and clenched in anticipation of her chastisement, made her really hot. Such macho strength at her disposal, wanting to satisfy her every whim. She slowly fondled her breasts, and dabbled her fingers against her clitoris, as she gazed at Max's predicament.

'Spread your legs a little farther.' She jabbed the whip against the inside of his thighs, and he shuffled his feet apart. She cupped his balls in her hand and he moaned in pleasure.

'Three strokes to initiate you, I think,' she said.

At each stripe Max bucked a little and groaned thickly. Miranda gently fondled each pink welt rising on his tanned buttocks, watching as the clenched muscles of his thick legs and thighs relaxed.

'Now you can stand up, turn around, and watch me undress.'

He obeyed as she slowly wriggled out of her silk dress. She wore a lace-up corset of pale silk, and her breasts were pressed together by its constriction. No panties. She kept her high-heeled sandals on. She rubbed the handle of the whip provocatively between her legs, inserting its butt into her vagina a little and wiggling against its smoothness, before replacing it on its pedestal. He watched hungrily.

'I don't know about you, but I feel really turned on. Are you ready to make love to me, Max? On my conditions?'

'Yes, mistress,' Max whispered.

'Good.'

Miranda fetched the whisky and KY jelly. She took a slug of the whisky and offered Max a swig, which he took gratefully. Then she dribbled a little of the amber liquid against his chest and licked it from his skin, nibbling gently on his nipples. He reached out to fondle her breasts, press them against his palms, squeeze her rosebud nipples. She turned away and sat on the chaise longue.

'Now worship me, Max, just to prove what you say.'

Max knelt between her parted thighs. He anointed her clitoris gently with his tongue and probed the inner folds of her sex until his tongue jabbed further and further inside her with a delicious, fast rhythm. She squirmed her fanny against his wide tender mouth as he sucked gently at the pink folds, lapping at the tender base, circling his tongue around the tip. He teased and licked the outside, before inserting his hot dense tongue inside her once more. She enjoyed his attentions while admiring the spectacle of his large, close-cropped blond head between her tanned legs, his concentration on pleasuring her. As she grew more and more excited she gripped his short hair and pressed him still closer into her orgasm.

Then she shoved him away.

'Very good. Did you like that too, Max?'

'Oh yes, mistress.'

'Then I shall reward you.' She sloshed a little of the whisky over his prick, then knelt down and licked the liquid off. She liked how hard and full his prick seemed between her lips, the way it twitched in response to little jabbing movements of her tongue. She could sense that he was doing his best to hold back from orgasm.

'Now turn around and bend over.'

Max looked disappointed, but he obeyed. She smeared a line of KY along his buttock cleft and over his anus. She smiled at the way it made him gasp when her ring finger gently probed his puckered hole until she could slide it deeper and deeper inside. All the while she was caressing his penis, his hard balls, his buttocks, with her other hand.

'Now, baby, you are going to fuck me while you are screwed in the arse.'

She kissed him then – a lingering French kiss. He reached for her sex, his fingers seeking her stiff little nub to stroke and tease.

'Sounds good to me,' he replied.

Slowly, guided by her instructions, he eased his arse on to the chrome prick. She could see that he was enjoying the feel of the metal dick inside him, as she had suspected he would. She was enjoying watching the chrome man slowly screw the flesh and blood version.

The reflection of Max's broad back, of her face over his shoulder, in the smooth sculpture, was sharply erotic.

When he was sufficiently impaled by the silent chrome man she straddled Max where he sat, in the lap of the sculpture, and lowered herself on to his prick, inch by delectable inch. His prick was so thick and lush and warm. She raised and lowered herself several times to relish the sensation. He gripped her thighs to gently govern the pace, so he could better control himself. She pressed her breasts against his eager mouth so he could lick and suck and tease each nipple in turn, while her fingers played with his short hair, his nipples, his hard balls in quick succession.

Slowly she felt herself losing control, rocking and circling against his generous cock hungrily until a sudden rush of desire flushed her skin and started fireworks behind her eyes. He moaned with her as she neared orgasm, and she felt doubly aroused, realising that each gyration they went through added to Max's own experience of being fucked. Max sucked hard at each of her nipples. Then he nibbled and sucked at the nape of her neck so fiercely, circling his dick inside her so eagerly that he made her come quickly, in a rutting tumult, as she sank her teeth into his broad shoulder to muffle her cries.

When they were spent Max took her in his arms and kissed her tenderly.

'Do you fancy getting a bite to eat now?' he asked shyly, rubbing the faint indentation she had left in his shoulder.

Miranda smiled.

'Why didn't you ask me that six months ago? Of course. Once you have cleaned the chrome man to my satisfaction. And after that we'll fuck some more.'

Pussy Willow

Liza Dallimore

*H*ow I came to be in that exclusive 'ladies' club' one night is not the subject of this story; it's what happened there that you want to know about. The venue and its whereabouts shall remain undisclosed: suffice to say that it is in a city famed for being 'European' whilst being very far from Europe. No doubt you'll find your own way there in your own good time. Remember, though, that one seldom simply arrives somewhere. While you dream of being somewhere new, your dreams are being divined, and a place is readying itself for you. Once you have come to it, made it yours, a place will expect something of you in return. And you must be ready to give, as you shall see.

Like so many straight women I often fantasize about my own sex. When I finally received an invitation to this house of dreams I became charged with a wild and erotic excitement coupled with nervousness. I had heard various stories about what happened there. Some of those tales were surely apocryphal, the result of wishful thinking, urban myths, but I had no way of knowing until I arrived. Much of the club's reputation rested on its mystique and its exclusivity.

It was a theme night at the club: French decadence. One was expected to dress accordingly. Virginal white seemed a fitting choice for me so I chose a romantic silk shirt with lace ruffles that could have been from any era. I added a waistcoat, snug black satin pants and leather boots that laced up. And a beret, of course.

After some elaborate security measures at the door conducted by a woman in an old-fashioned uniform with epaulettes (I wonder if frisking was *really* necessary) I was ushered upstairs into one of the most luxurious interiors I have ever seen, an exquisite *fin-de-siècle* French brothel. Had it not been a women-only establishment I'd scarcely have been surprised to meet the ghost of Toulouse-Lautrec glowering into an absinthe.

Heavily framed giant mirrors hung on the walls. There were wine-coloured damask drapes, plus velvet chaise longues and ottomans. The walls were papered in deep coral contrasted with black and gold and adorned with tapestries and oriental prints. The room was softly lit by ornamental chandeliers with lamps of delicate pink and green glass.

Part of one wall was a *trompe l'oeil* of Manet's famous *Déjeuner sur L'Herbe*, with its shadowy trees providing a perfect backdrop for the pale figure of the naked woman. Persian carpets lay on the floor. Near the *trompe l'oeil* was a dais covered with a mound of white satin pillows. The dais was enclosed in an oasis of light from a standard lamp. Under it a small black cat slept on a flowery fringed shawl. A bouquet of white, mauve and pink flowers spread out of a large porcelain vase.

The room was full of women, low-voiced and elegant, of varying ages. Some reclined on couches, sipping glasses of red wine, some sat in small groups at tables with champagne bottles in buckets next to them. I noticed one woman with an arm draped across her neighbour's shoulder. A glint of gold caught in the light as she moved her wrist: she was wearing cufflinks. A couple were involved in a deep kiss in one corner but otherwise everybody seemed to be simply conversing. Most of the women were dressed in dinner suits such as Colette and Missy might have worn when frequenting decadent bars in Paris.

There was a bar at one end of the room. Music from a single violin sent tendrils of sound over and under the hum of conversation, which seemed to fade as I looked about. Immensely self-conscious, I started across the room and wondered about the protocol of ordering a drink – was I supposed to go to the bar or simply sit at one of the tables? I nearly regretted my decision to come alone. Should I try to strike up a conversation with someone? I knew why I was here but began to wonder whether I had the courage to follow it through.

A woman dressed in a long diaphanous gown of a pale peachy shade came up to me. Around her neck was a thin black ribbon tied in a bow. One shoulder strap had slipped down. She was obviously naked underneath her dress and I could see the deep beige of her nipples. She knew my name.

'We've been expecting you. Come and sit down.' I followed her across the room. The little wooden-heeled slippers she was wearing clacked softly as she walked. She led me to a table near the dais. On it was a carafe of water and some glasses.

There was an air of watchfulness about, as if the room had been waiting for me. I became powerfully aware of my body, my muscles and skin, and the texture of my clothes. I wished that I were dressed entirely in silk. Or nothing at all – a thought that made me blush. At the same time I was lit with a lively teasing power, alert, responsive to the atmosphere. No one knew me here. I could do, could be, anything I wanted.

As I sat down a small movement caught my eye: I turned my head and with a shock saw that the *trompe l'oeil* was real! A *tableau vivant*. This was disorienting and surreal, giving me the feeling that I couldn't trust my own eyes. The naked woman looked over at me with a serene smile, elbow on one knee, her chin resting on her thumb and forefinger. What I had perceived to be the fully clothed male figures of the painting were really two women wearing dark velvet jackets and fez-style hats. They were all smiling at me now; no doubt the look on my face betrayed my surprise.

The light from the chandeliers was dimmed, leaving this corner with the picnic scene and the dais illuminated. The only other light came from spherical lamps hanging over the bar. An expression of pleasure took over the nude woman's face as the other two reached out and lazily began to caress her, stroking her legs and fondling her breasts. The woman who had greeted me went over and sat down with them, one leg appearing out of a split in the side of her gown. One of the clothed women idly ran her hand up her thigh and slowly slipped her hand under the silky fabric until it disappeared into the translucent folds of material. The woman in the dress closed her eyes, her nipples hardening under the sheer material. One rounded bosom was revealed as her shoulder strap slipped off.

Meanwhile the other clothed woman was pulling at the nipples of the nude, whose passivity I found disturbing and powerfully exciting. She continued to gaze calmly at me while her nipples grew stiff. She sighed at the touch of the woman who was fondling her freely with one hand, bold and proprietorial, whilst eating a pear with the other. Some cherries and plums spilled out of a picnic basket lying on its side. The other woman in a suit had slid her partner's gown up to her hips, casually pushing her legs open and playing with her now-exposed sex.

The suited figures lay back as the other two women languidly kissed each other, their slow movements enhancing the dreamlike quality of the scene.

I poured a glass of chilled water from the carafe. As I

sipped I glanced around the room. Surprisingly few of the others were taking any notice of the sensual play in front of them. I saw some women look over at me as if to determine my reactions.

I watched as the suited woman fed cherries to the nude, dangling them over her mouth, brushing her lips with them before allowing her to bite them. The other two women shared a peach, biting into it together so that their lips met and the juice spread over their mouths and down their chins.

The violin music rose and fell, trilling as the women caressed and petted each other. All four of them gently slid into a tangle of pale smooth limbs contrasted with the deep midnight and black of the velvet jackets. An air of anticipation caught me, snatched my breath. Was this inviting scenario truly being played out, as it seemed, for my titillation alone? I was both watching and watched, here a glance, there a smile quickly hidden.

Sighs and little mews of joy were coming from the four women. They rolled gently together, this way and that, their four bodies joining to create a constantly moving entity which pulsated with an increasing tempo. Soon the women were climaxing with high-pitched little cries and moans, their faces and bodies flushed and shimmering in the soft gold light.

After a while the woman in the slinky dress detached herself from the little group and walked over to the dais. She stood opposite me, illuminated in a glow of muted apricot. I couldn't take my eyes off her as she slipped the gown down over her hips and stood before me, naked and magnificent. Still wearing her slippers she reached down to take a deep salmon-pink flower from the vase, placing it behind her ear before lying back on the pillows. One hand rested on the mound at the top of her crossed legs. I laughed out loud with delight and recognition: Olympia! Her eyes challenged mine with all the presence and calm sexuality of the original.

Unmistakeably, this was for me. My fantasies were materialising in front of my eyes, conjured up by some unimaginable magic, but it no longer seemed strange. I was only too happy to suspend disbelief and watch to see what would happen next. Would it be as I had so often dreamt? Would she share her secrets with me as if there were only the two of us in the privacy of her boudoir?

The dull pink of the flower matched her lips. She lifted the corner of her mouth slightly, then smiled wider. She wet one fingertip in her mouth and then started to caress her bosom, bringing out the rosebud of her nipple with rhythmic strokes. I forgot the room, the other women, forgot even that I'd ever existed outside her gaze. She stroked herself with long sensuous movements. Her hands travelled from the peaks of her breasts down over her stomach, rested briefly at the fine coppery curls of her pubic triangle and then returned to pinch and rub her nipples.

With painstaking slowness she uncrossed her legs and shook off the slippers. They fell to the floor with a gentle clatter. As she opened her legs wider I could see the secret folds under the curls and a sliver of dusky pink. Then she touched herself with smooth, deliberate movements. I was just close enough to see her sex change colour and swell, growing wet as she parted the lips. Her fingers played around the beaded frills of her inner labia and slipped in and out of the crevice of her sex. I was mesmerised.

The little black cat stirred then. It arched and stretched before smooching its way up her leg, and settled in the space between her thighs. I could hear it purring. Olympia bent one knee as the cat was obscuring my view of her sex. The cat gave itself a few self-conscious licks then it, too, looked at me, waiting. The tip of its little pink tongue poked out of its mouth.

'Go on,' I whispered. It turned and buried its triangular head in Olympia's vulva – pussy to pussy. Its head bobbed daintily up and down as it licked furiously. The purring became louder. I imagined the exquisite feel of that rough little tongue rasping on my clitoris and the velvety softness of its fur against my thighs. I looked at Olympia's face, at the blush on her cheeks and her now half-closed eyes. Her hips rocked ever so slightly – restrained movements that were careful not to dislodge the throbbing little bundle between her legs. But soon it was obvious that she was finding it difficult not to move; I could see tremors and quiverings overtake her and hear her breaths become moans. Then she arched her back, reminiscent of the cat moments before, and let out heavy singsong sighs of contentment and relief.

I drank some more of the water and decided, once the thudding of my heartbeats subsided, to get a drink. I had to do something. I got up from the table. I breathed a musky, perfumed closeness and only just stopped myself from sniffing the air. I felt as if I were on heat and that my arousal must be ablaze in the subdued lighting. I became aware again of the sound of women's voices. I tried not to sway my hips as I walked. Was I prey or predator here? I longed both to keep control and to abandon myself completely. I suddenly felt the urge to drink recklessly.

I made my way towards the bar, where a heavy crystal fruit bowl on a stand caught my eye. It held bright tangerines, figs, pears and grapes. Perfectly ripe, of course. I smiled. Clichéd images of forbidden fruit. The luscious sensuality of a summer-ripe peach smiled back at me through the reflections of coloured light glittering from the cut edges of the bowl.

The low murmuring stopped. The air of erotic tension rose. And there she was, behind the bar – Manet's barmaid! Now I laughed out loud, shaking my head as I took another look at her. Her heavy fringe framed her soft face, her dark round eyes and those full rosebud lips. A black velvet choker encircled her throat, dramatic against her creamy skin. White lace flounced over her bodice and through it peeped her pink-tipped breasts, a posy perched daintily between them. Her pale forearms were turned out to me, her famous pose somehow expressing the inevitability of her presence.

I was completely undone. She smiled directly at me – quite the loveliest thing I have ever seen. I gaped. The room was suddenly smaller and hotter. In the mirror behind her I saw myself reflected and also the reflection of other women moving towards the bar. Something was expected of me. I was being drawn into a mysterious circle as they came closer, waiting for me to move or speak. My pulse was leaping. I tried very hard to keep my eyes on the barmaid's face. My nipples leapt up to salute hers. My mouth went dry.

More women surrounded the bar; surrounded me. I saw them gliding in the mirror, felt a gentle nudging and realised that I was being softly pushed towards Manet's vision.

I was near to losing control and wanted to leap over the bar in a ridiculous and dramatic gesture to ravish her.

'Would you like something to drink?' she said. I was besotted by her smile.

The circle of women crowded closer. It was all I could do to open my mouth to answer her.

'Yes. Do you have a cocktail list?'

She laughed. Her breasts shook in their lace bonnets.

'You won't have tried any of these before,' she said, handing me a elaborately printed card. 'They're our own.'

Sweet Honey on the Rocks
Pussy Willow
Madame de Pompadour's Breast
Rubyfruits of the Jungle

They all seemed to be champagne-based cocktails And she was right: I hadn't heard of any of them.

'Pussy Willow,' I read out. 'Suzon's speciality. Champagne, peach nectar and Suze over crushed ice. You, of course, are Suzon.'

Stifled laughter bubbled up around me. The barmaid exchanged amused looks with the women behind me.

'Yes. I am, of course, Suzon.'

'Ah.'

The mirror revealed all of the women watching me, their lips twitching and smirking. It must have been obvious how badly I wanted a drink. But I wanted the woman behind the bar more. I wanted her very badly indeed. And that must have been obvious too.

'What's Suze? A liqueur?'

The delectable Suzon grinned at me. I was entranced just by watching her open her mouth to speak.

'Suze is an apéritif from France. This drink is my invention. It's the way you drink it that makes it so special.'

'So how do you drink it?'

This time no one bothered to hold in their laughter, and feminine chuckles erupted around me. The women were clearly enjoying themselves a great deal at my expense.

'Would you like to try one?'

A few soft cheers. Well, why not? The women edged in. This wasn't going to be a lonely drink. Suzon dimpled at me as she carefully poured two fingers from a bottle over crushed ice in a glass and added champagne. She twirled the glass, very deliberately, all the while watching me. Breath was held. I felt breasts pressing into my back. A long thigh leaning into mine. Warm breath on my neck. Someone's hair brushing my ears. Hands gently nudging me closer.

'Now,' said Suzon. With a swift and elegant movement she knelt on the bar before me; my face was at the level of her hips. She was nude from the waist down. The black velvet bodice came to a stop above her navel. Sheer stockings and dainty suede ankle boots were her only other apparel. I gasped. I blushed. I hyperventilated. The women were pressing in on me now. Fingers crept around my waist. Lips nibbled my neck, ears. Hands stole inside my shirt and searched around my breasts.

Manet's barmaid slowly opened her thighs. I gazed into honey-blonde pudenda, pink lips glistening, the clitoris puffed redly upwards. I was being pushed closer. She raised the glass in one hand and with the other felt down and separated the inner lips of her sex. Slowly she upended the glass so that a stream of liquid coursed down between her legs into her vulva, dripping tantalisingly from her pubic hair. It was beyond resistance.

Someone pressed my head forward. I could hear whispers all around me:

'Drink.'

'Suck.'

'Enjoy!'

I closed my eyes and breathed in deeply of a rich odour – an exquisite smoky combination of musk, champagne and peach. I put my mouth to her stomach and licked. I sipped, slurped and sucked. I felt my shirt being unbuttoned and my pants being unzipped. Anonymous hands were squeezing my breasts, rolling my nipples, sliding up and down and around my body, insinuating themselves into my vulva, under my buttocks, rubbing between my legs.

I don't know how many women were touching me, caressing me, teasing me. Now I licked slowly down her stomach until my tongue reached her luscious and dripping cunt. I drank and was lost in her, lost to myself. My own sex was drenched and pulsating as strange fingers crawled into me, and thumbs massaged my clitoris. I felt the rhythmic orgasm beginning, and then I was no longer separate from Suzon or the other women. I reached up to those divine breasts and clasped my fingers over her burning nipples. I moaned into her sex as orgasm took me over and she arched her back and let out loud mews. She held my head against her as she gasped, sighing and writhing against me. Driving my tongue in and around her I grasped her buttocks as we climaxed together, with me nearly sinking my teeth into her, breathless and lost. I felt faint with sheer pleasure.

Eventually I raised my head to smile gratefully up at her. Suddenly I was hoisted on to the bar and my clothes pulled off me. I had become nothing but the naked toy of these unknown women.

Suzon straddled me and I sucked ferociously at her, straining at the last of the sticky liquid on her pubes. She hovered teasingly above my tongue and, like a baby, I sucked greedily at whatever part of her I could reach. Meanwhile the other women in the room took turns to apply little kisses all over me until I was screaming with the maddening pleasure.

Just when I knew that my clitoris could endure no more stimulation there was a lull. I lay aflame on the bar, aching for an ultimate fulfilment. I wanted to be filled up, fucked; fingers and tongues were no longer enough. I ground myself into Suzon's pubic mound, opened my legs as wide as I could and heard myself begging her, someone, anyone, to fuck me.

All of a sudden I was blindfolded. Fingers separated me and something hard was pressed against my clitoris. The pressure increased gradually and I writhed against the object until it found my vagina. Pressed in. It was a dildo, and bigger by far than any cock I'd ever had. My cunt was being stretched as it slowly made its way further into me, so slowly that I rose to meet it and thrust against it until it filled me completely. It withdrew a little and thrust in again. The muscles of my sex clamped around it as I was thoroughly and expertly fucked to the most powerful orgasm I have experienced. Spasms rocked my entire body and I was oblivious to anything but the enormous sensations in my vulva and my anus as the probing of the dildo was met there by the probing of a finger.

I climaxed until I ached. Eventually I started to feel the cold of the bar on my back. The blindfold was taken off. Suzon raised a most welcome cool drink to my lips. We locked gazes as I sipped from the glass. She wore the expression of a tiger after an especially heavy feed.

'I hope you enjoyed your drink.'

By now the other women had melted away and into each other. I scarcely noticed the moans and sighs from the corners of the room. Right then I could have sold my soul for the pleasure of lying naked on that bar, gazing at this sublime creature for the rest of my life. My face must have told her so, for she leant down and kissed me softly on the lips.

I wondered how many of those who ordered a cocktail were treated to the same delights. And just what did the other concoctions on the list involve? There was only one way to find out.

'Could I see that cocktail list again, please?'

Loaded

Miranda Stephens

The Highway Patrol officer stood motionless in the privacy of the bedroom, legs slightly apart, with the swagger of the righteous enforcer, a stance that can never be disguised, even when perfectly, perfectly still. The officer stared into the mirror through mirrored lenses. It was a long, hard stare; she'd worked on it, she liked it, it was cool.

A white, peaked motorcycle helmet, a lightly tanned face and sharp chin made threatening and anonymous by the icy lenses. The dark-blue shirt framed and shaped the upper body in a way that only uniforms can. A lean, muscled waist, cinched with a heavy black leather belt. At the hip, a holstered Smith & Wesson .38 conferred on her the power and permission to . . .

Trained to be neither cruel nor kind without due cause, her own stare penetrated her as it always did, filling her up with a terrible excitement. An expectant tautness tugged at her core, an electric stab, alive and dangerous, longing to have and be had.

Now she could not stop, could not focus on anything else – she felt a quickening pulse at her neck, a rising heat as she drank in the shape, the power and authority of that presence. An authority she had always wanted, always craved. Her eyes caressed the strength in the long line of the leg, accentuated by the fullness of her motorcycle britches at the thigh, gloriously shaped around the curves of the ass, tapering as they entered the high black leather boots.

She never wore a bra, so that even under the stiff fabric of her uniform everybody, men and women, noticed how her breasts moved in an easy rhythm with her body. She liked that too; she liked them to look and imagined how they might like to touch her. The men rough, squeezing, pressing with a man's unpredictable violence, the bulges in their pants happening to rub hard against her, while the women would be gentle, breast to breast, caressing her, feeling the softness of her skin, sharing the delicious sparks their touches set off. Her own hands, driven by the images in her mind, plundered her breasts, and she watched appreciatively as they moved. Then, lifting her hands, she felt the weight of her breasts, the flat palms of her slim hands rubbing the nipples to a delicious hardness beneath the uniform shirt.

Geordie Brown liked herself. So far in her twenty-three years she liked herself better than anyone else she knew. She wasn't particularly vain, but she had worked hard on herself, especially on her body, ever since the first boy who touched her under the protection of darkness in the back row of her hometown cinema had confessed that he did it for a dare and would not been seen with her in daylight.

She had always been tall for her age but very chubby, and her face had been strong rather than pretty. She'd had long, dark hair which she would wear like curtains, hiding from the world. But now, after the tearful misery of the cinema, she resolved to change all that – she would never be humiliated by rejection again. She would be in control.

She cut her hair so that it framed her face instead of hiding it; if others didn't like it, fuck 'em – and maybe she would. She worked out in the gym, embarrassed at first about her size, but gaining confidence as she compared her body to those of the svelte, athletic girls she saw in the changing room and realised that her weight was slowly coming off, her muscles gaining tone, and that her height was becoming an advantage. Her face, too, now enhanced by the urchin haircut, matured and strengthened. Standing proud and naked in front of the mirror, feeling the eyes of the other girls on her, she knew she would never be pretty – but she cut a sexy, striking figure, which gave her some satisfaction.

Geordie knew what she wanted and so, despite long, noisy opposition from her widower father, she achieved her ambition and graduated as a cop in the Highway Patrol.

Knowing her mind was an advantage in one way, but it meant that throughout school and then police college no boy she'd ever met had been quite right, so Geordie had stayed a virgin.

Some of the boys she'd met had been exciting – tall, fit and rangy. She had allowed herself the luxury of looking at and thinking about them quite a lot – in fact sex was rarely far from her thoughts. She loved the shapes they made under their uniforms; she eyed the bulge in their pants, enjoying the frightening implications and the way their muscles rippled as they moved. She loved the boys, especially the bad ones, loved their stupid humour and the shape of their necks and their deep, dirty eyes.

But for now the fantasy was good enough. She thought of the men she worked with watching her as she moved like this, wanting to feel her tits, bite her nipples – she hoped they talked about her in the locker room, their cocks growing huge as they fucked her in their minds. It always worked for her, that fantasy.

Sometimes she would think of them engorged with lust, coming at her like a pack of wolves, dragging her back to their lair, thick with the acrid, honey scent of sweat and sperm and socks and men. There they would take her for all she was worth, tear her apart, force her open, lick her cunt until she was drenched in their wetness and hers. A man would slick his cock with her juices and push it into her slowly, inching it into her asshole. It would hurt but she would ride it, enjoy it, feel it filling her, pushing her cunt out into space so that she needed fucking even more. He would pull her back down on top of him, curling his legs around hers, holding her wide open and powerless to resist. Another man would stand in front of her, sliding his hand up and down the thick length of his cock, rubbing it up just for her, long and thick and massive, so that he could fuck her from the front.

Sometimes she imagined a third forcing his penis into her mouth. She would take it slowly, tasting him, licking the shape of it, sensing the ridge around the head of it, sucking on it, before taking the whole length of it into her mouth, filling herself up with the thrill of it, while others she could not see would rub their thick cocks against her thighs.

They would use her like this without mercy until in a great simultaneous gush they would come in her, on her, around her, so that she was awash in their semen – it would be over her breasts and mouth, across her soft, flat stomach, between the cheeks of her ass; every beautiful shape she made would run with their juices, matting the beautiful curls around her cunt, and she would taste it, swallow the salty flavour of it down; she would drink it all in but she would give them nothing. No part of her would be theirs, because in this fantasy she always used them – they served her and they did as they were bid.

A terrifying new excitement tugged at her, an electric

stab, a longing to have and be had by something hard that she could trust. She pulled out the gun, opened the magazine and looked at the bullets, shiny lethal little cocks that could fuck your brains out. She licked each one, loving them, wondering which of them might explode inside her.

He was hard, this gun; he was smooth, he was strong; her hands caressed his muscular butt, feeling his power, knowing it worked just for her. When he came for you, he gave you everything he had – he knew how to treat a lady. She ran her hands over the muscular neck and shoulders, then rested them on the cock.

Eyes shut now in total fantasy – he is black for today. Her hands linger over the shapes his strength make. She feels the joyous, hard, hot weight that can only be a good, strong man going down on her; the weight on her chest, the fucking inside her. She feels the strong small of his back where it gives way to the rounded buttocks, feels the sinewy strength as he thrusts and fills her with his big, hard, glorious cock; she buries her fingernails in his ass, pulls him apart, slides in and round and down. His asshole takes the end of her finger and the buggery of it drives him on, thrusting harder; her hands take on his balls with their strange weight, full of spunk for her – he is thick and hard, thrusting with fuck just for her.

A dangerous pulse tugs at her clit. Slamming the ammo of sexy little fuckers back in, she rejoices in a deep guilty heat; nothing can stop it now. Her own raw sex hurls her to the ground – it hurts, but she needs the agony. She is crucified in the mirror, helpless, legs spread, nailed to it, gun moving hard over her breasts.

Hurt me with it, hard against my nipples, bring it off between my breasts; let me lick its end, feel its hole, suck, suck its hardness, suck it off – pistol fuck me, her cunt rages. Make me do it, make me do it, goes her brain in a frenzy of hands and gun and open juicy cunt to the mirror and men fucking her in every hole and women watching, legs spread wide, wet fingers frigging clitoris, biting each other's nipples and jerking off the men, all wanting a lick of her wet quim for themselves.

Spread it – fuck me – screams a voice from the raging centre of her cunt. The hands are on her now, tearing open the buttons of her shirt, hefting the soft weight of her breasts, pinching the bullet hardness of her nipples. The hands search her body till she has nowhere left, no orifice to hide in – her sex is out, exposed. The hands consume every curve, every muscle, every live softness and hardness her body has to offer. It's having me now, it has the power, I can't resist, can't stop, she thinks, and the thought tips her into a frenzy.

The uniform britches slide down her long smooth legs to the tops of her high leather boots. Her silk panties are pulled up hard against her clit, moving, teasing, tearing her in two. The pistol barrel caresses the soft fabric, taut against the open, deliciously swollen lips of her cunt, then finds its way between the juice-soaked silk and her mound with its soft curls and deep, deep need.

She can't bear the wait before the silk gusset tears. Breathing in hard gasps – she needs this – the hard, cocked weapon opens her up, moves deep in her, across her clitoris, nudging against the cushion of her G-spot with faultless aim, into her cunt, this gun-metal cock fucking hard and long and deep, as hard and long as she needs. She gives in and it has its way with her.

'Make me do it!' she screams. The smooth barrel of the pistol fucks inside her; he is hard and dangerous, unrelenting and beautiful.

Turning on her front, her ass wide open and up to the mirror, she moves one hand deep in her cunt while the loaded revolver moves down and round, into the crack of her strong, round ass, the barrel slick from her cunt juice, exploring the entrance to her anus, penetrating just inside. The trigger of her orgasm is squeezed, fingers working clitoris, Smith & Wesson fucking asshole.

The world explodes in purple waves running from her nipples through her womb, working every primal connection in her body until she shakes and cries and weeps and finally lies still, the gun limply hanging by its trigger guard from her finger.

The Bargain

Kathryn Anne Dubois

'*I* won't do it!'

He laughed sarcastically. 'Oh, I think you will.'

She was trying to look incredulous, but her erect nipples told him otherwise. Besides, the alternative was unthinkable.

'You would have been wise to consider that before you embezzled the money – the consequences, that is.'

Her eyes widened. Beautiful – large and brown. He wondered what her nipples looked like.

'Let me see them.' He motioned to her breasts.

'What?' If possible, she was even more incredulous.

'Your breasts.' He waited. 'Let's see them.'

'You're crazy!' She clutched her blouse convulsively. 'I'd rather go to prison.' Her chin lifted indignantly, her soft full lips lengthening into a line.

He chuckled softly. 'I don't think so. Now show me your breasts.'

'Not on your life,' she drawled.

He'd made a mistake. She was trying to dismiss him now as she turned from him and walked briskly towards the door. He needed to keep the upper hand – keep her on edge.

'Walk out that door and I pick up the phone,' he snapped.

She stopped abruptly and fixed him with a challenging glare. 'No you won't. You'd ruin your chances of carrying out your sick little fantasy.' She ran her fingers through the long silky strands of her hair and paced about before she turned to him again, thoughtful, as though weighing her options.

He didn't give her the time. Walking up swiftly, he spun her around and jerked open her blouse.

She gasped and stumbled back against the wall, lashing out at him with her fists, but he grabbed her wrists, locking them together with one hand, and raised her arms above her head. As he pressed against her, flattening her against the wall, he watched her full, gorgeous breasts heaving and falling before him, spilling over the lacy cups of her bra. He groaned inwardly – he couldn't let her know how quickly she aroused him. Jesus, his cock was already straining.

She gave him another shove and kneed his crotch, missing his balls by just inches.

'Goddamn it, Jamie.' He dragged her over to the couch and threw her down on her back, then leant the full weight of his body against her. 'If you think I'll let you walk out of here, you're wrong.'

'Get off me,' she hissed, tossing her hair off her face and pushing against him.

'Look,' he said, going nose to nose with her. 'We both want something so let's stop playing games.' He kept his tone casual and hoped she couldn't feel how hard he was. Just the scent of her was intoxicating, the clean scent of woman. He wanted to breathe her in when she was aroused. And she would be – he had no doubt of that.

She stopped struggling for a moment and took on a thoughtful expression. He eased off her and stood by the side of the sofa gazing down at her. She pulled herself up and leant back on her hands, her breasts tantalising him, the tips of her nipples straining against the sheer lace. He made himself glance away, but not before he took in her long silk-stockinged legs stretched out along the cushions. He skirt rode far up her thighs. He'd be damned if he let her know what she did to him.

He walked casually over to an easy chair placed along the windowed wall of the office and propped an ankle atop his knee – better for hiding erections.

He lit a cigarette and watched her out of the corner of his eye. For several long seconds she remained motionless, and then she swung her legs around and lifted herself off the couch and proceeded to walk slowly towards him, her short silky skirt rippling around her thighs. She perched on the edge of the chair and studied him. Her long lashes swept down once and then again before she let out a tiny sigh.

'What is it you want?'

He grunted impatiently. 'I thought we discussed this, Jamie.'

He shook his head and adopted a bored expression, repeating, as though speaking to a child, the terms for his silence: 'You remain available to me at all times – sexually that is – and to anyone else I want to share you with for a period of one week.'

He chuckled cynically. 'A little fantasy I've had that I'd like to indulge in now that I have the opportunity.' He leered at her. 'Of course I need to know if you suit me.'

'Are you suggesting . . . with strangers, too?' She gave a little snort, but he could tell she was rattled.

'Don't be naive, Jamie. Of course with strangers. Look, I'm through reviewing this.' He lifted himself as though to leave the chair, and her eyes narrowed.

'Wait.' She plucked the cigarette from his lips and

took a long drag as she looked away from him, thought-ful for a minute.

He watched the light flush travel up her neck and reach the high planes of her cheek bones. Her large doe eyes were liquid, and her blonde hair fell like a thick sheet to her shoulders as she clutched her blouse closed. For a brief moment he almost called it off. It wasn't as though he lacked available women – he had more than his share. But considering the circumstances, well, this was too hard to resist.

'What is it going to be?' he said in a businesslike tone.

She crossed her long legs and rested her arm over the back of the chair, bending towards him with her blouse open, her breasts inches from his lips, and gave him a knowing smile. She laughed softly and glanced down into his lap. Was she hoping to use his lust against him? Satisfy him now and he'd leave her alone, was that her idea?

He moved forward and dragged her bra down with his teeth. She was startled by his swift movements. Her nipples came spilling out and he grazed them with his teeth a little harder than she probably expected, letting her know the consequences of taunting him. She jumped off the edge of the chair and pulled her bra up, looking chastised. Good! A little fear would make this even better. He chuckled to himself.

She glowered at him, but he stood quickly, levelling his gaze on her, a hard glint in his eyes, daring her to refuse.

Her gaze faltered a bit, but she replied flippantly, 'Fine. One week. When do we begin?'

'Now,' he said, without missing a beat. 'Remove your blouse completely, and let me see your breasts.' He lowered himself leisurely back into the chair and drew a comforting hit on his cigarette, keeping his tone casual.

Upon dropping the blouse, she reached up and unhooked the front of her bra, and her breasts toppled out. He suppressed a groan, his cock swelling and engorging with the speed of light. A deeper flush spread over the white skin of her breasts, and her tits tightened under his stare, large and brown, the hard tips darkened to red now – gorgeous.

'They'll do. Drop the bra.' It fell to the floor.

'Now your skirt.'

She blanched, seeming to hesitate, but he would brook no argument.

'Remove it. And do I have to say your panties, too?' he drawled.

He caught the faint tremor on her lips as she dropped her skirt, hooked her thumbs into her lacy panties and began to slide them down. Her skin was so white and the soft triangle so dark. Jesus – her breasts swayed and hung before him as she bent to remove the scrap of silk. She stood before him, fully flushed now.

He almost broke at this point, but he checked himself. Whenever she wasn't aroused, he promised himself he would stop. What would be the point? And then to his surprise, she flung the panties at him.

He chuckled softly, drew the panties to his nose and inhaled deeply, watching for her reaction. She shivered lightly and looked away. He smiled lasciviously and leant back, locking his hands behind his head and sprawling out his legs before him.

'Turn around, Jamie.' His voice sounded husky to him. He had to work harder to hide his responses.

She turned and the smooth roundness of her bottom caused him excruciating pain in his crotch. He was constricted so badly he was going to have to take himself out. At least with her back to him he could respond naturally to her. When he dragged his cock out, he breathed deeply, but didn't dare stroke himself for fear of exploding.

'Bend over, Jamie.' He tried to sound matter-of-fact. She sighed heavily but then she did, and his groan was audible this time. 'Spread your legs.' He sucked in his breath. She was red and swollen. God, so wet.

He knew she would be. He smiled now.

Struggling to lift himself off the couch, his erection full and painful, he walked up behind her. Dropping to his knees, he reached up to separate her pouting sex lips with his fingers. He stroked along her labia, dipping in with one finger, sinking deep and thrusting. She squirmed with pleasure, although she made a pretence of annoyance, grumbling something incomprehensible, but then she swelled more. 'Bend over farther, Jamie. Part your thighs wider.' She no longer fought him but whimpered in surrender and complied.

He flushed, fighting for control. Her clitoris was swollen, hard and throbbing. God, he couldn't help himself. He settled his tongue on her sensitive little nub and sighed. She moaned aloud, and he suckled her gently, his thumb dipping in her, thrusting harder now, stroking the unbelievably soft skin of her bottom with his other hand.

She sobbed and shuddered, crying out to him. He plunged his index finger into her arse, and she came – violently, bucking against his hand and sobbing openly now, starting to collapse under him. He grabbed her waist with one arm and held her up until she was completely spent, not wanting her to miss one delicious wave of heat. He suckled her until she whimpered and fell against him, kicking at him half-heartedly in an effort to push him away, no doubt mortified.

He laughed sardonically. 'You wanton little bitch. You loved every minute of that.'

He lay her face down on the carpet, but she bucked against him, so he pushed her down and propped her bottom up, holding her tight by her hips as he guided his cock into her. With a deep grunt, he fucked her hard, but after a few deep strokes he was gone, expelling his come into her in thick squirts. He groaned and shuddered, ramming her deep, up to his balls, and then finally withdrew.

Leaning back on his heels, he thought to himself that nothing was more beautiful than watching his come drip from her glistening, lightly throbbing sex lips, and then she rolled over. He was wrong. She stretched out like a cat underneath him, running her tongue along her lips seductively – delectable.

He bent down to lick her nipples only to find himself flying off his feet and landing on his arse. She had lodged her foot against his ribs and knocked him off balance – hard.

He smiled and rolled on to his side to watch as she rose indignantly and slipped into her bra and panties, tossing her hair over her shoulder as she glanced at him with contempt. He'd let her go – this time.

'Don't forget tomorrow. Five minutes late and I call,' he warned her.

She slipped him a look of disgust. 'We'll see.'

'Oh, yeah,' he breathed to himself as he watched those long legs disappear through the door.

She kept telling herself she had no choice when in truth she did, but not much. Prison versus this? Was there any comparison?

It was a week of decadent sexual encounters beyond anything she could have imagined.

Tonight Neil was taking her downtown to the heart of the Mardi Gras. Again, imagining what he had in store was impossible. She found herself swelling instantly as thoughts of the previous nights flooded her.

The tight white tank top was a 'gift' from him. He took great pleasure in watching her dress, although he pretended otherwise. But then she pretended she wasn't enjoying his watching. Her nipples tightened when she glanced over at him, his long dark hair falling over his collar, eyes dark as the night, his jaw strong and masculine, the light scar above one brow. She shivered lightly.

'You're not cold, are you?' he drawled sarcastically. 'Because you'll be wearing far less when we get out of this car.'

He pulled the car to the curb and they began drifting through the streets. The crowd got thicker and the music louder. People all around were dancing and laughing, jostling each other, lovers grabbing each other openly.

He had insisted she discard her underwear, and she had to admit she found it very sexy. He said he wanted her available – conveniently available – at all times. Her short flared skirt of raw silk felt cool and sultry against her bare bottom.

A crowd gathered around a young woman who was dancing seductively, her tight skirt temptingly easing up her thighs, breasts thrusting out, nipples erect through her silky top. Jamie was mesmerised.

Neil laughed softly behind her and slipped his hand beneath her skirt. He stroked her bottom slowly, running his fingers down between her legs, teasing her as she watched the dancing girl. When he dipped his finger into her cunt, he growled playfully, leaning into her and pulling her ear lobe delicately between his teeth. 'You little wench. You're wet already.'

She winced at his choice of words but, even so, found them arousing. 'And you have as much class as a rutting hog,' she quipped.

They walked by a group of men leaning against a low brick wall as ·they surveyed the passers-by, and Neil lifted the back of her skirt for them. They groaned in unison, and she flushed, instinctively turning and pulling down on her hem, but Neil jerked her around again and whispered in her ear, 'Wiggle your beautiful tush for them.' He continued to hold her skirt up, bracing himself around her so she couldn't pass, her back to the ogling men. He stroked her bottom.

'Please Neil,' she begged, purposely parting her lips and gazing up at him. He seemed to soften and then actually bent to kiss her on the mouth. She bit hard on his bottom lip.

'Shit!' His hand flew to his mouth and he caught a drip of blood up with his finger. He yanked her skirt up again. 'Do it, Jamie!' he snapped and then bent and nicked her ear lobe with his teeth – just nicked it, but the message was clear. He wasn't going to argue with her. She knew he loved showing her off to strangers, and his look had turned threatening.

She pushed her bottom out to the men and shook it blatantly.

'Jesus Christ!' one man hissed louder than the rest.

'Shit! That is one nice ass,' another caterwauled over the moans of the others.

Neil looked down at her and smiled tenderly, which threw her off guard, and then he brushed his lips against hers. 'You're beautiful, baby.' He ran his tongue over her mouth and sucked her bottom lip gently. She squirmed in response, forgetting her whistling and howling audience for a minute: when Neil was gentle like this she just melted.

'This way, Jamie.' She followed him to a large crowd of men who were looking up towards a balcony overlooking the sidewalk. A group of women, heavily made up and in suspender belts, leant over the low rails, their breasts barely concealed in their skimpy bras, nipples poking out over the lacy edge. They swayed and moved seductively, invitingly, encouraging the men to part with their wages.

Neil moved her into the crowd and then, to her horror, left her. She was suddenly frightened and looked around, trying to find him. Before long the men noticed her, and she found herself in the centre, tall hard bodies surrounding her, the distinctly male scent all around.

She told herself not to panic, and then she felt the cool

breeze on her bottom and thighs as her skirt was lifted up.

A deep gravelly voice groaned audibly: 'Oh, Jesus!'

Thick arms circled her waist from behind, pulling her against a body of steel. She struggled at first, but the arms were both strong and gentle, and she felt her resistance dissolve.

Large hands stroked up her thighs, but not the same hands that were wrapped around her waist. She closed her eyes, enjoying the sensation of pairs of hands on her, the masculine smells, the male voices. One hard body held her firmly against him while the other slid his hands under her skirt and up her thighs. They were large, strong hands yet they stroked so softly.

She squirmed and lifted her bottom off the man behind her when she felt him reach down to unzip his fly. She groaned when she felt the velvety skin of his cock sliding against her, feeling herself swell and tingle in response.

The other hands were nudging between her thighs now, encouraging her to spread her legs, and she did, but rather than plunging his hand straight up, he feather-touched her inner thighs, working his way up, slowly, agonisingly, teasing her beyond endurance. She started to weaken and felt her legs buckling. She grasped the large biceps of the man who encircled her from behind and felt him tighten his hold.

The other man murmured to him, 'Hold her skirt up.'

She felt the breeze hit her thighs and tickle her crinkly hairs. She spread her legs wider without any coaxing and whimpered, aware of her wetness.

'Oh, God,' a voice groaned. He slid his hands up between her legs, and she felt his fingertips separating her and stroking her gently, barely touching her lips, which were now plump with arousal. He dipped a thick finger in a little and withdrew it. She arched to his

:ouch, begging for more. He dipped in again and then withdrew his hand completely.

'Mmm,' he murmured. She realised what he was doing – he was licking his fingers. He slipped a finger up her again, this time deep, and she moaned, lifting her hips to his touch.

'Sit her on the wall, John.'

He lifted her effortlessly, and the cool smooth brick felt good against her skin. She leant back against the broad chest, and she could feel his lips in her hair and the rapid rise and fall of his granite muscles, his cock, full and stiff, pressing against her bottom. She wondered now what he looked like – he felt wonderful, but she wouldn't open her eyes. He eased her against him so that she reclined back and the other one drew her knees up now.

He lifted her skirt and groaned.

'Jesus! She couldn't be wetter,' he murmured. 'She looks delicious!'

She throbbed in response, the aching unbearable now, and then she felt his lips on her tight, burning cunt. He licked her gently, dipping his tongue in for a taste and running its tip along her labia. His lips were warm and wet and his tongue smooth and slippery. A fire burned between her legs.

He lifted his lips, leaving her bereft, and then she felt him spreading her lips, gently, as though separating the petals of a flower. She knew he was simply looking at her.

She shuddered in arousal when she felt her top sliding up, and her nipples tightened against the cool night air. She was completely exposed now and the man behind her placed his large hands over her breasts and began stroking their fullness, pinching the erect tips between his fingers. She writhed and squirmed with the answering tug of her clit. Every time he pinched her nipples, her clitoris throbbed.

141

The other man was gently pulling her lips apart and back, and her clitoris peeked out now from its protective hood. The contrast of the cool air against the heat of her arousal was torture. The man pinched her tits again, and she moaned as her clit throbbed in response. He repeated it, and she thought she would die.

'Oh, yeah,' the man in front growled and then licked her clitoris playfully with the tip of his tongue. She jumped and moaned – it was torture.

She was tortured and too tight, badly in need of relief. He thrust his finger up again and kept it there as he licked her gently. Then he withdrew abruptly. Now she knew she would die! She reached down to touch herself but a hand gripped her wrist tightly.

Suddenly frightened, she opened her eyes to see a darkly handsome man gazing down at her, his eyes smouldering. The man behind her held both her wrists now and the Latin-looking one was unbuttoning his Levi's.

He chuckled softly. 'We can do just about anything to her, John. She's that hot!'

The man behind hissed through his teeth and grunted, rubbing against her. She realised a crowd of men had gathered – or maybe they had been there all along. One by one they unzipped their flies and pulled out their cocks, their eyes glazed over with lust. She looked down at herself, her legs spread wide and her breasts heaving, and was afraid. The man behind dropped her wrists, but to her horror he lifted her up and nudged the head of his penis between her buttocks, easing the head into the tight ring of her anus. She gasped, and he stopped, reaching around with one hand to stroke her breasts gently.

'Just relax – you'll like this.'

She moaned and shivered. The mixture of pleasure and pain was oddly arousing, and she looked around her to see the men moving closer and caressing her with their eyes, their cocks straining and rigid, jutting out against hard flat stomachs.

The cock eased in gently, and she sighed at the new sensation. The chest behind her twitched and tightened and she listened to his ragged breathing. The dark man bent down to lick her nipples lightly, first one and then the other, nipping them teasingly between his teeth between licks.

'I can't get all the way in, Kalim.'

The dark one, Kalim, dropped down to his knees and licked her clitoris lightly. She became bathed in sensation as he massaged her with his tongue, and then she felt John slide his prick completely into her.

'Oh – that's it,' he breathed. She could feel his heart beating fast. Kalim stopped suddenly, and her eyes flew open. She sat impaled on John, her legs spread wide, surrounded by a group of strangers, and, to her shame, she found it unbelievably stimulating. Her clitoris ached. She watched as the men's eyes devoured her. They stroked their shafts with one hand and cradled their balls with the other, no doubt holding back their impending climaxes. She vibrated with need and looked at Kalim, pleading with her eyes, gazing at his swollen, veined cock.

He smiled at her in satisfaction and approached her now, rubbing his cock against her face, teasing her lips with its head. Then, placing his hand on the back of her head and holding his penis in the other, he guided it into her mouth. She slid her lips around the head and ran her tongue in the little hole. He shuddered and groaned.

She felt hot, sticky droplets on her face and glanced to see a man in the midst of his climax, his come squirting over her cheek. Then several others groaned and shot thick, milky semen over her belly and breasts. She sucked deeply on Kalim. He came with a shuddering

groan, and she swallowed deeply, sobbing now and
begging for release.

John began to thrust gently, carefully. His hands came
around to squeeze her nipples, first gently and then
harder until she moaned and ached, lifting her hips and
sinking down on him with each thrust. More men
appeared, their cocks pointing at her face. She grabbed
hold of two and squeezed and slid her hands along their
hard, thick shafts. Running her thumbs along the thick
vein of their underskins, she revelled in the hard male
feel of them. She tasted each one alternately, listening to
their groans as she flicked her tongue along their swelling cocks and around the heads.

Then Kalim dropped down in front again and placed
his hot, wet tongue on her. He licked hungrily, and then
sucked her gently. He slid one long finger up her cunt
and then two. This took her over the edge.

She felt the shuddering power of her climax. Every
muscle became infused with heat and tremoring waves
rolled over her and through her, warming her, dissolving into liquid fire. Then the exquisite relaxation and
pleasant, gentle throbbing of sexual afterglow welcomed
her.

She sighed deeply, collapsing and then relaxing
against John, who held her firmly, still tight with his
arousal.

He made one hard thrust and she felt his explosive
orgasm, pumping deep within her. Pulling her against
him, locked deep inside her, he gasped with deep gulping rasps.

Kalim licked her nipples and traced his tongue lightly
over her belly. 'You did good, girl. So good.'

Neil appeared from nowhere. The two men weren't
sure what to make of him and just stared. He slid her
top down over her breasts and eased her off John, lifting
her effortlessly in his arms. She leant into him, resting

her cheek against his chest and wrapping her arms around his neck as he walked away with her.

He kissed her softly on her lips. 'You're beautiful, baby.'

He had never kissed her so fully and softly on her lips and she found the act oddly intimate after all they'd done. And she felt an unfamiliar sense of security – a safety with him.

He smiled at her wickedly. 'Wait till you see what I have in store for you tomorrow, baby.'

She shot him a look that could kill. If she weren't so sexually satiated, she might have hit him. But she just settled into his hard chest instead.

Primal Scream

Sophia Mortensen

*F*rom the edge of the forest she could see the head-lights of the dumper trucks wheeling around in the near distance. She had come far enough to get a view of the activity, and had halted to take stock of the situation. She could detect the now-familiar smell of diesel fumes, and the metallic taste they left in her throat reminded her once more that she was thirsty. She moistened her lips and swallowed, and the chill night air gave substance to her breath as it escaped in forked paths from her nostrils. The sound of active machinery and workmen's voices left no doubt that construction was underway for the night. Heavy industry ticking over; great caverns being gouged into the earth; roads being built; progress being made.

She'd been watching them for some time, and it seemed that the men liked working in a female-free environment. Their language was coarse and their manners were non-existent. When it was break-time they ate voraciously, then belched and farted without compunction. All boys together – working hard; labouring; building up a sweat. They joked with each other, loudly proclaiming their sexual conquests in the staff portacabin, their profanities booming out under the strip lights. Gradually – over a period of several weeks – they had all become less civilised, displaying signs of primal behaviour. That's how she liked them: raw and basic. No finesse. No false charms. Just the male human in his unadulterated, unperfumed state, reeking of hard work and obsessed with sex.

Distractions were welcome on the graveyard shift. When the governor had knocked off, and the small hours were taking their toll on concentration, that's when she made her move. To them she was a club kid who'd taken a wrong turning. Cold in spangly strapless nothing; thighs taut and shining from working up her own sweat on the dance floor. Irresistible and fresh; a little bit out of it and lubricated just enough. That's how she'd arrived at the cabin last Friday night, and tonight she had a date to keep with the one called Roy. He was big and meaty and he knew what he wanted: her, up-ended and wet for him. She knew that he hadn't believed his luck when she said she'd put out for him. She'd lay money on him counting the seconds until 1 a.m. – their arranged time for tonight's assignation.

She walked to the cabin and hid in the shadows; inside, one of the lads was holding court, in mid-story.

'I said two's up with the slag, you greedy fucker, and you know what the bastard did?'

Two voices: 'No, no, what happened?'

'He said, "Thank Christ. Put something in her mouth, will you, and stop her making that row." So I was in there like a shot. She loved it, too. Sucking on me and slurping all over it. After a few seconds Barry shot his load in her and fucked off, so I got a go at both ends. He doesn't half know some filthy tarts, that Barry.'

'I fucking wish I could meet some of 'em. I've forgotten what it's for, it's been so long,' said another, grabbing his crotch.

'Yeah, well, Tel, you'll just have to work another week in hand, won't you!'

Dirty laughter, then the door banging. She watched as five of the men made their way down the path and back to the machines, their banter gradually becoming indistinct. One man stayed behind. It was Roy. It was five to one. She emerged from the darkness and leant against the pebbledash coating of the cabin. She was prepared for him. In easy-access clothing she was a zipless-fuck dream. Her skirt was brief and silky. When she twirled around it flew up, skimming the tops of her thighs. Her T-shirt was two sizes too small and her nipples poked through the gauzy material. It wasn't the ideal get-up for the season, but it did the trick for her purposes.

'Well, Roy. I came,' she drawled.

Roy spun around, startled at first by the suddenness of her appearance. 'Christ, you made me jump out of my skin!' he said, his hand on his chest. 'I was wondering when you were going to show up but I hadn't expected you to creep up behind me like that.'

'I didn't want any of the others to see me. I don't want you to get into trouble.'

Roy moved her under the light from the cabin window. 'You're something else,' he said, taking a long look at her. 'Aren't you worried, walking around here at this time on your own, dressed in next to nothing?'

'I can always sense when I might be in danger,' she said. 'And I like prowling around on my own. I come alive at night.' She looked him directly in the eyes as the wind flicked her long black hair around her head like a dark sea anemone gone adrift. She burned with lust and life, and her green eyes glinted wetly in the darkness.

'Aren't you going to invite me in?' she asked.

'Sorry, love. I was mesmerised for a second there,' he said. He made to put his arm around her and she flinched, although he detected nothing. Closer to him she could see every millimetre of his face magnified: the tubble on his face; the dark hairs sprouting from the inner rim of his nostrils; the indentations in his temples left by the hard hat he was required to wear. His scent was intoxicating in its strength, and it aroused her. She loved it when men like him were desperate for it; she could feed off that urgency and take their energy from them. It invigorated her; gave her energy.

She gingerly stepped up into the cabin, her red satin fuck-me shoes clicking tartily on the concrete steps. As she looked around she felt almost sorry for him. It wasn't his fault he was a first-timer. Still, she wasn't going to allow human weaknesses such as pity to encroach on the Plan.

Inside, the cabin was a testament to men left to their own devices. Mugs with half-drunk teas and coffees cluttered the table and the air was stale with cigarette smoke and the scent of unwashed flesh. Fast food containers were scattered around the room and an assortment of overalls and muddy boots were piled on the benches fixed to the walls. A couple of small adjoining rooms were positioned at one end. One was a broom cupboard and first-aid kit storage place; the other was just big enough to take a mattress and a bedside lamp.

'Good idea, that,' said Roy, gesturing to the bed. 'You can take a kip when there's not much doing.' She registered no response. He smiled at her. 'Or nip in there for a bit of relief. Want a fag?' he asked, looking her up and down. He was getting excited; she could sense his anticipation. His breathing was getting faster and his body temperature was on the up. He wanted to fuck.

She shook her head and walked into the mattress room as Roy lit a cigarette, then leant one arm on the door frame and continued to take stock of his willing captive. A crumpled polyester sleeping bag lay curled at one end of the mattress. There was no pillow. To one side of the bed was a stack of men's magazines.

'Are these yours?' she asked, flicking through them.

'All the boys use them,' he said, sucking on th
cigarette. 'Gets a bit boring up here a lot of the tim
Especially when you've got the road protest lot runnin
around like a load of lunatics on a soap dodge. Can't d
anything then. Have to sit it out till the security hav
sorted them.'

She'd seen how the security had 'sorted them'; over
heard the protesters' claims of their brutality and tast
for inflicting criminal damage on their meagre propert
Nothing was to stand in the way of progress. But sh
wasn't going to dwell on that now. She wanted pleasure

She continued looking through the magazines. On
page featured a woman who looked similar to hersel
dark-haired, slender and athletic. She was positioned o
all fours, her chest to the floor and her arse pointing t
the ceiling. She wore the tiniest pair of almost trans
parent briefs which nestled deep in her crotch, the lip
splaying wetly either side of the white lace. Her fac
was turned to the viewer; her expression one of fox
invitation.

'Do you like her?' she asked. 'Have you touche
yourself looking at her? Tell me what you'd like to do t
her.'

'The same as I'd like to do to you. But I don't need th
porno mag now I've got the real thing.' He smiled.

'What's the real thing?'

'You are! Come on, girl, you know what I'm talkin
about.' Roy moved closer to her; his presence filled th
room. 'Why do you think you're here? You love it a
much as I do.'

'I want you to talk to me the way you'd talk with th
boys. Maybe this will help you.' And with that she lifte
her skirt and stood apart, showing how snugly her whit
knickers encased her swollen lips; rudely tight like th
swimming costumes worn by seaside-town beaut
contestants.

'You're one of those posh tarts, aren't you?' said Roy.
'Face like an angel but you love it as dirty as it gets. Am
I right, or am I not wrong?'

'That's for me to know and for you to find out,' she
said, beginning to stroke her middle finger along the
length of her crease. 'I bet you'd like to feel how wet I
am. How ready for it I get wearing clothes like these. I
get horny when I put these shoes on,' she said huskily,
then turned around and bent over so Roy got a rear
view of everything. On high heels her pelvis was pivoted
forward, giving an extra lift to her already pert arse.

He advanced and grabbed hold of her waist then ran
his strong rough hands between her legs. She turned her
head round and gave him a cheeky smile. 'Not so fast,'
she said. 'I'm not going to let you have everything you
want quite so quickly.'

Despite her request to slow events down a little, she
was aching with the need to be filled by him. She could
feel how hard he was already as he pressed himself
firmly against her buttocks. She stood upright and
rubbed herself against it. His thick work trousers chafed
at her bare legs, and his hot desperate breath came out
in little gasps next to her ear as he clenched her tight to
his body.

'You're going to get the fucking of your life from me
tonight,' he whispered. 'There's no way I'd let you out
of here, you've got me so worked up. Little sluts like
you are manna from heaven to blokes like me.' He
slowly inched a finger into her cunt. 'Gagging for it, are
we? Your knickers are soaking, you dirty little whore.'

He unzipped his fly and took his cock out, then
rubbed the pre-come over the head. 'Get down on the
bed,' he ordered. 'I can't wait any longer to fuck you.
I've been thinking about this all day. There's no point us
pissing about chatting. Go on. On the mattress.'

She went over to the bed and lay down. Without delay
she hoiked her skirt up and began rubbing herself as

lewdly as she could, putting on a real display for him
He stood at the end of the bed watching her, wankin;
himself.

'Go on, show it to me, you little tart. You're in for .
real treat. I could spunk all over you in a couple c
seconds but I want you to go home with a sore puss)
Well and truly greased and filled. I've never known suc
a pretty whore as you, either. It must be my lucky week

She writhed on the unsheeted mattress, and sprea
open the lips of her cunt to show him some pink. It fe
wet and swollen, and the heavy musk of her juices hun;
in the air. She brought her fingers to her lips and sucke
them, looking him in the eye all the while. He move
towards her and knelt on the bed. 'Time to suck a littl
cock, baby,' he told her, inching himself nearer to he
face.

She seized it hungrily, and slid the ample length of i
into her mouth. Roy began pumping his hips back an
forth. The rich dark scent of his sex was overwhelmin;
and she felt dizzy with the musky intoxicant. Betwee
sucks she held on to his cock and nosed around hi
balls, delighting in the amazing smell of man-sex. Afte
a minute or two he grabbed her by the hair and pushe
her off it.

'You're too good at that,' he said. 'You'll have m
shooting my load before I'm ready.' He reached betwee
her legs and gasped his approval when he was rewarde
with her whimpers of pleasure and the rhythmic swa
of her slender hips. She reached down and began t
languidly stroke her clit, enjoying the full indulgence c
seeing the power she was exercising over her lover. H
was almost drooling, so blatant was she in he
exhibition.

'Rub it harder. Bring yourself off for me. I want to se
you do it, you filthy little girl. I'm right up for bangin
you good and proper. So much nicer if your hole's a

juicy with your own come.' He was playing with himself again, and rubbing his swollen balls with his other hand.

'I can do this anytime,' she said. 'Right now I just want to feel you inside me. Feel that cock good and hard and ready to spurt.'

Roy needed no further encouragement. He unbelted his trousers and pulled them down just far enough to allow movement before pressing the full force of his weight on top of her and ramming it in. He sighed with relief and his eyes lit up with lecherous pleasure. Her arms above her head, she pressed against the wall behind her and pushed down on him, making their fucking all the more forceful and urgent.

On the floor beside them, the magazine lay open at the back pages, displaying a variety of phone line ads and pictures of tartily made-up girls spreading themselves for the camera. She could see Roy glancing furtively at them while he was pounding her to oblivion. Breathy and barely audible he began mouthing sentences made up from the slogans to the ads: 'I'm gonna slide in your oily cunt, you horny little bitch. That's right – spread it nicely and I'll come right up inside your dirty crack. I'll ram it in for you till you're begging for it. Yeah, you're making me do it . . .'

Then it began to happen. No, not yet, she pleaded silently. Please, no! But it was too late. She could feel the changes taking place in her body. It began from the legs. They felt as though liquid fire and gold were running through the veins, and an incredible heat spread all through her. She tensed the muscles in her face and bit down hard on his neck. She clawed at his back; the large expanse of pale flesh tore open where she sunk her talons and small beads blossomed on his skin and hung there like fledgling redcurrants before trickling downwards like condensation on a steamy window. As he roared his agony into the stale air of the tiny room his cock pumped its tribute into her, and she could feel the rush of his come pouring out of him like a boiling jet. The sight and smell of the blood was her catharsis. She hadn't planned for it to happen this way. With him. But it was too late for hypothesis.

As she ran back to her sheltering place she felt bad about the man called Roy. He was a simple soul and he hadn't deserved such a violent fate. Still, someone had to be the first sacrifice. The place where she rested was only half a mile or so into the woodland, but her thirst was so urgent that she was panting. She stopped to drink from a puddle on her way back, and the cool water felt good in her mouth as she washed away the traces of her feast. The night air was sharp and she was glad to have eaten. Winter was about to grip the country and she needed to keep her energy levels up. After five years in the west of Britain, she was still unused to the dark months. The wild food she'd been weaned on wasn't as plentiful here, and certainly not as substantial. She lifted her head from the puddle and gazed at the full misty moon. She was not sorry for what she'd done – her cause was a noble one – but she knew it was only the beginning of the killing – all of it unnecessary if only the construction companies would stop raping the ancient land.

The small hours used to be the only time she could roam free. Now she was having to skulk around unseen twenty-four hours a day. Since the tarmac of new motorway had encroached on the outer rim of her territory, she had been confined to the woodland; now that too was under threat. The sadness which filled her would not be contained, and she let out a mournful howl, her proud head bent back to give her cry its full power. Then she padded off to her hiding place, leaping over ditches and flattening herself close to the ground to get under the felled trees. It felt good to have the bare earth under her paws again. When she found her spot she sniffed the air for danger. Finding none she snuggled down and licked her fur, which was by now caked with mud from where she had pressed her underside into the damp ground. Satisfied with her toilette, she closed her amber eyes and waited for sleep. It had been an exhausting evening, but she had a moon cycle to recover before the next changing time.

At about 7 a.m. the morning shift of road builders arrived on site to find the portacabin cordoned off with police tape and two uniformed officers barring the way in. Groups of men wearing sheepskin coats or expensive wet-weather gear huddled around in bunches outside the cabin, smoking cigarettes and drinking tea from Styrofoam cups. A separate group comprising of several younger people – men and women from the road protest camp – badgered the police with questions and stood around waiting for confirmation of what had happened. One of them was banging some form of ethnic drum, making an arhythmic din until one of the labourers snatched it from him and put his size-11 steel-toe-capped workboot through the skin. A journalist was also on the scene, trying to get a statement from the Scene of Crime Officer, who was saying very little about the murder. He was better off talking to the men, who had plenty to say about the crime.

'They took the remains away at about five but there's a lot of cleaning up to do. Poor Jonno's being treated for shock in Exeter General. Can't be easy to deal with, can it, seeing your workmate torn in two pieces? Apparently the head was the only part of him left intact.'

'He was a sound lad, was Roy,' said another man. 'Hardworking; liked a laugh. Who would want to kill him?'

'Isn't it more a case of what rather than who?' asked the journalist. 'I've heard that he was savaged to death. They're not ruling out a wild animal.'

'Don't be daft. How would a wild animal – a lion or

something – get into the portacabin? No, it's some bloody mad bastard, probably escaped from the maximum security place about ten miles up the road.' He turned to his mate. 'Freddie worked on the new alarm system up there last year and said there were some right fucking psychos in there. You put that in your paper. This country should be more like the States. Do away with 'em. 'Lectric chair would do the job. Bloody taxes going on keeping that lot in steak and chips.'

The journalist sighed and turned his attention to the protesters, who seemed a lot calmer and less reactionary.

'We know nothing about this,' said a young woman with a complex top-knot of dreadlocks. 'We're always having confrontations but none of us are going to do anything like this. Mikey's being held for questioning. They came busting in the Eco-trip tent about an hour ago. He didn't know what was happening. Turns out they found a woman's clothes in there with the body. They reckoned they might have belonged to one of the protest-camp women. After firing all manner of questions at him, the police finally told him there had been a murder. Anything happens round here we get the blame. Bastards.'

She was obviously the spokesperson of the group, having a clear voice and well-pronounced diction. She didn't seem like the sort who would back down easily. The journalist saw this as a great opportunity to get involved with the story. He wasn't representing any one particular newspaper and the conflicting issues involved in the case meant that his piece might well be syndicated around the world. The pound signs began to roll through his brain. He got phone numbers from the workmen, contact fax numbers of the construction company, and the email address of one of the protesters' sympathisers who ran a website from Exeter University. At 9.a.m. the police still weren't revealing any details, so he set home to work on his piece.

* * *

It was ten days later before the autopsy report was faxed through to him. After persistence and a bit of side-stepping the formal procedures, he had managed to access the truth about the murder of Roy Byde. There was conclusive evidence that the lacerations to what was left of the body had been made by a big cat of some kind. Traces of black fur had been found at the scene of the crime. They could find no trace of any human involvement, however, other than the clothes, which were strangely devoid of anything useful to forensics. The portacabin had been towed away for further investigation, and it looked as if there was to be a verdict of accidental death recorded at the inquest. The family had been clamouring for clarification, and the local and national press had been giving their story considerable coverage, running features on everything from safety on building sites to unusual deaths in the West Country. Now the grisly truth was going to be revealed.

In the windswept wilds of Bodmin Moor she had found shelter in a copse of firs. There were no building sites here yet; no noise but the occasional RAF test fighter plane and the distant chatter of parties of outward-bound enthusiasts. She had taken care to remain unseen by the humans. She would lie low until the next changing time, resting after her long journey and feasting on small animals: voles and rabbits, mostly. But something else was happening to her: she was coming into her breeding time again, and her scent had brought a mate to her. He was younger than her – about three years old – and, like her, had escaped his cruel owner in his bid for freedom, shimmying under a wire fence to run free for miles without stopping.

He was with her now, biting playfully at her shoulder as she languidly stretched beneath his warm muscled body. This was how it should have been in their home-land, only they should have been romping in the night-time warmth, the sound of crickets and monkeys screeching around them as they coupled. But she wasn't too dismayed; it felt lovely just to have a mate – someone who would hunt for her when the young were born. He was insatiable today. They had already fed on a sheep and mated twice this morning, and now he was hungry for sex again, following his instincts. She felt him mount her once more. His front legs were tightly clasped around her middle and when his sticky pink member slipped out of his shaft he found her once more.

His hindquarters went like a jackhammer, and she revelled in the joyous sensation of realising her conception. He sunk his canines into her nape and barked his moment of completion.

Maybe they would run together for years to come. They needed each other; and when the cubs were born there would be strength in numbers. They would hunt together until then. It was half a moon cycle to the next changing; the next killing. She planned to take him with her this time. She would wait for the metamorphosis to begin, then make the journey to the site of destruction. She hadn't encountered her own species during a shape-shift before but she felt confident that her natural scent would act as a language; that he wouldn't notice any difference because she would smell the same then as she did now.

She purred in the afterglow of their mating; the possibilities would be very interesting.

Office Politics

Tina Harden

On the day of the interview I almost changed my
mind about going for the job. Personal secretary to
senior partner in a firm of solicitors sounded OK until I
turned up for the interview and saw the crumbling white
pillars at the entrance to the large building. It must have
been a gracious town mansion once, probably last century, but it was looking a little sad now. My present job
was in a bright modern office, and I wondered if I really
wanted to work in such an old-fashioned place. My
foreboding increased when I stepped inside the cool,
green-domed entrance. I felt as though I were stepping
back in time.

My worst fears were confirmed while I waited gloom-
ily in an old leather chair. I overheard the receptionists
talking about the senior partner, Mr Henry Dalrympole,
and I realised that he was on the point of retirement.
They were speculating on which of the junior partners
would take over his position. No doubt Mr Dalrympole
was as old-fashioned and crumbly as the building.

However, I had gone to a lot of trouble to come to the
interview. The pay was a good deal better than my
present job and I decided I might as well go through

with it now that I was there. At least I was confident that I looked the part. My suit was boring black, although the skirt was very short, to show off my best feature – my legs. I'd brightened up the ensemble with a lime-green silk shirt. I left the jacket open, as it was uncomfortably tight over my large chest. My long blonde hair was pinned up so I looked suitably prim and proper.

'Miss Linda Bryan?'

I was shown into Mr Dalrympole's large but cluttered office, and seated opposite him in another leather arm-chair. This one was deep and squashy and, to look elegant, I had to sit with my thighs clamped tightly together. After I'd positioned myself reasonably comfort-ably I took a proper look at Mr Dalrympole while he studied my CV.

I was pleasantly surprised. He was obviously well into his sixties – a couple of generations away from my nine-teen years – but he was tall, and held himself erect. His face was tanned, almost leathery, as if he spent a lot of holiday time in the sun. He wore an immaculate pinstripe suit with a crisp, white shirt and dark-red tie. He put on his glasses to read, which made him look fairly severe; I could easily imagine him demolishing the opposition in court if he were a barrister. When he finished reading, he took off the glasses and I noticed the penetrating blueness of his eyes. Yes, he was definitely fanciable.

It was his turn to scrutinise *me*, and he took his time. There was plenty of exposed ankle and leg for him to look at, clad in glossy, shimmering stocking. His shrewd, blue-eyed gaze travelled up my body and lingered on my bosom. Was he a breast man? I couldn't help wonder-ing. When his searching stare registered my full young lips and moved on to meet my eyes, I held his gaze boldly. The corner of his mouth twitched in what might have been a knowing smile.

He asked me a lot of questions then, about my qualifi-cations and so on. While I searched for the right words he used the time to stare lasciviously at my body. The interview seemed to go on for ages, and I felt like I was being cross-examined. But I managed to find an answer to all his questions. His gaze was lingering on my chest again, and I even glanced down to see if a button had popped open. It hadn't.

He asked me about my shorthand speed, and sat back with steepled hands to await my answer. I began to think about those long, strong brown fingers prying aside the thin silk of my blouse and crushing the soft white flesh of my breasts. My nipples began to harden at the thought. I knew Mr Dalrympole was staring at the erect peaks which were, by now, scratching against the thin silk. I swallowed hard and tried to turn my attention to shorthand speeds.

'Most satisfactory,' he said from time to time during the long interview, which I took to mean that things were going well. By now I had reversed my ideas about the job. I looked forward to the thought of working for Mr Dalrympole and teasing him with my young, attractive body.

After a while my leg muscles began to tremble with the effort of holding my thighs together. So I let them relax and spread apart ever so slightly. Sure enough, in the very next moment, Mr Dalrympole's gaze was tunnelling between my thighs, and I felt my pussy twitch.

When the interview was over, he stood up and shook my hand politely, but he made no attempt to hide the evident bulge in his trousers, and we both knew that he was horny as hell. I knew that he was going to offer me the job, but I had to wait a couple of days before I got a formal letter.

I soon mastered the office routine. After a week or two I decided it was time to start titillating Mr Dalrympole, or Henry as I now called him. This was easy enough to do. Often I would bend over the desk to show him plenty of cleavage. Other times I would give him an eyeful of bum as I filed some documents in the lower drawer. After all, I was doing the man a favour – I had learnt that he was widowed and I didn't think his masculine lust was being satisfied elsewhere. As for me, I was in the unusual situation of being 'between boyfriends'. Why not do a bit of prick-teasing?, I thought.

Henry often put piles of documents on the floor, which gave me plenty of opportunity to show him the colour of my knickers. One day, after I'd been there a few weeks, Henry was seated at his desk and I bent to lift some documents, making sure I waved my arse in his direction. I heard the chair creak and then I felt his cool fingers seek out the warm flesh at the top of my stockings. I wriggled my bum to show I was enjoying it, then I turned to face him. His crotch was straining to contain his hard-on. I had a sudden urge to get my hands on the thing that was squirming beneath his trousers.

I was surprised to find his fly was the old-fashioned sort, but it didn't take me long to undo the little buttons. I parted the equally old-fashioned white underpants, and watched the thing uncoil. It was pink, smooth and long. It waved gently from side to side, like a mesmerised snake. I knelt in front of the chair between his legs and grabbed it. I gave it a hard wanking and, in about fifteen seconds, I had creamed him off into my hand. His eyes were closed and his face was still screwed up with pleasure as I did up his fly.

I straightened up. 'Coffee, Henry?' I asked, speaking as if nothing had happened. I went out to make it before he could reply. When I came back he was still sitting at the desk. His face was expressionless. He seemed to be stunned – or so I thought. I felt pretty smug at that moment when I put down the drink on the desk.

He stood up then, and moved the drink to the coffee table. I thought he was going to sit in the armchair. Instead, the room was suddenly tipped sideways as I felt strong arms lift me up. I was placed on my back on the desk. I raised myself up in protest, but a firm hand on my belly pushed me back down again.

'Spread your legs,' he ordered. Something in his tone of voice made me obey him.

'Wider!' he barked.

I didn't need a second bidding. My hole was stretched wide to receive the three horny fingers which thrust roughly past my French knickers and up my passage. I let my head sink back on the desk, and I felt my pinned hair fall loose.

'Rub yourself,' he commanded.

His nostrils flared with concentration and his face beaded with sweat as he finger-fucked me. I thought his whole arm was going to disappear, he went at it with such vigour! Meantime I rubbed myself like crazy. Before long, I felt my mouth opening in a long 'Oh' of excitement, and I bucked myself to orgasm.

He helped me off the desk. My clothes were all rumpled and there were papers everywhere, but he looked cool as a cucumber in his pinstripe suit. He sat in the armchair and sipped his coffee, looking at me through narrowed eyes. 'Just remember who's boss around here,' he said quietly.

That was the start of it. From then on, it became a regular occurrence, which suited me just fine. Before five o'clock, it was all filing and 'Take a letter, Linda.' Even then, whilst I scribbled shorthand, I managed to let my short skirt ride up just a bit; well, quite a lot. But after five, when the building had cleared, was when we got down to the real business of the day.

He was an organised man, was Henry, and he soon established a routine. On Mondays, it was the filing cabinet. First he would pull up my skirt very slowly until it was around my waist. Then he would draw up the lacy edges of my French knickers until the taut satin was biting into my bum crack and crotch. Then he crushed me against the hard steel cabinet so my bum was slapped up against the cold, grey metal.

On that first Monday I was wearing a low-cut lycra top and no bra, and, as he pinned me with his pelvis, he pulled down the stretchy material and eased out each tit into his waiting hand. The top was tight beneath them and provided an impressive uplift. My tits were young and bouncy anyway, so they thrust out jauntily, with perky pink nipples which were just asking to be eaten. Being so tall, Henry had to bend in order to gobble and gorge on them. I ran my fingers through his thick salt-and-pepper hair, and savoured each pulse of sensation which arced from my tits right down my body. Meantime I could feel his hardening need pressed against my swelling mound.

While his mouth was still clamped to my right breast, and he was giving my left nipple a good working with finger and thumb, I felt him fumbling with his trousers. In the next moment he had kicked off his shoes and dropped his trousers and pants. As he stepped out of them, I just had time to look down and see his pink snake's-head rearing up at me. Then I was slammed up against the metal again, and his feet were between mine, spreading them wide so my crack was open and vulnerable.

Henry dipped down, then, when he straightened up, his snake went straight in, up to the hilt. It took my breath away. My head went back and I gasped out loud. But before I'd recovered from that first thrust, he'd pulled his organ out and then rammed it home again. And again. Soon he had a rhythm going, a good steady fucking. I felt his warm, panting breath in my ear.

After a while, he swayed back from me so he could get a grasp on my tits again. It also meant his rod was angled for even sharper thrusting. Every now and then he would stop and grind his pelvis against mine. In turn I gyrated my hips against his, the skin of my buttocks held fast to the metal with hot sweat. I could feel his snake twisting and squirming inside my body. I was amazed at his self-control. We'd been at it for ages, but it was clear he wanted to give me maximum pleasure as well as satisfy his own lust.

All good things come to an end. But even when he finally tucked his tired sticky dick back into his trousers, I knew that there was always tomorrow to look forward to.

Tuesday was carpet day. That meant that I was either lying on my back looking at the high corniced ceiling while Henry shagged me thoroughly from the front, or on all fours, doing it doggy style. By the time Henry had finished ramming his dick up my exposed fanny, the pattern on the worn Axminster was swimming before my eyes and I was practically eating carpet.

On Wednesday it was the desk. Fortunately it was one of those old-fashioned, sturdy mahogany jobs which could take a lot of punishment. And did I take some punishment on that desk of Henry's! It was just the right height for a table-ender, of course, and I could wrap my legs around his body to pull him in closer with each thrust. Sometimes he would hoist my legs up over his shoulders, so that when he leant forward I was practically doubled up and at his mercy.

Once, out of curiosity, I asked him where he had learnt to satisfy a woman so thoroughly. He narrowed his gaze and gave me a penetrating look through those clear blue eyes.

'Years of experience, my dear,' was all he would say.

He had a comfortable leather armchair, and each Thursday he would sit on the broad arm, and I would sit astride him. With his dick right up inside me. The chair was facing the mirror and hatstand. So when the ride got really rough I could hang on to the hatstand. In the mirror I could watch my tits bouncing every which way as I impaled myself again and again whilst he did his best to buck me off.

Fridays turned into a bit of a ritual. I'd be sitting on the opposite side of the desk while he put on his glasses and study some real or supposed typing mistake. Then he'd give me a severe look over the top of his glasses, just as he would look in court, I suppose.

'You should be punished for this mistake,' he'd say. 'Don't you agree?'

'Yes, Mr Dalrympole,' I'd reply meekly, acting my part.

Doubled over the back of the leather armchair, my toes barely touching the floor, my hands firmly gripping the arms of the chair, my bottom was thrust tautly upwards. Henry pulled my skirt up and my knickers down. The cheeks of my strained arse were already tingling in anticipation. The light slaps skated across the tops of my buttocks, making them quiver like twin jellies.

'Harder!' I demanded, remembering my role. 'Punish me!'

There followed half a dozen stinging smacks which made my arse jump with excitement. My breath was coming in harsh shallow pants, which seemed to intensify the smell of leather.

I could feel my buttocks reddening as he undid his fly. Henry squirted baby oil over my bum, and rubbed in the cold liquid with the head of his prick, not forgetting my exposed arsehole. His hungry weapon found my moist vagina and I braced my willing arse ready for another good poling.

One Wednesday he had me on the desk for a table-ender as usual. We had become careless about being disturbed – everyone knew what we were doing anyway and said 'What the heck. Good old Henry. It puts him in a good mood.' So the door was left ajar. We were hard at it when I looked over and saw the hunky junior partner, Adam Garvie, standing in the doorway watching. His handsome face was expressionless for a moment as he registered the scene. I smiled at him in mid-fuck and he winked back. The desk was at an angle to the door, so all Adam could see of Henry was his back and his clenched white buttocks dipping in and out between my raised legs.

From my angle, all I could see of Henry was his top half, still smartly dressed in jacket and waistcoat, his tie neatly tightened against his expensive shirt. Out of sight his naked bottom half was fucking vigorously. Really, he has tremendous stamina for a man of his age, I thought, as his thrusts shook my breasts up and down.

Henry quickened his thrusts and started panting his way towards a climax. Being watched by Adam turned me on, and I started moaning extra loud in time with Henry's thrusts. Adam stepped inside the room. His nostrils were dilated as his breath quickened. Suddenly Henry realised that some of the heavy breathing was coming from elsewhere. He turned and saw Adam. In surprise Henry jerked his organ out of my body. But he had already gone past the point of no return. With a lusty grunt, Henry grabbed his member just as it spilt its load. The spunk landed on my bush, where it clung in pearly droplets.

As Henry stepped back, Adam took up position between my legs. With a cheeky grin, he took hold of my ankles and stretched my legs wide apart, peering straight down into my pink wet slit. He gave me another wicked smile and a wink before attending to his belt, which clattered to the floor. Adam's longish fair hair flopped down attractively over his forehead as he bent to unzip his trousers, ever so slowly. He stepped athletically out of them. Crisp black hairs curled over the edges of his skimpy red briefs; briefs which only just managed to contain his equipment, I noticed. Adam hooked his thumbs under the narrow elastic across his well-shaped hip bones, and slowly pulled his pants down. His magnificent organ sprang out at right angles to his body.

Before I had time to admire its girth, it was in me like a hot piston, and Adam's hairy balls were slapping my buttocks. Henry was impressed; I could tell by the way his snake was beginning to twitch again. I reached out and took hold of it, rubbing it against my tit until it spunked again. The creamy spunk ran off my nipple and on to the dark mahogany desk. At just about the same moment Adam withdrew his cock and fisted it until a fountain of come spurted into the air and landed on my belly button. After that, the two of them massaged the spunk which had landed on my tits, belly and bush, all over my trembling body, until I had a long, noisy come.

After that, our sessions turned into a threesome. The scent of male musk soon got my juices going. Sometimes Henry would fuck me while I sucked on Adam's meat. Or else Henry would wank while Adam's organ slurped noisily in and out of the swollen lips of my cunt.

As Adam was so much younger – twenty-nine, he told me later – he could take up much more athletic poses than Henry could manage. One day I was twined round Adam's virile body while he stood and jiggled me up and down on his pole. Henry was in the armchair, wanking furiously. I heard him come just as Adam and I reached the peak of ecstasy.

It was after that session that Adam was made senior partner, in accordance with Henry's wishes, and took over his office. 'A man after my own heart,' said Henry in genuine admiration. We all knew he wasn't just referring to his legal skills. Not only that, Adam and I were married several months later. We have a nice house just out of town. Adam has fucked me in every corner of every room, and the garden.

Henry has retired to a cottage not far away. When he's not tending his roses, he sometimes calls for tea. Afterwards, we usually try out some variation on a sexy threesome which Henry has thought up while pruning his roses. But we still have some of our best fucks in the office.

Bloody Grunge Love

Airyn Darling

Sandwiched between Victor and Elizabeth, grinding away to the heavy bass beat, I realised my thighs were getting wet, and that it had been too long since I'd had any real sexual contact. I sighed, kissed each of them gently, and walked to the side of the dance floor. Leaning on the thick yellow pipe demarcating the small area packed with undulating bodies, I picked up my nearly empty cup of water from the floor, sucked on an ice cube and watched, careful to seem bored and detached from the goings-on. Victor was an amazing dancer; Elizabeth much less so, but they were my best friends, and I loved them dearly.

It was sometimes difficult being with them – they were lovers, and I occasionally felt like an intruder. Elizabeth's wife, Karen, sometimes felt that way as well, and was leaning on me heavily to become her concubine. Trouble was, I despised Karen. Part of it was jealousy that Elizabeth loved her so much, part was the fact that she looked like a small Arabic man (I like my women to look like women) and part was her borderline-obnoxious personality. Yet I had to pretend to get along with her, since she was an integral part of Victor and Elizabeth's lives.

Sighing again, I looked around for prospective lovers to take home. Jay was bumping and grinding, revolving those beautiful hips like they were made of ball bearings. Earlier in the evening he had said, 'Kate, whenever I'm around you, I get so horny.'

I looked back on the time I had taken him, only fifteen then, under my wing when his parents had thrown him out. Drugs, trouble in school, and miscellaneous other problems plagued him. I worried and fussed with a mother's love, and lusted with a twenty-year-old's cunt. He was so beautiful, so deceptively innocent-looking. Our two brief sexual encounters occasionally haunted me, and apparently he'd been thinking of them as well.

But now, he had blossomed into this amazingly mature young man. Most troubles behind him, he was in love, working and planning for his future. I began to understand the proud, joyous/sad twinge of parenthood when the baby leaves the nest and does well on his own. I was happy to have had a hand in his progression.

Grudgingly, I ruled Jay out as the night's toy. Chewing slowly on my plastic cup, I gazed about, smiling at my friends, and noticing Nick, the lights guy, staring at me now and then. He'd been a friend of Jay's way back when, and then they'd parted ways, due to some dispute. Nick was beautiful as well, although in a different way. He was also pretentious as hell, and hadn't spoken to me in quite some time. I ignored him.

There were more women here tonight than was the usual on gay night. And many of them were attractive, which was even more unusual. Being bisexual certainly has its advantages, I thought with a wry smile. A lean black man sidled up to the small space in front of me, thoroughly into the groove. He was wearing black vinyl pants, a gold lamé overshirt, skin-tight white T-shirt, and thick-framed black glasses. His dreads bounced up and down as he danced. He smiled at me, and I gave a small one in return.

A friend joined him, and began dancing in front of me as well. Upon first glance, she really was nothing special, but since she was only inches from me, I thought I'd look her over.

She was grunged up: two demerit points. I almost dismissed her right then, but she turned to face me and smiled shyly. Her face was so smooth, so beautiful! Her lips were a pale reddish-pink, her hair (as best I could tell in the flashing lights) was strawberry blonde, long and straight, with the cutest little bangs. She wore a white short-sleeved shirt with a heart on the breast (ack), overalls, and the requisite flannel shirt tied about her waist. She was charming, despite her obvious grunge fixation. She didn't dance flamboyantly, pretentiously or seductively; she just moved shyly to the beat and smiled to herself, sometimes glancing at me from beneath those bangs and long eyelashes. She radiated innocence willing to be corrupted, which was like a magnet to someone like me. I wanted to take her home, gently seduce her, and then show her things that would blow her mind.

I was absorbed. 'Bloody hell,' I thought, 'I'm hot for a grunge child.' I was almost disgusted with myself, but was too entranced to notice it much. I watched her and her friend intently, wondering if the man was bi or gay or what. My gaydar said 'flaming fag', but my naive hope said 'definitely bi', and envisioned the three of us in a snarl of sheets.

A song I could tolerate came over the speakers, but rather than dance, I stayed still to watch them. They were obviously not 'together' in the truest sense, but acquaintances, touching base with each other a little nervously, and then going back into their own little worlds.

Was she wondering if I was still watching her? Was

that why she glanced at me so often, or was it because I was only inches away, and made her uncomfortable? Did she sense my predatory intentions? I was dying to reach out and stroke that soft, fine hair, to say something along the lines of, 'You're so beautiful – do you live around here often?' Humour, my favourite defence. I looked about the bar, scanning the corners for intriguing faces. Finding none, I settled upon this lovely child as the night's target.

I stared at her until she looked back up at me. I locked her eyes, and gave her a look which made my intents clear. She stared back for the briefest of seconds before looking quickly down. I smiled to myself, knowing those eyes would be looking back before long. Indeed, only a few moments had passed before she gazed back up. Everything about her exuded shyness.

She turned coyly away and took a few steps towards the centre of the dance floor, dragging her male friend by the hand with her. The wiggle in her hips was a fine invitation, and the bounce of her small, lovely breasts even more so.

I placed my cup on the nearest table, fixed my eyes upon her and slid towards her through the crowd. Drawing a bit from my gift, I slightly parted the dancing bodies as I passed, so she would see me as graceful, not jostled about, or getting an elbow up my nose.

I moved into position behind her, looking her deliberately up and down as I did so. Smiling at her friend, I began on him, so as not to frighten her. He willingly joined me, slipping his knees between mine, and gyrating around seductively, moving up and down on my body.

I grasped his head with my hands and ground my pussy inches from his face. His dreads flew about as he played along with my cunnilingus scenario. Out of the corner of my eye, I saw we had captured her attention. I pulled him up and moved around behind him, pushing my hips into his ass, grinding hard, and my hands caressed his chest and pulled him into me.

He bent at the waist and stuck his ass up in the air, still circling his hips. I made like a butch-dyke, thrusting my imaginary dildo in and out of him. He tossed his head and reached back with both hands, pulling me in deeper and deeper. He straightened and I began moving down his back, rubbing my breasts up and down over his ass, while reaching between his legs and stroking his cock firmly and slowly.

She was entranced. Others around us smiled appreciatively. Dirty dancing was nothing new to the Peach Pit crowd; it was, however, duly appreciated when performed well, and ignored when poorly done. I had nearly perfected the art over the years. My thighs were strong and firm, and I could grind with the best of them all night. And often did, really.

He turned around and whipped me around, pushing his half-hard cock into my ass. I rotated and pushed back appreciatively. My tight leggings were like a second skin, as were his vinyl pants. That so little separated us excited me. He cupped my breasts and bit my neck, pinching my nipples as he did so. I pulled one of his hands between my legs and held it there, pushing against it. God, these boys could work it. I was so ready to come right there when the song ended, and a much less erotic beat came on.

We parted, and I turned to smile at him, giving him a kiss on the cheek. He winked at me and started doing this fancy-footwork number. I laughed. He grinned and turned to the man behind him, grabbing his ass and falling into easy conversatioin as they both danced minimally.

I chuckled and turned to make sure she was still there. Of course she was, smiling (again shyly!) at me. I stepped only slightly towards her and danced in a casual 'yeah, I'm dancing, but I'm not that into it' kind of way.

She turned her back to me which, oddly enough, is the standard invitation for closer contact. I turned to the camera that always follows me around in my ego and smiled confidently before approaching her.

I didn't touch her at first, just let her know I was behind her. The song wasn't particularly appropriate for erotic dancing, so I contemplated my next move quickly. Something non-threatening, but firm. I reached out with both hands, touching each side of her head and running my nails across her scalp and down through her hair. It was indeed soft as I had imagined. She didn't turn, but let her head fall back as I repeated the procedure. She had minimal personal shields, which I could have easily stroked down, but in a place like the Peach Pit, personal shields never hurt.

I felt her quiet inner strength, her quivering desire, and I was now certain that she'd never been with a woman before. I couldn't have asked for a more perfect gift tonight. I thanked the forces and moved just the tiniest bit closer to her, so the tips of my breasts brushed against her back now and then.

I placed one hand on her hip, just resting it there, following her movements. She was slightly stiffer now, more self-conscious, and more than a little nervous. This would be a delicious pursuit. I wondered if we would speak at all. Silent seductions are one of my favourite things. She was so young, though, and so nervous, I expected that she'd speak out of sheer terror soon, something to cut the developing tension. We continued moving together. Now and then, I stroked her side, just lightly, just for a moment, before returning my hand to her hip, reminding her of my presence, of my intent and of my desire.

The bloody song was one of those rave-type numbers, mindless thumping for seemingly hours on end, with no lyrics, just thump-thump-thump-thumpa-thumpa-thump-thump-thump. It was driving me nuts, but I was reluctant to leave her before I had really set the hook. I looked imploringly up at Roger, the DJ, rolling my eyes and gesturing around at the music/noise. He nodded and began rummaging through his collection. As a regular of five years and as a former employee, I had special privileges, which, might I add, I enjoyed tremendously.

Roger began mixing in the intro to 'Get Down Make Love' by NIN. I grinned up at him and mouthed 'Thank you.' It was one of my perennial favourites, and guaranteed to make me incredibly horny, as if I needed to be any more so. As the old song faded out, and NIN took over, all the boys groaned and left the floor. The girl started to leave, but I took her hand and held her with me.

She seemed surprised, unsure of what to do. I smiled reassuringly, and dropped her hand, beginning my industrial dancing mode. The floor was nearly deserted, populated by the 'old crowd'. We all knew each other, and longed for the good old days of Industrial Night at the Pit. We took what we could get now, though.

The Peach Pit is like a drug, like another world. It is addictive, and it is all-consuming at first. Lives revolve around it, and lives are destroyed within it if one isn't careful. I learnt my lesson years ago, when I could look around at the various levels and see perhaps eight to ten people with whom I'd had sex, twenty or so more whom I didn't want to talk to, and maybe another ten with whom I'd love to have sex, but hadn't. I knew everyone's little story, and I got completely wrapped up in the lifestyle and in all the little psychodramas.

Thank the gods it closed for a while to remodel, at which point I quit working there. Now I only visited. Scary thing was, people who had been working there long before I had still did, and they still loved it. I shook my head, thinking about this tiny little place with all its power.

Trent Reznor was screaming, and I began lunging

from side to side with each word, curving around her at each end. I moved my arms in a different pattern, but to the same beat, and reached around her, beginning the seduction for her and for those around us. Everyone appreciated a good seduction. We were all equally voyeuristic and exhibitionistic here at the Pit.

I simulated stroking her up and down, my hands several inches from her body, but forming each and every curve, circling her breasts. Finally I pushed her head to one side, reached around her stomach, pulled her tightly to me, and buried my face in her neck, biting softly and licking delicately before releasing her and resuming my regular dance.

The second time I pulled her to me, I didn't kiss her, I just held her and led her gently. With one hand held firmly to her tummy, I reached down with the other to stroke her thigh. I moved up and down her leg slowly, tracing up the inside with my fingertips, then pressing firmly with my whole hand on the downstroke.

She was relaxing slightly, giving in. I was leaning on her just the smallest bit with my gift, soothing her anxiety. Being a projective as well as a receptive empath has its benefits as well. I inhaled the smell of her hair, a patch of clean softness inside the room full of harsh cigarette smoke. Oh, this was divine. I hadn't been with a woman in months. 'Get Down Make Love' began to end, and I signalled Roger to play something similar, to keep the mood going for me. He grimaced but obliged with the 'I Sit on Acid' remix by Lords of Acid. Roger's a good guy.

The crowd cheered – this was acceptable, given its lewd content. As the boys began bopping about, the girl started to as well, but I once again restrained her, slowing her down, helping her find the slower underlying rhythm. I turned her to face me, but didn't look into her eyes. Yet.

I arranged myself so that we each had one leg inside

the other's, pulled her tight to me so that our bodies pressed together from breasts to thighs. I placed one of her hands on my ass, and put one of mine on hers as we slowly rotated against each other. Her breath was audible in my ear, even above the loud music. I was sure part of it was the physical exertion of keeping this strenuous activity up, but also that part of it was the lust between us.

At the next chorus of 'Sit on your face, I wanna sit on your face', I stared directly into her eyes, but didn't do anything as tacky as mouth the words to her. She didn't look down this time. In fact, she tightened her grip on my ass. I was so pleased at this action that I almost forgot to keep dancing. I quickly recovered my composure and smiled into her eyes with mine.

I began to wonder if this chick was having me on. Was she just an accomplished shy femme? I don't usually misread people. Buggery bullocks, Kate, I thought, all she did was grab your ass – she's just turned on, that's all. I was reassured by this and felt firmly back in control.

She was now pushing back towards me with equal intensity, but couldn't bring herself to look into my eyes directly again. She glanced up sporadically through those bangs in a most endearing way. I was firmly hooked, even if she wasn't yet. I was just dying to feel her breasts, already visualising her sitting on top of me, undulating and moaning, or alternatively, bound by my wrist restraints, writhing as I went down on her. My knees were getting as weak as my thighs were wet. It was getting to be time to leave; I couldn't take much more of this.

I turned my lips to her ear, sucking on the lobe gently before saying, 'Let's go. I'd like to take you home with me tonight.' She inhaled sharply before nodding mutely.

We gathered our coats from the coatcheck. I tipped for both of us and we left.

Ann Arbor on a Friday night is a busy place. I contemplated asking where she parked, but didn't want to break the mood. I just led her to my car, parked in the alley across the street. As we drove to my apartment, I played the stereo loud enough to discourage conversation, all the while caressing her leg. Her fingers played tentatively in my long, curly hair.

At a particularly long stoplight, she reached to turn the stereo down. I let her. 'Ann. My name is Ann.' 'Kate.' She smiled nervously. 'I just thought we should know each other's names.' 'Why?' At this, she paused. 'I'm not sure.'

I turned the stereo back up and drove on. I swore I would need a spatula to get me off of my car seat; I felt part woman, part snail. At my apartment (which I had hastily cleaned before leaving that night, in the hopes I would be bringing someone home) I took her appropriately grungey coat and hung it next to my leather in the closet.

'You have lovely art,' she said quietly, admiring all of the prints and statuettes placed about. I smiled and said nothing. Motioning for her to take a seat on the sofa, I walked into my bedroom and closed the door softly. I looked around, made sure everything was all set, and lit the incense waiting in the censer. I walked into the bathroom, tossed a pair of dirty panties into the closet, wiped toothpaste out of the sink, straightened towels, and spritzed a bit of Shalimar into the air. Seemed OK.

I came back out into the living room, and said, 'Go ahead and take a nice hot shower, and relax. I'll use the other bathroom.' 'Umm, sure. OK. I guess I am pretty sweaty.'

I showed her to the bathroom and told her to make use of anything she found in it. I had left several varieties of scented shower gels on the countertop, as well as some stimulating body brushes and scrubbers in the shower itself. I turned to leave, and pressed in the lock as I closed the door behind me.

Before it shut completely, I said, 'Take all the time you want. We're in no hurry.' She smiled again.

I closed the door and walked to the other side of the apartment to the other bathroom. I rinsed quickly off, wanting to make a few other preparations before she finished. Satisfied that I was generally club-odour-free, I towelled off, donned a dark blue silk robe, and went into my bedroom. I listened at the bathroom door; she was still showering. I fanned the incense about my room, made sure all sex-toy-type things were hidden yet easily available, smoothed the sheets, closed the shades and lay down on the bed.

I closed my eyes, listening to the sound of water running off her body, visualising tiny rivulets coursing over her breasts, in between her legs, dripping off her pubic hair (if indeed she had any). I reached between my legs and rubbed my clit lightly, moaning softly. I was totally soaking wet again. Much more of this self-pleasuring and I'd have an orgasm before she came in the room. It was difficult to stop, but discipline won out, and I waited quietly.

I heard her turn the water off and shuddered slightly with anticipation.

'Oh shit! The candles!' I thought. I jumped up and lit two on the wall above the bed, one on my altar, and one on the bookshelf on the wall opposite the bed. The overall effect was lovely: enough light to see well by, but not harsh like incandescent lamps. Exotic shadows cast by my many feathers and drapings danced about. I hoped she would enjoy the ambience; much of my pleasure would stem from hers.

'I thought you might like a massage,' I stated quietly.
'That sounds really nice.'

She fidgeted with her robe a little. I sat on the edge of the bed and motioned her towards me. She stood before me, and it took every ounce of will not to ravish her right then and there. Instead, I stood and removed her robe from behind, sliding it off over her shoulders slowly, watching every inch of flesh revealed.

'Lie down on your stomach, please, Ann.' She did so, making herself comfortable.

'Make sure there's no undue pressure on your neck.' She shifted more.

Satisfied that she was comfortable, I asked if she would prefer almond or clarey sage oil. She said that the sage sounded more exotic. I opened the nightstand drawer and removed the bottle, placing it on top. I then removed my robe. Her head was turned away; too bad. I looked at the contrast of her pale white skin on my dark green duvet. Beautiful.

'I'm going to start at your neck and work my way down to your feet.' She nodded silently. I poured a small amount of oil on my hands, smoothed it up my arms to the elbow, and made sure my hands had a generous coating. I then warmed a small bit more in my hands, and said, 'I'm going to begin now.'

Her hair was already off her neck; a good thing – I'd forgotten to check before I oiled my hands. I began very softly, spreading the warm oil from the base of her skull down over her trapezius muscles. She was relaxed on the surface, but had tension in the deeper muscles. I gently worked her neck and shoulders for a long time; she carried her stress in this area. As the knots came loose, I moved down her spine and outwards, always visualising the tension moved by my hands out of her body as I felt the flow of energy out of me and into her.

I moved to the base of her spine, just before the swell of her buttocks began. There was little tension here, but I gave the area special attention, as she reacted strongly to my touch. I stroked downwards to the outside of her hips, pressing firmly. Her flesh was so resilient and so soft. It was as much a pleasure for me to be touching her as it was for her to be touched.

I used a heavy amount of oil on her ass; it trickled into the cleft and she shuddered. I smiled. I squeezed her gluteal muscles to get to the tension from dancing moving downwards. I pushed and squeezed and pulled. I could see her anus tighten in pleasure when I pulled her cheeks apart. I could see that she was at least partially shaven. Shaven women are such a turn-on for me; I can see everything, and there's no hair to get in my mouth, either.

Her thighs were specially tight; the dancing had taken a lot out of her. I projected a strong amount of healing energy into this area, loosening the grip of the lactic acid. Her calves were equally tense. She had strong, well-formed legs. She was very fit without being muscley.

Finally, I reached her feet. I used enough oil to squish around between her toes and make luscious noises. She moaned appreciatively as I eased all the accumulated body tension out through her toes. I used particularly hard pressure on the soles of her feet, using various pressure points corresponding to areas on her body. As I finished up, I used soft, smoothing strokes all over her body.

'That was incredible. You have the most amazing hands,' she said lazily, turning over with as little effort as possible. 'I haven't felt this relaxed since, like . . . God, I don't know.'

She really was young. Perfectly fine by me. As she lay on her back, I couldn't help but admire her breasts with their pink, firm little nipples. I looked down, and she had a small patch of darker blonde pubic hair.

'Kiss me,' she said softly. I was more than happy to oblige, but held up a finger for her to wait. I poured oil down my front, and smoothed it over my breasts and belly; oiled flesh against oiled flesh was one of my favourites. I slid up her belly and over her breasts with my own, and straddled her with my legs as I leant in to kiss her. She had full, yielding lips, which I kissed gently. I used my non-supporting hand to caress her side. Her skin was enchantingly supple. I licked the corners of her mouth, and she opened it to me. I teased her, darting my tongue in and out quickly, not giving her the full hard kiss she wanted. She lifted her head to me, but I backed away. Finally, she grabbed the back of my head and forced my tongue into her. She sucked on it, played with it, nibbled at it with her teeth.

It had finally begun. I began rubbing my breasts up and down against hers while still kissing her passionately. Small moans emanated from both of us. I took each of her wrists in my hands and pinned them above her head; I have a bit of a bondage fetish, and this was a way to test her reaction. She didn't go totally passive, and she didn't struggle against me, she just used her body to communicate her passion.

I released her and began kissing her neck, nibbling, sucking, biting, licking it all over, from front to back, top to bottom. The back was particularly sensitive. Each time I grazed it with my teeth she inhaled sharply and pushed her hips up towards me. I couldn't stay away from her breasts any longer. I had to touch them, to taste them. I worked down her chest, cupping each breast from the side, pushing them slightly together, as she murmured the sorts of things people do when helpless with desire. I took her left nipple in my mouth, sucking hard and long. I nipped at it, laved it with my tongue, squeezing with my hands. Her breasts were perfect C cups, perky but not overly so, naturally firm, with perfect nipples. I could have spent days worshipping them.

She was moaning louder now, and breathing faster. She pulled me up and slid down simultaneously, positioning herself under my breasts, and began sucking on them furiously as her nails dug into my back. I arched into her, murmuring appreciatively. My hair swished across my back, giving me goosebumps and making me shudder.

From beneath me she asked, 'Is this right? Does it feel good?' I told her it felt wonderful.

I moved back down, so we were face to face and kissed her deeply again. I then began kissing down her body, paying close attention to those marvellous breasts, then venturing further, sampling her belly button, her waist, her sides. I didn't stampede to her pussy the way most men do; I paused to caress, to admire, to suckle.

When I lowered myself to her pubic mound, I could smell her delicate aroma. I blew softly on her hairs, and she gasped, 'Oh please, oh please,' but I was going to make her wait, to make her crazed for it. I pushed her legs apart so I could fit in between them, and lowered my face to just inches above her pussy lips. She was so slick and wet and fragrant, I wanted to dive in, but restrained myself. I blew on her again, and she raised her hips, desperately trying to obtain any pressure on her beautiful, plump little clit.

I raised myself up.

'Not yet; I'm not going to let you have it yet. I want to tie you up. May I?'

'Yes, yes, God, if you'll make me come just do anything!' She was writhing.

I reached down between the bed and the nightstand and came up with one of my prized possessions: thick leather wrist restraints, lined with even thicker lamb's wool, with big, chrome buckles. I had it linked to its mate on the other side of the bed with a length of heavy chain. As I gently tightened the buckle, she started looking anxious.

'Shh, shh, shh,' I soothed. 'I won't hurt you. If you want me to stop, say so and I will. I won't do anything you don't want, and we can stop at any time you want. If you want me to stop, say "panic".'

She nodded and said, 'OK, go ahead.'

I kissed her gently but passionately and crawled across her to get the other restraint, bringing my cunt within inches of her wet lips. When she was properly tied down, I smiled wickedly, and said, 'Now that you're buckled up, let's take you for a ride.'

I reached up and grabbed a peacock feather from one of the drapings around the bed. I ran it lightly up and down her body. She shivered. I stroked her with it between her legs, and knew how tantalising this was for her – it was enough to feel, but not enough to get any true satisfaction from. The chain links were clinking together as she struggled to get the tip of the feather to touch her clit harder. I wasn't about to let her. Putting the feather aside, I lay down on top of her, covering her entire body with mine, and pulsing my pubic bone against her pussy. She groaned.

'Please make me come. Please, God, please make me come. I want to come so bad.'

I was loving this. It's not a power trip for me; it's knowing how good she's going to feel when she finally does come. All the teasing, all the tantalising pays off in the end. I stroked her brow, soothing her, calming her, bringing her down a few levels to where she was less crazed for an orgasm. I went to the foot of the bed, cradling her right foot in my hands and blowing on the sole. I took her little toe in my mouth and sucked on it gently, repeating the process for each toe on each foot. Her feet were sensitive, but not ticklish, so I could get away with flickering my tongue over the soles of her feet.

I took one foot in each hand and pushed her legs apart, keeping them straight as I did so. I could now look directly up into her pussy. I could see the wetness, the fullness, the redness of it in all its perfect beauty.

I found the ankle restraints and gently wrapped one around her right ankle – gently wrapping, but firmly buckling it. I completed the other ankle, and stood, looking down at this gorgeous woman, spread out and tied to my bed. It was the best gift someone could give to me.

'You're so beautiful, Ann.' She moaned. 'Do you wamt me to suck your pussy?'

'Please.' She arched her back and spread her legs even further.

I licked and kissed my way up her thighs, making sure to lavish attention on the backs of her knees, a little-known erogenous zone for many people. I scraped my nails up the insides of her thighs, hearing her breath hiss in and come out with an 'aaaaaahhhhh'.

Finally, I was at her gateway. I framed her little pussy with my hands, pulling the lips gently apart, and again blowing on her clit, this time harder. She gasped.

'You smell so good, Ann. I can't wait to taste you, to suck on your clit, to put my fingers inside you, to lick your asshole. I want to make you come so hard, so hard . . .'

My words were exciting me as well as her. The chain rattled against the wall as she moved. I traced her labia with the tip of my tongue, loving the absence of hair, loving the smoothness of her inner folds, loving the smell of her. After much teasing in this manner, I positioned my tongue just below her clit, and thrust it lightly up against the bottom of it. Finally obtaining some pressure on her clit nearly sent her over the edge, but I slowed to a steady pulse.

I was dying to fully taste her, so I flickered my tongue down to her vagina and buried it there. Her wetness began running down my chin and I explored her inner depths with my tongue. She pushed her hips up against me, and I could feel how much she wanted to grab my head and pull it to her with her little hands.

I moved back up to her clit, and began to suck on just the little tip of it. She thrust her hips up to meet each pulsing suction, moaning, trying to grind herself into me, and failing each time. I wasn't going to let her come yet; I wanted this to last, and then to do it all over again.

'Mmmm . . . I can feel how much you want to come. I want to make you come. But not yet.' I looked up at her to see her looking down at me, and I smiled wickedly. She let out an exasperated sigh and flopped her head back on to the pillow.

I reached into the nightstand drawer – it was my drawer o'tricks. Various vibrators, dildoes, lotions, oils, powders, feathers, handcuffs, miscellaneous other items, and the delicate, shiny, chrome objects I was after: the nipple clamps. Intricate and well-made, these little beauties often made me come by themselves. The chain linking them clinked lightly as I brought them into her view. She squirmed a bit, again unsure.

'All right then, I'll wear these.' I teased my left nipple, almost letting the rubber-tipped clamp all the way down, taking it off, putting it on rapidly. The reddish-brown pigments darkened and I moaned softly. She was watching with wide eyes, her hands straining towards me, but unable to reach. I attached both clamps to my nipples, and gazed down at my quarry. She was looking more and more like she wanted them to be put on her as well.

I licked my lips and turned around, suspending my pussy above her face, and positioning my mouth so it was less than an inch away from hers. I could feel her neck lifting, trying to push her face into the wetness presented. I wiggled my ass, dipped my hips so that the soft, shaven skin brushed against her mouth. Her tongue darted out to taste me, but I lifted myself away before she could get more than a tiny bit.

I reached back into the nightstand drawer and came out with a duplicate pair of clamps. I turned and saw her pupils dilate with excitement. I blew on her nipples, licked them, pinched them with my fingers lightly, bringing the blood in to sensitise them. I placed one very lightly on her left nipple, not clamping it down tightly at all.

'Tighter,' she said. I put more pressure on and she let out a sharp moan. 'Yesssss . . .' I put the other one on her with equal pressure.

The ankle restraints allowed her a limited range of motion, and she was bending alternate knees, lifting each leg up and down. I took hold of each knee and forced it to the mattress before shoving them apart. She thrust her hips up and I finally buried my face in between the luscious folds. Her slightly salty taste had a hint of bitterness, just the faintest tinge of sweat. As I sucked on her clit she let out a loud 'aaaah!' of relief. I flickered my tongue over her, into her, down her thighs and back up again. All the while, I taunted her with my own pussy, lowering it and raising it again before she could do much but catch my clit between her lips.

I slipped my hands under her ass and around to her pussy again. Dipping a finger into her, I gently began probing her asshole, which tightened delightfully. With each tentative insertion, she gasped and her hips jerked. Finally, I drove my index finger all the way into her, at the same time sucking as hard as I could on her clit, rubbing my tongue over it through the suction. She shuddered, she cried out and she came.

And by the gods she came hard. She was one of those rare women who ejaculated when she came – juices squirted out of her and on to my face, surprising me, then turning me on all the more. As her little shivers and moans subsided, I turned around to face her and shoved my cunt into her mouth, tugging on my own nipple clamps as she eagerly nibbled and sucked on my clit. I rocked my hips back and forth, feeling the friction of her teeth on me, feeling her tongue catch my hood piercing and pull on it firmly, feeling . . . feeling . . .

As I came closer and closer to orgasm, I reached over and released one of her hands, and pulled it up to my breast, squeezing and pinching, rocking and pushing, panting and gasping. She almost had me there, so close, so close. I grabbed the back of her head with both hands and pressed her hard against me, moving her head in opposition to my hips until I felt that beautiful moment when I know I'm going to come and there's nothing I can do to stop it. That beautiful release, the sounds coming from my mouth that I have no control over, the sweet fire coursing through my body, centering on my clit but pouring over my entire body . . .

I began to come gently down from the peak, still gasping, still pressing her face to me. She was softly stroking my clit with her tongue, letting me come back down. I practically collapsed next to her, first releasing her other hand so we could hold each other. When I regained a clearer state of mind, I released her ankles and we wrapped around each other, smiling slightly to ourselves, kissing now and then.

After perhaps half an hour, she sat up and stretched. She looked for a moment at me, and then at the restraints, and then back at me. She smiled evilly.

'Your turn,' she said.

A wild fluttering in my belly began.

And I submitted myself to her care.

The Western Whore

Kristina Lloyd

I needed water. More than anything else in the world, I needed water.

The walk from the pension to the bus station was only a couple of minute's worth of dirt track, and during that time, all I could think about was water, water, water.

Pretty dull, considering all the major-league stuff that was somewhere in my brain. But when your body's got needs, it screams a lot louder than your head ever can.

So once I'd got past the first hurdle – sneaking away from you when the muezzin was wailing from the mosque – I didn't agonise about the rights and wrongs of what I'd just done; I didn't agonise about the dangers of being a single white female in this land of lechers. I just agonised about the bus station's café: please Jesus-Allah – whoever has the biggest say in the matter – let that café be open for business. And let that café sell plastic bottles of water with the stopper sealed – which meant mineral water – rather than plastic bottles of water with a broken seal – which meant tap.

Someone holy was on my side because my oasis was open. But when I entered, that's when it hit me: travelling alone was going to be a helluva lot more difficult

189

than travelling with you. And that had been difficult enough.

Even though it was early morning, the café was full of smoke. Men with leathery faces and dark moustaches sat at Formica tables, alone or in small groups. They drank tea from dinky little glasses, tucked into rough breakfasts, played backgammon, or just sat, elbows on knees, staring into space and twiddling with their worry beads.

As I walked into the room, I could feel all those eyes turning on me. Some of the men merely glanced up while stuffing soupy hunks of bread in their mouths; others watched me like I was television, their gazes sleepily placid, oblivious to the fact that my eyes worked just as well as theirs did; one or two gawped, slack-jawed like kids at a toyshop window.

No surprises there then.

Rucksack crouched on my back, I made my way to the counter and asked for *su*. I paid over the odds for it, but I was in no mood to barter.

There was some old guy in a bobble-hat near the door who ogled me with beady little eyes. Feeling insolent, I tried staring him out as I headed for the exit. His gaze never faltered, and when I neared him, a tobacco-stained grin cracked open beneath his grizzled 'tache. He tilted his head back and made a clicking noise in his throat. I think that's Kurdish for 'you and me babe, how about it?'

All in all, it was a pretty average trip into no-woman's land. The difference this time was that you weren't waiting for me: I had no bodyguard boyfriend; I had no Western man around to signify, in their eyes, 'has an owner but no wedding ring so obviously a goer'. Of course they didn't know I was suddenly single, but I did. And so the usual stares were far more intimidating. 'Has a man in every bus station,' I heard them thinking. 'A Turkish man. Just like me.'

In your dreams, matey.

It's amazing that the novelty hasn't worn off for them yet. I mean, I know the town isn't exactly tourist-central, but it's still high on the list for us backpackers dumb enough to do the Eastern Turkey trawl. So you'd think the locals just might have got used to the fact that there are women with blonde hair rather than dark; that there are women who do not cover up virtually every inch of flesh with headscarves and swathes of grubby floral cloth; that there are women from civilised lands who have lives rather than husbands. But no. For them, Western woman is still an object of fuckable fascination.

In the morning heat, glugging back my water, I wandered around the bus park, checking out the ramshackle offices for ticket prices and departure times. A scruffy little shoeshine boy kept hassling me, waggling his brush at my dusty feet in a frantic bid to polish my trainers. There were a few parked buses and one man, standing by his vehicle and shouting in tongues, starred an open hand at me and promised, 'Fife minutes! Bus go in fife minutes, lady.'

I didn't know where I was heading. I just wanted to get out of the place a.s.a.p. – before my escape was discovered – then take stock and make plans. 'Fife minutes,' though I knew it was a lie, looked like the best thing on offer.

Things didn't improve much on the bus. It wasn't one of those long-distance German brutes with air conditioning and leg room. It was cramped and stuffy and when I boarded, it was standing-room only.

A sea of eyes confronted me as I began nudging up the aisle, rucksack at my feet.

In my rush to flee the pension, I'd packed badly and the rucksack was awkward and bottom-heavy. I half-kicked it along and all those bad slip-on shoes, with little tassels, gilt chains and fancy bits of latticework, shuffled aside. Then a sudden yammering broke out and there was a rush to help me – men clicking fingers and shouting and I saw my rucksack being lifted high and bobbing effortlessly over heads until it found a vacant slot in the luggage rack above. I smiled gratefully at no one in particular.

Sometimes it's tricky when the culture which leers and gropes is also unspeakably generous and kind. I never know whether I love these people or loathe them.

Several minutes later we were off, churning up clouds of dust as we rumbled out of the bus park.

That's when I felt I'd truly left you. I wondered if you were awake yet, perhaps reading my note which said: 'No, I haven't popped to the loo. I've popped out of town. Will send a letter to you in Urfa, poste restante. Hope your hangover's a killer.' Or were you still in an alcoholic stupor? Probably the latter.

The bus bumped through parched, lunar landscapes, and the driver's radio played a constant noise of singers warbling to jingle-jangle tunes. As usual, the windows remained closed. Cigarettes, sweat, engine fumes and heavy air-freshener clogged up my lungs.

All around me were swarthy faces and bad blouson jackets. Apart from a couple of big-bosomed peasant women at the back, I was the only female – and certainly the only female who had bare shins, bare arms and bare shoulders. I was the centre of silent attention. My shoulders seemed particularly popular.

Their gazes bored into me. I was an affront to their Moslem morality. I disgusted them because I was from a faraway land of easy money and easy sex. I was the wicked whore of the West, and because of that they hated me. And because of that they ached for me. Lust sparkled in those deep brown eyes. Every now and again, one of them would shift his weight, change position, and I knew the fleeting brush of an arm against mine or the brief press of a thigh was not accidental.

But I wasn't going to be cowed by it. Let them, I

thought. If it means so much, then let them steal their sly little touches. Let them lie in bed at night, handling their cocks, guiltily recalling the moment they stood near the Western whore and felt her smooth, honeyed skin warm against theirs. Let them be tormented with lust and with the dread of Allah's wrath and the heat of hellfire. What did I care if I lured them into sin? All I intended to do was get a bus out of town – a bus labelled 'fast-track out of a relationship, destination elsewhere'.

So I coped with the stealth of uninvited touches. But an uninvited erection is a different matter.

I froze when I felt it, a solid bulge pressing lightly against my arse. A few seconds later, it retreated.

I didn't turn around; I knew who it belonged to. He was a vigorous-looking guy with an army-boy crop, an army-boy body and a clean-shaven army-boy face. That was some comfort. If the swollen cock had belonged to a greasy middle-aged moustache, I might have kicked up a small fuss. Thankfully, it didn't.

Nothing happened for a while. Scared and excited, I just hung on to the leather strap above me, gazing beyond heads as the rugged dry plains swept by. Then I felt him again, firmer, harder, and my body was all butterflies and pulses.

I'd been a bad girl from the word go that day and so – though I know I shouldn't have – I pressed my arse back, ever so slightly. I was rewarded with an answering push. His groin stayed there a while, digging an insistent ridge into my soft buttock. My pussy flushed with dangerously sweet arousal.

In a surge of daring, I lifted my heels up, then down. I did it again and again, covertly bouncing on the balls of my feet, making my cheek rub gently along his hard-on. He responded by rubbing back.

And no one knew a thing. It was just me and my army-boy rubbing each other up in a crowded, sweaty bus.

You know, when we had our blazing row, one of the things which really pissed me off was you saying I had no sense of adventure, that I couldn't accept a challenge. OK, so I get weary of staying in hovels with no hot water; I get sick of eating bread and yoghurt for days without end; I tire of feeling grimy and I yearn for a few home comforts. But it does not follow that I have no sense of adventure.

My army-boy thrilled me. I encouraged his attentions, edging nearer to him and taking full advantage of the bus whenever it swayed or lurched. Once, when we feigned a minor collision, I felt his steadying hand on my waist and heard him breathe in my ear: *'Pardon.'* I turned to acknowledge him with a smile and my eyes locked with his: blue-green jewels set in a deep-brown face. My cunt, already heated, went up a few extra degrees.

As we approached destination elsewhere, his lips came to my ear again and in a whisper which was warm and ticklish, he enquired: *'Ben sen seks?'*

'Me you sex?' My heart went 'boom'. A breath which was close to a gasp snagged in my throat.

I craned around to meet his gaze. My pulses thumping, I gave a little nod. 'Yes, OK,' I murmured, quiet and cool.

At the bus park, we disembarked along with half the other passengers, army-boy gallantly carrying my luggage. He looked somewhat stunned. On the dusty ground, he hooked an arm into my rucksack strap and slung the thing at an angle on to his back. He looked at me, his brow furrowed with confusion and wariness.

'Yes?' he frowned.

'Yes,' I said brightly, fixing him with a bold, brazen stare.

He gave an uncertain smile which broke into a little laugh. I don't think army-boy could believe his luck. Maybe he'd just been playing games. Perhaps he hadn't expected me to understand the *'ben sen'* part of the sex question. But I did.

I reckoned army-boy had merely been wondering how far he could push it with Western woman. He'd heard tales about them, about how they all took oral contraception; how greedy they were for cock; how easily they would spread their legs and open their supple wet pussies and you didn't even have to ask them their names. Maybe he'd tried it on before but had received only abuse. So he'd stopped believing those tales. And then all of a sudden this one was saying 'yes'. Which meant either those tales were true after all, or she had a hidden agenda. She was a police informant, a spy, a murderess, a castrator.

But I wasn't. I was being what he wanted me to be: the Western whore.

And I was horny as hell. My sex was melting into my knickers. The cotton gusset was damp against my vulva.

I wanted him there and then. I wanted him to fling my pack from his shoulder and push me up against the bus. I wanted him to drag my shorts to my ankles and fuck me hard, both of us pumping and grunting, oblivious to the stares and all those worry beads going click, click, click.

But we had a few practicalities to sort out, like was there anywhere for me to stay in this one-horse town?

'You want room?' he asked.

'Pansiyon?' I enquired hopefully.

He made a tutting noise. 'Room,' he said flatly. Then he smiled. 'For you, is no money.'

Ah, I thought: a bed for services rendered. Well that suits me just fine, army-boy. And so, together, we headed into town.

His name's Sabri. He is my pimp and I am his whore.

I'm staying on the edge of town, with a family whose English is zilch. Between them, they might just have enough teeth to fill one mouth. Tourists don't come here. Tourists go somewhere. I've come elsewhere.

When we left the bus station and walked down the rubbly streets, kids stopped playing their games and stared. Some of the braver ones danced after me. Sabri brought me to this house and after some animated gabbling, I was shown a room: pretty primitive but it's got a bed.

We didn't fuck straight away: not appropriate and besides, the big brawny mamma made certain I was never alone with army-boy.

I get the sense she's protecting my honour.

So I had the afternoon to myself. I caught up on some sleep and masturbation. (Very, very quiet masturbation.)

You know, there was something else you said which really pissed me off. You said I had no stamina. OK, so maybe I am a bit lacking when we go traipsing up and down in desert-dry heat. But if you'd seen me last night, you would have well and truly eaten your words. I had the stamina of a dozen whores.

The centre of town's busier and more civilised than the part I'm staying in. The market square's got fruit and veg stalls, a few shops, a mosque close by, and a couple of *lokanta* – though I'm not eager to sample the cuisine. Down one of the narrow streets leading off, there's a crude stone building which looks, for all the world, like any other house around here.

But it's really something special.

Last night, Sabri took me there.

We walked along streets which were spookily dark. The sky was a black, star-spangled canvas. There are so many stars out here. Why is that? There were mountains in the distance. You couldn't actually see them, but parts of the sky were completely black, completely without stars. It looked as if someone had put stencils up there, chucked glitter across the heavens, and the mountains were the shapes left when all the stencils were removed.

I was hot for my army-boy. 'Sabri,' I kept saying as we walked along. 'Sabri, fuck me. Here, down this street. Now. *Lütfen*. No one's around.'

'No,' he would reply in a hiss. 'We must wait. It is not safe.'

And with every step my hunger intensified. My nipples, already sharpened by the cool night air, grew doubly sharp in their need to be touched. My sex was a pouch for milky lust and my labia were so beautifully swollen, so plump and fuzzy with desire. I ached for the good solid thrust of cock. I wanted it everywhere, in every orifice.

To look at me, no one would have dreamt I was capable of such appetite because I was dressed like a village girl at a wedding feast. Well, almost.

The women of the house had kitted me out, giggling, gawping and stroking as they turned me this way and that. I wore those baggy shalwar pantaloons which look like confused skirts. They were black cotton, sprigged with tiny flowers, and the hammock-like crotch hung somewhere below knee-level. On top I had a flowery blouse thing with a scooped neck. It was far too small. My midriff peeped and the fabric over my breasts was stretched tight, the button in the middle threatening to ping off if I took too deep a breath. The scrawny little girl of the house had kept on shyly proffering more and more trinkets and I tinkled and clinked, rings on my fingers and bells on my toes.

The idea, I assumed, was to make me less conspicuous. The finishing touch – that dash of authenticity – was a mustard cardigan, full of holes, and again far too small. I'd tried to refuse it – it was rotten – but my dressers had insisted, hugging their own bodies and miming shivers. A thin yellow shawl, fringed with tassels and bits of metal, was draped over my head, and my new friends had laughed and chattered as the English Rose in fancy dress gave them all a twirl.

English Rose. Ha! I was the Western whore.

'What is this place?' I said to Sabri, when he knocked on the door of the building which looks ordinary but is really something special.

'Inside I have many friends,' he said.

'And will you fuck me in here?' I asked, foolishly thinking that perhaps this was his mates' house. 'Or have you gone all Moslem on me?'

He grinned broadly, his eyes glinting, his teeth clean and white in the darkness. It was the most confident expression I'd seen on his face so far. Then he fixed a clawed hand on one of my breasts and gave the soft flesh a deliciously long squeeze.

'We will all fuck you,' he replied, and he bent into my shawl to lick briefly along my neck. 'I think this is what you want. Yes? I am right?'

My cunt was quicker than my brain. It flared in a burst of greedy excitement while my head swirled with 'many friends' and 'oh my God' and 'yes please' and 'no thank you.'

Before I could reply, the door was opened by a moustache-man who was just plucking a cigarette from his lips. He beamed at Sabri, releasing a cloud of pungent smoke, and the two shook hands and slapped shoulders while exchanging eager foreign chat.

I kept my head low, hearing rowdy jeers and tinny music which sounded just like the stuff on the bus. We were in a short, stone-floored corridor and about the only thing my eyes noticed was a descending flight of steps. At the foot of those steps was a half-drawn curtain, and beyond it just dim light and a fog of smoke.

It's hell, I thought. He's taking me to hell. And hell is a room full of moustache-men with octopus arms, all gawping and groping and wanting to fuck me while bus-driver music played.

Then I felt the shawl being folded back from my head on to my shoulders. Fingers under my chin forced me to raise my head and I shot a challenge into the eyes of our doorman.

'*Güzel*,' he said in a gravelly drawl. '*Çok güzel.*'

That much I understood. I'd heard it often enough. But as ever, I didn't know if he was saying I was 'very good', 'quite pretty' or 'stunningly beautiful' because '*çok güzel*' seems to cover all those things. In my opinion Turkish can be fairly limited as a language. Perhaps we should learn it. Might help our relationship.

'So, lady,' began the doorman. 'You like cock, ah? You want it, ah?'

He said something which was obviously very funny and the two men laughed raucously.

'You want it up you?' grinned the doorman, and he took a heavy suck on his cigarette.

I drew the deepest breath I could, wary of the stress on my too-tight top, and flexed my shoulders back in a posture of pride.

'Yes,' I said. 'But not yours.' Then, bold as brass, I cupped a hand to Sabri's groin. 'I want his,' I said firmly. And I truly did because Sabri was hard beneath my palm and my touch made him twitch even harder.

The doorman guffawed and with a nod of his head directed us down the steps to hell.

It was a stone-pillared cellar. Kilims and carpets, coloured like earth and autumn, covered the walls and floors. Candles burned in arched recesses. The tables were slices of tree trunk; the seats were cushions and low stools. And the people sprawled and perched there were men – and those men looked like army-boys. There wasn't a moustache in sight. Instead it was strong brown arms and smooth shorn heads gleaming in the amber half-light. It was like seeing Sabri through a kaleidoscope.

It wasn't hell. It was heaven.

And heaven didn't notice the angel-slut who'd just

landed because they were too busy whistling at an angel-slut who was dancing.

Sabri led me to some cushions. First things first, I got rid of the mustard cardi. Then, half-hidden by my shawl, I watched the dancer.

She was nothing like those belly-dancing tourist-tarts we saw back in Istanbul. She was beautiful – like a spice stall at a bazaar. Her skin was nut-brown, her hair dark-henna, and her clothes were all saffron, cinnamon, cayenne and mint. She looked far too young – obscenely so – but she had the wiggle and tease of a harem-harlot.

There was another angel-slut, lying on some cushions between the open thighs of an army-boy. Both slut and soldier were watching the dance but soldier had his hands down angel-slut's top. Beneath the cloth, he was idly massaging her tits. She looked less than excited.

But it made me hot. So those sort of antics were OK here, were they?

With half an eye on the floor-show, I rolled my body into Sabri's and drifted a stealthy hand along his thigh to his groin. I palmed the bulge.

'I want you,' I said, close to his ear.

Some guy came over and set a jug of water and two tumblers on the tree-trunk table beside Sabri. Sabri poured water in the glasses and the clear liquid already in there turned cloudy white. Yeah, we were on raki: the devil's drink. I sipped, letting the sweet anise warm a path to my stomach.

'I still want you,' I said, turning so we were chest to chest and fondling his crotch again. 'When can I have you? Tell me, Sabri. I can't wait much longer. I'm so horny. My cunt's on fire. I'm –'

'Your . . . your what?' he said, giving me a quizzical look. Shadows flickered over his dark handsome face and his blue-green eyes twinkled with mischief. I think he was bluffing.

'My cunt,' I whispered, and I took his wide calloused

hand and guided it under the elastic waist of my shalwar. I wasn't wearing knickers.

Unaided, his big broad fingers ruffled through my springy hair and down to my hot, wet flesh.

'Ahhh yes,' I sighed as he dabbled in my folds and juices. 'That's it, army-boy. That's cunt.'

He was no novice. He penetrated my slipperiness and proceeded to give me a slow, two-fingered fuck while circling my clit with a perfect-pressure thumb.

'You like that?' he breathed, and I groaned a husky response.

It briefly crossed my mind that someone might just notice what we were up to; that someone might clock the fact that Sabri's forearm was half-way down my trousers and my groin was a hump of moving fabric. But I didn't really care. We were in heaven and this part was seventh.

With languid expertise, he teased me ever closer to orgasm. My breath rushed in tiny gasps and as the tension coiled I murmured, 'Yes, oh yes,' over and over.

'Sabri!' came a cheerful holler and I heard the voice as if it belonged to another world.

'Ingiliz!' he called back by way of an explanation, his hand still working steadily in my trousers.

Then, as if to prove I was English, he nuzzled into my top, nosing down the gathered neck to suckle on a half-exposed breast. His hot humid mouth made me squirm and moan, and moments later, he made me come like a thing possessed.

On my enormous cushion, I arced and writhed, crying quietly and then shamelessly as the convulsions burst open and tore through every vein. When I drifted back to earth – or was it heaven? – cheers, applause and huge whooping whistles were ringing in my ears.

All eyes were on me. I smiled back, ignoring the flare in my cheeks. Now I'd done it. My metamorphosis was complete. I was well and truly their wicked Western whore.

The thought brought a charge of fresh heat into my sumptuously moist sex and I tingled from head to toe, goosebumps dancing everywhere.

And to make it perfect, the angel-sluts had disappeared. I had no competition. It was just me, devil-slut, with a pussy full of appetite and a room full of army-boys.

I gave a challenging little laugh, and half a dozen or so men took the bait and surged forward. They lifted and dragged me into the centre of the room, then a crush of men closed in, eager-eyed and boisterous. My body was being jostled, my clothes were being tugged. A flurry of hands moved over me, touching my hair, my arms, my legs, my lips. They didn't seem to know quite what to do. I sucked on someone's finger, much to the crowd's delight, and one hand grew bold enough to latch on to my breast. But it was all too much of a commotion.

So I said, 'Wait,' and I gently pushed a couple of bodies away. Then I said, 'You can look but you can't touch. Not until I say so.'

Some of them appeared to understand and they fell back. Sabri gave a translation and the rest retreated. I had a fascinated, obedient audience forming a wide circle around me. Some grinned expectantly; others frowned in bemusement.

That vulnerable button on my blouse had gone, and between my breasts the fabric gaped in a vulva shaped split. I decided I would dance for them, but not the way angel-slut had danced. I wasn't going to shimmy my hips in a teasing little nothing-show. I wasn't going to wiggle around to bus-driver music.

I was going to strip for them. I was going to dazzle them with my fair English skin and nipples pinker than any they'd ever seen. So I did, swaying and turning, stroking up and down, caressing my lush curves and dips. The men started to clap, a steady rhythm of lewd encouragement. I unfastened my top, button by button. If I hadn't been so wild with lust I might have spun my performance out. But I didn't. I was far too horny.

Edging the blouse from my shoulders, I gradually revealed my firm, high tits with their English-rose nipples. The handclaps grew louder, faster, harder, chasing the beat that was pounding in my sex. I massaged my breasts, filling my palms with their tender weight, then smoothed a path down to the waist of my shalwar.

I tantalised my army-boys, stretching the elastic this way then that, giving them one hip at a time, then a little bit of arse and a little bit more. I had them fired up to a frenzy, and their heat and noise and rabid urgency was almost enough to make me come. Their greedy eyes were like greedy fingers, swooping over my flesh and penetrating deep.

I was going to have Sabri first.

So I eased off my trousers and kicked everything away. Apart from the glinting trash of bangles, rings and necklaces, I was naked. In the cloudy orange haze, my skin was champagne to their coarse, untutored palates, and my pubes were as precious as spun-gold. The clapping grew a bit ragged and disorderly. Somebody whistled; somebody groaned.

I was in my element. They could look but they couldn't touch. I padded around my circle of men, drifting my fingertips across chests and jawbones. They all followed me with pleading eyes. Not once did they touch.

There was one guy whose eyes were pistachio-green, and whose T-shirt had a dark patch in the middle: fresh male sweat. Delicious. I stopped in front of him and tugged the T-shirt from his jeans, wafting it up. Eagerly, he finished the job, whipping it over his head and presenting me with a muscular, sweat-glinting torso. It was like a slab of burnished teak.

Smiling like a prick-tease, I spread strokes across its firmness then cupped his groin. Rock-hard. I rubbed at the straining ridge and he moaned throatily, his lower lip sagging in a lustful pout, his eyes fixed hopefully on mine. I liked him. I'd have him after Sabri.

Further along the circle, I did the same to a second army-boy. I got another teak chest and another rock-hard groin. This was fun.

Sabri was standing just behind a couple of guys and when I got to him, I reached my hand to his T-shirt and drew him into the ring. I stripped him of his top-half then pressed my hand to his crotch. His prick was pushing against his fly. My cunt wept for him and a trickle of juice ran secretly down my inner thigh.

Somebody called out to him and he shouted back, beaming like a mad man.

'Ben sen seks?' I whispered, and quick as a flash he scooped me up off the ground and carried me across the cellar. (He's much stronger than you. In his arms, I am a feather.)

The crowd roared, surged in, then scattered to let us pass until Sabri set me on my feet again between two stone pillars. The army-boys regrouped in a noisy jostling horseshoe and Sabri hurried with his zip. His cock sprang free, thick, gnarled and gorgeously meaty.

I wanted to look, touch, suck, but Sabri just stamped out of his trousers and turned me around. I was arse-facing him, arse-facing my audience. Lifting my arms, he pressed my left hand to one pillar, my right to the other. I spread my legs wide for him, feeling the wet gape of my vulva and the dampness on my thighs. His body nuzzled up behind me, his prick nudging to find my hole.

Then he was there. With a noise like 'hrrrmph' he penetrated me, packing my depths in one clean, hard thrust. The force of him rocked me. My knees went to jelly and I wailed openly because the pleasure of being filled was so blissfully explosive. Slowly he withdrew, lingering at my opening. Then he did it again – 'hrrrmph,' slamming so high my body jumped and my tits bounced.

'You like that. Yes?' came his voice in my ear. 'English girl, you like it in your cunt?'

'God, yes,' I said, my voice several octaves too low, and I locked my elbows, bracing myself against the pillars, steadying myself for his next punishing jerk.

I was ready. So were my army-boys, because as Sabri did his slow withdrawal and linger, some of them started to make a kind of football match noise – a low steady rumble which rose louder and louder until it burst into a shout as Sabri rammed his cock deep.

Again and again they did this, matching each boorish crescendo to Sabri's grunt and shove. My breathless gasps were drowned out, and my body went into rag-doll mode, shaking on every lunge.

I could hardly stand. I was aching for speed. Bearing my arse backwards, I clamped my vagina to his shaft and begged frantically for more.

That quickened him, and he soon stopped playing up to the crowds and began playing for me. Wrapping an arm around my waist, he held me tight and gave it to me fierce and fast. His hips pumping furiously, he pounded away, gasping in my ear and snatching at words.

'*Hadi! Hadi! Hadi!*' he kept saying, and I was gulping at air and crying in delight, breasts jiggling, orgasm about to hit.

Stamping feet and clapping hands vibrated through my blood and when I came, the place erupted. Moments later, so did Sabri, and the two of us were left heaving for breath in the midst of that hungry, army-boy rabble.

When Sabri slipped out of me and I'd regained some

composure, I scoured the room for pistachio-eyes. There he was: bare-chested and big-groined. I smiled, fixing him with a locked gaze.

'Who's next?' I demanded, and Pistachio grinned roguishly as the cheers broke out yet again.

That night, I had cocks everywhere: in my mouth, my cunt, my arse; sometimes separately, sometimes all at once.

Money changed hands. The army-boys counted it out with licked fingers and slapped it into Sabri's open palm. There were a lot of notes, but as you know that doesn't mean much out here. It might just have been a few quid. Anyway, over half of it's mine.

Me and Sabri are saving up to go on a package holiday, somewhere clean and lazy with nice food and hot showers.

That's what I wanted to do with you. Remember? Stupid idea of yours to go backpacking on a shoestring. I said it wouldn't work. I said it'd be stressful and we'd only end up fighting. But do you listen? Do you care?

So this letter's just to let you know the state of play: I've been sold into white slavery and I might not bother coming back.

And you know when we had our final row? Do you know what really pissed me off? What pissed me off the most?

It was you saying I had no imagination.

I did not deserve that.

The Best of Hands

Portia Da Costa

'Yes, I understand perfectly,' murmurs Madame Guidetty, escorting us into the room. A silver coffee jug stands on a tray, on her desk, flanked by two fine bone-china cups and the usual paraphernalia of milk jug, sugar bowl and tongs. There are just two cups because I won't be taking coffee.

'Do be seated,' Madame continues, smiling almost flirtatiously at my Master, 'and we'll have our coffee while I outline our range of services.'

'Thank you, that sounds most pleasant,' my Master answers genially, sinking down into a comfortable, deeply upholstered chair set at right angles to Madame's spacious desk. He glances at me and I blush furiously. He has noticed my transgression – the fact that I am staring about the room, and at Madame, and at him, when I am supposed to keep my eyes lowered at all times – and I realise that I will suffer for it soon.

It seems that Madame has observed my slip-up too. 'Perhaps Susan could stand in the corner while we chat?' she suggests pleasantly, although there is, I detect, a faint thread of excitement in her barely accented voice. 'In a display position, possibly? I always find that tends to curb a wilful streak quite nicely, don't you, Monsieur?'

'A good idea, Madame,' returns my Master, his own voice rather vibrant too. 'Would it offend you if Susan removes her skirt and her slip? I always find a greater degree of exposure more effective ... Although if that isn't your practice here, perhaps I could trouble you for the loan of a couple of safety pins?'

'No need for that,' says Madame, 'we too recognise the subduing qualities of partial nudity. It is a measure we rely upon heavily.' She pauses, and I hear a slight click, then the sound of a bell ringing somewhere else in the house. 'There, I've summoned a maid to take Susan's slip and skirt.'

My heart begins to lurch around in my chest. Yet another stranger to see me embarrassed. I colour even harder and feel sweat prickle and run beneath my arms.

'Well, Susan?' my Master prompts, and with shaking fingers I unfasten my skirt. Just as I am stepping out of it, there is a knock at the door.

'*Entrez*!' calls out Madame, and a maid enters, a beautiful dark-haired girl, with a sullen, sultry mouth. Her uniform is old-fashioned and immaculate; her apron is snow-white, and her buttoned shoes shine like polished jet.

'Ah, Florenza, Susan here doesn't need her skirt and underslip for a while ... I wonder if you would take care of them for her?' Madame speaks to her maid in almost an intimate manner. Against my will, I begin to speculate on the type of duties this Latin beauty might perform. She gives me an expressionless look as I hand her my skirt.

Sliding down my lace-trimmed half-slip, I become more and more conscious of my undies. They are chosen by my Master, as always; and, as always, they are costly and luxurious. The slip is heavy satin, pure white, and was bought at an exclusive Knightsbridge boutique. I sense both Madame and Florenza silently pricing it, and thus estimating how highly my Master values me.

My stockings and suspender belt, which I will retain, are both equally extravagant. The former are fine deniered, smoke-grey – to match the formal suit I wear – and with a thick welt of lace; and the latter is white silk to match my underslip. My panties, however, are very plain, just the simplest of white cotton interlock, bikini-shaped, but not especially brief.

I pass my slip to Florenza and she folds it neatly, placing it upon a chair, on top of my already folded skirt.

'Florenza,' says my Master, his voice appreciative, although I do not know whether this is in regard to the sight of me, skirtless, or due to the dark girl's undeniable loveliness. 'I wonder if you would be good enough to lower Susan's knickers for her? Just as far as mid-thigh, that will be perfect for our needs.'

'Of course, sir,' replies Florenza dutifully, her voice rather more accented than Madame's and clearly indicating quite a different nationality.

I start to shake as her deft hands go about their business. My Master has not exposed me a great deal to the eyes of strangers, so this is relatively new to me. There was of course the time he invited a few male friends around to watch him cane me, but then I was blindfolded, and the resulting darkness calmed my shame.

Nevertheless, I don't resist as Florenza eases my panties down my thighs, revealing my belly, and the silky blondness of my pubic grove. I am tempted to try and cover myself, but I fight the need. As if sensing my discomfiture, my Master says, 'Hands on head, Susan. There's a good girl.'

Florenza is crouched beside me, seemingly intent on adjusting the position of my bunched white panties, but what she is really doing, I guess, is studying the sight her Madame has not yet seen. A phenomenon that will soon embarrass me even more. As the pretty servant finally straightens up, my Master abruptly calls out, 'Turn!'

I obey.

'*Quel cul ravissant!*' cries Madame, as her eyes light upon my mortifying secret. A naked bottom that's already a brilliant pink.

I feel the scrutiny of all in the room fix on me. They study my soreness, the warmed state of my buttocks. The evidence of my intractable behaviour ... There is silence for a few moments, then Madame dismisses Florenza. That she has allowed the maid to see me at all is a punishment in itself.

'Yes, I have already had to deal with her,' observes my Master as the door quietly closes. 'Susan is often disobedient and disrespectful in public, but I find a smacked bottom tends to settle her somewhat. We never leave the house without making sure she's nice and red.'

How true that is! I think if my Master had his way, I would spend my whole life with a hot, crimson bottom. Dinner parties, the theatre, the ballet; every function I attend, I attend it feeling sore. Every time I sit down, I'm reminded of his preference.

Today is a typical example of my life. My Master came to collect me at my work place, and when he was ushered into my office, and we were alone, he locked the door. Within moments, I was face down across my own desk, skirts up, pants down, whilst he belaboured my bottom-cheeks with my own plastic ruler. The snapping impacts soon raised a glow of stinging pain.

'An excellent regimen,' comments Madame, her voice approving.

'You may move to the corner now, Susan,' says my Master.

Again, I obey, my steps rendered tiny and awkward by the pants that are bundled around my thighs. I hear the tinkle of spoons and china, and smell the delicious aroma of fresh coffee. As Madame and my Master enjoy their refreshment, she outlines the facilities offered by 'Maison Guidetty'.

'As I described on the phone, Monsieur, we provide a service to dominants like yourself, who, for one reason or another, are unable to attend to their charges themselves. Whether it is due to family circumstances, or to foreign travel or work commitments, we administer discipline, in your stead, and to your exact specifications.' She pauses, then goes on with pride, 'Or if you prefer, we will create an appropriate programme for you . . . We – that is my husband, my son, my daughter and myself – are all extremely experienced with all devices, and conversant with all classic scenarios.'

I can well imagine. Madame is very handsome, with her elaborately chignoned hair, and her Parisian clothes, but she exudes an exciting air of hidden strength. Beneath her hand, a hapless bottom will sting and burn furiously, that's evident. And her eyes, beneath her long, dark lashes, are those of a true, impassioned zealot.

'And we offer a variety of arrangements to suit every need,' she continues, warming to her theme. 'For instance, a charge may simply attend once or twice a week for a sound punishment to see them through until the next visit. On the other hand, we also offer boarding facilities, for those submissives who require continuous attention.'

'I think an arrangement somewhere between those two will suit Susan best,' interposes my Master. 'She has commitments . . . Employment of her own. I wouldn't want to interfere with that . . . Perhaps she could come to you each weekend?' he suggests.

Yes, employment of my own. How ironic. What would my colleagues and subordinates think if they knew I was chairing a meeting with a bottom still raw from the lash? That beneath my Ralph Lauren skirt I was pantieless, because my inflamed cheeks could not stand the slightest brush of underwear? That my buttocks were bruised and wealed by the man I love?

'Of course,' says Madame, concurring. 'Many of our clients specify "weekends only". I would say it's our most popular option.'

They go on to discuss the finer details. And money, which seems so meaningless in this strange and special world. My Master specifies Madame herself to be my disciplinarian, and that my 'treatments' be morning, noon, and night. Especially night. It seems that even though night will not occur at the same time for us during the next few months, he wishes to dream of me lying in my bed with my buttocks scarlet.

Madame coughs delicately. 'And is she to be provided with . . .' Her voice lowers. 'With "release"?'

'Oh, yes, I think so,' replies my Master. 'Perhaps Florenza could oblige?' he suggests, his voice playful.

I shiver in dread anticipation. The dark-eyed servant does not look very kind to me. Pleasure with her might be as testing as the pain.

'A splendid suggestion,' agrees Madame. 'And perhaps I might supervise, to ensure it is correctly dispensed?'

'Of course,' concurs my Master suavely. He well knows how it shames me to be watched while I lose control.

'And now, perhaps a brief tour of the facilities? And a demonstration?' offers Madame, her soft voice full of anticipation. My instincts tell me she can't wait to get her hands on me.

'Yes! Capital!' My Master can't wait for her to get her hands on me either. 'I would like Susan to be fully acquainted with the tests that lie ahead of her.'

With that, Madame escorts us from the room, still describing the many advantages this establishment offers. I follow, at a slower pace, hampered by my underwear around my thighs, my pulses racing at the prospect of further treatment to my already smarting rump. Progress up the stairs is particularly difficult for me, with my hands still on my head, but my Master gently guides my faltering steps.

The first room we enter offers quite a sight. A young woman, completely nude, is draped over a thickly upholstered couch. Her bottom is a blazing pink, all over, and she's sobbing. Behind her stands another young woman, a breathtaking beauty; her face is flushed, her arm is high, and in her narrow, patrician hand she grasps a paddle.

'My daughter, Mariette,' announces Madame proudly, and the enchanting disciplinarian bobs a curtsey.

'Charmed, Monsieur,' she answers prettily, her fingers moving on the paddle she still clutches, as if she is anxious to continue with her task. Her fine eyes settle momentarily on my semi-nakedness, and her lips – so like her mother's – quirk with longing.

'Pray do not let us disturb you, *chérie*,' encourages Madame. 'Monsieur here is anxious to see how we deal with our charges ... He will shortly be putting Susan into our hands.'

'Of course, *Maman*,' says the young woman pleasantly, returning immediately to her task. She lifts her arm and the paddle descends with unexpected force. Mademoiselle Guidetty is far stronger than she looks. The owner of the unfortunate, becrimsoned bottom wails piteously, her hips shifting and weaving against the surface of the couch. She bears a fresh patch of deeper red on her rounded left cheek, and beneath her pelvis the moquette upholstery is visibly damp. I bite my lip to contain my moan of sympathy.

In the next few minutes, the younger Guidetty treats us to a virtuoso display with the paddle, whilst her charge puts on a show of equal vivacity. The round tongue of leather crashes down with almost metronomic regularity, its point of impact constantly circling its chubby target. The punished girl bucks and heaves across the couch, her strident squealing unrestrained and deeply stirring.

'Valerie has much to learn,' observes Madame Guidetty, and just as she speaks, Valerie howls loudly, her torso stiffening.

It is clear what has happened. Remaining rigid for a couple of seconds, the girl then flails her legs and pumps her crotch against the edge of the couch.

'Oh, Valerie,' murmurs Mademoiselle, accusingly, as the body she has been chastising jerks in orgasm. As we leave the room, she is lifting a cane from a selection in a drawer.

'My daughter is quite a stringent disciplinarian,' says Madame fondly as we move along a corridor. 'I believe she inherits her gift from me.'

My Master nods discreetly, in congratulation. I hobble behind them, my bottom bare, my flesh aroused. Other rooms pose other tests to my frazzled nerves . . .

In one, an exquisitely good-looking young man is hand-spanking an older woman whom I seem to know. I start to sweat again and I gasp, recognising her as a formidable adversary across the bargaining table – my opposite number in another prestigious company. Briefly craning her neck she looks up at me, her eyes languorous, her mouth working as the pretty youth pounds her cheeks. If she recognises me, it seems to be of little importance to her. All that matters now is the growing torment of her reddened bottom.

As we leave, Madame names the gorgeous boy as her son, Jean-Louis. I feel a sense of awe that in just one family there could be such fearsome gifts.

We do not see Monsieur Guidetty. Although we hear his work . . .

Before a closed door, we pause, listening to the sounds issuing from the hidden room beyond. I hear a heavy thudding slap, a ponderous doleful sound, then a low, weak groan. The slapping comes again, and the answering cry is ragged, extenuated, redolent with suffering. The slaps repeat. And repeat. The voice of their recipient gurgles. There is no way to tell whether the cries stem from agony or reflect a state of bliss.

'This client has requested a closed room for his charge,' says Madame in hushed tones. 'And the severe attentions of my husband. No observers . . . No manual pleasure to be given.' Although I am not supposed to, I look up and see her roll her expressive eyes. 'Just the strap. Laid on with energy. For extended periods.'

'And this will be Susan's room,' she says a little later, conducting us into a bedroom decorated in a delicate Victorian style. There is a proliferation of chintz, a very beautiful armless nursing chair, an elegant chaise longue. It is warm and cosy, and the air is rich with the essence of quiet, domestic discipline. I already see myself in a long, white nightdress of perfect purity, my buttocks uncovered as I lie across the bed, waiting to receive what is due to me.

The picture is so vivid, so meltingly appealing, that I long for it immediately to be real. Without thinking I gyrate my naked bottom, and my Master – ever watchful – notices the movement.

'Perhaps Susan can be punished here now?' he suggests, striding over to a dressing table cluttered with antique knick-knacks. He lifts a simple wooden hairbrush from amongst the profusion of gilt and crystal, and holds it out towards Madame, whose eyes light up with undisguised glee.

'Of course, Monsieur, I would be happy to accommodate you,' she says gaily, already seating herself on the chaise and arranging her skirts. My Master catches my eye, then nods in Madame's direction.

Silently, obediently, I shuffle towards her, and skilfully she tips me across her lap.

It takes just a few moments to position me correctly. Madame slides my knickers down to my ankles, but leaves them there. 'I find that underwear left around the feet impedes kicking . . . Especially when tangled around high heels.' My arms are forward, but she asks me to cross my hands at the small of my back. When I comply she firmly grips my wrists.

Waiting, I stare at the patterned carpet, aware that my Master has handed the brush to Madame Guidetty. I smell his cologne as he sits down beside us on the chaise, then feel the gentle touch of his caressing hand as he strokes my hair.

When the first hard blow smashes on to my bottom, I start to cry . . .

That was over a week ago, and now my Master is far away, and overseas.

I miss him, of course, but other pains are soothing the pain of us being apart. These pains are less abstract, and more absorbing; they divert the mind.

And this is why I'm lying face down, my buttocks bare, on my chintz-clad bed.

A little over a quarter of an hour ago, Madame Guidetty finished giving me a rigorous caning. My nightly punishment. I can still feel the savage line of each sharp cut she laid upon me; the grid of fire she worked so cleverly across my flesh. My snorts of distress are still ringing in my ears.

I cried pathetically, of course, but my Master will enjoy that. I can just imagine his secret pleasure when he receives the video.

Maybe he'll find amusement in the interlude which followed too. The sight of my engorgement being resolved by Florenza's tongue.

So, here I am, my dearest Master, I think, mentally composing an intimate letter to accompany the tape. *My bottom's hot, and it's caned bright red, just how you like it. But because it hurts, it reminds me of you, and I don't feel lonely.*

That's true. Reaching behind me, I finger my weals, their fire my solace.

I miss you madly, but I know I'm in the best of hands . . .

Sweet Revenge

Wendy Harris

*E*mma nodded mechanically as she dug her fork into a sweet and sour prawn ball. She wasn't listening to what he was saying and was in no mood to care whether a nod was an appropriate gesture or not. He was ugly and had no right to expect her full attention. Why didn't he just shut up and eat his meal?

She had only agreed to come out with him to get back at Steve for cheating on her with that skinny bow-legged tart at Samantha's party; a pancake-chested bubble-head in skintight tiger-print leggings. She'd caught them in the bathroom together, the girl with her leggings round her ankles and Steve with lipstick on his cock and a stupid grin on his face. Bastard! Emma stabbed her pancake roll with her knife.

'Take it easy,' said Rick. 'I think it's dead already.'

She looked up at his face and forced a smile. 'I'm sorry, I was miles away,' she said, wondering for the umpteenth time what had made her agree to a date with this broken-nosed oaf. He'd been at the right party at the right time, she supposed, and had caught her in a moment of weakness, boiling over with anger and fixated on revenge. He had been the first man she'd clapped eyes on after discovering her boyfriend *in fla-grante* in the bathroom. His bulldog face hadn't mattered then. In fact, she'd hardly looked at it. But now that her anger had simmered down, she was bitterly regretting her mistake.

'I've seen you before at other parties,' Rick was saying, 'always with that handsome blond guy. Steven, isn't it? You've never noticed me, of course.' He sighed and gazed wistfully at her. 'I still can't believe my luck. I never dreamt you'd go out with me. You're so beautiful.'

She smiled guiltily. Poor sod, he couldn't help being ugly. She murmured something banal and stared at his hands. They were massive, like his rugby-player's shoulders. She couldn't have chosen anyone less like Steve. Lean, svelte Steve with his fine chiselled features. This man was a gorilla by comparison, all corded muscles and thick hairy arms. She set down her knife and fork with a clatter.

'Aren't you hungry?' he asked her.

She rubbed her forehead, feigning tiredness. 'To be honest with you, Rick, I'm not feeling too well.'

His face dropped. 'Jesus, that's a pity. I was enjoying this evening. Still, if you're not well, I'll get the bill.'

He did most of the talking as he drove her home. She answered his questions politely and volunteered one or two comments of her own but her mind kept wandering. Why hadn't Steve called her? Who was he with tonight?

'Here we are,' Rick said, stopping the car outside her flat. He turned off the engine and faced her. 'Do I get a goodnight kiss?'

Emma considered a moment. She'd just as soon kiss a pig's arse. But would it hurt her to let him kiss her? He'd spent all that money on the meal. It was the least she could do. 'Sure,' she said and, closing her eyes tightly, pursed her lips and leant towards him. But he was not about to settle for a peck. His seatbelt twanged as he released himself to gather her into his arms.

His lips were surprisingly warm and firm as he pressed them lightly against hers. Experimentally at first; a butterfly kiss which gradually deepened in pressure until he was nudging open her mouth to receive his tongue. Wow, she thought, as his French kiss stirred an unexpected response in her. This man was no novice; he moved his lips with incredible sensuality. Caressing and probing with his tongue, and turning her legs to liquid. She gasped as he released her.

'Any chance of a coffee?' he uttered hoarsely.

Emma started to say no to his subliminal message but her lips were still tingling from his kiss. She was curious to know what had triggered such a powerful sensation within her. Could he fuck as well as he kissed? The train of her thoughts appalled her. How could she even think of having sex with this crooked-nosed Bluto of a man? Was she so intent on revenge that she'd sleep with just anyone to get even with Steve? She thought about it, and in a strange way it made sense. After all, it wouldn't matter what Rick thought of her in the morning. She could just use him and throw him away.

'OK,' she agreed. 'You can come in for coffee.'

But as she opened the door to her flat and switched on the light, she started to have second thoughts. This was ridiculous. She didn't even fancy him. That kiss had been a fluke. She must have been subconsciously thinking of Steve.

She decided to make him coffee in the literal sense and steered him into the kitchen. She'd get rid of him as soon as he'd drunk it.

She could feel his eyes boring into her as she reached into a cupboard for the coffee jar.

'Have you any idea how beautiful your legs are?' he murmured. 'A man could worship legs like that.'

Suddenly, before she could stop him, he was kneeling down in front of her and had lifted her foot in his hand. She leant back against the sink, her stiletto heel resting on his knee, a flutter of anxiety hammering at her heart as he began to kiss and caress her ankle. It crossed her mind briefly that he was some kind of kinky foot fetishist but, as his mouth and hands began travelling up her calf, the idea dismissed itself and she found herself experiencing a warm flush of pleasure as his erotically climbing fingers and soft searching lips explored her knees and thighs. Alarm bells rang in her head as his hands slithered up under her skirt and his hair brushed against her pubis.

'Rick, I don't think . . .' she started to say, but as he lifted his head, the expression in his eyes arrested her. They were the most attractive thing about him. Dark, Latin eyes with long curly lashes. How hot and hungry they looked.

'This isn't a good idea,' she uttered. Her protest sounded weak to her ears.

He rose to his feet, letting his hands slide up her thighs so that her skirt lifted with them as he reached his full height. She gasped as he gripped her buttocks and raised her by her haunches. God, he was strong; almost lifting her from her feet as he nuzzled into her neck.

The scent of his male musk and the warmth of his probing lips sent her fingers crawling into his hair of their own volition. But as the swell of his erection pushed against her groin and her internal muscles scrunched in response, Emma knew that she had to stop him before she lost control completely.

'How do you like your coffee?' she croaked. It seemed an odd thing to say, standing there with her skirt hiked up round her waist and his hands clamped firmly to her buttocks.

'Hot,' he rasped hungrily, lifting his hands to her breasts. Her nipples stiffened like bullets as his thumbs slid over the silk of her blouse, rotating and stroking until her breasts were straining against her bra.

'Please, Rick, let me think. I can't think,' she pleaded helplessly.

'I don't want you to think,' he said, and closed her mouth with a passionate kiss which turned her legs to jelly again. With every subtle, sensuous movement of his tongue, Emma could feel herself submerging deeper into a sea of lust and, like a drowning man clutching a straw, she thrust her hands against his shoulders and wrenched her face from his.

'We can't do this. I hardly know you,' she reminded him.

Reluctantly, he let her go. 'I understand,' he told her. 'I'm going too fast for you. But you're so damn gorgeous, I just can't help myself. I've never wanted anything as much as I want you.'

'Please, can we just cool it?' she suggested. 'Why don't you go in the other room and let me make the coffee? I need to get my head together.'

'Sure,' he agreed, 'if that's what you want.'

Was it what she wanted? Emma hardly knew as she watched him go out. Her thoughts were in turmoil. Why did her body keep saying yes to him? There was no denying that he was an accomplished seducer with a masterful touch. But didn't her brain have a say in all this? You don't want him, she reminded herself, you just want revenge. It wouldn't be fair to fuck him just for the sake of convenience. He'd get the wrong idea and think she actually fancied him. Which, of course, she didn't. He was ugly. But so was that French actor with the big nose; a lumbering ox of a man, oozing with sex appeal, who had featured in her erotic fantasies on more than one occasion. Perhaps Rick had sex appeal too. After all, you didn't learn techniques like his out of a book. Other women must have fancied him.

As the kettle boiled, Emma noticed that her hands were shaking as she laid out the cups. Surely Rick was not responsible for this sudden flurry of nerves? Emma tossed the ridiculous thought from her mind and mentally cautioned herself to dispel the absurd idea of ugly Rick being in any way similar to the French actor.

She mixed the coffee and carried the sploshing cups carefully into the lounge, almost dropping them when she saw that he had unbuttoned his shirt to the waist and was leaning back with his hands behind his head, exposing a forest of hair on a torso rippling with muscles. She stared at his chest with distaste. She liked her men smooth-skinned like Steve, not hairy like a chimp.

'What are you doing?' she asked, plonking the cups on the coffee table before moving into a chair on the opposite side of the room.

He looked at her innocently. 'Don't you think it's a little hot in here?'

He was right. She was feeling decidedly warm herself. 'I must have turned the heating up too high,' she commented.

He smiled as he reached for his cup, prompting Emma to decide that, actually, his smile was the most attractive thing about him. Good teeth; a wonderfully sensitive mouth. It was a pity about his crooked broken nose.

His dark eyes, peering at her over the rim of his cup, held a look so intense that she felt he was stripping her naked with his gaze. She shifted uncomfortably in her seat, her eyes darting towards the bedroom door. Damn, it was open. She cursed herself as she realised that his eyes had followed her gaze. What on earth did he think she was thinking? But he'd lifted his cup and lowered his eyes and she couldn't even begin to guess at his thoughts until the black crescents of his eyelashes swept upward to reveal a smouldering glow that confirmed he was thinking the worst.

She forced herself to yawn and say, 'I'm really very tired, you know.' Then her cheeks flushed as it occurred to her that he might interpret this as an invitation as well.

Sure enough, he grinned and said, 'We could always go to bed.'

'I don't make a habit of sleeping with strangers,' she snapped.

'I was only joking,' he pointed out. 'And I wouldn't say that we were strangers. I know your name and you know mine. We've had a meal together and three hours to learn about each other.'

Yes, but she hadn't been listening. In fact, the only knowledge that her brain had bothered to retain was the fact that he played scrum half and liked chicken chow mein.

He was looking at her legs again, brazenly studying them with his head to one side. She fiddled nervously with her hem as his eyes scrolled up to meet her gaze. There was no mistaking the question they posed.

'Don't look at me like that,' she said irritably, wishing that he would finish his drink and go.

'Like what?'

'You know,' she insisted, getting up and reaching for her own cup.

'Do I?' he asked, catching her hand and pulling her gently towards him. He stroked her wrist with his thumb. 'I'm not responsible for the way you make me feel,' he told her. 'If there's desire in my eyes then blame it on your beautiful face or your sexy body, but don't blame me. I'm only a man with a hard-on that won't go away.'

Her eyes flicked down to confirm the bulge in his trousers. 'I thought we agreed,' she protested feebly, wondering why her mouth was so dry. But she mustn't lick her lips; not after looking at the evidence of his erection. He'd think she was curious to know what kind of prize marrow was creating such a mountain.

His arms snaked around her hips. 'I agreed to a coffee break,' he conceded, drawing her on to his lap. 'But now it's over. So, let's get back to business.'

His dark eyes mesmerised her. She could feel her head

drooping towards him. 'Kiss me, Emma,' he commanded her softly.

What the hell, she thought. Some things were just inevitable. With a sigh of capitulation, she slid her arms over his shoulders and as he parted her lips with a bruising kiss which sucked the breath from her lungs, her body squirmed in ecstasy. As his warm lips moved sensuously over every part of her mouth, the lazy, rolling motion of his tongue wove promises of pleasure with every languid caress. Then as his kiss deepened and quickened, the thrills surging down her spine to her loins grew ever more frantic until she was clutching his head and gnawing at his lips in an agony of passion so overwhelming that her desperation to devour him became almost frenzied. Only then did he break off the kiss and nuzzle his face against her cheek.

She clung to him, exploring his bear-like shoulder with her lips, marvelling at the powerful sinews of his strength. As if he guessed her thoughts, he lifted her up and carried her into the bedroom as if she were made of feathers.

He undressed her eagerly and yet so skilfully that she hardly knew what was happening. She only knew that she was naked when she felt the tickly roughness of his chest hair on her breasts. Rotating over her nipples until they tingled and ached. The novelty of his teasing furry pelt excited her insanely and she heard herself moaning over and over with pleasure as he brushed his powerful chest up and down her body, caressing her with the mink-softness of his lush manly fleece.

She brushed her face along his bristled arm, exalting in the feral feel of him, in the earthy aroma that emanated from his skin. And as his hairy leg stroked against her thigh, she snarled as if he'd awakened something dark and primeval within her. Suddenly, she was tearing at his shirt like a tiger, wrenching it savagely from his shoulders so that she could sink her nails into his back.

He winced but continued to torment her with his tickling caresses until her desperate hands were grappling at his fly. As his zip slid down, her fingers plunged inside and released his engorged penis.

What she felt in her hands made her gasp – he was built like a stallion and as hard as tungsten steel. He groaned as her hands made the long journey up and down his shaft, throwing back his head as she pulled down his trousers and fondled his balls through the slit in his boxers. With mounting urgency, she tore at his clothes until he was naked and when she saw his beautiful body – honed like a heavyweight boxer's – a shiver of exquisite expectancy made the goose-bumps rise on her skin. She feverishly explored his muscular thighs, his taut buttocks, his massive rippling shoulders. He was beauty and the beast. Half man, half animal. And she wanted him. So desperately that her whole body ached with longing.

She spread her legs, signalling her readiness. But he was determined to take his time and moved slowly down her body, brushing her belly, then her thighs, with his hairy chest; his hands followed behind, caressing and kneading, as he descended to the mound of her sex and pushed his tongue deep inside her crevice.

She clasped his head as he lapped at her clitoris, her hips bucking to his rhythm. And then, as she started to come, he lifted himself up and pushed his swollen helmet into her labia, gently nudging her lips apart before slowly squeezing his huge cock into her sopping-wet vagina.

The walls of her sex clamped around his shaft as it plunged deep inside her and began pumping in and out; long luxurious strokes that made her wail with delight. As her muscles began to spasm, he rammed his cock harder and faster; violent, powerful strokes that would have pushed her up the bed if he hadn't been clasping her hips with his powerful hands.

The great engine of his buttocks drove his shaft like a piston as he rode her into an explosive orgasm which triggered his own thundering climax. They clung to each other, sharing a moment of pure joy, then he flopped into her arms and she hugged him to her body, smothering his neck and shoulder with grateful kisses.

'That was wonderful,' she told him, tracing his features with her fingers. 'You were amazing.'

'I had an amazing partner,' he said. 'Come on, let's get into bed and cuddle up.'

As they snuggled together beneath the sheets, wallowing in the afterglow, Emma silently thanked her body for its persistence. Had her common sense prevailed, she might never have known the glory of his lovemaking.

But her smile of happy contentment was abruptly erased when, suddenly, like a detonation, the phone rang and shattered her blissful thoughts. Reluctantly, she pulled out of Rick's hairy arms and stumbled into the lounge.

'Who is it?' she barked into the receiver.

'Hi, baby. I've missed you. Have you forgiven me yet?'

'What do you want, Steve?' she snapped.

'I want you back,' he replied.

'I'm sorry, Steve,' she told him flatly, 'I'm afraid it's all over. I don't want you back.'

'But why?' He sounded astonished, as if couldn't believe his ears. She'd always thought he was too conceited, too sure of his pretty face. 'Come on, baby,' he crooned. 'I know I've misbehaved. But I've done it before and you've always taken me back. What's changed?'

'I have,' she answered. 'I don't want you any more, Steve.'

'Why?' he persisted.

'Why?' she echoed. 'Because you're just not hairy enough.'

She smiled as she returned the receiver to its cradle. He hated riddles. It was the perfect way to leave him. She'd got her revenge after all. But somehow it didn't matter any more.

As she walked back into the bedroom, Rick's sexy dark eyes lazily scanned her body, making her deliciously aware of her nakedness.

'It's a little late for phone calls,' he said. 'Nothing wrong, I hope?'

'Wrong number,' she lied, opening the bedcovers and slithering back into his warm furry embrace. He gave her a bear hug and smiled at her. Such a beautiful smile, she thought. And, actually, his nose rather suited him.

Private Dancer

Magdalena Salt

*L*aurie's mind was elsewhere that day and nothing could bring her down to earth. Even her only employee, Serena, could not get through to her. Laurie owned and ran a small bookstore which specialised in foreign poetry and literature. She was proud of her business, especially as it was running so smoothly now. But matters at home were not.

'What the hell is it?' demanded Serena.

'Oh, I just don't look forward to seeing Justin anymore.' Serena's eyes urged her to elaborate: 'He doesn't come over for the right reasons. He comes to eat, to sleep and to –'

The conversation was abandoned as a very handsome man in his late thirties swaggered in. He was greeted by the unblinking stares of the two contrasting beauties. Laurie was dark, with creamy beige skin and a peachy body shape; Serena had pale hair, flushed cheeks and a slim figure. Elegant hand gestures accompanied her every word or thought.

He sauntered towards them only to idly pick something from the desk they stood by, quickly lose interest, and disappear between the floor-to-ceiling shelves.

'Looks like he just woke up from a long sleep on the beach,' Serena whispered. He had close-cropped but messy golden hair and a weather-tanned face; he looked like a lost beachcomber thinly disguised in stylish clothes.

'As for Justin,' said Serena, a wicked glint in her eye and her forefinger resting upon her lower lip, 'why don't you teach him a lesson?'

At first, Laurie looked blank. Then, an idea forming, her eyes glittered in response. 'Yes, perhaps you're right. Let's shut up shop, even if Mr Sandman over there is still browsing.'

Laurie returned home to find her post included the Arabic folk music she had ordered to encourage her to practice belly-dancing. She put the tape on, flung on a loose long skirt and a small top, and wrapped a scarf sown with hundreds of thin gold coins about her hips.

The soothing tones reminded her of snake-charming music, and affected her accordingly. Uncurling and twisting her arms about her head, she began to sway her broad hips in a very slow figure of eight – the scarf whispering a tinny accompaniment – whilst keeping her upper torso still. The trick, she recalled her teacher Shama saying, was to isolate the movement of different body parts. Transferring the movement to her breasts and ribcage, she made her bosom swell and relax in waves whilst her shoulders remained inert. She rolled them back and forth in a slow shimmy as the piece ended and wondered again at the perspiration generated from such subtle movements.

She looked up from her reverie to see the curtains in the flat opposite swish shut. Laurie's heart raced as she wondered who might have seen her performance. She fell back on her beige velvet sofa; for the first time since she had moved into the flat she felt acutely self-conscious, and wondered how long she had been watched, and by whom.

The sofa and bare pine-floored lounging area faced large bay windows stretching from the ceiling down to low window seats. A couple of metres from these windows lay an identical flat, whose interior was now obscured by heavy dark-coloured curtains. Laurie's flat was open plan and the massive windows her only natural light source. She had no desire to filter the light with gaudy lace curtains, so she resigned herself to the thought that she would never find the privacy she sought whilst living in the city.

Laurie watched Serena as she climbed the ladder up to the top of the third bookshelf to retrieve some over-stock. She had just finished relating her story of the previous evening, drawing it out and embellishing it to capture Serena's easily distracted attention.

'Laurie, that's really exciting. Did you catch a glimpse of them?'

'No, and I'm not sure I want to. They could be old, or anything. They might be dangerous for all I know!'

'What? In Docklands?' Serena quipped mockingly.

'Some of the most brutal serial killers have been yuppies, I'll have you know.'

'Look who's coming.' From her superior position Serena could spot people halfway down the street. It was the rugged handsome man whom they had hastily ejected the evening before. Today, he strode directly to Laurie's side to enquire after a book, and she was disappointed to find his manner to be imperious and rude. She directed him to his goal, and made a point of not responding when he blithely thanked her. Later, Serena giggled and suggested that Laurie's coldness had somehow fired the man's passion, as he had not stopped eyeing her since.

This left an indignant ember in Laurie's heart. When she got home and found that Justin had let himself in, she became still more agitated. As she entered he gave her a lazy grin from his prone position on her sofa and muttered, 'Hi, honey'. In the kitchen she discovered he had devoured much of the fridge's contents.

'Justin,' she called with the sweetest tone she could muster, 'come here, I want to play a game.' His imagination sparked, Justin coaxed himself from his place and went to where she waited at the foot of the steps which divided the split levels of her apartment. He looked rather like an over-eager schoolboy, Laurie mused.

At her instruction he removed his clothes to reveal a smooth, lean body. 'Stand here, Justin. Yes, that's right, legs apart and arms away from your sides. That's the ticket, sweetheart,' Laurie went on soothingly.

She tied him tightly to the banisters, much to Justin's growing perturbation. Feeling satisfied with her handiwork, she returned to the kitchen and collected wine, a glass, cigarettes, a lighter and a high stool. Bit by bit, with a measured slowness, she brought the items through to where Justin stood. She slipped off her shoes and skirt to leave just a suspender belt, stockings and a black basque covered by a crisp white shirt. This she unbuttoned with the tantalising finesse of a stripper.

'Laurie, baby, come here,' Justin pleaded.

'I'll come when I'm ready to come, Justin, baby.'

She made herself comfortable on the stool and sat with her stockinged legs a little apart; just enough for Justin to see her barely covered sex. She toyed with a cigarette for some time. When she lit it, Justin's face took on a frustrated aspect. She blew the smoke toward him and he begged her to let him have a drag. Wordlessly, she stood and moved close enough for him to taste the smoke; then, after one more long and considered inhalation, she stubbed the cigarette out by his left wrist. He yelped slightly and his bright green eyes flashed with anger. 'Christ, Laurie, what are you up to?'

Laurie was really enjoying herself now. This was, she

observed, the most emotion she had seen in Justin's face for a long time, and she felt powerful being the one to incite him to lose his indolent cool. Ignoring him she sang, 'I'll be right back.'

In the bathroom, Laurie could not resist putting her hand between her legs and gently caressing her clitoris. She settled her behind on the cold enamel of the bathtub and her mind wandered to the image of the impertinent blonde man who had so annoyed her that day. The memory of his strong bronze hands aroused her and she began to slide her clitoris against the enamel and finger her dark brown nipples. Eventually Justin's wails became too wrathful to ignore. Laurie restrained herself, grabbed the neroli massage oil from the cabinet, and, distinctly aware of her own wetness, returned to Justin's side.

Justin had also worked himself into a sweat, but a sweat of impotent rage. His forehead was studded with salty pearls, and his pale skin was flushed.

'Laurie, you're a bitch. Let me go!'

'Calm down! I'm sorry, I got a bit carried away in the bathroom.' As proof she dipped her forefinger in her juice and took it to his lips. 'Taste me, Justin.'

Laurie could see that despite his resentment she was succeeding in arousing him, but he refused to suck the moist finger she offered. He turned his face away, looking humiliated. Laurie picked up the oil and poured it generously into her palm. She rubbed it for a few seconds to warm it and then started to massage her full, firm breasts. She started at her already hard nipples and circled outwards slowly, paying particular attention to the sides. Laurie's face took on a dreamy expression, and when she opened her eyes, she saw that Justin's eyes were no longer averted and he was hungrily watching the lingering movement of her hands.

She dropped to her knees where she was face to face with Justin's large proud cock, which pointed straight at her. Justin was breathing hard. She took more oil and began to massage his thighs. As her hands rose nearer to his groin and she slid her thumb into the crevice of his buttocks, Justin groaned loudly. She took firm hold of each of his buttocks, and leant forward, so that she could lick and nibble his balls whilst her oily breasts slipped and bounced against his knees. She dug her nails in hard as she increased the pressure of her mouth. Justin moaned at the pain and pleasure, his rigid penis purplish with neglect. Laurie got to her feet and ripped off her basque to reveal her perfectly rounded belly and the dark silky fur which glistened beneath it.

'You're a fucking tease,' Justin whispered hoarsely.

'Don't speak.'

'Suck my cock, Laurie.'

She took the last of her Chinese scarves and gagged Justin. She then brought the stool closer and, facing away from him, she leant over it so as to give him a close-up view of her arse tilted in the air and her soaking-wet vagina. She fingered herself from between her thighs until Justin began to sob with frustration.

The tip of Justin's penis was barely an inch away from Laurie's ripe body, and he was straining desperately against the ties to meet it. Laurie, too, was finding it hard to hold back now so, slowly, she edged back until she felt the burning sensation of his glans kissing her anus. She tilted her bottom further into the air and the end of his cock found the mouth of her vagina. She cried out, all her composure deserting her, as she slid down it. She felt her buttocks bump into his hard stomach and his balls swing against her clitoris and she slid forward again, so that only the very tip was still being held tightly by her labia.

Through the muffled sound of the gag, Justin was sighing and moaning his gratitude. Laurie continued the rhythm: ramming back to the hilt and sliding out to the tip. She steadily increased the pace until, her insides on fire and her clitoris mercilessly teased by the soft whack of his balls, she came, grinding herself back against his rigid body as it contorted with its own exploding orgasm.

Laurie collapsed to the floor. After pouring a glass of wine, she studied Justin's beautiful, young, hairless chest. His eyes avoided her. His head hung dejectedly to the side, his hair in his face and the gag wet with sweat. Taking pity on him, Laurie untied his bonds. Without a word, Justin collected his clothes, dressed, and left the flat without once looking at her. Still naked but for her stockings and belt, Laurie walked to the sofa, where she languidly studied the television guide.

Without looking up, she remembered the flat opposite. In the corner of her eye she could see light coming from their window, and a movement of some sort. Slowly, she looked up to find no one there, but again felt as if she had just missed them, as if there were something in the room still moving from a hurried exit.

Laurie wrapped herself in a gown, and seating herself comfortably on the window seat, perused the flat's interior in the hope of finding a clue as to its occupants. She saw a large black leather armchair facing the window. Apart from this imposing piece of furniture, the place was quite empty. The walls were unadorned but for pine shelves carrying a stereo. Laurie eventually gave up trying to play detective, and retired to her bed feeling vaguely dissatisfied, despite the evening's events.

A few days later, Laurie hadn't heard a word from Justin. At this she was neither surprised nor particularly disappointed. Her thoughts were mostly occupied with the exquisitely haunting feeling that someone was watching her every movement.

In a moment of anxiety, Laurie telephoned Serena. 'Look, I'm sure I'm being watched. They're just too quick for me. Whenever I turn my head the lights go out, or the curtains close, or the door shuts.'

'Laurie, take the day off. That'll surprise them. Keep your curtains closed and peep through the side. I can manage here.'

'Thanks, Serena, you're wonderful. I'll give it a go.'

Laurie spent an hour peering through a tiny crack in her curtains at the flat opposite. Today there was a man's shirt strewn across the leather seat, but nobody entered the room. The only thing she learnt was that the occupant was male, had good taste in shirts, and that it is extremely easy to watch without being seen. Bored with such an unfruitful occupation and anxious to get out into a fresh and sunny May day, Laurie put on a button-through dress in light cream cotton and took the train to work.

Laurie walked into her shop to find it empty of people. Walking cautiously to the back between the high shelves, she heard a soft sigh.

'Serena?' Turning a corner, Laurie came upon a man with Serena's silky slim legs wrapped tight around his waist. Their faces were buried in a passionate kiss.

'For God's sake, Max, can't you wait till after 5.30?' yelled Laurie.

Max, taking his time, turned around. 'Hi, Laurie, it's lovely to see you, too.' Serena looked pink and sheepish whilst trying to hide behind him.

'Get out of my shop, now,' Laurie demanded in a measured tone.

Max kissed Serena's face tenderly and strolled out.

'Laurie . . .' Serena began beseechingly, her hands fluttering.

Furious, Laurie grabbed Serena's wrists to shake her, but Serena leant over and kissed Laurie firmly on her lips. Dumbfounded, she froze, and saw just past Serena's shoulder the haughty blond man walking softly away from them. Laurie gasped and motioned to Serena, who stifled a giggle, and bold as only she could be, jogged over to where he stood browsing. 'Do you need any help there, sir?' she asked.

'No, I would like to speak to the owner, if you don't mind,' he replied, his face impassive.

Rebuffed, Serena returned to where Laurie still stood, feeling dazed. 'He wants you, I'm afraid.'

Laurie approached him. 'What can I do for you?'

'My name is Charles. If I may be so bold, I would like you to come out with me tonight so that I might put a proposal to you.' Laurie was half-listening whilst thinking about Serena and wondering what had just happened.

'Well?' he asked impatiently.

Flustered, Laurie nodded. He told her he would meet her at nine o'clock in a Soho bar.

Before Charles had even left the shop, she regretted the arrangement. She had accepted an invitation from the most disagreeable man she had ever come across. He was formal yet over-familiar. They had barely exchanged ten sentences and he had invited her out. How presumptuous.

'Oh, Serena, what have I done?' she wailed.

'I don't know, what have you done?' Serena replied, having tentatively reappeared from the back of the shop.

'I'm having drinks with Charles, tonight.'

'Charles is it? Well, well, I might have known. I could tell his interest in Hungarian poetry was waning,' Serena teased.

'Actually I think it's a business matter.'

'So how come you look so uptight about it?'

'It's his manner.'

'You never know. It might be fun,' Serena said. 'And about earlier: I'm really sorry . . .'

'About kissing me? No, it was –'

'No, I mean Max. It was really unprofessional of me.'

'And kissing your boss without warning isn't?!' At

this they both dissolved into giggles, and the matter was closed.

Laurie wafted into her flat and put on her belly-dancing music. The last of the day's sun was still gleaming through the windows as she began to warm up to the slow, hypnotic beat of the *kahnu*. She wore just an ivory satin bra and G-string with gold detail. She also had a matching slip which she pulled down to rest on her hips. Closing her eyes and relishing the smooth breeze from the window tops, she bent her torso forward and wound her hips round in a full circle. Her arms dropped lazily forward as her hips went back, and fell behind as she swung them to the front again.

Steadily, the music gained momentum, and her hips jutted out to each side in synch. She shimmied and flicked her hips with abandon, until the music reverted to a slow tempo, which she used to slide her ample breasts from side to side and unfurl her fingers above her head. She alternated between these two styles, and, opening her eyes as the music picked up for the last verse, she saw that a figure was seated in the room opposite.

The room was barely lit by the electric light that shone faintly through the door behind him. Laurie's body was so taken by the music that it barely illustrated her shock. Gulping a breath she led her dance into an exotic frenzy. The appearance of an audience had brought the most salacious smile to her lips and a playful coquetry to her movements. Sweat was trickling down her neck, and her bosom heaved and blushed as she shimmied provocatively to the last bars.

She couldn't see the face of her observer, as the lighting behind him threw his figure into silhouette. She bowed down to the floor flirtatiously. Slowly rising, her body bent at a right angle to her legs, and her dark curls half covering her face, she saw the man clapping, slowly.

This jolted Laurie back to reality, where she found herself half naked and being mocked by her voyeur. She rushed to the windows and whisked the curtains shut.

Laurie showered and, feeling extraordinarily alive, put on in a peach satin dress which fitted neatly around her hourglass middle, and a grey linen blazer. As she made her way to Soho, the thick air washed away all her euphoria, and her heart sank at the realisation of who she had to spend the evening with. On entering the bar she immediately wished she had worn underwear and a longer dress. She scanned the tables before her for some thirty seconds before spotting him with his stiff posture and lazy eyes staring boredly at her.

'You could have waved.'

'Yes, I could have,' he replied, and stood to plant a hot-lipped kiss at her temple and slip the jacket from her shoulders in one easy motion. He sat down and stared at her intensely. 'Can I get you a drink?'

'I'll have a large vodka and lime please,' said Laurie with as much bravado as she could muster.

'I like the way you move, Laurie.'

Affronted, Laurie looked down at her hands. Suddenly desperate to take his gaze and the conversation away from herself, she questioned him brightly. 'Tell me a bit about yourself, Charles. I'm sitting with a stranger and . . .'

'Yes of course. I spend most of my time flying between Dubai and London. I have a hotel there. Now I intend to spend more time here as there is, at last, something to keep my attention for more than five minutes.' He continued with a brief summation of his expatriate background. His words appeared confident, and his casually thrown together clothes gave him an air of nonchalance that nagged at Laurie, who was over-dressed by comparison. He had on a camel-coloured V-neck sweater over a white T-shirt, and wore crisp dark blue denim on his legs. And yet, for all his self-assurance, his hand shook a little as he lit Laurie's cigarette.

A few drinks later, and Laurie was no more comfortable than when she had arrived. 'Look, why did you invite me to spend the evening with you?' she asked, emboldened by the steady flow of vodka.

He looked deep into her eyes and she held her breath. 'Frankly, I grew tired of watching you through the cracks in the curtains and between bookshelves, like some sort of pervert.'

Laurie's mouth fell open.

'I want to touch you,' he said simply.

'Oh God, you're crazy.' Laurie jumped to her feet to leave, but he grabbed her wrist and said, 'You knew you were being watched, Laurie.'

'I don't know what the hell you're talking about,' she faltered.

'I saw it in the way you moved.' Charles murmured, holding her eyes in his. 'Your dancing flowered under my gaze; every movement you made became more erotic when you realised you had an audience; even if it was just stretching to change the volume on the stereo or –'

'Stop it, shut up!'

Charles's eyes glinted sadistically at her protests. 'And what about your little performance with the young man? Did it never occur to you to close the curtains?'

'Christ, I'm so stupid.'

'No, you're just a very beautiful exhibitionist, and now that you've taunted me these last weeks, I want to have you.'

His dark, handsome eyes crinkled at the corners a little, as if her horror were quite amusing to him, and she was reminded of his mocking applause earlier that evening. Laurie's heart was beating hard as she pulled away from the hand that still held hers and ran from the bar like a frightened child.

* * *

She fell through the front door and it suddenly dawned on her that her lovely new home was no longer a haven. She stripped off the damp peach satin, fell into her bed, and listened to her breath quieten.

After an hour or two of fitful sleep, Laurie awoke to an aching feeling between her legs; her fingers discovered that she was slick and warm. Her clitoris became quickly swollen beneath the deft circling movement she made with her fingers. She wanted to have an orgasm so that she could sleep properly, but every time she came anywhere near a peak her mind snapped back to the incident in the bar. The intensity of Charles's stare had terrified and shamed her. Everything he had said was true.

Giving herself up to frustration, she dragged herself from the bedroom to the kitchen, where she poured herself a large glass of pink grapefruit juice. The bittersweet taste stung her dry lips. She proceeded to the lounge after wrapping herself in a bath sheet and tiredly reflected on the week's events.

Suddenly, for all her reservations about Charles, she couldn't help going to the curtains and whipping them wide open. There he was, sitting easily in the great leather chair, which was revealed for the first time by full lighting. He was sipping a liqueur of some sort and he smiled sardonically at Laurie. This discovery sent a ripple of intense pleasure down her spine which settled in the crook of her groin. Feeling bold, she opened the window to let some fresh air inside.

His bare tanned chest was decorated with a fistful of blond curls. Dropping her arms to her sides, she let the towel fall at her feet and stood there in her naked glory. He took a large gulp of his drink and adjusted his position in the seat. Never leaving his eyes, she rested one foot on the window seat so that her vagina was open and started to stroke herself again. She kept a slow pace, and found herself shivering uncontrollably at the sight of his penis swelling against the stiff denim of his jeans and his strong jaw tightening with repressed desire. She looked at him as if to say, is this what you want?

Laurie collected a dildo from her bottom drawer. When she slid the tip into her sex, Charles got to his feet and walked to the window. He pressed himself right up against the glass, and Laurie was made aware of how close he was, with only a few metres separating their windows. His stare had dropped from her eyes to her pussy, and, as she slid the black staff further inside, his body flinched. Pressing it in until she was full she let her head fall back and groaned, exposing her neck and arching her back so that her breasts thrust towards him enticingly.

Laurie had become feverish with pleasure and was on the verge of becoming abandoned to it, when her provocateur beat hard on the window. Laurie saw determination in his eyes. Then he disappeared. The next thing she knew, someone was ringing the doorbell. Of course, it was him.

Once inside, he smiled an almost predatory smile and said, 'Now for a taste of your own medicine.'

First he blindfolded her, and then, taking her hand in his, he led her through to the bedroom, where he instructed her to kneel on all fours on the raised futon. His voice was cold and businesslike. Laurie felt that she would not question anything he asked of her now. She abandoned all power.

She heard nothing for a couple of minutes. Then, suddenly, there was a large smack as the flat of his hand landed on her bottom. Her skin smarted but she did not complain or cry out. He spanked her twice more and then all was quiet and still. Eventually she felt him place his hot, dry hands on her behind. He stroked the pain and it magically transformed into pleasure.

Every so often his hand brushed the springy fur which

hid her outer lips; it was like a current running through the hairs to electrify the whole surface of her sex. Next, she felt a feather caressing her face, her cheeks and then her lips, so that she suddenly ached to be kissed. It occurred to her that she was naked and blind with someone she had never kissed.

Then the feather travelled insufferably slowly down her silken throat, and circled each of her breasts. Instead of feeling the soft caress reach her nipples, she was startled by his fingertips squeezing them so hard that she cried out involuntarily. He twisted and rubbed them until their brownness turned to dark crimson.

As he caressed her inner thighs and bush with the feather, she felt her clitoris harden. She grabbed the duvet in her fists tightly so as not to give her desire away by arching toward it. Then she felt his hot breath on the backs of her thighs, and she realised he must be on his knees at the foot of the bed. Presently, she felt his fingers gently part her labia and his tongue delve deeply into her pussy. She moaned long and loud. Charles responded by flicking his tongue on her clitoris, and gently blowing on its wetness.

She heard him move. Now his hands guided her back on to his upturned mouth, and she straddled his face. Laurie rocked back and forth, and rotated her hips, so as to alter the pressure of his mouth.

Her whole body began to tense up and shake above him in anticipation. Charles eased out from between her thighs and seated her on the edge of the bed, where she soaked the duvet with her honey. She heard the sound of his belt being unbuckled, and the sexy denim slide down to the floor.

Like a blind woman she reached out to where she thought he stood. She felt the curls that nestled between his firm pectorals first, and, running her hands slowly down his ribcage to his narrow hips, reached the fuzzy trail which began at his navel and led her fingertips down to the base of his stallion-hard cock. She leant forward so that her silky hair fell like water on it, each lock clinging momentarily like a ghostly finger. Her mouth found the end of his cock. She licked its circumference, pushing the foreskin back with her tongue, and lunged forward to envelope the whole length in her mouth.

She rose and fell petulantly on his cock whilst cupping his balls in both hands. Eventually he pushed her back, lifting her curvaceous creamy legs into the air and squeezing his penis between her thighs and into the warm wet slit of her sex. As he eased himself into her, she felt the first wave of ecstasy course through her body. The end of his cock burnished her insides whilst his pubic bone rubbed against her clitoris. He rested her ankles on his muscled shoulders and then, at long last, he kissed her.

He was utterly in control of the thrusts that pulsed into her, whilst Laurie was at the mercy of the violent contractions that seized her insides. As she cried out with mad bliss she ripped her blindfold away, and she saw his face lose all its stately composure as his hot liquid surged into her body.

After they had rested a while, Charles said, 'Come, let's dress, I have something to show you.' Laurie was intrigued: what more could there be after such a performance? Charles took Laurie's hand and led her to his own flat. They entered the room she had only seen as an outsider. She fingered the leather armchair.

'Sit down, sit in the chair, Laurie.'

She did as he said. Behind her she heard the soft click of the light switch and the room was plunged into black. After blinking for a moment she saw her flat and the remnants of their love-making. Then she saw that there were other flats lit up besides hers. To her left there was a couple watching television, and to the right, another couple gesturing at each other wildly.

'Look through these.' Charles handed her a pair of weighty binoculars. With them, to her astonishment, she could see that the seemingly innocent couple snuggling on the sofa were actually watching a porn film whilst fondling each other, and the couple who had been arguing were now ripping at each other's clothes with a savage energy. Laurie could even see the way their eyes glittered with arousal.

'They do that regularly: fight and make up.' Laurie jumped at the sound of his voice, having become so involved in their passion.

'Now do you see what I see?' He breathed into her neck. 'The only difference between you and them is you knew you were being watched.'

Laurie felt the full force of his words and it suddenly dawned on her what she had let herself into; she was inextricably tied up in his risqué pastime. Was what he was doing against the law? She'd read about men with hobbies like his. Was she risking prosecution by aiding and abetting his fun?

She felt Charles begin to gently massage her shoulders. He did it in such a sensuous way that she was almost distracted from her feelings of anxiety. The lease on her flat bound her for the coming year, so if she couldn't handle Charles watching her she would have to shut her curtains for good. And yet he is such a masterful lover, and my dancing *has* improved over the last week or so, thank to Charles's little kink, thought Laurie.

In an expressionless tone, Charles said, 'Now let me show you my bedroom.' She searched out his face in the dark and caught a familiar glint in his dark eyes. Laurie laughed, put her apprehension to the back of her mind and, grasping his warm hand, she followed him.

The Red Petticoat

Rhiannon Taliesin

*M*adlen gazed out across the valley that stretched below. She breathed in the sweet mountain air that could only be found at the top, and slowly descended into the valley's hot ire. The steam from the nodding pit wheels rose into the air, settling on her burning skin.

She gaily skipped over the puddles of scum that lay about her, red petticoat catching the dulled sun that peeped through the steamy haze. This was what had become of her beloved South Wales.

The boys wolf-whistled from the distance, their beady eyes lingering on the sweetness that only a young eighteen-year-old body could exude. She'd not married. Not yet. They all wanted her. Wanted her long slick black hair on their chests, her high breasts on their lips. Iolo, the foreman's son, wanted her more than anything else. He was a strapping boyo – tousled hair of coal-black and sinews reaching all the way down to a powerful muscle of love.

Iolo called out through the hot haze. 'Madlen.'

She stopped and slowly turned around. 'Ai, what do you want, Iolo?'

Her tone was quite rough. She had been brought up

in a stinking hovel in Llanboidy, the next town over, where language was irrelevant to survival.

'Madlen, he stuttered. 'I . . . I want you to go down North Pit today.'

'North Pit? Christ, it's full of the boys. How am I to work in this heat with all them boys, Iolo?' She smiled a secret cat-like smile. Iolo knew exactly what she was saying. The heat was so unbearable that the women and men stripped at least to the waist to work. Cramming them in together only meant one thing for Madlen. Fun.

'It can't be helped, we need a tram maiden quick. I'll join you later to see if there's any problems.' Madlen was grinning by now.

'Oh you will, will you, Iolo? I can guess what that means, you dirty bugger.'

Humming an old tune she skipped away to the giant cage that would take her down, down into the bowels of the earth where men and women become beasts of the dark.

Madlen's eyes scoured the black until she got her bearings. She could hear the soft chorus of a hymn deep down in gate four; the men were already hard at it. She dragged a huge wooden tram from the holding area and pushed it towards the gate. As the tram trundled down-hill she jumped in for a free ride; but the ride she had in mind for later – once she had loaded the first stack – would be far more fun.

The boys saw her coming, petticoat flapping in the down-draught.

'Here she comes, boys. We're in for a treat today. Old Iolo's up to no good sending her here.'

Dirty laughter filled her ears as the tram came to a lurching stop.

'All right, boys, she said. 'I've been sent as your tram maiden, so get to bloody work and let's fill this bloody truck before you all burst.'

The boys hacked away at the wet coal, filling the tram

with every intake of breath. Madlen was the best cure for any lazy bastard who wouldn't work and Iolo knew it. She could be trusted to help any lagging mine, boosting productivity.

There was always a gap between filling and trucking away. It was this gap that kept Panty mine going all these years. Madlen's family had a history of fine women, and they were all used in the same way. The preacher called them the heathen sluts of Llanboidy, and it was no coincidence that Madlen had battle scars from the jealous wives working the other side who couldn't get near their loved ones. They never knew if their men had slaked their lust with her or not. The whole mine was awash with the scandal. The women even threatened to strike.

The last shovel of coal was piled high and the men stood around relaxing their tense, hard muscles for a few minutes. Madlen smiled their reward and pulled the red petticoat high over her knees. The men licked their lips with longing. She hadn't visited them for a while.

Madlen placed herself delicately against the tram. The boys were bursting, their engorged cocks pulsating and their eyes filling red with lust. Thomas, standing nearest to her, felt the pressure unbearable as Madlen rubbed herself hard. She let out an initial gasp and quickly found her prize. Her fingers, bobbing in and out of her warm place, were moist with her liquid.

The boys were terrified. She had an aura of complete sex about her. They sniffed the coal dust air as her juices and musky scent permeated it. She was the mossy Welsh earth beneath the strength of great oaks. The boys' branches bowed down to her every whim. They were transfixed. Encroaching footsteps approached the rear of the queue. Iolo strode purposefully through the scene of seduction and stood like a great fired-up engine in front of her.

'OK, boys, watch me and follow on if you got spunk.'

His words dispelled the mystery that had been set up by her prodding and pushing inside her secret place. Iolo removed his belt and let his braces down. He was clean all over, shining like a pearl in a shell, and she was like a black puma; eyes glistening through the soot, a caged animal that could only be satisfied in the wilds of the mountains. Iolo slowly undid each button of his trousers, popping them one by one, the sound of bed time – end of shift. A nice sound.

His giant Celtic penis reminded Madlen of Cernunnos, the great three-horned lover whose power and awe kept the Romans shaking in their boots for hundreds of years. She was his Cerridwen, the enchantress of the wild mountainous woods, who would use her cauldron, filled with his juices, to bring forth Gwion as a sign of her fertility.

'Well, Madlen. This what you want, ai? All these boys looking at you, isn't it?'

He lurched towards her, grabbing her thin arms, and threw her red petticoat up about her like a reverse lampshade. He violently ripped away her underclothes, exposing her glistening fur to all around. Grabbing her buttocks hard, he tweaked them as if they were coals in the walls. The boys cheered around them in a circle, pushing and shoving for the best view.

'Come on my pretty. This is what you're paid for, to be a showgirl.' His voice was so masterful now he was below ground with the bucking rabbits, his usual stutter diminishing with every violent pound that he gave her aching quim.

His arse bobbed up and down, pushing her into the tram's side. She could feel the fire welling up inside her with every thrust of his cock. With her wetness increasing, she could feel her juices dripping slowly down her leg, leaving a trailing tongue of passion, a glistening jewel of love and desire. Iolo's love.

'Go on, Iolo,' shouted Thomas.

'He's going for first prize,' shouted another.

The jeering and shouts just inflamed Iolo more and more. He suddenly stopped, looked into Madlen's eyes and, grinning, said, 'Thomas – come here, boy. Give us a hand. She's good for two.'

Thomas's face burned with desire. He ripped his trousers open and his cock sprang out.

'Get behind her, Thomas – there's a lad.'

Thomas immediately fell in behind Madlen, who was in ecstasy.

He spat on his coal-dust hands and covered his cock with the warm liquid. He parted her buttocks as gently as he could and placed his staff between the clefts. With a little push he had his tip inserted into her globes.

'Yes,' she cried out.

With indrawn breath, Thomas pushed his cock hard until he was right up inside her, balls slapping against her back. She screamed out her passion. The sensation was overwhelming. Her whole being felt on fire; she burned with the valley's hot ire, with the anger and passion of millions who had slaved for the English over the years. She burned for her mother who had died in childbirth. She burned for Iolo. She needed him. He alone understood her desperate sexual yearning.

Thomas could feel his old school pal, Iolo, inside her other entrance. Madlen's breasts were now held in a vice lock by Thomas, who was playing with them, a look of delight on his face. The greasy smears of coal-dust were over her whole body. Madlen felt truly dirty. The dirt made her laugh out loud. It made her feel free from the bonds of womanhood. She was not the virginal pure spirit, dead from the waist down, she was a pioneer, getting dirty with the boys, working alongside them, searching for the black gold – the mineral God had given her people.

Her thoughts evaporated as her body started to jerk with the ensuing orgasm. The boys standing around the show shouted with excitement. Madlen was carried on wave after wave of wetness and orgasm. Her sex, pounded and swollen, couldn't hold any longer. She could feel Thomas reaching her soul. The cheering and clapping about her reached a crescendo as Thomas finally gasped his last.

'My God, Iolo, I'm done. Keep giving it to her.'

Some of the boys around the edge of this sideshow could not help stroking their own cocks. One boy, nineteen years, couldn't wait his turn. He moved over to Iolo, who was still rhythmically pounding her, and pushed him slightly apart from her. He stood over her stomach stroking his stiff cock towards her red petticoat. Madlen released a muffled gasp. The boy spent and Thomas collapsed. Sweet juices filled her very soul.

A second after, Iolo spent his vibrant liquid, flooding her. All four collapsed on to the damp ground. Madlen felt at peace with this bunch of young bucks. She was happy that, even in the surrounding industrial wasteland, she could still see beauty – beauty in the passion and vibrancy of Welsh loins.

Iolo slowly stood up, doing up his trews. He helped Madlen to her feet.

'OK boys, get back to work now. I'll be back later in the shift.'

With a gentle kiss on Madlen's burning face he walked away, spitting into the dust to clear his throat. The boys grumpily returned to work, many wet and uncomfortable in their trews. A young lad looked up at his uncle working near him. 'My mam will kill me. She says I'm a dirty sod with my undergarments creamed up.' His uncle smirked.

Madlen straightened herself out. She looked haughtily about her and, with a hoarse, husky whisper, implied she'd be back later. She tied the chains around her waist and pulled the heavy-laden tram. The chains cut into her hot flesh; this gave her an idea for some fun she could have later.

The lunchtime bell rang out across the valley. People were eating tuck and meeting their wives from the other side. Everyone relaxed in the hazy sunshine. Madlen sat on the warmed grass and supped on her bread and Caerphilly. The food gave her strength and she felt almost ready for the afternoon.

Some of the women were gazing at her. She heard one call out to her: 'You're nothing but a tart, you. Yes, you, Madlen slut Jenkins. Your whole family is scum. Your mam were found fucked to death over the tramlines. That's how you'll end up.'

Madlen smiled wanly at her; she was used to their insults. At least she was still beautiful, could afford a little extra for herself. Where they were wilting she was blooming. Another voice joined in. 'Look at her. She's like the cat that got the bloody cream. If she's had my husband I'll have her in strips dangling on hooks.'

Madlen stood up and proudly walked away.

The bell rang for the end of break. She stepped into the giant cage and felt the jerking of the old motor as it slowly crept down to hell. The next time she'd see it would be the end of the shift. The cage grumbled and she could hear over the other side the echoes of cackling women, no doubt laughing at nothing. She disliked women. She needed only men. And lots of them. Their smell pumped through her veins and their delicious cocks kept her happy.

The cage stopped and she daintily stepped back into the darkness, her eyes gradually adjusting to it. Her tram was waiting for her. As she pushed it back towards gate four, where her strong boyos would be waiting with their pick shafts and flaming cloth caps, she thought about her future with these beautiful people whose community she had been born into. She thought of their bodies, sweating, glistening in the moist, lurid air.

The smell of coal gases mixing with sperm and sweat was irresistible to her and, at that moment, she felt the happiest girl alive. As her tram moved towards its destination she could feel herself wet all over again. A bitch on heat, full of desire, she could satisfy the men's choir if she desired. The boys stood up from their crouching positions, waiting for her. They removed their caps in respect and asked if she was all right. The young lad of nineteen was red in the face and desperate to say something.

'Oh for heaven's sake, Moisen. What does the boy want?' Madlen was impatient.

His uncle spoke up for him in stutters. 'Well, my lad is a virgin.' The boy went purple as the others sniggered.

'You see, I don't know a lovelier person than you, Madlen. Other women I know think different and that's 'cos you're lovely and they – well they . . . Anyway, will you give my boy a treat?'

Madlen laughed at the forlorn boy standing before her. She took his hand and disappeared up the coal shaft, shouting as she pulled him behind her, 'I'll be back soon. Don't tell Iolo. It's not fair play to the lad if you see.'

Madlen found a crevice and sat the lad down. She crouched beside him.

'You never touched a girl afore?'

'No miss, I . . .'

'Don't worry, my pretty, we'll soon sort you out.'

Madlen took his small hands and placed them down her flimsy top. She pulled out one breast and let the young lad have a feel.

'It's soft. Like your head, boy,' Madlen laughed sweetly. She undid his trouser buttons with her teeth; gradually the swelling penis, unsheathed, protruded out of his underpants. In the darkness Madlen could see his cock shining like a great sword. She tasted its sweetness and covered his whole cock with her mouth. She worked up and down slowly, titillating and teasing its raw end. Gradually, she changed her tactics and aggressively nipped at the edges. The lad let out a gasp of longing. Madlen stopped. He was near.

'Not yet, my lovely. We've got loads to do.'

Just as she moved herself around for a better position in the cramped space, Iolo came whistling down the corridor. He saw his girl entwined with the young lad and exploded.

'What the bloody hell do you think's going on here?'

He grabbed Madlen roughly and threw her to the other side of the pit. The boy's trousers, wrapped around his ankles, trapped him, and he could run nowhere. Iolo towered above him and boomed out: 'Listen, my lad, you better get going quick afore I rips your ears off! Go! Try yourself out on some other maid and leave my Madlen be!'

The boy scampered away as fast as he could, stumbling back to work.

'Now,' he said, turning to Madlen, who was grinning like a fool.

'It's no laughing matter. You've been a very naughty girl and you need to be punished.' Iolo pulled her roughly towards him and pushed his tongue into her budding mouth, but he was still angry.

'Come on, my pretty. I've got a new game for you.' He was looking at the chains on the tram. Madlen had noticed their restricting beauty earlier; he'd read her mind. He roughly placed her against the end of the metal and chained her legs apart. The uneasy positioning made her feel stretched. She was slightly uncomfortable but willing and ready. Iolo then tied her arms up against the tram cage. Her whole body was lifted clean off the floor. The tram could be moved on its tracks with

her there, open to the whole world; the vulnerability
was intoxicating.

'Come on, we're going on a little trip.' Iolo pulled the
other end of the tram and led her up towards gate four.
As he walked he spoke a little more calmly: 'Madlen, I
know you're a tyke but I want you as my wife; you can
work with me up the top in the office.'

Madlen could not believe her ears. She'd been here
since she was five years of age. The blackness was part
of her life but it seemed that Iolo had other plans for
her. The tram stopped and Iolo hit the safety brake. He
stared at Madlen tied up – all red petticoat and black
hair tumbling down to her waist. He slowly took his
jacket and cap off. He pulled down his braces and slowly
undid his belt. The belt lingered for a second in his
hand.

'Shall I teach you some manners?'

The belt cracked the air around her and she braced
herself for a delicious flogging, but Iolo dropped it to
the floor.

'No, I want you welt free, my pretty.'

He carried on removing his clothes slowly. Madlen
thought of his muscular body, his protruding biceps and
firm legs. Most of all she thought of his massive cock
which, when he stood naked, made him look like the
god she'd prayed for on the mountain. On its top were
ancient standing stones like giant penises protruding
towards the sky. They had been left as a testimony of
the power of Welsh fertility. And now she was here, in
the mine, awaiting the wrath of her god in the bowels of
the earth. The thought made her wet.

He slowly approached her, grabbing handfuls of her
hair and forcing her to meet his prying tongue. She
exhaled in shudders as he gently lapped his tongue
down her neck, throat and breasts, biting her nipples
here and there. She could feel little explosions of desire
through her breasts. She could feel his cock rubbing

itself up and down slowly along her leg, getting harder and more urgent with every light touch. She could feel his piercing end seeping a delicious liquid; a liquid that she wanted to feel inside her mouth, its dripping, honey-like substance covering her lips with all its sweetness and goodness.

'Oh, you vixen.' Iolo saw her thoughts in her dark eyes. 'Do you want to suck old Iolo, eh?'

She couldn't speak. Her voice was lost somewhere in her throat. She nodded longingly, like a mute animal asking for food.

'Come on, then.' Iolo untied her arms and removed the chain that held her wide open. He turned her around and retied her. She was now forced against the end of the tram facing the carriage itself, her breasts and lower body pressed hard against the cold steel. Iolo, stood behind her to check the fastenings. As he did, he lifted up her petticoat from behind, pulling down her bloomers at the same time. He fingered her roughly and exposed her beautiful globes.

'Now, my dear, you will have your wish.' Iolo jumped into the carriage and stood in front of her. His groin was level with her head and his cock pushed into her face. She couldn't wait. Iolo pushed himself towards her lips and she gladly sucked the glistening honey that had been building up. He let out a gasp of relief. He pushed her head to receive the full length of his cock and Madlen happily let him.

Iolo could hold no more: 'I'm coming, my Cerridwen, hold on.'

A stream of pale nectar ran down Madlen's cheek and he bent down to cover her with all the kisses he could muster. It was now her turn for this luxury.

Iolo jumped out of the tram and went back to Madlen's rear side. He fell to his knees and started licking her legs from her ankles. She tasted of mulled wine and he happily licked his way slowly up the inside of her legs. She moaned and lurched to move but, held fast by the chains, couldn't stop his prying tongue from invading her very being.

Slowly, slowly, he reached his goal. Lapping her clitoris like a kitten at its milk, Iolo gently built up the pressure against it. He got harder and harder until his tongue disappeared completely, deep into her quim. As it darted it in and out she could feel wave after wave of restricted fucking from his tongue. She couldn't move an inch and she longed to press her legs together to squeeze her clitoris completely into submission.

He then changed tactics and came away from her sex, licking back towards her exposed behind. He loved her arse. She had solid globes like two fresh cottage loaves coming out of the oven, toasty hot and ready to be dripping with sweet Welsh butter. With that thought in mind, he feasted on her. His tongue seem to grow longer, reaching crevices previously unknown, and Madlen ached to be properly fucked.

'Oh Iolo, untie me now and fill me up.' Iolo gently untied her arms and waist and spun her around to meet his face. She was longing for his cock. He smiled and against the solid iron tram he took her deeply. She cried out even though she knew his cock. She was always surprised when he took her so masterfully. Her stomach lurched as he pounded his hardened flesh into her. She was afire, her nipples hard and raw as she rubbed them against his furry chest.

He plunged into her wet and slippery depths. As she lurched forward, crying out in gasps, he continued his mission. Madlen moaned, saying filthy things to him in Welsh as the invading cock pounded her. Iolo held her hard in a vice-lock of love.

She couldn't hold out any longer – wave after wave of orgasm came over her, flooding her quim with scented waters. Her cries could be heard along the mineshaft two miles down the valley at gate one – an affirmation of the joy and unbridled passion which filled her very being. She wanted to give Iolo everything.

Iolo dressed and stood back to let Madlen breathe.

'Madlen, will you be my wife?'

'Ai, you've passed the test. I still have my petticoat in one piece. It'll scrub up lovely for the wedding.'

Iolo bent down to his discarded coat and pulled a beautiful red silk camisole and matching bloomers out of his deep, inner pocket. Madlen gasped at the finery.

'Will this do you? It's about time we changed a few things around here, including that old petti you live in.' Iolo planted a dainty kiss on Madlen's nose and whispered: 'We'll start by getting you up the top and into a hot tub. Scrubbed up, you'll shine like new.'

Madlen let herself be carried like a child and placed gently into the tram. Iolo smiled at her and gently set about putting the chains around his own waist. As he pulled he shouted out up ahead.

'Look boys, I've got myself a tram maiden!'

Mindless Raptures

Larissa McKenzie

Natasha boarded late and walked almost the full length of the dusty old train before she found the compartment she'd been looking for. Or more exactly the contents she'd been looking for. The compartment had a sole inhabitant: a smartly dressed, ruggedly handsome young man, his easy bearing discernible in the way he had spread himself in his seat.

Entering and taking her seat directly opposite and forcing him to begrudgingly shift his long legs, she eyed him a little more closely; he had strong but elegant features with short, dark, curling hair.

He glanced up at her with limpid blue eyes. Both eyed each other in that brief instant.

Hearing the guard's whistle Natasha settled back with her head against the headrest. The train eased out of the station and began to rumble along the track.

'Strange weather,' Natasha said.

The young man gave her a tight, dismissive smile. It was a non-stop journey to Brighton and Ben had hoped to have the place to himself so that he could work on his best man's speech. He was looking forward to it. He knew he was a natural in front of an audience: confident,

258

witty, assured. Some girls he'd been out with had accused him of arrogance – but they loved it really.

As she gazed out of the window, Ben gave his travelling companion a more thorough once-over: a brunette, with thick, dark, bobbed hair hanging just above her shoulders; pretty. In her mid-thirties, he surmised. She had a stern but attractive air and seemed buxom in a matronly, rather than overtly sexual, way. But he had to admit she had incredible green eyes. So, no, she wasn't exactly the stunning, lithe, young blonde type that he went for, but then she wasn't exactly a hairy old drunk either.

Natasha returned her attention to the compartment and caught the young man watching her. She smiled inwardly. There is an inescapable intimacy in these situations, she thought. Two adults alone in an enclosed space, aware of each other's presence.

'I'm sorry if I've interrupted you,' she said in a soft, low, well-spoken voice, a suggestive smile animating her full burgundy lips, and her musky perfume enveloping him.

'Not at all,' Ben replied, making it as obvious as he could that he wanted to be left alone. But he studied her a little more closely now that she'd made the effort to speak to him. OK, she was quite attractive, and there was definitely something sexy about the crow's feet around her green eyes. But she looked slightly imposing and he preferred pretty, girlish blondes who smiled easily and hung on his every word. Like Nicola, who he was hoping to see at the wedding reception; his girlfriend, Anna, hadn't made the trip so it was a great opportunity to try and get Nicola into bed. Besides this woman was just too old for him.

I'm sure if you just sit back and enjoy the journey, you'll soon forget I'm even here,' Natasha said.

'Mmm,' Ben grunted, looking down at his newspaper. But not if you keep fucking yapping I won't, he thought.

Natasha was aware that he was bristling at her attention. Still, he shouldn't be any more of a challenge than the others, she smiled quietly to herself.

After about five minutes she said, 'I find train journeys so relaxing.'

Ben looked up from his paper. 'Look, I hate to be rude, but I've got a lot to think about at the moment. So, if you wouldn't mind . . .'

'It's just that I find the softly rocking motion of the train so lulling,' she said, ignoring his request. 'Feel it. Feel it rock you. Gently. Like a cradle. I've always thought there was something very maternal about trains, almost womb-like in the way they relax you.'

The cadence of her voice was soft and coaxing, gently persuasive. In spite of himself Ben found his attention tuning into the rhythm of the train, his head falling back on to the headrest, his gaze drifting out of the carriage window.

'I find it so hard to stay awake on these long train journeys, don't you?' she prompted softly. 'You can't help but be lulled by the gentle motion of the train as it moves along the tracks. You feel your limbs becoming heavier and heavier. After a while you look out of the window but stop taking in the scenery and just let everything wash over you. Letting your thoughts glide through your emptying mind . . . through time and space. You feel your whole body becoming heavy. Heavier and heavier. Your eyelids starting to flicker with the weight of this peace, this quiet. Listening to the gently rocking train.'

Ben felt himself sink into his seat, his breathing becoming deeper, more regular, more even. A heaviness was settling over him. She was right: it was hard to stay awake.

'That's it,' she coaxed. 'Listen to the train. It's such a wonderful sensation. Like a lullaby of sleep that you dimly recall from childhood, and before . . . before you were born, safely cosseted in your mother's womb. Think of darkness. Think of sleep. Your limbs are so heavy now. All the muscles in your body feel totally relaxed. Your eyelids are so, so heavy. It's becoming a struggle to keep them open, to keep your gaze focused outside you, on the calming swash of the landscape going by. Heavier and heavier. Heavier and heavier. So tired. So warm. So relaxed.' Natasha was leaning in now, lowering her soft, lilting voice further as she whispered her suggestions.

Then, suddenly, the door slid open and the ticket inspector walked in interrupting her flow. 'Tickets please,' he said brightly, oblivious of the situation.

Natasha flourished her ticket briskly, annoyed that he had burst in on her work.

'Ticket please,' he said to Ben.

Ben gazed up at the man. Who was he? Why was he in uniform? Why was he looking at him so expectantly?

'Is he all right?' the inspector asked Natasha.

'Yes, he's fine. He's just come out of hospital and he's still a little groggy from the anaesthetic.'

Ben looked at the two people talking over him, puzzled. He decided that their conversation didn't relate to him. Their voices floated somewhere just outside his comprehension.

'Here, let me get his ticket for you,' Natasha said helpfully, noticing that it was sticking out of his top pocket. She leant over and removed it, softly whispering, 'Heavier and heavier, my dear,' into his ear as she did so. 'So comfortable, so relaxed.'

Ben smiled, revelling in her gently commanding voice and rich perfume.

The inspector thanked her, punched his ticket and handed it back to Natasha, who slipped it into her handbag making quite sure her subject would not be able to leave the station without her. Not that she expected to resort to any cheap subterfuge.

The inspector left, closing the door behind him with a loud thud.

'W-what's going on?' Ben stammered, suddenly roused from his reverie by the slamming door. He felt sluggish, as if he'd just woken from an aborted sleep. Strange – he hadn't felt tired at all a moment before.

'Don't worry,' said the woman opposite him.

But Ben couldn't help thinking that something was going on here. He tried to focus on his female companion but all he could do was stare helplessly into her deep green eyes. He tried to get to his feet, but his limbs felt heavy, almost rubbery.

Natasha looked on impassively as the young man wobbled on his feet, feeling an early satisfaction at the difficulty he was having trying to struggle free of her hypnotic grip. A moist excitement tingled in her cunt. She didn't bother to try and stop him but simply remained in her seat and intoned in a soft, luxurious voice, 'Heavier and heavier. More and more relaxed. Warm. Loose. Heavy. Completely relaxed. No urgency. No desire. No will of your own.'

Ben felt light, disembodied. The woman was whispering and yet her words were incredibly clear, as if they were being spoken from deep inside his own head. He froze for a moment, finding it difficult to think straight. Then, as the train took a bend, he collapsed back on to his seat, unable to coordinate his limbs or maintain his balance.

Natasha smiled wickedly and said, 'Now I want you to notice that the more you try to struggle against my will the more you will want to obey my every command. And the more you try to understand what I am saying, the less you will be able to understand it. Do you understand?'

Ben's mind reeled, trying to make sense of her last statement. For a while he struggled to think and fight his way clear, but finally he gave in and accepted her authority.

'Yes, I understand,' he said.

'Good boy. Gazing out of the window now,' she said, continuing to effortlessly condition her subject. 'No longer able to make out individual shapes. Just differing patterns of light and colour. Soothing you. Sending you deeper and deeper. Deeper and deeper down inside yourself. Tell me your name.'

'Ben,' he said automatically.

'I'm Natasha. Listen to the train, Ben. Listen to me. Feel yourself becoming immersed, surrounded by a wonderful, warm, red darkness. Associate this with the sound of my voice, Ben. As safe and relaxed as a baby suspended in his mother's womb. Your eyelids are so heavy now. You can no longer keep them open.'

Ben's eyes closed as he felt himself sinking deeper and deeper into his seat; as if the seat was moulding itself to the shape of his body. Drifting in time and space.

'Now then, Ben, I want you to concentrate easily and loosely on the end of your nose. Concentrate on it until you quite naturally turn your attention completely and utterly to the soft, compelling sound of my voice. All the time going deeper and deeper into sleep . . . into relaxation. Everything is just as it should be. There are no worries, no fears, no anxieties. Only peace and relaxation. Only my voice. Only your desire to please me. You are so comfortable, so relaxed. Too comfortable to think, too relaxed to think. Thinking only gets in the way of relaxing. Doesn't it, Ben?'

'Yes,' he murmured.

'Good, Ben.' Natasha smiled, watching this virile young man lapse into sleep. 'Now, in order to continue relaxing you know you will have to stop thinking and refocus your whole mind on pleasing me. Is that understood?'

'Yes, Natasha.' He felt an overwhelming desire to cooperate with her. He wanted to please her.

Natasha sat back in her seat, delighted with the way this was going. He was a good, receptive subject – and soon he would be a good, loyal, obedient subject.

'Now Ben, do you remember where you are taking the train to?'

Ben had to think for a moment. His thoughts felt soupy and slow. 'Yes,' he said finally. 'To Mark and Laura's wedding.'

'But you don't like Mark and Laura, Ben. They're ugly and selfish. Relax, Ben, and realise that you never wanted to go to their wedding in the first place. In fact you've been trying to think of an excuse ever since your invitation first arrived. You remember that now, don't you, Ben?'

'Yes,' Ben said. He couldn't believe he'd forgotten.

'Well, now you have an excuse, don't you?'

'Do I?' he asked weakly.

'You're thirsty. You're thirsty, so you won't be able to make it to their wedding.'

'Yes,' Ben murmured. Of course. Why hadn't he thought of that before? It was the perfect excuse.

A victorious smile spread across Natasha's lips. She loved it when she got them to this stage. They were so easy to manipulate. But it wasn't enough to simply hypnotise Ben. If that was all she did he would gradually ease out of his trance, and after about three days or so he would be back to his normal self. She needed to reinforce Ben's new-found subservience by implanting post-hypnotic suggestions, then working on him whilst he thought he was more 'himself'. He had to believe that it was his decision to change.

Feeling a sense of mischief mingled with curiosity Natasha sat down next to her transfixed subject and unzipped his trousers, nuzzling her lips into his ear and telling him to relax whilst gently stroking his cock into life. She loved the way it responded to her touch, becoming hard and thick for her. She gripped it and watched Ben's mind spin as he tried to make sense of his strange predicament.

Careful not to arouse her young man too much in case she jogged him out of his trance, Natasha nevertheless let her hand casually, almost absent-mindedly, glide up and down his cock, comforted by its girth and the way it pulsed under her caress.

Then, as the train drew into the station, she returned Ben's erection to the confines of his trousers and counted him out of his deep sleep, giving him instructions to wake up and follow her without question and remember nothing of this 'uneventful' journey. She steered him along the platform and out of a side exit to avoid any confrontations with friends who might be waiting to meet him.

Natasha opened the boot of the car and told him to carefully load her bags. When they were inside, she said, 'Now then, Ben, you will feel as relaxed by the motion of my car as you were by the rhythm of the train, and you will fall into a deep sleep before we have even left the car park. Do you understand me?'

'Yes Natasha,' he said in a voice that sounded flat and distant to him.

Natasha turned the ignition on and backed the car out of her parking space. Ben was asleep beside her. She smiled. This way he would have no idea of the route from the station to her house and wouldn't be able to retrace his steps if somehow he broke out of his hypnotic state.

The next thing Ben knew he was carrying Natasha's bags into her house. He looked around him and he had no idea where he was. The house stood alone, surrounded by greenery. He followed Natasha through to the kitchen.

'Just put the bags down on the table, Ben,' she said, directing him to a large pine table in the centre of the room.

'Fetch me a drink, Ben,' Natasha ordered in a soft but commanding tone. 'G and T.'

Ben walked over to the drinks cabinet, took out a bottle of Bombay gin and poured a glass for Natasha, adding ice, tonic and a slice of lemon. It did not occur to him to make a drink for himself.

Watching Ben fix her drink Natasha slipped off her coat to reveal a smart open-fronted silvery grey jacket with a black low-cut top that exposed her full cleavage. She was wearing a black satin Ultrabra that gave her a wonderful uplift. Around her neck hung an emerald pendant that complemented the colour of her eyes.

Natasha watched her lovely young man wander around her house in the sweetest of dazes. She opened the door of her dresser and took out a set of new candles, lit them and placed them around her house. She liked to bathe the place in soft light for times like this. She didn't see why there shouldn't be an element of romance to the procedure simply because he was so deeply under her control.

She could see that his eyes were attracted by the sparkle of her pendant and watched purringly as his dreamy eyes lingered over her cleavage. Natasha was pleased with his lascivious response. That was a side of his personality she would not be suppressing.

After slowly undressing him she walked over to the pine sideboard and removed an old stocking from one of the drawers. She beckoned him over with a crooked finger, tied the stocking into a figure eight around his cock and balls and used it to lead him upstairs to her bedroom. She loved that dazed expression on his face, his heavy and sluggish eyes, the look of total submission.

Once in the bedroom she stood back to admire her new toy, as if he were a sculpture or any other inanimate exhibit. Then she walked around him, studying him closely. He had smooth pale skin, a lean, well-toned body, trim, sleek lines and a nice firm bum. Soft dark hair covered his chest.

By tomorrow, if everything went to plan, nothing would remain of this transfixed and blissfully unaware boy: all his old personality traits, memories and physical mannerisms would be wiped clean. She would remake him in an image more suitable to her tastes. Certainly that brusque arrogance could go.

Sighing, Natasha made up a bed in the spare room upstairs.

That night she lay back on her bed, sinking into her soft mattress and red silk sheets. Her fingers gently twisted her pubic hair, then glided over her moist clit. She always felt incredibly aroused by the power she gained over a new boy, but it was important that she did not give into her urges before he was fully fashioned. If she used him for sex right now it was still possible that, in her abandon, the carefully controlled image she was presenting might slip and jar him out of his trance. But by tomorrow she wouldn't need to keep him in a trance. His newly learnt self-image and sense of innate subservience would be so deeply ingrained that the thought of disobeying her command would seem completely foreign, even frightening, to him – even in his fully conscious state. So, despite the temptation to do otherwise, she resolved to remain here tonight and enjoy this exquisite frustration.

Natasha woke Ben early the next morning in order to deny him sufficient sleep. She slipped off her damp knickers and dangled them in front of his expressionless face, allowing the tired and bleary figure to breathe in the musky, evocative sex smell. He looked pale and flat, a shadow of the man who had glanced at her on the train yesterday, dismissing her in that one, brief, cursory look. But this would be temporary, just one phase in his treatment. Once he had been reconditioned his face would return to its previous state of animation; but his mind would remain Natasha's.

'Take a deep breath, Ben. Take a deep, deep breath of Natasha's warm, damp knickers. Breathe it in. Hold it. And exhale. Now relax. Fill your lungs with the smell of my beautiful pussy. You find the smell so erotic. Dazzling your senses, twisting your brain. You will respond to this smell whenever it is wafted in front of your face. You will find the desire growing and intensifying with incredible force, overwhelming you, until the very faintest trace of my sex smell sends you into mindless raptures. You will only need to catch the subtlest aroma of my smell on the breeze and you will prostrate yourself in front of me in the hope of being allowed to kiss and worship at the altar of my body.'

Ben had no time to think; Natasha had reasserted control of his dazed mind. He looked up at this beautiful, voluptuous woman standing over him, at her cello-like curves, her thick, dark hair slightly mussed from sleep and her spellbinding green eyes. As he blinked and struggled to clear his head Natasha moved closer and pushed her warm damp knickers into his face.

She said, 'Remember, Ben, the more you try to understand what I am saying, the less you will be able to understand it. Do you understand?' His lack of sleep, and the strange memories of yesterday coupled with this morning's sudden awakening were all too much for him. Once more he capitulated.

Natasha watched his beautiful face become calm – the outward expression of a mind suspending critical judgement and accepting her orders without thinking.

Gently, her hands pressing down on his firm pecs, Natasha pushed Ben back down on the bed. She climbed on top of him, undid the sash of her creamy silk kimono and adjusted herself so she was kneeling above him.

Then she slowly lowered herself until she was sitting on his face.

He moaned and squirmed beneath her.

It would be just as if he had been visited by a succubus in the night, Natasha smiled contentedly to herself.

When Ben awoke later that day he felt incredible. The muddle of yesterday had cleared, leaving him feeling fresh and revitalised. He knew who he was.

Natasha checked her appearance in the mirror, keen to look her best despite having assured herself of his undying love and admiration. Her kimono with its faint blue brocade design was tied in around her waist to accentuate her curves. The erect nipples of her heavy breasts were clearly outlined beneath the robe. 'Good morning, Ben. How are we feeling today?' she asked in an easy conversational tone, as if yesterday had never happened.

'Amazing, thank you. I haven't slept that well in ages,' he said.

'Good. I'm glad to hear it,' Natasha said casually, walking over and sitting down on the edge of his bed. Looking him in the eyes and seeing that he was unquestioningly hers she leant in and ran a caressing hand along his cheek. He hadn't shaved and the dark shadow added a rough depth and charm to his face. She pulled him to her and kissed him. His mouth opened compliantly and she ran her tongue along his teeth, then pushed it against his own. He was placid but responsive, letting her take control and dominate him.

Natasha climbed on top of him and Ben experienced a strangely haunting sense of *déjà vu*. But just as he was beginning to wonder why, Natasha lowered her pussy on to his face and his mind went crazy. It was the most incredibly arousing smell he had ever known and he found himself hungrily licking and stroking her cunt with his tongue, waves of submissive lust crashing through his mind and body.

Natasha arched her back and gripped the wrought iron bed-rest as she rocked backwards and forwards. She came almost instantly, smearing her come over Ben's lips and then covering him in kisses.

Now that she owned him it would be a cinch to train him up in bed. Soon she would be having the most perfect sex of her life. And if he enjoyed it, well, so much the better, but his pleasure was irrelevant. His needs were secondary, in all matters. He was here to please her. He had been trained to serve the superior sex and his young mind had been frozen into a blank acceptance of his lowly status. Her emerald eyes were wild and greedy as she slid down his body and lowered herself on to his surging erection, hot pangs of delight shooting through her body.

Natasha leant in and whispered, 'You will not come until I say that you can. Do you understand me, Ben?'

'Yes, Natasha,' he groaned breathlessly. This time Ben's eyes were glazed with lust.

They rolled around on the bed, ruffling the sheets, scattering the pillows and knocking over the table lamp as they panted and sweated. Ben found himself unable to leave Natasha's sweet pussy alone for very long and soon he was going down on her again, stroking and massaging her aroused clit, licking and nibbling her.

Before long a second consuming orgasm started to well up inside Natasha and she ran her hands over her sensitised flesh, gripping and massaging her heavy breasts and tugging at her nipples, heightening the pleasure. Ben's hot mouth kissed and bit her neck.

The orgasm broke, and wave after wave of extreme sensation spasmed through her thrashing body, shaking her with an ecstasy of sweet inner screams. She moaned and dragged her nails down his back, leaving long red tracks from his toned shoulders to his buttocks.

After a while her movements slowed and the intense pleasure subsided into an overall feeling of wonderful satisfaction. She rocked him gently, back and forth, savouring the last eddying currents of her orgasms. Then, as her mind cleared and her composure returned, she realised how pleased she was with her new acquisition. Gripping the back of his head she looked straight at him.

'Look deep into my eyes, Ben.' Ben's dazed, soft, blue eyes stared helplessly into her own; his face was smeared with her red lipstick and come, his short hair clumped and tufted. 'You've done very well,' she said in a warm, coaxing voice. 'I'm very pleased with you. And –' she smiled wickedly, gripping his hard cock and palming his heavy balls '– you've been very well controlled.' She kissed him. Their lips were wet from the mixture of lipstick and come.

She couldn't wait any longer and, straddling his lap, lowered herself slowly on to his throbbing erection. This time her orgasm shot through her as if every nerve ending had been set alight. A long, soft, groan of pleasure escaped her mouth as she felt it slide deeper and deeper within her. Riding him, she slid her cunt down every beautiful inch. Feeling yet another sweet, squirming orgasm threaten to blow her away she looked deeply into his eyes and whispered in a rich, huskily hypnotic voice, 'You are mine now, Ben.' And as the ripples swept through her she moaned, 'Come for me, Ben, come for Natasha. Now!'

Ben immediately shot his hot, limpid jets deep into his dark seductress and Natasha collapsed on her hypnotised sex-slave as they came together, a sated smile glowing over her face.

Later that week Ben meekly followed Natasha around the local town centre carrying her shopping. Natasha stopped to talk casually with friends and acquaintances.

'Very nice,' Monica said, eyeing Ben enviously. 'Where did you find him?'

'Oh, I went shopping for him at the weekend,' Natasha said, a wicked smile darting across her face. 'Found him, liked what I saw, brought him home, trained him up.'

Monica, of course, didn't think she was talking literally. 'Quiet, isn't he,' she said.

'Knows his place,' Natasha said.

They both laughed.

Ben smiled dimly, vacantly, not fully comprehending the fact that he was being talked about as a piece of property.

To Natasha's friends, meeting him for the first time, he simply appeared to be a pretty but rather dumb and compliant young man who was hopelessly infatuated with this striking older woman. And if he was obviously under the thumb, well, good for her. What woman wouldn't want to control her partner like that? Especially one as handsome as he was. And especially after the ill fortune Natasha had had with other men in her life. Well, her luck certainly had changed. She seemed to bring home a different young man every other month or so. But when they asked her what her secret was she would always smile enigmatically and shrug and say the same thing: 'You just have to know what to say.'

Then, after a couple of months, which was about average, Natasha let Ben go. Released him back into the wild with a pat on the bum and orders to forget that this had ever happened. Before long he would regain something of his old self, although his friends would notice that his old, brash personality had been replaced with a more thoughtful side. He would treat women with a new reverence. After all, they are the superior sex.

Natasha watched his train pull out and then walked back over to the kiosk. It was time for another shopping trip, she thought, and bought a return ticket to London.

Mistress Sheila

Kate Dominic

*H*er exquisitely tasteful business card said it all: MIS-
TRESS SHEILA, DOMINATRIX. Accepting both experienced and novice submissives. Will train to suit.

Like everyone else I knew, I admired her from afar.
Mistress Sheila was the most beautiful drag queen in all
of New Charleston. It was an honour to escort her, and
she insisted on being formally escorted to all of the
functions in her highly visible life. Every dinner was a
formal affair, and those whose arm she took wore tail-
ored designer suits to the most exclusive of restaurants.
Her perfectly manicured blood-red nails would curl
around a crystal wine glass while she purred her dinner
order, and she always ordered for her escort as well.
Certain positions were, shall we say, assumed before she
accepted an invitation.

I was amazed at the men who sat at her table: civic
leaders, clergy, business executives. And no one sat at
her table who hadn't knelt before her. It was whispered
that her escorts were never allowed to wear underwear,
so that she could reach over at her whim and feel the
heat of their well-warmed buttocks through their
trousers.

I'd actually seen her once. Up close. It was at Bernardi's, that new Italian restaurant on the hill overlooking the city. I was there with friends, and our conversation, like every other in the restaurant, came to an abrupt halt when she walked through the room to her private table in the corner.

She was exquisite. Her dress was her signature red – a deep crimson; I presumed it was silk from the soft folds flowing across her breasts. She showed just enough creamy cleavage for everyone present to wonder how she could make it seem so real. A strand of pearls was draped seductively around her neck – I'd heard tales of what she did with them – and the matching earrings were accentuated by the way her long brown tresses were swept up off her neck into a beautiful French braid.

And her legs. My God, they were gorgeous. Long and curving and encased in real silk stockings that stretched from her four-inch red stilettos all the way to where her glorious cock would have hung had she not confined it to the silken prison of her feminine undergarments.

I'd heard tell that her cock reached all the way to where her garters attached to her stockings. Of course precious few had ever seen it. Certainly not I. But I dreamt that she kept her whole body shaved as smoothly as her legs, so that her cock would slide like satin all the way down my throat. In fact, I dreamt about it rather often. I'm one of her biggest fans.

That night in the restaurant, I watched her escort closely, too. He was a bit older than I, probably in his early thirties, and I recognised him as one of the deputy district attorneys. He wore a grey wool suit and stark white shirt that emphasised both the width of his muscular shoulders and the deep warmth of his tan. He was the epitome of service to her, attending to every detail of her comfort. And as he again reached to fill her glass with the chilled Dom Perignon, I could see that the man was definitely not wearing underwear. He'd taken off his jacket to eat, and the round curve of his ass was smooth from hip to thigh.

As his arm stretched out, her hand slid towards him and she dragged just one fingernail delicately over that curve. His whole body stiffened as he gasped, but he didn't spill one drop. When he set the bottle back down, she removed her hand and said something to him – I couldn't hear what. But he blushed all the way to his hairline. Then his hips moved as he said, 'Thank you, Mistress.' And he kissed her fingertips.

I almost came in my pants. Instead, I dropped my wine glass. The fragile crystal shattered against the tabletop and the burgundy stained deeply into the white linen. I was mortified. I tried to wipe it up, but I only succeeded in spreading the stains on to the crisply starched napkins. My dinner mates hadn't been watching me, so I let them assume that my glass had just slipped. The waiter graciously cleaned up the mess and I relaxed a bit, assuming no one had noticed why I'd committed my little faux pas.

But as I glanced up, I saw Mistress Sheila looking directly at me. And I became very aware of the intelligence behind those velvet brown eyes. I was suddenly reminded of that time in third grade when my mother discovered that I'd cheated on a math test. Mama was a gentle woman, but that night she'd led me into the back yard to peel a poplar switch. Mistress Sheila looked at me that same way now, disappointed but very decisive. I felt the heat on my cheeks as I flushed and looked away. When I dared to look up again, she was still looking at me. She nodded once, a glint lighting her eyes in the candlelight. Then she turned away in dismissal, letting her silver fork resume its trip to her lips, a daintily skewered bite of shellfish trapped on the tines.

The next day, I told everybody at work about seeing Mistress Sheila at the restaurant. Seeing her in person is an event in this town! But I left out the part about my spilling the wine. After all, I'm the boss, and they didn't need to know about that. They were all suitably impressed, especially my assistant manager, Jon. He's a big fan of drag queens in general, and Mistress Sheila in particular.

That Friday was my birthday, and it was one helluva day. Not only was I turning 30, but our bookstore was doing inventory. Even the sick were called back in out of bed to count merchandise. To top it all off, I'd gotten a call from corporate the night before informing me that a representative would be coming at five o'clock for two full hours of my undivided attention because of some discrepancy in a computer database.

I was frantic. I couldn't very well reschedule the whole damned inventory. So I announced that as a reward for the extra effort of the inventory (after all, we are a large bookstore), I was treating everyone to dinner at Le Papillon, a local steak house known for its delicious food and unbelievably slow service. The reservations were for five o'clock, and I told them no one was expected back until seven. Believe me, with that crew, I knew nobody would come back early.

As soon as they left, I ran to the bathroom. I figured I had just enough time to brush my teeth, shave and change into my suit. At exactly five o'clock I was back in my office, tidying up, when I heard the bell tinkle as the front door opened. I was surprised. Jon always locks the door behind him when he leaves. Then I heard the lock turn again and the steady click of heels on the hardwood floors.

'Mr McGuire?' The husky voice wasn't loud, but it carried.

I stepped to the office door, ready to ask if corporate kept keys to all its stores. But as I looked up, my voice froze in my throat.

There, standing next to the Damron travel guides, was

Mistress Sheila. She was wearing a long winter dress coat, and she carried a large leather purse on a strap that curled over her shoulder.

'Mr McGuire,' she said curtly. 'I am neither accustomed to rudeness nor do I find it acceptable. We have an appointment this evening. I expect you to invite me into your office.'

I stumbled all over myself holding the door open for her as I stammered, 'Yes, ma'am. Excuse me, ma'am.'

'There is no excuse for this type of behaviour, young man. But we will deal with that later. Now offer me a chair.'

Although I supposed she was probably my age, I suddenly felt very young and very aware that I was being carpeted for unacceptable behaviour. When she was seated in my desk chair – the most comfortable one in the room – I started to sit in the straight back chair across from her.

'What are you doing?' she snapped.

I froze, halfway down, looking up at her in surprise. 'Ma'am?'

'I've not yet directed you to sit. You will stand or kneel in my presence unless directed to do otherwise. Is that understood?'

I nodded mutely and carefully stood back up. Her voice was too low for a woman's. It radiated a caressing heat that slid over my skin. And again, I was very aware of my error.

She tapped a fingernail impatiently on the arm of the chair. 'Are you going to offer me something to drink? Good lord, boy, didn't your mother teach you any manners?'

'Yes, ma'am. She did, ma'am,' I said, stumbling all over myself as I handed her a glass of ice water from the tray I'd set on the credenza. 'It's just . . .' I stopped and looked at her. 'Mistress Sheila, I'm one of your biggest fans, and I'm really honoured to have you in my office.'

I raked my fingers through my hair, then blushed as I realised I'd just ruined my carefully coiffed look. 'I'm expecting a visit from my corporate headquarters. The representative is late now. And I have no idea why you're here. And . . .' I stopped, totally at a loss for words.

'Mr McGuire,' she said, sitting up in the chair as she sipped the water and carefully set the glass back on the desk, 'I shall cut to the chase. There is no visit forthcoming from corporate. Your assistant manager is my nephew by marriage, and I am here at his request to help you celebrate your birthday.' She paused for just a moment, letting her words sink in. 'And I do indeed remember you from the other night in the restaurant.'

My shock must have shown on my face. I felt myself go pale as she added, 'Now, young man, you are overdressed for a first meeting with me.'

Mistress Sheila stood and walked around the desk, then took off her coat and handed it to me, shaking her head. 'Hang up my coat. And for God's sake, close your mouth.'

My fingers felt like they weren't attached to my body as I draped her luxurious coat on the coat rack in the corner, but it wasn't because of the feel of her coat. My eyes were now feasting on the glorious sight of Mistress Sheila's body. And she was glorious.

She was still wearing red, but this time there was no silk dress. She was wearing a red leather bustier that laced tightly down the valley between her breasts. The leather miniskirt was black, as were the silk stockings and the thigh-high leather laced boots. I stood there frozen, my nostrils flaring at the smell of Chanel mixed with the faint aroma of the soft lambskin. Her skin was beautiful, and I knew even as I felt my cock fill that there was no way I was going to control my erection. All I could think of was dropping to my knees and licking up the inside of her thighs, letting my tongue and nostrils search out the prizes hidden under the cloak of her skirt.

Her voice brought me rudely back to reality. 'Mr McGuire, you will now strip naked for me. I do not suffer the presence of those who have not felt the kiss of my correction on their bare skin.'

Again, my surprise must have shown on my face, because she sighed heavily, then walked over and gently raised her hand to my cheek. She stroked once, softly, and I felt glad that I'd shaved. Then she turned her hand and dragged just the fingernail of her index finger lightly down the side of my neck.

'Mr McGuire, I understand you are a novice at such things, and because of that I am trying to be patient with you. However, you need to understand that I am here to help you celebrate your birthday. And celebrate we shall.'

The fingernail lifted at the edge of my collar, scratching lightly over my shirt as her fingers slid lower and then curled around my tie. She twisted the patterned silk gently but firmly, making me just vaguely aware of the soft stricture around my neck.

'Keep in mind, though, that your bottom is still quite tender.' I could feel her other hand steal around behind me, the fingernails scratching over my trousers. 'And you have already earnt punishment for spilling your wine and for your lack of courtesy tonight. Trust me, Mr McGuire: that will be quite enough for your first time.'

With that she stepped back and snapped her fingers at me, and I started fumbling quickly with the buttons of my shirt. I know her eyes never left me while I undressed. I could feel them on me even though I wasn't looking at her. It took me a bit longer than I'd expected to get all my clothes off. My hands were shaking pretty badly, and my cock was so hard it seemed to get tangled in everything. But eventually I stood in front of her in all my naked glory, hard as a steel-blue flagpole, my face first flushing with embarrassment and then paling with apprehension as I looked up and saw the small black leather paddle she'd drawn from her purse.

Mistress Sheila walked around me, nodding as her eyes travelled up and down my body. The closer she stood to me, the more aware I was of the scent of her perfume. I jumped as she touched the leather to my skin, gently rubbing the smooth hard surface of the paddle all over my backside.

'We will start with your birthday spanking.' As she spoke she tapped lightly on the fullest part of my bottom cheek. 'Now bend over your desk.'

Her voice was firm and quiet. Disobeying was unthinkable. I bent over the cherrywood desk I'd inherited from my grandmother, vaguely aware that the precome seeping from my cock was probably soaking into the stack of purchase orders I'd slaved over all week.

'In groups of ten, Mr McGuire. Count them.'

'Yes, Mistress,' I said.

The words were barely out of my mouth when the first sound smack stung across the right side of my butt.

'One,' I yipped, but I was more startled than hurt. Actually, I was surprised that it didn't sting more. My surprise didn't last long though. By the time I choked out 'ten' I was fighting back tears and my ass felt like it was on fire.

'You're doing very well, Mr McGuire.' I smelled the leather and her perfume as she came closer. 'Now stand up and turn around.'

My cock led the way as I turned. The red skins that covered her breasts appeared to shimmer as I blinked to clear my eyes. My cock twitched again at the sight of her leather-clad body and she smiled her approval.

'Touch yourself, Mr McGuire.' My eyes flew up to meet hers, then quickly dropped submissively back down. But I had seen the ghost of a smile touch the edge of her crimson lips. 'I like my men hard when they take the leather. See to it.'

I was already hard as a rock, but I dutifully took my cock in my hand, ignoring the burning in my backside as I slicked the precome over the head, stroking until my balls pulled up tight against my body. I couldn't believe how turned on I was, how close I was.

I think Mistress heard my breathing change. She snapped out, 'That's enough!'

My hand froze in mid-stroke, my cock quivering as I let my fingers drop to my side, my groan of frustration coming out more like a whimper.

'Turn around and we will resume. Begin counting with eleven.'

This time even the first stroke hurt. It was heat and pain, and I felt it all through my ass. She repeated number thirteen because I didn't say it loudly enough. After that I said them all clearly, although I was gasping and there were tears running down my face by the time I got to twenty.

This time when I turned around, I stepped from the desk. I could almost feel the heat reflecting back at me from where my scalded skin came close to the cherrywood.

'Hard, Mr McGuire. I want it hard.' She reached out and touched the paddle to the tip of my cock. I jumped at the feel of the warm leather, and she smiled at the clear strand of precome that followed the paddle back.

I stroked myself a few times, but I was so hot I was afraid I'd shoot right then if I touched myself too much. I just knew Mistress would consider that discourteous. So I tugged on my balls instead and tried to concentrate on catching my breath and clearing the tears from my eyes, not on the hot pressure that was pushing to the surface of my prostate. She was so beautiful, so masterful, and the pain she wielded was so delicious. I couldn't look away from where her long red nails stroked over the edge of the paddle as she watched my hand move over my heated flesh.

I don't know how I found the voice to count the last ten. My ass burned red-hot and I was sobbing when she finished. And, oh God, it was all I could do not to come as the heat radiated forward from my ass to my cock. The pleasure pain was almost unbearable. I turned around and Mistress seemed to swim in front of my eyes. The red and black leathers flowed together until they seemed almost a part of her creamy soft skin. She moved closer to me. I could smell her perfume through my tears. Then suddenly she was next to me, and her long red fingernail was reaching towards my almost purple cockhead.

'I believe you've had enough for one night, Mr Mc-Guire.' Her voice was husky. 'You've done well, I am pleased.'

As she spoke, she pressed her full painted lips to mine. I could taste her lipstick and the musk of her perfume as she leant into me, ever so slightly, and kissed me. I gasped as I felt the bulge between her legs press against my thigh. Felt her rubbing against me. Then the pad of her finger, just one finger, dragged slowly up the base of my cock.

I came all over her hand.

When I stopped shaking, she was still pressed hard against my thigh, though now she wasn't moving. She held me a moment longer, until her own breathing had slowed. Then she took a deep breath and stepped back. She lifted her hand to her face, inhaling deeply, then held her fingers to my lips. Without even being told to, I licked her hand clean, kissing her palm when I was finished. And she smiled at me, a genuine smile that reached all the way to her sparkling brown eyes.

'I gather, Mr McGuire, that you are satisfied with your birthday present?' Her voice was suddenly huskier, and I'd said 'Yes, Mistress,' before I realised that she was trying not to laugh. Then I couldn't resist grinning back up at her, too. My ass was so sore I could feel the heat radiating off it, I was standing naked in my office with my now-flaccid cock glistening with drying come, my employees were about to return to find their boss kissing a leather-clad drag queen. And I felt great.

I dressed under her watchful eye, hissing as my trousers slid over the exquisitely tender skin of my bare ass. At her direction, I had tucked my briefs in the pocket of my backpack. She straightened my tie for me, then I helped her into her coat.

As she picked up her purse, I noticed she had forgotten the paddle, and I politely held it out to her. She looked at me for a long moment, then she said quietly, 'You are free for dinner next Friday night, Mr McGuire?'

Surprised, I nodded.

'Good.' She reached into her purse and drew out a parchment business card.

'Then we shall have dinner at Bernardi's at nine o'clock.' She looked at the paddle in my hand, then picked up her purse and walked towards the door.

'My driver will pick you up here at five. You will present the paddle to me then, kneeling, and I will provide you with the correction you need for your lack of manners both tonight and when you spilled the wine. And, Mr McGuire –' she paused with her hand on the door, ' – when we walk into Bernardi's, I will feel the heat from your skin each time I run my finger over your pants.'

My cock was getting hard again, but I kept my eyes respectfully downcast as I whispered, 'Yes, Mistress.'

Her heels clicked across the floor of the store, then I heard the tinkle of the bell as she let herself out. I glanced over at the clock on the bookshelf. It was 6.55. My cock was making a tent in the front of my trousers, and I had exactly five minutes to get it under control, move the ruined purchase orders, and decide whether I was going to shoot Jon or kiss him. I reached back and felt the heat glowing off the surface of my ass. Probably kiss him, the son of a bitch.

I put the purchase orders and the paddle in my backpack with my underwear, closed my office door, and walked out into the store to count postcards.

Visit the Black Lace website at
www.blacklace-books.co.uk

**FIND OUT THE LATEST INFORMATION AND TAKE
ADVANTAGE OF OUR FANTASTIC FREE BOOK OFFER!
ALSO VISIT THE SITE FOR . . .**

- All Black Lace titles currently available
  and how to order online
- Great new offers
- Writers' guidelines
- Author interviews
- An erotica newsletter
- Features
- Cool links

**BLACK LACE – THE LEADING IMPRINT
OF WOMEN'S SEXY FICTION**

**TAKING YOUR EROTIC READING
PLEASURE TO NEW HORIZONS**

LOOK OUT FOR THE ALL-NEW BLACK LACE BOOKS – AVAILABLE NOW!

All books priced £6.99 in the UK. Please note publication dates apply to the UK only. For other territories, please contact your retailer.

MIXED SIGNALS
Anna Clare
ISBN O 352 33889 X

Adele Western knows what it's like to be an outsider. As a teenager she was teased mercilessly by the sixth-form girls for the size of her lips. Now twenty-six, we follow the ups and downs of her life and loves. There's the cultured restaurateur Paul, whose relationship with his working-class boyfriend raises eyebrows, not least because he is still having sex with his ex-wife. There's former chart-topper Suki, whose career has nosedived and who is venturing on a lesbian affair. Underlying everyone's story is a tale of ambiguous sexuality, and Adele is caught up in some very saucy antics. **The sexy *tour de force* of wild, colourful characters makes this a hugely enjoyable novel of modern sexual dilemmas.**

SWITCHING HANDS
Alaine Hood
ISBN O 352 33896 2

When Melanie Paxton takes over as manager of a vintage clothing shop, she makes the bold decision to add a selection of sex toys and fetish merchandise to her inventory. Sales skyrocket, and so does Mel's popularity, as she teases sexy secrets out of the town's residents. It seems she can do no wrong, until the gossip starts – about her wild past and her experimental sexuality. However, she finds an unlikely – and very hunky – ally called Nathan who works in the history museum next door. **This characterful story about a sassy sexpert and an antiquities scholar is bound to get pulses racing!**

PACKING HEAT
Karina Moore
ISBN O 352 33356 1

When spoilt and pretty Californian Nadine has her allowance stopped by her rich Uncle Willem, she becomes desperate to maintain her expensive lifestyle. She joins forces with her lover, Mark, and together they conspire to steal a vast sum of cash from a flashy businessman and pin the blame on their target's girlfriend. The deed done, the sexual stakes rise as they make their escape. Naturally, their getaway doesn't go entirely to plan, and they are pursued across the desert and into the casinos of Las Vegas, where a showdown is inevitable. The clock is ticking for Nadine, Mark and the guys who are chasing them – but a Ferrari-driving blonde temptress is about to play them all for suckers. **Fast cars and even faster women in this modern pulp fiction classic.**

Published in September 2004

CLUB CRÈME
Primula Bond
ISBN 0352 33907 1

Suki Summers gets a job as a housekeeper for a private gentlemen's club in London. Club Crème has been founded by the debonair Sir Simeon for chaps who want an elegant retreat where they can relax and indulge their taste for old-fashioned frolics. Her first impression is that the place is very stuffy, but it isn't long before she realises that anything goes, as long as it is behind closed doors where she is required to either keep watch or join in.

BONDED
Fleur Reynolds
ISBN 0352 33192 5

Sapphire Western is a beautiful young investment broker whose best friend Zinnia has recently married Jethro Clarke, one of the wealthiest and most lecherous men in Texas. Sapphire and Zinnia have a mutual friend, Aurelie de Bouys, whose life is no longer her own now that she her scheming cousin Jeanine controls her desires and money. In a world where being rich is everything and being decadent is commonplace, Jeanine and her hedonistic associates still manage to shock and surprise.

Black Lace Booklist

Information is correct at time of printing. To avoid disappointment check availability before ordering. Go to www.blacklace-books.co.uk. All books are priced £6.99 unless another price is given.

BLACK LACE BOOKS WITH A CONTEMPORARY SETTING

☐ SHAMELESS Stella Black	ISBN 0 352 33485 1	£5.99
☐ INTENSE BLUE Lyn Wood	ISBN 0 352 33496 7	£5.99
☐ A SPORTING CHANCE Susie Raymond	ISBN 0 352 33501 7	£5.99
☐ TAKING LIBERTIES Susie Raymond	ISBN 0 352 33357 X	£5.99
☐ A SCANDALOUS AFFAIR Holly Graham	ISBN 0 352 33523 8	£5.99
☐ THE NAKED FLAME Crystalle Valentino	ISBN 0 352 33528 9	£5.99
☐ ON THE EDGE Laura Hamilton	ISBN 0 352 33534 3	£5.99
☐ LURED BY LUST Tania Picarda	ISBN 0 352 33533 5	£5.99
☐ THE HOTTEST PLACE Tabitha Flyte	ISBN 0 352 33536 X	£5.99
☐ THE NINETY DAYS OF GENEVIEVE Lucinda Carrington	ISBN 0 352 33070 8	£5.99
☐ DREAMING SPIRES Juliet Hastings	ISBN 0 352 33584 X	
☐ THE TRANSFORMATION Natasha Rostova	ISBN 0 352 33311 1	
☐ SIN.NET Helena Ravenscroft	ISBN 0 352 33598 X	
☐ TWO WEEKS IN TANGIER Annabel Lee	ISBN 0 352 33599 8	
☐ HIGHLAND FLING Jane Justine	ISBN 0 352 33616 1	
☐ PLAYING HARD Tina Troy	ISBN 0 352 33617 X	
☐ SYMPHONY X Jasmine Stone	ISBN 0 352 33629 3	
☐ SUMMER FEVER Anna Ricci	ISBN 0 352 33625 0	
☐ CONTINUUM Portia Da Costa	ISBN 0 352 33120 8	
☐ OPENING ACTS Suki Cunningham	ISBN 0 352 33630 7	
☐ FULL STEAM AHEAD Tabitha Flyte	ISBN 0 352 33637 4	
☐ A SECRET PLACE Ella Broussard	ISBN 0 352 33307 3	
☐ GAME FOR ANYTHING Lyn Wood	ISBN 0 352 33639 0	
☐ CHEAP TRICK Astrid Fox	ISBN 0 352 33640 4	
☐ THE GIFT OF SHAME Sara Hope-Walker	ISBN 0 352 32935 1	
☐ COMING UP ROSES Crystalle Valentino	ISBN 0 352 33658 7	
☐ GOING TOO FAR Laura Hamilton	ISBN 0 352 33657 9	

☐ THE STALLION Georgina Brown	ISBN 0 352 33005 8
☐ DOWN UNDER Juliet Hastings	ISBN 0 352 33663 3
☐ ODALISQUE Fleur Reynolds	ISBN 0 352 32887 8
☐ SWEET THING Alison Tyler	ISBN 0 352 33682 X
☐ TIGER LILY Kimberly Dean	ISBN 0 352 33685 4
☐ COOKING UP A STORM Emma Holly	ISBN 0 352 33686 2
☐ RELEASE ME Suki Cunningham	ISBN 0 352 33671 4
☐ KING'S PAWN Ruth Fox	ISBN 0 352 33684 6
☐ FULL EXPOSURE Robyn Russell	ISBN 0 352 33688 9
☐ SLAVE TO SUCCESS Kimberley Raines	ISBN 0 352 33687 0
☐ STRIPPED TO THE BONE Jasmine Stone	ISBN 0 352 33463 0
☐ HARD CORPS Claire Thompson	ISBN 0 352 33491 6
☐ MANHATTAN PASSION Antoinette Powell	ISBN 0 352 33691 9
☐ WOLF AT THE DOOR Savannah Smythe	ISBN 0 352 33693 5
☐ SHADOWPLAY Portia Da Costa	ISBN 0 352 33313 8
☐ I KNOW YOU, JOANNA Ruth Fox	ISBN 0 352 33727 3
☐ SNOW BLONDE Astrid Fox	ISBN 0 352 33732 X
☐ THE HOUSE IN NEW ORLEANS Fleur Reynolds	ISBN 0 352 32951 3
☐ HEAT OF THE MOMENT Tesni Morgan	ISBN 0 352 33742 7
☐ THE WICKED STEPDAUGHTER Wendy Harris	ISBN 0 352 33777 X
☐ DRAWN TOGETHER Robyn Russell	ISBN 0 352 33269 7
☐ LEARNING THE HARD WAY Jasmine Archer	ISBN 0 352 33782 6
☐ VALENTINA'S RULES Monica Belle	ISBN 0 352 33788 5
☐ VELVET GLOVE Emma Holly	ISBN 0 352 33448 7
☐ UNKNOWN TERRITORY Annie O'Neill	ISBN 0 352 33794 X
☐ VIRTUOSO Katrina Vincenzi-Thyre	ISBN 0 352 32907 6
☐ FIGHTING OVER YOU Laura Hamilton	ISBN 0 352 33795 8
☐ COUNTRY PLEASURES Primula Bond	ISBN 0 352 33810 5
☐ ARIA APPASSIONATA Juliet Hastings	ISBN 0 352 33056 2
☐ THE RELUCTANT PRINCESS Patty Glenn	ISBN 0 352 33809 1
☐ HARD BLUE MIDNIGHT Alaine Hood	ISBNO 352 33851 2
☐ ALWAYS THE BRIDEGROOM Tesni Morgan	ISBNO 352 33855 5
☐ COMING ROUND THE MOUNTAIN Tabitha Flyte	ISBNO 352 33873 3
☐ FEMININE WILES Karina Moore	ISBNO 352 33235 2
☐ MIXED SIGNALS Anna Clare	ISBNO 352 33889 X
☐ BLACK LIPSTICK KISSES Monica Belle	ISBNO 352 33885 7

☐ HOP GOSSIP Savannah Smythe   ISBN0 352 33880 6

☐ GOING DEEP Kimberly Dean   ISBN0 352 33876 8

☐ PACKING HEAT Karina Moore   ISBN0 352 33356 1

BLACK LACE BOOKS WITH AN HISTORICAL SETTING

☐ PRIMAL SKIN Leona Benkt Rhys   ISBN 0 352 33500 9   £5.99

☐ DEVIL'S FIRE Melissa MacNeal   ISBN 0 352 33527 0   £5.99

☐ DARKER THAN LOVE Kristina Lloyd   ISBN 0 352 33279 4

☐ THE CAPTIVATION Natasha Rostova   ISBN 0 352 33234 4

☐ MINX Megan Blythe   ISBN 0 352 33638 2

☐ DEMON'S DARE Melissa MacNeal   ISBN 0 352 33683 8

☐ DIVINE TORMENT Janine Ashbless   ISBN 0 352 33719 2

☐ SATAN'S ANGEL Melissa MacNeal   ISBN 0 352 33726 5

☐ THE INTIMATE EYE Georgia Angelis   ISBN 0 352 33004 X

☐ OPAL DARKNESS Cleo Cordell   ISBN 0 352 33033 3

☐ SILKEN CHAINS Jodi Nicol   ISBN 0 352 33143 7

☐ ACE OF HEARTS Lisette Allen   ISBN 0 352 33059 7

☐ THE LION LOVER Mercedes Kelly   ISBN 0 352 33162 3

☐ THE AMULET Lisette Allen   ISBN 0 352 33019 8

☐ WHITE ROSE ENSNARED Juliet Hastings   ISBN 0 352 33052 X

☐ UNHALLOWED RITES Martine Marquand   ISBN 0 352 33222 0

☐ LA BASQUAISE Angel Strand   ISBN 0 352 32988 2

☐ THE HAND OF AMUN Juliet Hastings   ISBN 0 352 33144 5

☐ THE SENSES BEJEWELLED Cleo Cordell   ISBN 0 352 32904 1

BLACK LACE ANTHOLOGIES

☐ MORE WICKED WORDS Various   ISBN 0 352 33487 8

☐ WICKED WORDS 3 Various   ISBN 0 352 33522 X

☐ WICKED WORDS 4 Various   ISBN 0 352 33603 X

☐ WICKED WORDS 9 Various   ISBN 0 352 33860 1

☐ WICKED WORDS 10 Various   ISBN 0 352 33893 8

☐ THE BEST OF BLACK LACE 2 Various   ISBN 0 352 33718 4

BLACK LACE NON-FICTION

☐ THE BLACK LACE BOOK OF WOMEN'S SEXUAL   ISBN 0 352 33793 1   £6.99
    FANTASIES Ed. Kerri Sharp

☐ THE BLACK LACE SEXY QUIZ BOOK Maddie Saxon   ISBN 0 352 33884 9   £6.99

To find out the latest information about Black Lace titles, check out the website: www.blacklace-books.co.uk or send for a booklist with complete synopses by writing to:

> Black Lace Booklist, Virgin Books Ltd
> Thames Wharf Studios
> Rainville Road
> London W6 9HA

Please include an SAE of decent size. Please note only British stamps are valid.

Our privacy policy
We will not disclose information you supply us to any other parties. We will not disclose any information which identifies you personally to any person without your express consent.

From time to time we may send out information about Black Lace books and special offers. Please tick here if you do _not_ wish to receive Black Lace information.   ☐

Please send me the books I have ticked above.

Name ....

Address ....

....

....

....

Post Code ....

Send to: Virgin Books Cash Sales, Thames Wharf Studios, Rainville Road, London W6 9HA.

US customers: for prices and details of how to order books for delivery by mail, call 1-800-343-4499.

Please enclose a cheque or postal order, made payable to Virgin Books Ltd, to the value of the books you have ordered plus postage and packing costs as follows:

UK and BFPO – £1.00 for the first book, 50p for each subsequent book.

Overseas (including Republic of Ireland) – £2.00 for the first book, £1.00 for each subsequent book.

If you would prefer to pay by VISA, ACCESS/MASTERCARD, DINERS CLUB, AMEX or SWITCH, please write your card number and expiry date here:

....

Signature ....

Please allow up to 28 days for delivery.